Pamela Evans was born and brought up in Hanwell in the borough of Ealing, London. She has two grown-up sons and now lives in Wales with her husband.

A SMILE FOR ALL SEASONS

Pamela Evans

HEADLINE

First published in 1999 by
HEADLINE BOOK PUBLISHING

First published in paperback in 2000
by HEADLINE BOOK PUBLISHING

10 9 8 7 6 5 4 3

ISBN 0 7472 5992 5

Typeset by Palimpsest Book Production Limited,
Polmont, Stirlingshire
Printed and bound in Great Britain by
Caledonian International Book Manufacturing Ltd, Glasgow

HEADLINE BOOK PUBLISHING
A division of the Hodder Headline Group
338 Euston Road
London NW1 3BH

www.headline.co.uk
www.hodderheadline.com

A SMILE FOR
ALL SEASONS

Chapter One

Eve Peters was in a cheerful mood as she put the finishing touches to the food. Chops lightly grilled, jacket potatoes crunchy just as they liked them, salad fresh and crisp. Having the evening meal ready when her husband got home was something of a challenge when she worked overtime, but she always tried to do it because it gave them more time to relax together.

A tall, striking figure with blackish hair and dark shining eyes, her attention was drawn to the window of this top-floor flat by the sun sinking behind the rooftops opposite in a blaze of orange, a stunning contrast to this gloomy little kitchen with its ancient sink, prehistoric gas stove and battered old kitchen cabinet.

Taking the cutlery from the drawer, she glanced at the clock. Seven thirty. Ken would be home any minute and everything was ready. Good. Looking down to the street to see if he'd already arrived, she saw by the absence of his builder's van that he hadn't but was struck by the way everything was transformed by the fiery sunset, windows and car bonnets glinting, dusty flowerbeds enriched in the front gardens of the Victorian terraced houses that made up this West Ealing back street.

In days gone by this large property would probably have been a family home; now, in the early summer of 1963, it was entirely converted into small furnished flats. The accommodation was overpriced, draughty and bitterly cold in winter, but it suited Eve and Ken for now.

Having laid the table and left the food served in the

1

kitchen, Eve turned on the TV and sank into an armchair, glad to sit down since her job in the packing department of a mail order company in Acton required her to be on her feet all day. Casually dressed in a pair of ski pants and loose summer top, she curled her long legs beneath her and became engrossed in the latest happenings along *Coronation Street*.

Half past eight and still no sign of Ken. She went to the telephone in the hall and rang the office at his builder's yard. No reply. Surely he wouldn't still be out working at this time? He was doing a painting and decorating job this week and customers didn't usually want a workman about the place in the evening when they were trying to relax.

Disappointed to have her efforts wasted and her evening spoiled, a dull ache was beginning to nag in the pit of her stomach. This situation had a familiar feel to it. Ken had been late home quite often these past few months. Usually he'd been held up on a job or out somewhere doing an estimate. But he really should call her if he was going to be late. For all she knew he could have crashed his van and been rushed to hospital.

Her stomach was beginning to complain because she'd had nothing to eat since lunchtime, so she decided to have her meal without him. Too agitated to sit down while she waited for the food to warm through, she stared out of the kitchen window, longing to see his van draw up outside and stop in its usual place under the street light.

Darkness had fallen but it was well lit outside. People walked by, a constant resonance of footsteps in the evening air. Cars passed with headlights beaming. But still no sign of Ken.

'Sorry I'm late, love,' he said sheepishly when he finally appeared just before ten and confronted her in the living room.

'Where the hell have you been?' She was angry, relieved, hurt.

'I've been doing an estimate over in South Ealing,' he explained 'Quite a big job too, knocking through a dividing wall and decorating the whole lot afterwards. It'll be worth a few bob if I get it.'

'Until this time?' she queried, facing him with her eyes blazing.

'They kept me talking.'

'Really?' she said coldly.

'Eve, love . . .' His voice was persuasive as he moved towards her, vivid blue eyes brimming with contrition. 'I'm doing all this work for us.'

She moved back quickly. 'There *are* such things as telephones, you know,' she pointed out, her voice raised in anger.

A tall man with a mop of thick blond hair, he was wearing a black T-shirt and blue denim jeans which showed off his fine physique. He raked his hair from his brow with strong, builder's fingers, handsome face lightly tanned. 'I should have phoned you, I know,' he said remorsefully.

'Then why didn't you?' she demanded 'I've been worried sick. You could have had an accident for all I knew.'

'This request for a quote came up out of the blue,' he explained. 'It was a recommendation from the people where I've been working today, some friends of theirs, apparently. They wanted a price, sharpish, so I had to go as soon as I'd finished work.'

'That's no excuse for not letting me know, Ken,' she said 'It's so damned inconsiderate.'

'Honest, babe, I didn't realise it was so late,' he said, looking shamefaced. 'We got talking about the job – they were trying to get me to drop the price – and, well . . . the time just sort of disappeared.'

'The dinner's ruined . . .'

'I hope you've had yours,' he said.

'Mine was ruined too by the time I'd waited hours for you and then warmed it up,' she told him. 'I didn't want it by then anyway.'

'My poor Eve,' he said, coming towards her with arms outstretched.

'You're not gonna get round me so easily this time, Ken,' she said determinedly. 'This sort of thing is becoming too regular.'

'I know, love, but I can't let the chance of a job go,' he explained. 'The harder I work, the sooner we'll have the deposit on a house.'

'But all these late nights . . .'

'You want us to have a place of our own and security for the future, don't you?' he appealed to her.

'You know I do,' she said, beginning to melt.

'Well then, the more time I give to my business, the more money I'll make for the things you want, a house of our own, babies and all of that.' He looked at her tenderly, raising his hands expressively. 'You know me, Eve, I'm happy to stay as we are, living here at the flat, just the two of us. I'm doing all this work because I know you want those things.'

It was true. A home of their own and a family was Eve's idea of the future. Ken was quite content as they were, free to come and go as they pleased. He would rather spend their money on clothes and outings than save for a house, and he had no real desire for children at this stage.

Eve wasn't desperately broody at the moment either – they were both still only twenty-six. But she wanted to start a family while she was still quite young, and they couldn't try for a baby while they were living here, because children were strictly forbidden by the terms of the lease.

Their joint savings towards the deposit on a house had been seriously depleted when Ken had set up in business on his own as a builder and decorator. As well as all the initial expenses, it had been a while before he'd actually started earning.

All of Eve's wages had gone into keeping them, which meant they hadn't been able to save anything for a long period. But she'd given him her full support in his business venture because she knew he wanted to make something of himself.

'We both knew I wouldn't be working nine to five when I started on my own,' he continued. 'No one ever got rich doing that.'

She looked at him, his boyish good looks registering with as much vibrancy as ever. By any standards he was gorgeous and she was still as much in love with him as the day she'd married him three years ago after a whirlwind romance. They'd met one Saturday night at the Hammersmith Palais and had been mutually smitten. 'I know you're working hard for us, Ken,' she said now in a softer tone, because he was irresistible when he was penitent. 'But we never seem to get any time together lately. I'm out at work all day, I look forward to spending the evening with my husband.'

'And I look forward to spending time with you,' he said, his eyes full of sincerity. 'But when the opportunity to earn some decent cash comes up, I can't just let it go.' He paused, looking at her. 'I can see your point, though, and I'll try to be more disciplined with my work in future, and get home earlier.'

'Promise?' She was smiling now, and glowing inside.

'I promise.' He slipped his arms around her and this time she didn't resist. 'I'm really sorry I didn't phone to let you know I'd be late.'

'And so you should be.' She was quite firm about it even though she had relented.

He kissed her on the lips. 'I'll take you out somewhere nice to make up for it sometime soon,' he said casually.

'I might hold you to that.' She grinned.

'You do that,' he said 'And in the mean time I'll pop down the chippy to get us some food, since I ruined the meal you cooked.'

'That'd be lovely,' she said.

'I'll be five minutes,' he promised, kissing her briefly before hurrying from the flat.

She was still smiling as the door closed behind him.

The following evening Eve met her brother George on her way home from work. He was passing in his car when she got off the bus and offered her a lift. It was only a few minutes' walk to her flat but she accepted his offer because she'd been to the supermarket in her lunch hour and was laden with heavy carrier bags.

'You finished work for the day?' she enquired casually as she settled in the passenger seat.

'No. I've been out on business all afternoon. Been to see a bloke about some motors,' explained George Granger, a sturdily built man with the same dark hair and colouring as his sister. 'I've gotta go back to the car lot to clear up a few bits and pieces before I can go home.'

'You going out tonight?' she asked in a chatty, sisterly manner.

'Might go down the local for a pint and a game o' darts later on,' he said, deep-brown eyes focusing ahead as he turned off the main road. 'Depends what time I get finished.'

'Stay in or go out, you've only yourself to please,' she remarked.

'That's right,' agreed George, who was twenty-eight and happily single with a small bachelor flat in Ealing.

'How's business?' she asked.

'Pretty good, thanks.' Two years ago George had given up his job as a car mechanic in a garage and set up as a self-employed car salesman, in a very small way at first. Renting a piece of waste ground on the busy main road, he'd started with a couple of old bangers and gradually built up to the healthy stock of vehicles he now carried.

The project had been so successful that his father had resigned from his job on the assembly line in a factory to become George's general assistant. He and his dad had always been good mates and worked well together. For the first time in his life, George had something worthwhile to aim for and he was determined to eventually achieve his dream and open car showrooms trading in good-quality used cars. His ambitions filled his life to such an extent, he didn't even have a steady girlfriend at the moment.

'I'm glad it's still going well,' said Eve.

'How are things with you, sis?'

'Fine.'

'Ken?'

'He's fine too,' she told him. 'But working too hard.'

'Par for the course when you're self-employed, I'm afraid,' he replied.

'That's what he says,' she sighed, rummaging in her bag for her keys. 'But he's promised to try and get home earlier of an evening. I'm fed up with being on my own at night.'

'That's why I'm glad I'm single,' George confessed. 'I can get home as late as I like as I've no one to answer to.'

'You'll meet someone one day and all this confirmed bachelor stuff will go out of the window,' she said with a smile in her voice.

'Maybe. But not until I've got my business plans up and running,' he said. 'Marriage would hold me back and I don't want that.'

'Time will tell,' she said sagely.

When they got to her place, he carried her bags up to the flat for her but wouldn't stay for a cup of tea because he had work to do. She said she didn't mind because she wanted to start getting dinner ready for her and Ken.

'He's a lucky man,' George said.

'If I have to bin the meal again tonight, he'll be a dead one, I know that much,' she grinned.

'Oh, dear,' said George. 'Let's hope he doesn't get held up, then.'

He didn't. He was in on the dot of seven armed with a bunch of flowers.

'Peace offering,' he said with one of his most melting smiles.

'Thanks, darling. 'She kissed him deeply. 'It's a lovely thought, even if it was inspired by a guilty conscience.'

'It was inspired by the fact that I love my wife,' he corrected.

'I believe you, thousands wouldn't,' she joshed, but she couldn't help being touched. There was something so special about receiving flowers.

The atmosphere over the meal was relaxed and happy. Eve washed the dishes, anticipating the rest of the evening with pleasure. But by the time she went into the living room, Ken was fast asleep in the armchair. When he woke up, an hour or so later, he seemed very preoccupied.

'Penny for them,' she said when they were about to go to bed.

He stared at her blankly, as though he hadn't heard her properly. 'What, what was that?' he asked.

'Penny for your thoughts,' she repeated. 'You seem miles away.'

'Oh . . . do I? I'm just thinking about work, love,' he explained. 'Various jobs I've been given the chance to quote for.'

'You and that bloomin' business,' she said. 'You're becoming obsessed.'

'The more obsessed I become, the sooner we get that house,' he reminded her.

'Yeah, I know,' she said with a stab of guilt.

'Tell you what,' he said, suppressing a yawn. 'Let's go out for a meal on Friday night. I'll make a point of finishing early and we'll go to a restaurant. I'll book a table somewhere nice.'

'That'd be smashing, Ken,' she enthused. 'I'll look forward to it.'

She hurried home from work on Friday, had a bath and got dressed in a plain black dress that she'd had a while but kept up to date with regular shortenings. Her hair was cut in a simple Mary Quant-style bob and gleamed from fresh washing. She was putting the finishing touches to her mascara when Ken phoned to say he'd been held up and couldn't get home in time to make the restaurant.

'This is the last straw,' she said and hung up on him.

She refused to have anything to do with him when he finally arrived full of apologies at nine thirty. She told him she was in no mood to listen to his excuses and maintained a steely silence for what was left of the evening. When they went to bed, she turned her back on him.

'I did phone and let you know,' he pointed out lamely.

'And that's supposed to make it all right, is it?' she mumbled into her pillow.

'Of course not. But just let me explain . . .'

'I've heard it all before, Ken. We had this out the other night,' she reminded him. 'You promised you'd stop putting work before our life together. And still you let me down.'

'I'll make it up to you, I swear,' he said. 'If you'll only stop turning your back on me.'

'Leave it, Ken,' she said. 'Turn the light off and go to sleep.'

'Please, Eve,' he begged her. 'Just turn over and listen to what I have to say. I promise I won't touch you.'

Slowly, she turned on to her back, staring at the ceiling and keeping her distance from him.

'I know I keep letting you down and I hate myself for it,' he said, and there was a catch in his voice that touched her heart despite herself. 'But I feel I must put the hours in now while there's plenty of work about, in case I get a slack patch. It's very insecure being self-employed. I want to get something solid behind me before I ease up.'

'But surely it isn't necessary to work so often in the evenings?' she suggested.

'I don't get time to go out doing estimates during the day while I'm actually working,' he explained. 'So I have to go at night.'

'Mm. I suppose so.'

'If you could just bear with me until I get the business more firmly established,' he said. 'It'll benefit us both in the long run. And I'll try to get home at a reasonable time as often as I can.'

'I don't want you killing yourself with work,' she told him. 'I'd rather wait longer for the house.'

'I don't want that,' he said.

'But all this work, work, work isn't good for you,' she said.

'I'm young, I can take it.'

Now she was full of compunction because he was doing it all for her. 'Oh, Ken,' she said, 'I shouldn't go on at you.'

'Shush.' He was stroking her arm now. 'You're perfectly entitled.'

'It gets lonely when you're out so much,' she said, edging towards him.

'I know, I know,' he said softly. 'I'll really try to do better.'

She lay still, listening to the hurrying beat of her heart as their bodies touched.

'So am I forgiven?' he asked.

'When do I ever not forgive you?' she said lovingly, turning to face him and noticing that his eyelids were drooping and his arm felt heavy as he put it over her. He looked exhausted.

'Thanks, Eve,' he said. 'Love you.'

'Love you too.'

She got out of bed to go to the bathroom, and when she got back he was asleep. That business of his is going to give him a heart attack before he's thirty if he isn't careful, she thought worriedly, and got into bed, careful not to disturb him.

Eve's parents, Dot and Ned Granger, lived quite near to Eve, in Marshall Gardens, in the same house that she and George had been brought up in. Their proximity meant that Eve was able to see a lot of them.

On Saturday afternoons, Eve and her mother always went shopping together. Usually they were looking rather than buying, and would scour the West Ealing stores and sometimes get the bus to the Broadway for a mooch round Bentall's and a cup of tea and a buttered bun in the cafeteria there.

Today they didn't bother with the Broadway and had their tea in Lyon's. But Eve was still preoccupied with the events of the previous night and not her usual chirpy self.

'What's the matter, love?' enquired Dot when they had unloaded their tray and settled at the table in the crowded café.

'I can't hide anything from you, can I?' said Eve, looking at her mother. Dot was a sweet-faced woman with warm brown eyes and a youthful look about her despite the matronly clothes she wore because she thought – wrongly, in Eve's opinion – they were the sort of thing a woman of forty-seven should be wearing.

'Not usually, no,' she admitted with a grin.

Eve spread butter on her bun. 'It's Ken,' she said, looking up.

In contrast to her children, who had both inherited their father's dark looks, Dot had wispy light-brown hair and a round, plump face. She frowned, stirring her tea. 'Not in trouble, is he?'

'Only with me.'

'Oh?'

'He's working too hard, Mum, and I'm worried about him,' she explained.

'Hard work never did anyone any harm,' Dot pointed out, looking relieved that it wasn't anything more serious. 'He's young and strong, he'll be all right.'

'I don't want him to make himself ill just so that we can get our own place quicker,' Eve said. 'I want him to ease up.'

'Have you talked to him about it?' Dot wondered.

'Yeah, we discussed it last night.' She wouldn't dream

of discussing the personal details of her marriage, but it was nice to share this problem with someone she was close to.

'And has he agreed to slow down?' Dot chewed her bun slowly, waiting for her daughter to reply.

Eve nodded. 'Oh yeah, he's promised to try,' she said. 'But he's said that before and it never seems to happen.'

'Oh, dear.'

'His work dominates our lives,' Eve told her. 'We hardly get any time together these days. And when he is at home, he's worn out.'

'Hmmm.' Dot pondered the problem. 'What you need is a holiday.'

Eve thought about this. 'I've got two weeks' holiday to come in June but I don't suppose Ken will take any time off,' she said. 'So we won't be able to go out for days anywhere.'

'I'm talking about a proper holiday away, just the two of you,' explained Dot.

'Oh.' Eve's mood brightened. 'It's a good idea but I don't suppose Ken will agree.'

'Then talk him into it,' Dot advised her. 'A holiday away is what you both need, so don't take no for an answer.'

'I'll give it a try,' said Eve, fired with a sudden determination.

'A holiday!' exclaimed Ken when she broached the subject to him that evening over supper. 'I can't take time off to go away on holiday.'

'Only for a week,' she said, sprinkling parmesan cheese on to her spaghetti bolognese.

'How can I go away when I've got jobs booked in?' he asked her.

'They can be rearranged,' she suggested hopefully.

'And lose all the goodwill I'm trying to build up?' was his answer to that.

'People will wait an extra week,' she pointed out. 'Builders are known for keeping people waiting.'

12

'Not me,' he said, his voice rising.

She put the cheese sprinkler down and stared at him. 'You're entitled to a holiday, Ken.'

'Being entitled doesn't come into it when you're self-employed,' he declared, sounding cross now. 'I don't get holidays with pay like you do.'

'No, but you do earn well when you're working,' she reminded him. 'We can certainly afford a week at the coast somewhere.'

'And what about our savings?' he wanted to know.

'I'm talking about something cheap,' she said.

'We'd still be spending money,' he pointed out. 'And holidays always cost more than you expect.'

'There are times when it's more important to spend than to save,' she said. 'And this is one of those times.'

He fell into a thoughtful silence. 'We wouldn't get anywhere to stay at this late stage anyway,' he said with obvious relief. 'It's almost June now.'

'There are always last-minute cancellations,' she reminded him. 'I could look down the holiday accommodation in the local paper.'

'No, it isn't a good idea, Eve.'

She twirled spaghetti around her fork. 'Why are you so much against it?' she asked, looking up.

'Pressure of work,' he said quickly. 'You know that.'

They continued with their meal in silence for a while. Then Eve gave him one of her wide, uplifting smiles, and said, 'Okay, we can't agree about this, so I'll do a deal with you.'

'Oh?' He looked at her warily.

'As you've said, we probably won't get in anywhere at this late stage.' She looked at him, a twinkle in her eyes. 'But if I do happen to find accommodation, I'll book it and arrange everything. All you have to do is come with me. Deal?'

Their eyes were locked in conflict. She wouldn't allow her gaze to falter.

'Deal,' he surrendered at last with a half-smile 'But I'm quite safe, 'cause you won't find anywhere.'

'We'll see about that,' she said with a determined gleam in her eye.

Chapter Two

Eve was awake first on the Saturday of the holiday. A week in glorious Devon, just her and Ken. She couldn't wait. Eager to be up and doing, she all but leapt out of bed, controlling her exuberance because Ken was still asleep.

Instead she slipped carefully out and padded barefoot to the kitchen to make a pot of tea, long legs emphasised by a short scarlet nightdress. Back in the bedroom, while the kettle boiled, she drew back the curtains, filling the room with sunlight.

'Time to get up, Ken,' she said, sitting on the bed, gently stroking his shoulder.

After some drowsy grunting and mumbling, he muttered, 'What's the time?'

'Nine o'clock.'

'What!' He shot up. 'Why didn't you wake me? I'll be late for work.'

'Not today, you won't.' Her slightly husky voice was squeaky with excitement. 'Because we're on holiday, remember.'

There was a silence while the information found its way into his half-awakened brain. 'Oh yeah, so we are.' He lay back and closed his eyes, letting out a growl of pleasure. 'So, draw the curtains and come back to bed.'

'There isn't time.'

'Why not?'

'George will be here soon to take us to the station in his car.'

'Oh, no!' he groaned.

'I told you I'd arranged it with him,' she reminded him.

He peered at her over the sheet. 'Yeah, I remember now,' he said, yawning and stretching. 'But I'm not sure I can face your brother so early in the morning.'

'Don't be horrible about George,' she admonished firmly. 'It's very kind of him to give us a lift to the station to save us paying for a taxi.'

'Okay, okay,' he said. 'There's no need to get the hump.'

'I'm not, I'm just stating the facts,' she told him, defensive as ever about her relatives.

'Point taken,' he said.

Originally from south London, Ken didn't keep in touch with his own people. He said he didn't have anything in common with them now that he was an adult. Given his attitude towards his own family, it wasn't surprising that he didn't understand how important Eve's was to her.

Whilst they were the embodiment of goodness and stability to her, Ken had never hit it off with the Grangers. They went through the social formalities but there was an underlying mutual antipathy between them which Eve sensed but which was never mentioned by any member of her family because they were sensitive to her feelings.

The confidence that Ken exuded in such abundance and which Eve found so attractive didn't appeal to everyone. She supposed that must be the problem. She wished things could be different, but accepted the fact that some people just didn't like each other.

'Any tea going?' he asked.

'The kettle's on.'

'That's my girl.'

'You *will* get up as soon as you've had your tea, though, won't you?' she urged. 'Or you won't be ready when George arrives.'

'I promise.' He looked at her persuasively. 'But do we have to go away?'

'We certainly do,' she said with ebullience. 'It's all booked and paid for.'

'Oh, God,' he moaned. 'How come I'm getting dragged off to some caravan in a godforsaken place near Torquay?'

'Because we made a deal,' she informed him brightly.

'I really came unstuck, didn't I?' he sighed. 'I honestly didn't think you'd find anywhere for us to stay.'

'You should never underestimate a woman,' she laughed.

'I wouldn't dare.'

'Seriously though, Ken,' she said more solemnly. 'We both need a holiday. Especially you. And if the only way I can get you away from your business is to drag you off to the seaside, then so be it.'

'You're a hard woman,' he said playfully.

She wriggled her shoulders with pleasure. 'Oh, I'm so looking forward to it.' She breathed deeply. 'All that lovely sea air will do us the world of good. It's really exciting to be going away.'

'Dunno about exciting . . .'

'You and me together on our own for a week in a cosy caravan by the sea,' she said, tossing her head and making a clicking sound with her mouth. 'What could be more exciting than that?'

'Not much,' he said, because her vivacity was very appealing.

She looked towards the window. 'It's a lovely morning.'

'Always a bad sign.'

'Now stop putting a damper on things,' she ordered, laughing because she knew he was teasing her.

'Just being realistic,' he said lazily, eyelids drooping, long lashes curling. 'In this country, if the weather's nice on the day you go away on holiday, it rains for the rest of the week.'

'That isn't true,' she denied, slapping his arm in a playful manner.

'It's a recognised fact that British sun doesn't have the stamina to stay out for more than a few days at a time, and we've already had a spell of nice weather this week.'

'I'm not listening to any more of your doom and gloom.'

17

She saw his eyes closing. 'Don't you dare go back to sleep.'

'I'm tired.'

'Mm, I'm not surprised, after what we were doing in the early hours of this morning,' she giggled.

He opened his eyes and gave a slow, languorous smile, remembering. 'Yeah, that was really quite something,' he said.

The understatement of the decade, she thought, all the more so because it didn't happen often enough lately, with Ken working all hours and being exhausted when he got home. They needed this holiday *so much* – time to relax and have fun together, to talk and make love. It could rain the whole week for all she cared. 'It certainly was,' she agreed. 'It must have been the holiday spirit.' She leaned over, smiling wickedly into his eyes. 'Which, I might add, is noticeably absent in you this morning.'

'I'll be all right when we get there,' he said, smiling.

'I shall make sure that you are,' she told him. 'We'll have a great time.'

The sound of the kettle whistling sent her hurrying to the kitchen, laughingly daring him to go back to sleep while she was gone.

Returning a few minutes later with the tea, she found him with his eyes closed. 'Oh no,' she wailed. 'I told you not to doze off again. George will be here and we won't be ready.'

'That had you fooled, didn't it?' He was laughing as he grabbed her and pulled her down on to the bed, kissing her.

'You rat.'

'Come back to bed.'

With enormous difficulty she managed to resist. 'There'll be plenty of time for that in Torquay,' she chuckled, pulling away. 'I'm going to get us some breakfast. And I'll expect you to be out of that bed in five minutes.'

'Spoilsport.'

'You won't be saying that when we get to Torquay,' she grinned.

He gave her one of his most charming smiles. 'In that case, the sooner we get there the better,' he said, sitting up.

'I thought that would shift you,' she said, and headed for the kitchen, feeling warm inside.

'That really is a smart motor, George,' said Ken as he and his brother-in-law loaded the luggage into the boot of George's blue Zephyr.

'Not bad, is it?' agreed George.

'Are you keeping this one for yourself?'

'No,' said George. 'It's for sale like all the others.'

'Why not have this one for your own personal use?' suggested Ken.

'There's no point.'

'Surely you're entitled to a car of your own when your business is doing well?' opined Ken.

'Time for that later on when I've got money behind me,' George told him. 'Until then, it suits me to use the cars I have in stock.'

'I'd want a car of my own if I was a single man in your line of business,' said Ken.

George's dark eyes rested on Ken as he silently counted to ten. 'It's a question of priorities, mate,' he said patiently. 'The more money I put into my business, the sooner I'll have enough to build showrooms, all supposing I can talk my landlord into selling me the land, o' course. Anyway, it doesn't matter if I use a car from stock, since they all belong to me.'

Ken gazed admiringly at the sleek contours of George's vehicle. 'A car like that would suit me down to the ground.'

'Well, when you're ready, come and see me and I'll get you fixed up,' offered George.

Glancing towards Eve, who was waiting for them in the back of the car, Ken turned back to George and spoke in a confidential manner. 'God knows when that'll be,' he said wistfully. 'We're saving for the deposit on a house.'

Shrugging his shoulders, George said, 'You can't have everything.'

'You know what women are like,' continued Ken with the over-emphasised masculinity of someone who wants to be one of the lads but can never quite make it. 'They want babies and a house with a fitted kitchen . . . the whole domestic thing.'

'Surely it isn't only women who want that,' George corrected. 'Most men want a nice home and a family too, eventually.'

'*Eventually* being the operative word.' Ken paused, looking at George. 'I'm in no hurry to have a mortgage around my neck and a lawnmower to push round the garden at weekends. But it's what Eve wants.'

'It's what marriage is all about, isn't it?' said George. 'Making a home, having a family.'

'Yeah, I suppose so,' agreed Ken.

Being of an amiable disposition, it was unusual for George to dislike anyone. But he'd spent the past three years trying, unsuccessfully, to like his brother-in-law. It shouldn't have been difficult. Ken was a bit of a bighead but he was a decent enough type and Eve thought the world of him. But for some reason he made George's skin crawl.

Still, as long as Eve was happy with him, George would continue to act the congenial brother-in-law, for her sake.

Inside the car Eve was looking idly out of the window into the street where children were already playing. The roar of traffic from the nearby main road throbbed in her ears, but she was miles away, imagining the fresh sea breeze in her hair as she and Ken walked along the beach together.

Ken settled in the back seat with Eve, and George drew away, hooting loudly to disperse a game of rounders that was in progress. The weekend got off to an early start for the kids in this street.

'Are you going straight to work when you've seen us off?'
Eve enquired casually of her brother, who was dressed in a
business suit.

'Yeah,' replied George.

'Dad might have sold a car while you've been away,' said
Eve, who was very close to her father.

'He'll be chuffed to bits if he has,' remarked George
lightly.

'Yeah.' She smiled at the thought. 'I've never known Dad
to be so cheerful as he is since he went to work for you.'

'I'm the same,' remarked George. 'Selling cars for a
living beats being a grease-monkey any day o' the week.'

Eve sat back in her seat as they got on to the main
road, the traffic at a crawl as they progressed through the
crowded West Ealing shopping area into the Broadway,
with its elegant shops and imposing town hall dating back
to the last century. They moved on past Ealing Common,
where the grass was lush, the magnificent chestnut trees in
full bloom. People were already out enjoying the sunshine,
strolling beneath the trees.

Skirts seemed to get shorter as beehive hairstyles got
higher, Eve noticed, watching a crowd of young girls walk
across the common. She'd always loved trendy clothes and
fashionable hairstyles, though she preferred a simple bob
to the heavily lacquered, backcombed styles. As a teenager
she'd always had the latest thing. Nowadays, she could only
keep up to date within the limitations of her budget because
everything she earned went into their home.

But a special knack of teaming things up and reinventing
old clothes with the clever use of scarves and cheap jewel-
lery meant she usually managed to look reasonably smart.
Today she was casual in a white T-shirt and jeans.

The glorious sunshine put her into the holiday mood
with even more enthusiasm. This time tomorrow we'll be
stretched out on the beach, she thought, or sheltering from
the rain somewhere. So long as she and Ken were together,
it really didn't matter.

George was complaining about the traffic, which got denser the nearer they got to central London. 'I knew it would be bad, being a Saturday,' he said, 'but it's worse than ever. We're gonna be pushed to catch your train at this rate.'

'We won't be able to go if we miss the train,' said Ken, turning to Eve and adding with irony, 'what a terrible shame.'

'Of course we'll be able to go,' she said, taking the joke in good part. 'We'll get a later train.' She gave him an assertive look, but there was laughter in her eyes. 'You're not getting out of this holiday, Ken, so you might as well accept it. If we have to wait at the station all day for a train, we're going to Torquay.'

'Okay, I give in,' he said, slipping his arm around her.

Main-line railway stations always made Eve feel emotional. The excitement of going somewhere combined with the frenetic bustle of people on the move brought tears to her eyes.

'You're as daft as a brush,' said George, standing on the steamy platform as she hung out of the window of the corridor, sniffing into her handkerchief. 'You're only going to Torquay for a week.'

'It's ridiculous, I know.' She blew her nose. 'It's other people's partings that get to me. Some of them might be going away for years.'

'Not very likely,' said Ken, who was standing beside her. 'If they were going to the other side of the world, they would be at the airport, not the train station.'

'I suppose so,' she agreed. 'But that doesn't stop me filling up.'

The guard shouted, 'Mind the doors,' and they slammed all along the train.

'Thanks for the lift, George,' said Eve.

'Yeah, cheers, mate,' echoed Ken.

'You're welcome,' said George. 'See you in a week's time.'

*   *   *

Inside the compartment, Ken squeezed her hand. 'All right now?' he asked affectionately.

'I'm fine,' she told him. 'I've always had this thing about big stations. Probably because going somewhere outside of London is such an event. I don't suppose seasoned travellers take any notice.'

'You wait till we can afford to go abroad for our holidays,' he said. 'You'll be so used to travel, you won't turn a hair.'

'That'd be lovely,' she enthused. 'But Torquay will do me for now.'

'Me too.'

'What's that I hear?' She turned and gave him a quizzical look. 'I thought you were only here on sufferance.'

He smiled. 'I am, but I'm getting in the mood now,' he said. 'As you've made me come, I might as well enjoy myself.'

'That's the spirit,' she said.

He opened his newspaper and she settled down to read a magazine. But the little girl sitting opposite her had other ideas. 'Hello,' she said, 'I'm Lesley.'

'Hello, Lesley,' said Eve.

'We're going to the seaside,' announced Lesley, a thin little thing of about six or seven with brown saucer eyes and hair worn in bunches.

'That's very exciting,' said Eve, putting her magazine down and giving the child her full attention. 'So are we.'

'Daddy's going to buy me a bucket and spade when we get there,' she informed Eve.

'You'll be making lots of sandcastles then,' responded Eve warmly.

'Yes.'

'I used to love doing that when I was little,' Eve told her.

Lesley nodded. 'Can you swim?' she enquired solemnly.

'Yes. Can you?'

'No. But Daddy's gonna teach me in the sea while we're on holiday.'

A man of about thirty-five appeared from behind a newspaper and smiled politely at Eve, then said to his daughter, 'Leave the lady to read her magazine in peace, Lesley.'

The woman sitting next to him, who Eve assumed to be the child's mother, said, 'Lesley could win prizes for yapping,' but her tone was more proud than apologetic. 'She never stops.'

'I'm enjoying her company,' said Eve. 'I'm not in the mood to read anyway.'

'Me neither.' The woman glanced at the newspaper her husband was holding, the front page full of the Profumo affair. 'Though I must admit, I have been interested in the latest steamy goings-on in the government.'

'I think most people have been following that story, whether they admit it or not,' said Eve in a friendly manner.

Lesley brought the conversation back to a more whole-some topic. 'Have you got your swimming costume in your case?' she asked Eve.

'I certainly have,' she told her. 'I wouldn't go to the seaside without that.'

'I only hope we get the chance to wear them,' said the child's mother with a wry grin. 'I never trust the weather when it's nice the day we're travelling.'

'That's exactly what my husband said, wasn't it, darling?' said Eve, nudging Ken, who lowered his paper and nodded at the woman.

Eve and Lesley's mother became engaged in conver-sation. The family were also going to Torquay so would be changing trains at Newton Abbot along with Eve and Ken. Ken peered out from behind the newspaper to comment appropriately when required. It was a pleasant way to pass the time as the train sped through the countryside.

'I think I'll go and stretch my legs,' said Ken after a

while. 'I fancy a wander along to the buffet car for a drink. Coming, Eve?'

'I'll stay here, if you don't mind,' she said, because she didn't fancy a drink and was enjoying the company in the compartment.

'Sure you don't want anything?' he asked considerately.

'Positive, thanks, love.'

'Shan't be long then,' he said, rising and grabbing the edge of the luggage rack to help him keep his balance against the rocking of the train.

Eve and her travelling companions continued to chat for a while, eventually falling silent listening to the monotonous clickety-clack of the wheels on the track. Lesley seemed sleepy. Eve was feeling a bit drowsy herself, watching meadows and cornfields flash past. Quite suddenly she experienced a moment of such intense happiness it brought a rush of tears to her eyes.

'How long till we get there, Mummy?' asked Lesley, livening up and becoming impatient.

'Not long now, dear,' her mother replied. 'We'll be changing trains soon. Then we'll be almost there.'

'I wish we were there now.'

Noticing how fidgety the child was becoming, Eve made a suggestion to her mother. 'I'm a bit bored myself, so I think I'll go and join my husband in the buffet car. Would Lesley like to come with me for a change of scene?'

'Yes, please,' chirped Lesley.

The woman thanked Eve for asking. 'You be a good girl for the lady,' she said to her daughter with obvious affection.

Making her way to the compartment door, Eve clutched Lesley's hand to keep her steady. She had just opened the sliding door to the corridor when the train seemed to slow down and started juddering violently. There was a scream of metal as the driver slammed on his brakes, then a thunderous crash.

A heavy blow battered Eve's shoulders just before she

and Lesley were thrown across the compartment, landing on top of Lesley's parents as the carriage left the track and turned on to its side. Suddenly there was broken glass and luggage flying everywhere, suitcases bashed open and spewing out clothes, black smoke pouring in through the shattered windows.

When the carriage finally stilled, there was a deathly silence as the terrified passengers took in the horror of what had happened.

'Bloody hell,' said a man eventually.

'We must have hit another train,' said someone else shakily.

Then there was screaming, shouting, and Lesley began to cry. People were sitting dazed among broken suitcases and holdalls, some struggling to get to their feet now that the train was still. The seats were smashed in the wrecked compartment. The carriage door was beneath them, the corridor overhead, the compartment door open as Eve had left it.

Stunned, Eve's first coherent thought as she scrambled to her feet was for Ken. But events here were pressing and she focused her mind on her fellow passengers, several of whom were cut and bleeding from the flying glass. She herself had to hold a handkerchief to her forehead to stem the flow of blood. The blow to her shoulders which had left her with a searing pain, she realised vaguely, must have come from a falling suitcase.

'Is anyone badly hurt?' she enquired loud enough for everyone to hear.

There was a muddled response, but at least everyone was conscious. The smoke was getting thicker, people were coughing and retching. Eve was expecting the compartment to burst into flames at any moment. The sound of people calling for help in other parts of the train added to the panic, especially for Eve, who was frantic with worry about Ken. There were flashes of light and the sound of fire crackling.

'We're trapped,' said a woman hysterically. 'Help, help . . .' Her voice was rising. 'Someone please help us, for God's sake, help us.'

'Don't panic . . . we're not trapped,' said Eve, managing to stay calm and positive despite her own paralysing fear. 'We can climb up and get out through the broken windows.'

Somebody muttered something about it being possible.

'I think we should get the little girl out first,' Eve suggested.

There was a murmur of agreement. Lesley's father stood up on the broken seats and battered suitcases. He wrapped a handkerchief around his hand, pushed the remaining glass from the window frame and climbed out. Eve lifted the sobbing child up through the window frame and handed her down to him on the ground. Lesley's mother went next. People waited their turn in a surprisingly orderly manner considering the horrific circumstances. Despite the crying and obvious sense of panic, they were all magnificently brave, Eve thought. Nobody bothered about finding their mangled luggage in their urgency to escape.

An elderly man displayed immense chivalry by insisting that Eve go before him. He would take no argument about it. Heart pumping and chest aching from the smoke, she hauled herself up through the window frame. As she jumped to the ground, the chaos and carnage around her was so shocking she couldn't take it in.

It was obvious now that they had hit another train. Both engines were on fire, as were several of the carriages, many of them lying on their sides. There were mangled carriages everywhere. The injured were lying groaning on the ground, cries of help still coming from passengers trapped inside the train.

The sight of blood-stained bodies by the side of the tracks made Eve vomit. People were hysterical at the sight of them. She could taste blood running into her mouth from the gash on her head; her clothes were soaked with sweat.

The emergency services were already pouring on to the scene. Police, fire brigade, ambulances. Eve found herself being forcibly ushered towards an ambulance by a police constable.

'Not me,' she sobbed. 'I'm not going in the ambulance. I have to find my husband.'

'You'll have to leave that to us,' he informed her in a kind but determined manner.

'He went to the buffet car . . . must have been in there or on the way back to the compartment when the train crashed,' she told him.

'Everything is being done to get everyone off the train as quickly as possible,' he informed her.

'He might be trapped.'

'He'll be found in due course,' the policeman tried to assure her. 'You need to go to the hospital to get checked over.'

'But I have to find him *now*,' she said, moving away. 'He might be hurt and needing me.'

'Keep away from the scene of the accident, please, madam,' he said, pulling her back.

'I *must* find him,' she cried, hardly aware of what she was saying.

'No,' shouted the policeman. 'It's too dangerous for you to go near the accident.'

Grey-faced and desperate, she broke away and ran towards the devastation in search of the man she loved. Her head was throbbing, her chest felt as though it would explode and her wound was gushing with blood . . .

Chapter Three

Dot Granger opened her front door, kicked off her shoes and headed straight for the kitchen. She was gasping for a cup of tea after trudging around the shops in this warm weather. The weekend wouldn't be complete without her Saturday afternoon wander, though. But it wasn't nearly so much fun without Eve. She smiled, imagining her daughter enjoying the sunshine in Torquay.

A short woman of rounded proportions, Dot threw open the back door to let in the fresh air, made some tea and went into the living room to watch the wrestling on television. With her husband out at work, she could enjoy it in peace, without a critical running commentary from Ned, who reckoned that professional wrestling was more carefully stage-managed than *Sunday Night at the London Palladium*. Dot thought he was probably right, and was sure she wouldn't enjoy it so much if she believed it to be authentic.

Tea and biscuits by her side on the coffee table, she settled in an armchair to watch these slick muscle-men apparently inflict pain on each other in spectacular style.

Dot's home showed about as much evidence of contemporary style as her clothes but was nicely furnished in the traditional way. The whole house shone with cleanliness because Dot found housework positively uplifting. She'd always enjoyed anything connected to homemaking – cooking, cleaning, knitting, sewing and even gardening. Dot's family and her home were her life. The problem was, she had too little to do with her time now that the children had left home.

She'd once thought of getting a part-time job, but Ned had been so appalled by the idea she hadn't pursued it. He was old-fashioned; he thought a man should be the bread-winner and any suggestion of his wife going out to work was seen as a threat to his manhood. She hadn't made an issue of it because she was happy to be just a housewife most of the time. It was only occasionally that she felt as though she wasn't making the most of her life.

On the screen the wrestlers were ostensibly intent upon killing each other. Dot laughed at their antics. All that pseudo male aggression was great fun to watch. Ned teased her, said it was an odd thing for a woman to like. As she pointed out, if it was that odd, why were there always women at the ringside?

The programme was interrupted by a newsflash. Dot nibbled a biscuit, only half listening as they returned to the studio, where the newsreader informed them that the death toll had now risen to twenty in the train crash near Newton Abbot in Devon. What train crash? Dot knew nothing about any train crash. But then she hadn't heard any news since early this morning on the radio. Devon? Her mouth went dry and her heart pumped horribly in the realisation that Eve and Ken had gone to Devon by train.

She told herself to stop overreacting; lots of trains would travel through Devon on a Saturday in summer. 'Which train was it?' she demanded of the face on the screen. 'Which bloody train are you talking about?'

'The eleven o'clock train from Paddington hit a goods train not far from Newton Abbot . . . many of the passengers were holidaymakers,' the newsreader obligingly told her.

Newton Abbot. That sounded ominously familiar. She was sure Eve had said something about changing trains there. And they must have left Paddington about eleven o'clock, because George had called in to see Dot on his way back from the station at about half past. *God almighty!*

An emergency telephone number came up on the screen for people worried about relatives travelling on that train.

30

She leapt up and grabbed a pencil from the sideboard drawer and something to write on from behind the clock on the mantelpiece, her hand shaking so much she could hardly get the number down on the back of the gas bill. Rushing to the telephone in the hall, she dialled the number. Engaged. Dammit! She tried several more times but couldn't get through.

Leaving the wrestlers to entertain an empty room, she tore from the house and headed for the car lot.

In the early evening of the following day, George's Zephyr travelled through the Devon countryside in the soft, persistent rain on the return journey to London. He and his parents had dropped everything yesterday to be with Eve. Ned Granger was in the front of the car with George; Eve was sitting in the back with her mother, her hands clasped tightly together on her lap. Her clothing was dirty, the suitcase of clean clothes still somewhere at the scene of the accident. She had a large dressing on the left side of her forehead.

'How are you feeling now, love?' enquired her mother with concern.

'I'm all right, thanks, Mum.'

'I still think you should have had another night in hospital.'

'They need the beds for the seriously injured,' she said dully, dry lips barely moving. She was rigid with tension and unable to cry. 'I'll be okay. I'd rather be at home.'

'How's your head?'

'Not too bad.' The wound was actually throbbing like mad but it seemed too trivial to mention compared to what other crash victims had suffered.

Silence fell. Eve was glad, because she was finding it difficult to follow a conversation. Her thoughts kept drifting back to the terrible events of yesterday afternoon . . .

She'd been so relieved when she'd found Ken lying on the grass at the side of the railway track, his face bruised and scratched, but his eyes open. 'Oh, Ken, thank God you're alive,' she'd said. He'd just stared, not moving. Then she'd seen the blood trickling from his mouth. A policeman had had to drag her away when one of the medics had covered him completely with a blanket, because she'd been begging them to leave his face free so that he could breathe. Silly of her to delude herself when it had been so obvious that he was dead.

'At least he didn't suffer,' her mother was saying now in an effort to console her. But no one could. Eve couldn't imagine ever feeling normal again. 'I mean, he wasn't trapped for ages, like some of the poor buggers. He wouldn't have been in pain.'

'There is that,' acknowledged Eve.

Ken had been flung through a door near the buffet car which had been thrown open by the impact of the crash. She'd been told that he'd died instantly from head injuries caused by his hitting the ground at such high speed.

That horrific scene yesterday was ingrained in her memory. She would never forget seeing Ken being taken away – not a person, but a corpse, just another fatal statistic of a disaster that would make headline news. She could hardly believe she hadn't fainted or had hysterics. But somehow she'd managed to carry on.

Now she dug into her handbag for a handkerchief and mopped her face. The vivid memories had brought her out in a cold sweat. But still she didn't cry.

'Nothing anyone can say can help you much now,' said her father, twisting round from the front of the car to talk to her, his booming voice noticeably subdued. 'But your mother's right about him not suffering.'

'He shouldn't have died,' said Eve.

'Of course he shouldn't, twenty-six is no age to die . . .' began her father.

'I mean that he wouldn't have died if it hadn't been for me,' Eve cut in.

'Whatever makes you say a thing like that?' said her mother, aghast at the suggestion.

'It was my idea to go away on holiday to Devon,' she explained in a flat voice. 'Ken didn't want to go.'

'You mustn't think like that,' said Dot.

'Course you mustn't,' agreed Ned, his big craggy face unusually pale against his greying dark hair. His wife and family were everything to him and he felt Eve's pain as his own. 'That sort of reasoning is just plain daft.'

'Maybe it is,' said Eve. 'But it doesn't alter the fact that Ken would be alive now if I hadn't insisted we go away on holiday.'

Her mother thought about this for a moment. 'It was me who suggested the idea to you in the first place,' she pointed out. 'So does that mean I'm to blame?'

'Of course not,' said Eve.

'There you are then. That proves how pointless it is to think along those lines.' Dot was shocked and saddened by Ken's death but her sorrow was all for her daughter. 'It was an accident. If anyone is to blame for what happened, it's the person responsible for the goods train being on the wrong line.'

'You've quite enough on your plate without guilt an' all,' her father put in.

'Okay, Dad.' Her intellect told her they were right but the need to punish herself persisted. The rain trickled down the car windows and dripped through the lush foliage in this muddy country lane which was overhung in places by trees. Every so often a gap in the hedge revealed cornfields and cattle-dotted pastureland, hazy with a rain mist.

But all Eve could see was the carnage of yesterday and the face of her dead husband. Although the thoughts and images were agonising, she had a perverse need for them to keep coming; her penance for being alive when Ken wasn't. She was at once guilty and grateful, and poignantly aware of the fragility of life.

'I'll be having Ken brought back to London for the

funeral,' she heard herself say, the practical sound of the words giving the whole thing a terrible reality.

'Yeah, o' course,' said her mother with an understanding nod.

'We'd never talked about anything like that,' said Eve. 'You don't at our age, do you?'

'Course you don't,' said her mother.

'But I think he'd want to be buried in Ealing,' said Eve.

'Don't worry about any of that,' said George. 'We'll help you get it organised.'

By the time they got back to Ealing, the rain had stopped but a humid dampness permeated everything. George pulled up outside their parents' house in Marshall Gardens and they all got out of the car. Except Eve.

'Come on, love,' urged her mother through the window. 'I'll get us something to eat.'

'I appreciate all you're doing for me . . . coming all the way to Devon and everything,' said Eve. 'But would you mind very much if I went home to my own place?'

'Well, no.' Dot looked surprised and worried. 'I just assumed you wouldn't want to be on your own tonight, and would rather stay here with us.'

'I think I'd rather go home.'

'I'll come with you,' Dot quickly offered. 'I'll just pop indoors and get some overnight things.'

Eve bit her lip. She didn't want to upset her parents, who were being brilliant. But she was hurting too much for pretence. 'I think I'd rather be on my own, if you don't mind.'

'Oh, love,' said Dot, full of concern. 'You shouldn't be by yourself. Not tonight.'

'I feel as though I need to be,' she tried to explain. 'I'll see you tomorrow.'

'But we can't let you be on your own at a time like this,' protested her father.

'I'd really rather . . .'

George made a hasty intervention. 'I think we should

let Eve do what she feels most comfortable with,' he said in a quiet but firm tone. 'She knows where we are if she needs us.'

'If you're sure, then,' said Dot with obvious reluctance.

'I am,' said Eve.

Dot insisted on giving her milk, bread and a few other essentials, since Eve had expected to be away so didn't have anything in.

'Thanks, Mum, you're a dear.'

'Ring if you need us,' she said.

'I will.'

'Take care, love,' said her father.

They were both standing at the gate as the car rolled away. When they drew up outside Eve's place, George offered to go in with her.

'Thanks, but no,' she said.

'Are you sure?'

'Tomorrow I'll probably want to surround myself with people, but . . .'

'But tonight you want to be on your own,' he finished for her.

'I don't *want* to exactly,' she said, trying to define her feelings, which weren't at all clear, even to herself. 'It's more that I feel it's something I have to do. Going home for the first time as . . .' She swallowed hard. 'As Ken's widow instead of his wife is something I must face on my own. And there's no time like the present.'

'See you tomorrow then.' He got out and opened her door for her. 'Give me a bell if you need me. It doesn't matter how late.'

'Will do.'

Kissing her on the cheek, he stood by the car, watching her walk down the short path to the front door. His heart was aching. Even in the glow of the street lights, the building looked stern and shadowy, its contours blurred by the mist. Large and impersonal, it seemed to swallow her up. It lacked the friendliness of their family home in Marshall Gardens, which always seemed welcoming, even from the outside, whatever the weather or the mood you were in.

He stood by the car, waiting until the lights went on in her flat. He and Eve had always been close and the thought of her all alone up there was almost too much for him to bear. He wanted to be with her to offer solace at this terrible time.

But there was only so much comfort anyone could give her at this early stage. Her grief was something she would have to work through on her own. She was obviously already aware of that, which was why she wanted to be alone tonight.

Life was going to be hard for her, *very hard*, he thought. With a heavy heart he got back in the car and drove away.

Because Eve felt like a different person to the one who had left home so full of joy and excitement yesterday morning, she expected the flat to be different too, somehow. It was, of course, exactly as they'd left it, only achingly still and silent.

The first thing she did was to strip off her mucky clothes and have a bath in the creaky old bathroom with its sloping floor and unreliable water heater. Dressed in a clean blue nightdress, but no dressing gown because it was in her missing suitcase, she went into the kitchen to make coffee, hands shaking, stomach tight. Bothered by hunger pains because she'd hardly eaten a thing since the accident, she took a digestive biscuit out of the packet, but had only one bite before throwing the rest in the bin because her throat was too constricted to swallow.

She made coffee, but it was left untouched in the kitchen while she wandered aimlessly around the flat, all the while expecting to hear Ken's voice, or his key in the lock.

He was everywhere – his clothes in the wardrobe, the scent of his shaving cream in the bathroom, his building magazines stuffed untidily in the rack by the television. She picked up a sweater he'd left hanging over the back of the chair in the bedroom and buried her face in it, inhaling the poignantly familiar smell of him.

The dull ache of sorrow turned to blistering rage, so ferocious she had to rush to the bathroom to retch over the sink. Back in the bedroom, she threw the sweater on the floor and kicked the wall in a fury at this appalling twist of fate that had taken her husband and shattered her world. She hated her vulnerability – her powerlessness to change anything.

Anger finally spent, her body crumpled and she lay on her stomach on the bed, her face buried in the pillow – *his* pillow, impregnated with *his* scent. Then she cried, an outpouring of self-pity and despair and the sheer torture of knowing she was never going to see him again.

She wept for a long time, personal anguish turning to deep sorrow for the real loser in all this – Ken, who had still had so much of life to live. She felt stiff and achy when she got up, but the tension had lessened, leaving her empty and sad.

Her coffee had gone cold. She poured it down the sink and made another, which she took into the living room. The release of tension meant that she was able to sit still for long enough to drink it, feeling utterly drained.

Her parents came into her mind. She recalled the anxiety on their faces and knew how worried they were about her, how much they needed to feel they were helping.

It was almost midnight. Too late to phone them under normal circumstances. But she knew they wouldn't be asleep, not tonight. About the last thing she felt like doing was talking to anyone, but she dragged herself to the telephone and dialled their number.

'Mum . . . hi,' she said, forcing herself to sound strong.

'Eve . . .' Dot sounded cautious, as though expecting trouble.

'There's no need to sound so worried,' Eve told her with a deliberate lift to her voice. 'I know it's late but I thought I'd just give you a call to let you know that I'm all right.'

'You're sure, now?'

'I'm coping, anyway.'

'Oh.' Her mother's relief was obvious. 'Well, I suppose coping is the most you can expect in these early days.'

'I expect so too,' said Eve.

'It's a start.'

'Perhaps you could come round in the morning,' suggested Eve.

'I'll be there.'

'We'll get started on what has to be done,' said Eve, because she knew she must face up to practicalities and guessed her mother would want to be involved in that side of things.

'We'll sort things out together,' said Dot.

'Thanks for everything.'

'No need to thank me.'

'Night, then – see you tomorrow.'

'Night, love.'

Eve felt better for having made the effort. At least her parents could go to sleep believing she was managing, even if she was actually falling apart inside. Heavy with exhaustion, she went into the bedroom and stared at the double bed – *their* bed.

She couldn't possibly sleep there, knowing he would never lie beside her again. She took a pillow and the quilt off the bed and went back into the living room and lay down on the sofa.

This simply won't do, Eve, she told herself a few minutes later. You're fudging the issue, running away. You have to get used to living without him, and the sooner the better. It won't get any easier for putting it off.

Heaving herself to her feet, she plodded back to the bedroom. Bracing herself, she climbed into bed to face the first night of the rest of her life without him.

How Eve got through the funeral she never knew. She seemed to pass through the entire proceedings in a state of unreality. Everything seemed distant and irrelevant to her. Must be nature's way of helping, she supposed.

It wasn't a large gathering; just her family, a few friends and Ken's parents, who made no effort to be sociable and had obviously only put in an appearance out of duty because Eve had found their address and notified them of their son's death. They neither came back to her place for food with the other mourners after the burial nor showed any interest in keeping in touch with their son's widow. Whilst Eve was hurt on Ken's behalf, she was too deeply immersed in her own grief for it to wound her personally.

With the drama of the death and the funeral behind her, and the routine of day-to-day life back in place, Eve faced the grim reality of Ken's not being there to share ordinary, everyday things with her. Sometimes it didn't seem possible to function, but somehow she was walking, talking, going to work. Being among people all day helped, but packing parcels was not sufficiently absorbing to distract her from her grief for long.

One thing that did distract her was the financial problems she found herself with, because the rent on the flat was too high for one person to comfortably manage. Ken hadn't considered life insurance to be necessary for a young man with no children. So she had to raid her savings on a regular basis to subsidise her wages.

When her father gently broached the subject of her claiming compensation from the railway for Ken's death, she was horrified because it seemed so brutal and materialistic.

'Money can't compensate me for losing Ken,' she told him.

'Course it can't,' he said in his calm but firm manner. 'And I'm not suggesting that it can. But you've gotta be practical about this. Sentimentality isn't gonna pay the rent.'

'I've no intention of trying to make money out of Ken's death, Dad,' she insisted, the mere thought of it causing her pain.

'You're making it sound as though you'd be making a profit out of it,' he said.

'I would be,' she was quick to point out, 'since there wouldn't be any question of my getting money if he was alive.'

'That's a cock-eyed way of looking at it, I must say,' he told her.

'Maybe it is, but the very idea of compensation makes me feel sick.'

'You wouldn't need money if Ken was alive to provide for you,' he reminded her. 'You wouldn't be finding it hard to keep the flat going on your own if it wasn't for the accident. The relatives of the other victims will be claiming compensation, you can bet your sweet life on it. The railway will be insured for that sort of thing, anyway.'

In the end, because the family seemed to think it was the right thing to do, and because Eve was feeling so tired and unwell – presumably because of the shock – she agreed to put the matter into the hands of a solicitor. She was told she should get a payment of some sort but it would probably be a very long-drawn-out affair. These things always were. She was too busy surviving from day to day to give the matter much thought.

But as the weeks went by and her savings were rapidly disappearing, she was forced to apply her mind to the reality of her situation. Her mother suggested that she go back home to live – for a while anyway, until she found a cheaper flat.

'It's the only sensible thing to do, 'Dot said one Sunday when Eve and George were having lunch with their parents. 'If you can't manage the rent on the flat on your own without using all your savings, you'll have to move out and come home.'

Eve had grave doubts about such a plan. As much as she loved her parents, she was long past the stage in her life where she could comfortably share a roof with them. Anyway, they were used to having their home to themselves. It wouldn't be fair.

'I appreciate your offering,' said Eve, 'but I need my own space, and so do you.'

'I wasn't suggesting that you stay forever,' Dot hastily pointed out. 'Just until you find a cheaper place of your own.'

Flats with affordable rents were few and far between in this crowded area of London. The only other alternative was a bedsit. There were plenty of those about. But they were expensive for what they were, and some of them were quite grim.

'I think I'll stay where I am for the moment.' Despite the struggle to make ends meet, Eve didn't want to move from the place where she and Ken had been happy. There were so many memories. She felt close to him there and didn't want to lose that. 'I'll carry on for a bit longer and see how it goes.'

'You might get a decent amount of compensation,' her father suggested hopefully. 'That'll help to put you on your feet.'

'I don't even want to think about that,' she told him. 'You know how I feel about it.'

'Only because you're looking at it from the wrong angle,' said George.

'I'm not looking at it from any angle,' she informed him briskly. 'Because I'm not thinking about it at all.'

'Then you should be.'

'Leave it, George, please,' she urged him.

'Just hear me out.'

'Oh, go on then,' she sighed.

'You've been widowed because of the railway's negligence,' he stated categorically. 'So they should be made to pay. You're not claiming for anything to which you're not entitled.'

'If you say so,' she agreed wearily, immediately dismissing the subject from her mind. There wouldn't be much left by the time the solicitor's bill had been paid anyway.

But it was a strain trying to keep the flat going with only her wages coming in. Advertising for a lodger wasn't an option, because there was only one bedroom. Anyway, she couldn't bear the idea of sharing her home – hers and Ken's – with a complete stranger.

Determined not to be beaten, she lived frugally and took any overtime that was going, which meant she was permanently tired. But at least she was managing to pay the bills.

She was considering the idea of getting a more lucrative job on the production line in a factory when something happened that turned her life upside down yet again, and took the choice of whether or not to stay at the flat out of her hands.

The revelation happened one morning in August when she emerged from the bathroom sweating and exhausted, having been violently sick for the sixth morning in a row. Feeling faint and weak, she collapsed on to the bed and faced up to the fact that she was pregnant and, as such, no longer qualified for the tenancy of the flat.

Her first reaction was anger – irrational fury towards Ken for getting her pregnant and then promptly expiring and leaving her to face this problem alone; rage towards the landlord for being mean-spirited enough to prohibit children in his property; and most of all, anger at herself for being careless enough to get pregnant when the circumstances strictly forbade it.

This was what happened when you allowed yourself to get carried away by passion, as they had done that Friday night before the accident. Ken was usually so careful about that side of things, because he was so much against having children until they were ready. He'd always insisted that he would take care of it so that he could be sure there would be no accidents. Well, he'd slipped up good and proper on this occasion and she was really in the soup. A baby on the way, with no husband, no home and no job once she had a child to look after. What a mess!

Realising that she would be late for work if she didn't shift herself, she got up and shuffled queasily to the kitchen to make some toast and weak coffee which were the only things she seemed able to keep down in the mornings.

As the dry toast settled her stomach and she began to feel a little less nauseous, she was imbued with an unexpected rush of light and hope. For the first time since Ken's death, her life seemed to have a purpose. Being aware that she was pregnant made her feel even more vulnerable, but stronger too, in a curious kind of way.

All right, so she hadn't planned to get pregnant yet, and a baby was going to make her life impossibly difficult. But she wanted it. She wanted Ken's child – *so much*.

How she was going to manage motherhood under her present appalling circumstances she had no idea. But she did know that she was going to give it her very best shot. Somehow she would make a good life for her baby and herself.

Chapter Four

'I'll finish the drying-up when I've done this, Eve,' offered Dot, her hands in the washing-up bowl. 'You go in the other room and sit down.'

'I don't mind doing it, Mum,' she said, drying some cutlery and putting it away in the drawer. 'I'd have done the whole job if you hadn't beaten me to the sink when we'd finished eating.'

'You need to put your feet up after being at work all day.'

'I'm not ill, you know,' she reminded her.

'No, but you are six months pregnant and doing a full-time job with overtime,' Dot pointed out. 'You must look after yourself.'

'I do,' Eve informed her patiently. 'I eat all the right things, take my iron pills and go to bed at a reasonable hour at night. You don't need to fuss over me.'

'I don't,' Dot denied.

But she did, and Eve was beginning to find it rather cloying, which in turn filled her with compunction because her mother was so well-intentioned. 'You mustn't try to wrap me in cotton wool,' she suggested in a friendly manner. 'I am a responsible adult.'

'You're still my daughter, no matter how old and responsible you are,' Dot informed her. 'Anyway, you should be glad someone's making a fuss of you. I wouldn't say no to a bit of pampering myself.'

Eve laughed. 'Fat chance of anyone being able to pamper you,' she pointed out. 'You won't even go to bed when you're half dead with flu in case someone upsets your housekeeping system.'

Dot grinned; she couldn't deny it. 'Well, we all have our own way of carrying on.' She turned, peering at the cup Eve was about to put away in the cupboard. 'Have you dried that properly?'

'Of course.'

'That's all right then. And make sure you put the knives and forks in the right compartment in the drawer,' she requested. 'You mixed them up yesterday, and one thing I can't stand is an untidy cutlery drawer.'

'Sorry,' said Eve, trying not to be irritated by her mother's fastidiousness.

'I'd rather you left it to me,' said Dot. 'I know how I like things done.'

At this point Eve conceded defeat and went into the living room, where her father was sitting in the armchair by the fire with the newspaper on his lap, watching *The Flintstones*.

'You all right?' he asked as she sat down in a chair at the other side of the hearth.

'Yeah . . . fine.'

'Feeling a bit suffocated?'

His sensitivity to her feelings was unnerving. 'You and Mum are great and I'm lucky to be able to stay here,' she replied diplomatically.

'But you need some space . . . ?'

She grinned. 'You always have been able to read me like a book.'

'I like to think I haven't lost the knack,' he told her.

'It isn't that I'm not grateful . . .'

'I know that,' he said emphatically, 'but you're bound to miss the freedom and privacy of your own place.' He paused thoughtfully. 'Why don't you go out for an hour or so, to have a break? You could visit a friend, or go and see your brother.'

'Good idea. I think I will,' she said, loving him even more

for understanding her so well. She kissed the top of his head on her way to the kitchen. 'Thanks, Dad.'

Her mother had finished the dishes and was now energetically wiping the worktops with a cloth. Eve hugged her from behind.

'Oi, oi, what's this all about?' Dot wanted to know, turning to look at her daughter with an enquiring smile.

'Just to let you know that I appreciate everything you do for me,' she explained.

'Oh, that's nice.' Dot's warm eyes softened with pleasure, plump cheeks pinkly suffused. She dried her hands. 'I've nearly finished here. I'll make a pot o' tea and we'll watch the telly. *The Dick Van Dyke Show* is on later.'

'Actually, I thought I'd pop round to George's for an hour or so,' said Eve cautiously.

Predictably, Dot was concerned. 'It's quite a walk and it's cold out. It *is* December, you know.'

'A walk in the fresh air will do me good,' said Eve, heading for the door to avoid further objection. 'I won't be long.'

'Mind how you go, then,' warned her mother. 'And get George to give you a lift home.'

'I'll see how I feel,' Eve told her. 'See you later.'

The weather was cold, with a sharp wind blowing icy rain into her face, as she headed past the neat terraces of Marshall Gardens, her pace impeded by the extra weight she was carrying. The weather wasn't conducive to an enjoyable walk, but it felt good to be out of the house.

It made sense to stay with her parents until after the birth; indeed, her mother would be disappointed if she didn't. But once that was over, she simply must find a place of her own. Even apart from the fact that being under her parents' roof made her feel like a twelve-year-old again, it wouldn't be fair to them to stay on for longer than she had to when the baby arrived. They'd raised their own family and deserved some peace and quiet. Finding somewhere suitable was a real headache, though, because most of the rented accommodation in her price range had a strict 'no children' rule. Still, she was on the council waiting list, and her chances would be improved once the baby was actually here.

Her mother had offered her services as child-minder when Eve went back to work, which she would have to do to keep herself and the baby. So that was one problem solved.

She was breathless by the time she reached George's flat on the first floor of a block.

'Eve.' His smile was warm but questioning as he opened the door and led her into his living room. 'What are you doing here?'

'I needed a change of scene,' she explained. 'I hope you don't mind.'

'Course I don't mind.' He looked at her, concerned because she was still out of breath. 'But should you have walked all that way in your condition?'

She threw a cushion at him. 'Don't you start,' she wailed. 'That's exactly the sort of comment I've come out to get away from.'

'Mum's being Mum, is she?' he guessed.

'Very much so.'

'How about we go down to the pub for a quick one?' he suggested. 'I think I can afford to buy my sister an orange juice.'

'That's the best offer I've had all day,' she said. 'It'll make me feel like a grown-up again.'

'Did you enjoy yourself at George's last night?' enquired Dot over breakfast the next morning.

Eve nodded. 'It was nice to get out,' she said, struggling to eat some toast even though for some reason she was feeling queasy. 'George is always good for a laugh. We went to the pub and back to his place for coffee afterwards.

48

We got talking and I didn't realise the time. That's why I didn't get back before you went to bed.'

'It doesn't matter about that,' said her father. 'As long as you had a good time.'

'I did,' she confirmed, covering a yawn with her hand. 'I'm tired this morning, though.'

'You weren't that late back,' commented Dot. 'We heard George bring you home just after we went to bed.'

'That's true,' said Eve, 'but I feel exhausted for some reason and I've still a full day's work to do.' She sipped her tea, feeling most unwell, which was odd because the morning sickness had stopped after three months. 'I'll soon liven up once I get going.' She finished her toast and looked at the clock. 'I must get ready or I'll be late.'

She left her parents at the table and went upstairs, returning a few minutes later, pale with fright and trembling. 'Could you ring the doctor for me, please, Mum,' she said shakily. 'I think I'd better go back to bed.'

The doctor finished examining his patient and regarded her thoughtfully. 'You say the bleeding has stopped now?' he said.

'It seems to have,' said Eve, her face almost as white as the pillow.

'Mm.' A grey-haired man of diminutive stature, he stroked his chin. 'That's a good sign, but it doesn't mean we are out of the wood yet. You must keep a close eye on it.'

'Am I . . .' She hardly dared ask the question. 'Am I going to lose the baby?' she blurted out.

'I can't tell you that,' he said frankly. 'Obviously the bleeding is cause for concern . . .'

'Oh God,' she breathed, brushing her damp brow with the back of her hand.

'You really must try to stay calm,' he advised, peering at her over the top of his horn-rimmed glasses.

'My baby means everything to me,' she said, her voice breaking, this unexpected development making her even more aware of her feelings.

'A show of blood doesn't always result in a miscarriage,' he told her.

It often did though, she knew that. 'Is there anything that can be done to stop me losing the baby?' she asked.

'Most of it is up to you,' he told her. 'It's important that you rest. You must stay in bed, and you *must* try to stop worrying. I know you've had a fright, but anxiety isn't going to help.'

Something was nagging at the back of her mind. 'I went for quite a long walk last night,' she said. 'Could that have triggered this off?'

'No.' He seemed quite definite about it. 'If there's a weakness in the pregnancy, this would have happened anyway.' He gave her a watery smile. 'However, there's to be no walking for you for a while. You must rest if you want to keep your baby.' He picked up his black bag. 'I'll come and see you tomorrow, but ring the surgery if you see any more blood before then.'

'I will,' she said, dreading that that might happen. Her baby was the last thing left of Ken and she couldn't bear to lose it.

As the days passed with no more worrying symptoms, she began to regain her confidence and think about getting back to normal, especially when she was up and about again and feeling fit.

But she was in for a shock when she visited the surgery to get signed off so that she could go back to work.

'What does your job actually entail?' the doctor asked.

She told him.

He frowned. 'I can't recommend that you go back to work,' he informed her.

'You want me to have another week off?'

'A bit longer than that,' he said, pushing his spectacles

up his nose. 'It wouldn't be wise for you to go back to work for the rest of this pregnancy.'

'What?' she burst out involuntarily. 'I can't afford to stay at home until after the baby's born.'

'You'll have to, I'm afraid,' he told her evenly.

'But I feel fine now,' she pointed out.

'I'm not suggesting you take to your bed or anything like that,' he explained. 'But it would be too risky to go back to a job as demanding as yours. You've had a warning and you must take heed of it. You need to take things easier from now on.'

'I'm a widow,' she explained. 'I have to earn money.'

He gave her a stern look. 'I know how much you want this baby, Mrs Peters,' he said, meeting her eyes, 'so I'm sure you'll manage.'

'Yes.' The gravity of his message hit home. 'Yes, of course I will.'

'Jolly good,' he said with an air of finality, glancing briefly at her notes. 'I see you have an appointment for a check-up at the antenatal clinic at the hospital next month.'

'That's right,' she affirmed.

'If you have any problems before then, come and see me,' he said, putting her file to one side in a valedictory manner.

'Thank you, Doctor.'

Her thoughts were racing as she walked back to Marshall Gardens. Things were going to be very tight for her financially, but her baby's life was far too precious to put at risk. She would just have to supplement any state benefit she was entitled to by dipping into what was left of her savings. If she used every penny, it would be worth it.

'I'm sorry you're not coming back to work,' said the manager of the mail order company when he'd heard what Eve had to say. 'But the doctor knows best.'

Eve looked at him across the desk, a large man with thinning ginger hair and cool blue eyes. His manner was always businesslike; not unkind but distant. His job depended on the efficient running of the company and he didn't like to be hindered in this by staff problems.

'I'm sorry to have sprung this on you,' she said 'I know you were expecting me back soon.'

'Can't be helped, my dear,' he said, managing to inject a note of sympathy into his brisk tone. 'You must look after yourself.'

She nodded. 'I intend to, for the baby's sake,' she said. 'But I've made arrangements for afterwards. My mother has agreed to look after it while I'm at work. Obviously, being a widow, I shall have to come back to work.'

'Hmmm.' He leaned on the desk, his chin resting on his linked fingers, his eyes not quite meeting hers. 'If you need a reference I'll be happy to oblige.'

'Oh,' she said with a sinking heart. 'I was hoping there would be a job for me here.'

He raised his eyes to meet hers for a second before lowering them. 'There's nothing I'd like more than to have you back but I'm sure you understand that I can't keep your job open for that length of time,' he told her. 'By the time you've had the baby and are ready to return to work, several months will have passed.' He shook his head. 'It just wouldn't be viable from the company's point of view.'

'I've always been a good worker,' she pointed out desperately.

'No one can argue with that,' he agreed, impatience beginning to show. 'But now that you're leaving us I have to find a replacement. And it will be a permanent position because it isn't the policy of this company to take on temporary staff.'

She knew it would be both pointless and unreasonable to persist because the man did have a business to run. 'I understand,' she said dully.

'Of course, there's nothing to stop you applying for a job here at some time in the future if there happens to be a vacancy,' he said crisply, 'but nothing can be guaranteed.' He looked at his watch and stood up. 'I'll see to it that anything owing to you is sent on.' He managed a smile. 'Good luck, my dear.'

'Thank you.'

As she left his office, fraught with anxiety for the future, she remembered what the doctor had said about the importance of staying calm. Worrying about how she was going to support her baby could cause problems with the pregnancy and she wasn't prepared to risk that. When the time came, she would have to deal with the problem. In the meantime, she must try to relax. She took a deep, calming breath and walked slowly to the bus-stop.

Eve was feeling a bit low on the afternoon of her appointment at the antenatal clinic at Perivale maternity hospital in January. She'd had a bad night, with vivid dreams about the train crash which lingered disturbingly in her mind.

Early for her appointment, she headed straight for the Ladies', her bladder being extremely demanding at this stage of the pregnancy. She was washing her hands at the basin when another heavily pregnant woman rushed in and shut herself in a cubicle. Eve was tidying her hair in the mirror when she reappeared.

She glanced towards Eve's stomach protruding from her ancient winter coat, which was gaping open. 'This baby of mine is playing havoc with my waterworks,' she said with the instant sisterhood of pregnant women.

'Mine too,' Eve told her, running a comb through her hair and speaking to her in the mirror. 'What with that and heartburn . . .'

'Don't talk to me about heartburn,' said the other woman, washing her hands under the tap. 'I thought it was some sort of sporting injury until I got pregnant and became the world's leading expert.'

Smiling at her turn of phrase, Eve said, 'Still, the end result is well worth the discomfort.'

'Sure,' agreed the woman, who had blonde hair and the most brilliant blue eyes.

Finishing her hair, Eve put her comb back in her handbag. 'What time is your appointment?' she found herself enquiring, even though she hadn't felt like being sociable a few minutes ago.

'Two fifteen.'

'I'm after you, then, at two thirty.'

'They're never on time at these sort of places, though, are they?' the woman remarked, and Eve noticed how well-spoken she was, in a natural, unaffected way.

'They do sometimes run late,' agreed Eve.

'Well, they'd better not keep me waiting today,' announced the blonde, 'because I have to get back to work.'

'Perhaps you'll be lucky,' Eve suggested hopefully.

'I'm banking on it.' She had long, straight hair that looked good with her loose black coat. There was an air of stylishness about her, despite her advanced state of pregnancy. 'I have my own business and time is money to me.'

'I'd have thought being your own boss would make it easier to get away,' said Eve.

'I used to think that too, before experience taught me otherwise,' she said, smiling at Eve. 'You're your own boss in theory but if you don't look after your business, you won't have it for long.'

'What sort of business is it?'

'A boutique,' she said casually. 'Trend, near Ealing Broadway station.'

'Oh, I've been in there.' Trend was a shop that stocked the sort of clothes Eve enjoyed wearing, up-to-date but not expensive.

'I haven't seen you, but I'm not at the shop all the time,' she explained. 'I'm often out buying stock or looking around London's boutiques to keep up to date.'

'Sounds fascinating,' said Eve.

'I enjoy it.' She finished drying her hands on the roller towel and they left together.

Having checked in and changed into billowing hospital gowns, which made them both giggle, they took their place among the other expectant mums to wait their turn.

The waiting didn't seem at all tedious, because Eve and her new acquaintance seemed to have struck up a rapport. Christian names were exchanged; her name was Meg.

'You lose your identity when you come to these places,' said Meg. 'You stop being a woman and become just a stomach.'

Despite Eve's earlier doldrums, she couldn't help laughing at Meg's entertaining manner. There was something endearingly vulnerable about her despite her self-confidence. 'Inevitable, I suppose,' she said, 'since it contains such a valuable cargo.'

'Just lately I've been feeling as though I'm carrying a full-grown elephant rather than a baby human being,' mentioned Meg.

'I know the feeling,' said Eve, and went on to tell her about her recent scare.

'That must have been really frightening,' Meg said sympathetically.

'It was,' said Eve. 'Still is. I'm very careful not to overdo things.'

'I can imagine,' said Meg in an understanding manner. 'My business would have to manage on its own if anything like that happened to me.'

'Is your husband supportive of you in that way?' asked Eve.

'I'm not married.'

'Oh.' Eve hadn't noticed the absence of a wedding ring and tried not to embarrass her by sounding too surprised.

'How about yours?' asked Meg.

'I'm a widow,' explained Eve, experiencing a stab of pain.

Meg looked surprised. 'Really?' she said. 'It must be quite recent.'

'Seven months ago,' explained Eve. 'My husband died without even knowing I was pregnant.'

'Ah, what a terrible shame,' Meg said warmly.

'We hadn't planned to start a family yet,' Eve told her.

Perceiving Eve's pain at the mention of her bereavement, Meg didn't pursue the subject. 'So, like me, you'll be bringing the baby up on your own.'

Eve nodded. 'When are you due?' she enquired chattily.

'March the seventh.'

'I'm due on the tenth,' said Eve.

'We might be in hospital at about the same time then,' remarked Meg, sounding pleased.

'Yeah,' agreed Eve, cheered by the prospect.

A nurse appeared, carrying a folder, and called for Meg Myers; Eve's new friend disappeared behind the screens.

Eve was still waiting to be called when she reappeared.

'Everything okay?' asked Eve.

'Yes. Everything's progressing as it should be, apparently,' Meg told her cheerfully.

'Good.'

'I hope all's well for you too,' said Meg. 'I'm sure it will be.'

'Thanks,' said Eve. 'Might see you here again.'

'I'll look out for you,' said Meg, and went to get dressed.

Feeling a whole lot more cheerful than when she'd arrived, Eve found herself hoping that they would indeed meet again.

They met at the same place a month later and took up where they had left off. They got on so well that Eve felt as though they were old friends. As more personal details were exchanged, they discovered that they both lived in Ealing, though in vastly different types of neighbourhood. Meg was a resident of the salubrious area of Ealing Common.

Again, Meg was first to be called for her appointment, and

Eve was with the doctor when her new friend had finished. But Meg waited for her and invited her home for a cup of tea because she was taking the rest of the afternoon off.

'I've got my car outside,' she told Eve. 'I can still just about squeeze behind the steering wheel.'

'I'd love to come,' said Eve.

If Meg's cultured accent, car ownership and career status hadn't already convinced Eve of their different backgrounds, her home certainly did. It was a flat in an imposing converted house overlooking the common. The accommodation was luxurious, with pale walls, big windows and modern fittings. The furniture was sleek and contemporary, the curtains boldly patterned.

'What a lovely place.' Eve was standing by the window in the lounge, looking out over the common, which had a bleak kind of beauty about it this afternoon, the trees stripped bare, the grass looking murky beneath grey winter skies. The red buses added a welcome splash of colour to this stark backdrop. 'A nice view too.'

'Thanks,' said Meg without a hint of conceit. 'I like it here.'

'Would it be too rude of me to ask if it's bought or rented?'

'Bought,' Meg informed her. 'What sort of place do you have?'

'I don't,' she said. 'I had to move back in with my parents temporarily because children aren't allowed at the flat my husband and I were living in.'

'Oh dear,' said Meg, seeming genuinely concerned. 'It can't be easy fitting into your parents' routine again after having your own place.'

'It isn't,' she admitted. 'But I'm grateful to them for putting me up.'

They wandered into a sleek fitted kitchen so that Meg could make the tea. 'If I had to go back home to live for any reason, my mother and I would probably end up murdering each other,' said Meg lightly, swilling hot water from the kettle around in the teapot to warm it before spooning the tea in.

Eve looked at her enquiringly. 'You don't get on with her, then?'

'Not really,' she said, pouring the boiling water into the pot. 'Mummy and I have different ideas about practically everything.' She gave Eve a wry grin. 'And my getting pregnant hasn't helped. She's positively incandescent with rage about it. The family reputation and all that.'

'I understand,' said Eve.

'I get on very well with my father, though. He's an absolute sweetie.'

'That's good.'

'Of course, I'm terribly grateful to both of them,' Meg went on to explain. 'They've given me everything money can buy, a private education and all that goes with it. They gave me the deposit on this place as a present, and my father lent me the money to start up in business. All paid back now, though.'

'An only child?' guessed Eve.

She nodded.

'My parents aren't in a position to give me or my brother the deposit on an armchair, let alone a property, bless 'em,' said Eve.

'Daddy has a wholesale kitchen and hardware business.' Meg took some biscuits out of a tin and arranged them on a plate. 'He's been well-off ever since I can remember, so I've never known anything else.'

'I see,' Eve said.

'Will you be getting your own place eventually?' enquired Meg casually.

'God, I hope so,' Eve told her. 'I can start putting pressure on the council once the baby has arrived.' She emitted a wistful sigh. 'My husband and I were saving for a house of our own before we started a family. Things don't always work out as you plan, do they?'

'You're telling me they don't!' exclaimed Meg. 'A baby was the last thing I had in mind.'

'Really?'

'I was shattered when I found out I was pregnant . . . I just didn't know what to do.' Her expresssion became grim. 'I was so desperate I even thought about adoption – and abortion crossed my mind fleetingly. But when I got used to the idea, I decided I liked it. Now I can't wait for my baby to be born.'

For all Meg's smart talk and self-assurance, Eve sensed a profound sadness in her somehow. There was a bleakness about her every now and then. She turned away to pour the tea, but not before Eve saw tears in her eyes. Eve wanted to reach out to her, to ask how such a beautiful and intelligent woman came to be facing motherhood alone. But such a personal enquiry would be too presumptuous at this stage.

When Meg turned back to Eve, she had reverted to her cheery manner, and they took their tea into the lounge, where dusk was falling. At the touch of a switch, the wall lights emitted a soft glow, the central heating a luxury to Eve, who was used to living with icy draughts.

As they talked, it became even more obvious that their ideas and opinions were similar despite their different backgrounds. They were the same age too; they would be twenty-seven within days of each other later in the year.

Eve asked Meg about her working arrangements now that the birth was getting close. She said her manageress was looking after things, but that she went into the shop herself for a short time each day to make sure everything was under control.

'I've always been interested in clothes, even though I haven't been able to afford many these past few years,' said Eve, sipping her tea.

'Fashion is very exciting at the moment with all the trendy new styles,' said Meg, offering her a biscuit.

'They say London is acquiring quite a reputation for it,' remarked Eve, choosing a digestive.

Meg nodded. 'Even men's clothes are beginning to get interesting.'

'I've heard all about Carnaby Street,' mentioned Eve.

'That's getting to be the "in" place for modern men's fashions,' Meg informed her, nibbling a biscuit. 'It used to be a run-down back alley behind Regent Street. But not any more. I don't cater for men myself, but I like to keep up to date with all branches of fashion retail.'

'How will you manage your business after the baby is born?' Eve wondered.

'I'll have to find someone to look after the baby while I'm out working,' she said.

'Would your mother help out?' suggested Eve.

Meg roared with laughter, but there was a false ring to it somehow. Again Eve was aware of sorrow beneath Meg's bright veneer. 'I think I can safely say that my mother won't be doing anything in the way of child-minding.'

She asked what Eve did in the way of work and what she was planning to do when the baby arrived. Eve filled her in on the details. 'I shall have to look for a job when the time comes,' she told her. 'My old job was boring, but it was steady income. I've lost that security.'

'You should come and work for me,' said Meg jokingly. 'We'd make a good team. Two working mums together.'

'Working in a boutique is something I really would enjoy.'

'I don't have any vacancies,' Meg said, looking worried.

'It's all right, I know you weren't serious,' Eve assured her. 'I wasn't angling for a job.'

They talked about other things, then Meg said, 'You're very young to be widowed, Eve.'

Eve nodded, her expression darkening. 'There aren't many widows of my age about.'

'It was insensitive of me to mention it,' said Meg. 'Trust me to put my foot in it.'

'Apologies aren't necessary,' Eve assured her. 'It's only natural for you to comment on it. I don't talk about it because it still hurts so much. But I've gotta get over that.'

'It might help to talk,' suggested Meg.

Eve nodded. She thought Meg was probably right. 'My husband, Ken, was killed in a train crash – the big one near Newton Abbot last June,' she told her. 'I expect you heard about it.'

Meg turned pale. She seemed stunned, which was understandable after receiving such dramatic information. Eve was used to this sort of reaction from people shocked to meet someone who'd been involved in something horrific they'd read about in the papers and seen on the television news. 'Yes, I heard about it,' she said after a pause. 'It was front-page news for quite a while. It must have been dreadful for you.'

'It was horrendous. I still have nightmares about it.' She went on to tell Meg more about it. 'It's a wonder I didn't lose the baby in the trauma of it all. If I'd known I was pregnant I'd have been in even more of a panic.' She paused, her expression softening. 'But the baby had barely had time to take root. I conceived the night before the accident.'

'Really?'

'Oh, yes. It was definitely then.' She looked sad. 'At least I've got something of Ken left to live for.'

'A happy marriage then?'

'We had our ups and downs like everyone else, but it was a good marriage.' Tears filled her eyes. 'Very good. Then, suddenly, he's gone. It's all over.' She touched her stomach. 'Thank goodness I have his child to look forward to.'

Meg cleared her throat, obviously moved by Eve's story. 'Yes, at least you have that.'

Noticing that Meg's eyes were moist, Eve was warmed by her empathy. Because they had moved on to more personal matters, Eve felt bold enough to say, 'That's enough about me. Your turn now – if you feel like talking.'

'You mean how is it I'm about to become an unmarried mother?' she said.

'Not that especially,' said Eve. 'I just thought that as I'd been doing all the talking, you might like to get a word in.'

'Not really,' said Meg, seeming suddenly depressed. 'My baby is a result of a relationship that didn't work out.'

'Are you still in touch with the father?'

'No,' she said in a definite tone. 'He isn't in my life any more and I want to forget him.'

'I won't say another word on the subject then.' Eve looked at her watch. 'It's time I was going anyway.'

Meg went to the hall to get Eve's coat.

'Well, it's been lovely,' said Eve, slipping into it. 'Thanks for your hospitality.'

'My pleasure,' said Meg.

They had already discussed the fact that they both had an appointment at the antenatal clinic in a month's time, unless they had given birth by then.

'Maybe the next time we'll meet will be in the labour ward,' said Eve lightly.

'Could be,' agreed Meg.

Pausing in the hall, Eve had an idea. 'Maybe we could get in touch before then,' she suggested, because she liked Meg so much. 'We could get together for coffee or just have a chat on the phone. They say the last month of pregnancy really drags.'

'Yes.'

'If you've a pen and paper handy, I'll give you my number,' said Eve.

Meg handed her a small notepad and pencil from the telephone shelf and Eve wrote down her full name and number. 'You'd better let me have yours, too,' she suggested.

There was a brief hiatus, as though Meg was thinking about it. Then she scribbled down her number, tore the page off the pad and handed it to Eve.

'See you soon,' said Eve happily. 'Take care.'

'You too,' said Meg.

*   *   *

'How long have you got to go now?' Bea Myers asked of her daughter one evening a couple of weeks later when she and her husband were visiting Meg at her flat.

'Two weeks, according to the hospital's reckoning,' Meg told her.

'Have you got everything ready?'

'Yes. Cot, pram and other paraphernalia ordered, my case packed.'

Bea Myers tutted, her blue eyes full of pique. 'And you're still determined to have this baby on the National Health?'

'Of course,' confirmed Meg. 'And if I wasn't, it's a bit late to do anything about it. These things have to be booked a long time in advance.'

'Would you agree to it if I could get you a bed in St Joan's,' asked her mother, referring to a private nursing home where the daughters of the women in Bea's social circle went to give birth.

'No.' Meg was adamant.

'Your father will pay.' She turned to her husband, Frank, who was sitting next to her on the sofa, a tall, slim man with greying brown hair and friendly grey eyes that always had a worried look about them on account of his wife's expensive tastes and demanding nature. 'Won't you, Frank?'

'If it's what Meg wants, of course I will, dear,' he agreed.

'Thanks, Daddy, but I'm not having you spend the earth on something that isn't necessary,' said Meg, looking at her father.

'Please reconsider, dear,' urged Bea worriedly. 'What will people think of us if you go into a National Health hospital?'

'They can think what they like,' said Meg. 'I pay my insurance stamps, I'm perfectly entitled to have my baby on the NHS.'

'That isn't the issue,' said Bea, a tall woman with large hips, angular features, thin lips and tightly permed grey hair. She was immaculate but dull in appearance, tending to wear expensive tweed suits and flat shoes. She took a dim view of the new fast-changing fashions as well as the major social changes that were sweeping the country.

'No, the issue here is your status among your friends in cocktail-clan Gunnersbury,' asserted Meg. 'And as there's nothing you can do to alter the fact that your unmarried daughter is about to give birth, you might as well accept it.'

'There's no need to be so blasé about it,' Bea said critically.

'I'm not going to go around hanging my head,' Meg told her.

'It's nothing to boast about,' Bea pointed out.

'And neither is it a hanging offence,' said Meg, hurt and exasperated. 'Anyway, you shouldn't be touchy about the situation. You've had nearly nine months to get used to it.'

'I'll never get used to it,' said Bea, genuinely upset by her daughter's condition. 'But if you were to have the baby privately, at least that would give the thing some sort of respectability.'

Meg gave a dry laugh. 'That's the most ridiculous thing I've ever heard.'

'It is a bit silly, Bea,' added Meg's father, who managed to retain a certain presence even though he was dominated by his wife. 'The place where Meg gives birth won't alter anything.'

'It'll tell people we can still afford the best,' Bea said.

'You're such a snob,' said Meg.

'I've never denied it.'

Neither of them could argue with that.

'People won't find it so odd if you go private, dear,' continued Bea, struggling to find some way through the scandal without losing face completely.

'What are you going to do when this baby actually arrives, Mummy?' Meg enquired. 'Are you going to pretend it isn't mine, tell people I'm looking after it for a friend?'

'Now you're being silly,' retorted Bea.

'I wouldn't put it past you to tell your friends that I have a husband stashed away somewhere,' said Meg.

'Are there any developments in that direction?' Bea wanted to know.

If it hadn't been so irritating, Meg might have laughed at such a ludicrous comment. But she was straight-faced as she answered her mother. 'If you mean have I found some man to marry me just to save you from disgrace at the eleventh hour, the answer is no. Of course I haven't.'

'Oh dear.'

'What do you expect me to do?' asked Meg irascibly. 'Go out on the street and ask the first man I see to marry me . . . or put an advertisement in the personal column of the paper – heavily pregnant woman needs husband to save her family's reputation?'

'There's no call for sarcasm,' snapped Bea. 'You know perfectly well that wasn't what I meant. I'm talking about the child's father, whoever he is, being made to face up to his responsibilities.'

'Forget it, Mother . . .'

'He shouldn't be allowed to get away with it,' Bea persisted.

Meg looked sad. 'I've told you, he knows nothing about it,' she said.

'Well, for goodness' sake tell him and give him the chance to do what's right,' said Bea.

'No.'

'Tell us who he is then, and we'll go and sort him out,' pleaded her mother.

'Just leave it, please,' begged Meg, staring at her hands clasped together in front of her.

'The least you can do is try to bring your child into the world without a stigma.'

'I didn't intend to start a family this way,' said Meg wearily. 'But it's happened, so I just have to get on with it and do the best I can.'

'You've always had terrible taste in men,' announced Bea.

'You know nothing about my love life,' corrected Meg, who, since she'd left home, had been careful to keep her boyfriends at a safe distance from her mother's scathing criticism.

'Not recently,' agreed Bea. 'But I used to know all your boyfriends when you lived at home, and you never went out with anyone from your own class. Oh no, that would have been too dull and ordinary for you. You always went for arty types, or yobbish riff-raff. I seem to recall a terrible Italian waiter who was always hanging around the house.'

'I was seventeen at the time, and he wasn't terrible,' said Meg.

'Be that as it may,' Bea went on, 'if you'd found yourself a decent chap, you wouldn't have been left in the lurch now.'

'Yeah, yeah.' Meg felt tired and dispirited. The pregnancy was beginning to exhaust her. 'Look,' she said to her mother in a grimly patient manner, 'I've said a hundred times over that I'm sorry to bring disgrace on you. I can't keep repeating it. But the baby is mine. I shall bring it up and do my very best for it. It's *my* responsibility, not yours, so why don't you just leave me to get on with it in my own way?'

'Easy for you to say,' Bea said. 'You wait till you're a mother yourself. You'll soon find out it isn't that simple.'

'But you don't have to be involved,' Meg pointed out. 'It isn't as if I'm some penniless teenager who'll bring her disgrace home. I have my own place, and an income. I haven't asked for your help and I don't intend to after the baby's born. All I want from you is for you to accept what's happened – that I'm about to become a mother – and stop being so shocked by it.'

'I'm trying,' said Bea.

'If it will make it easier for you, I won't bring the baby to your place at all, then you won't be embarrassed by it,' said Meg, biting back the tears. 'None of your snobby neighbours need know you've got a bastard grandchild then.'

Bea wasn't completely heartless or she might have taken

her daughter up on that, such was her shame about Meg's pregnancy. Bea's standing among her peers was paramount and she lived within a narrow set of values which meant a family scandal was almost physical pain to her.

The daughter of a bank manager, Bea had been brought up in an atmosphere of comfort and respectability. Falling in love with Frank Myers could have been a disaster given that he didn't have a high-flying career and earned his living in a relatively humble way behind the counter of the small hardware shop he had inherited from his father. But Bea could see a great deal of potential in the situation and it didn't take her long to set the wheels in motion for better things.

Having no intention of living in the flat above the shop for a moment longer than she had to, she had persuaded Frank to sell the shop and set up in business as a wholesaler, making use of his experience of the hardware trade. She'd moulded him into the man he was today, and was the driving force behind the nationally successful wholesale kitchen and hardware business he now headed.

She took no part in the business herself, but she did take credit for its existence. If she hadn't pushed and pressured Frank, he'd still be working behind the counter and they'd be living over the shop. Instead, they enjoyed an excellent standard of living, and all because of her persistence and foresight.

They had an expensive house in a classy avenue near Gunnersbury Park, and a place in middle-class suburban social life. Her women friends were all the wives of professional men or business tycoons, and she could mix with them on equal terms.

Her daughter had been to one of the best private schools in west London, and had been given everything a girl could want – good clothes, piano and ballet classes, riding lessons. And she had repaid them by being so uninterested in her school work that she'd failed her exams and left at fifteen with no qualifications.

After leaving school, she'd got a job in a dress shop in the

West End. Bea Myers' daughter, a common shop girl with a penchant for mixing with the hoi polloi. Now she'd brought the ultimate shame on her parents by getting herself pregnant with no sign of a marriage proposal. And she wouldn't even tell her parents who the father of their grandchild was.

'It's easy for you to come out with remarks like that,' said Bea now, responding to her daughter's comments. 'But it will be difficult for us, knowing everybody's talking about us.'

'I know, Mummy, and I've said I'm sorry until I'm blue in the face,' said Meg. 'But you'll just have to try and let all the gossip go over your head.'

'Give the girl a break, Bea,' urged Frank. 'All this arguing can't be doing her any good.'

Needing to escape, Meg stood up. 'I'll make some coffee,' she said.

'I'll make it, you sit down,' offered her mother in an attempt to assuage her guilt for being so unsympathetic to her daughter's plight.

'No, I'll do it. I need to move about, I get stiff if I sit for too long,' said Meg, and left the room swiftly because she knew she was going to cry and didn't want her parents to know how vulnerable and alone she felt. The confident front she put on for the world kept her going and gave her strength. But she wasn't impervious to the problems of her situation. Having a regular income and money in the bank didn't stop you feeling pain.

Her father followed her into the kitchen. 'Don't upset yourself,' he said. 'Your mother will come round once the baby is born.'

She wiped her eyes and turned to look at him, meeting those gentle grey eyes that had always had a soothing effect on her. He was a good man, completely in thrall to his wife. 'I'm not so sure about that, but don't worry, Dad,' she said thickly, 'I'll be all right.'

'I want you to know that we're always there if you need us, no matter how your mother makes it seem,' he told her.

Her father had quite enough problems of his own, satisfying his wife's demands; he didn't need his daughter bending his ear with her troubles too. He was weak when it came to Meg's mother. His valiant attempts to stand up to her never really came off, partly because of her dogmatic personality and partly because he adored her despite all her faults. 'I'm okay, really I am,' said Meg firmly. 'I'm going to manage fine with this baby.'

'You'll be a great mum.'

'I shall certainly do my best.'

She was taking some teacups out of the cupboard when the telephone rang in the hall. Frank went to answer it.

'It's someone called Eve,' he said, coming back into the kitchen.

'Oh.' Meg's face dropped.

'She says you haven't returned any of her calls and she's wondering if everything is all right,' he informed her.

'Can you tell her I'm not in, please, Daddy?' asked Meg in a whisper.

'But she knows you're in,' he reminded her. 'I told her I'd go and get you.'

'Tell her I'm in the bath or something then.'

'But . . . she'll guess it's just an excuse,' he said worriedly. 'I've already indicated that you're available to talk to her.'

'That doesn't matter,' said Meg.

Her father looked puzzled. 'Shall I tell her you'll call her back later?' he asked.

'No.'

'Tomorrow then?'

'No.'

'What message *shall* I give her?'

Meg spooned coffee into the cups through a blur of tears. There was nothing she wanted more than a friendship with Eve, with whom she felt such an affinity. Eve would understand more than anyone how alone and vulnerable she felt at this time. Just the thought of having Eve's companionship to sustain her through the months ahead gave her a feeling of hope. But she said sadly, 'There's no message, Daddy. Just tell her I can't come to the phone and leave it at that.'

'But won't she be offended . . . ?'

'Perhaps, but I'd still like you to do it,' she told him.

'It isn't like you to be so hurtful to anyone,' he said.

'I know.' She bit her lip. 'But please do it for me and don't ask me to explain why.'

He sighed. 'All right,' he reluctantly agreed. 'If that's what you really want.'

'It is.'

As he went back to the telephone, Meg thought sadly that Eve was sure to get the message soon, and would stop calling her.

Chapter Five

Eve replaced the receiver feeling puzzled and hurt. She'd sensed a change in Meg on the phone the other day but had been hoping she'd imagined it. Now it would be extremely naïve of her not to accept the fact that she had just been given the brush-off.

The most likely explanation was the inequality of circumstances, Eve thought. Meg had money, an interesting career and a foot on the property ladder, while Eve had to watch every penny and council accommodation to look forward to if she was lucky. Meg must have found her company too dull to pursue, even though it hadn't seemed like that when they were together. It was disappointing, but Eve could take a hint. She wouldn't call her again.

She did wonder if she might see her at the hospital on the day of her next antenatal appointment, but as it happened, Eve didn't make her appointment that day.

'It's probably just indigestion,' George suggested hopefully when his sister informed him that she thought her contractions had started at a moment that could hardly have been more inappropriate. He and Eve were stuck in a traffic jam in Ealing Broadway on their way to the hospital for her appointment. He had offered to take her in his car to save her waiting for a bus.

'Let's hope you're right,' she told him anxiously. 'The last thing I want to do is give birth in a car outside Bentall's.'

'I'm not mad about the idea either,' said George, turning

pale at the thought. 'But surely it wouldn't happen that quickly, would it?'

'They say it's often a long labour with a first baby,' she informed him, adding wryly, 'which is just as well, because I'm pretty certain these pains are more than just indigestion.'

'Bloody hell,' said George, peering ahead at the traffic in the hope of some movement.

'Oh God, there's another one coming,' she said a few minutes later, trying, unsuccessfully, not to tense against the pain.

'Don't panic,' he said. 'The traffic will start moving again in a minute . . . we'll get to the hospital in time.'

'I'm not so sure,' she said, sounding breathless as the pain grew stronger. 'This is really beginning to feel serious.'

'Can you try to concentrate on what they taught you at relaxation classes?' he suggested.

'I'm trying . . . I'm trying.'

'Looks like we're on the move at last, so that's something,' he said with relief.

The traffic moved, and so did the intensity of Eve's contractions – from excruciating pain to unimaginable agony. When they got caught in another tail-back, at the Hanger Lane junction with the Western Avenue, George was frantic. He managed to maintain a calm front, though, and kept up a steady flow of sympathetic dialogue, constantly assuring her that they would get to the hospital in time. By this time Eve was past caring where she gave birth, as long as she did – *and soon*.

They made it to the hospital with time to spare, in fact.

'How much longer is this gonna last?' Eve asked the midwife, sweating her way through endless waves of torment on a high bed in the delivery room.

'It shouldn't be too long now,' said the nurse in a matter-of-fact tone.

'I hope not,' gasped Eve. 'I don't think I can stand much more.'

'You'll stand it for as long as you have to, my dear,' said the nurse, a brisk, efficient woman of the old school who considered sympathy unnecessary during such a natural function as childbirth. 'You're doing fine.'

The pains kept coming. It felt like nothing Eve had experienced before, and she was unable to hold back her screams. This earned her the nurse's scathing disapproval. She said there was no need to let the whole of west London know that she was in labour, and that she was upsetting the other patients.

At last it was over.

'You've a lovely little girl, Mrs Peters,' said the nurse, handing the baby to Eve.

And Eve was staring at the squashed, angry countenance of her daughter, red and wrinkled and astonishingly beautiful. There were no words to describe the sense of joy and tranquillity that imbued her at that moment.

'She's beautiful,' she said, breathless with awe, her feelings intensified by having once thought she might lose her. 'Absolutely beautiful.'

'She is, and she's a fine pair of lungs on her, too,' said the nurse as the baby's first cries filled the room. 'I'll take her now and get her cleaned up.'

'Thank you.'

'Someone will bring you a cup of tea in a minute,' she said, thawing a little now that the baby was safely delivered.

'Lovely,' said Eve, knowing instinctively that there would never be another moment in her life to match this one.

There were only two women in the ward who weren't visited every evening by their husbands – Eve, and Meg Myers, who'd had a baby daughter three days before Eve. Meg was in the bed nearest the door, Eve at the other end by the window, so there was no need for them to speak to each other directly. Eve didn't want to talk to Meg anyway, after the way she'd been snubbed.

Meg's attitude had been friendly but impersonal when they'd first met on the ward, as though Eve was just one of the other new mums and their earlier palliness had never happened. Eve thought it was odd but went along with it and kept her distance because this was neither the time nor the place for a confrontation.

One evening after visiting time, when her parents and George had left, Eve found herself plunged into the blackest of moods, a depression so deep it was a physical ache. It had been threatening ever since the post-delivery rapture had worn off, and Eve could no longer keep it at bay. For some reason, motherhood seemed to have produced a resurgence of her grief for Ken.

Feeling isolated from the others by this inner blackness – as the rattle of cups indicated the approach of the cocoa trolley – she couldn't stop thinking about Ken and how he would never be able to share the joy of their daughter with her. Unable to hold back the tears any longer, she slipped out of bed and headed for the toilets, where she locked herself in a cubicle and cried her heart out.

Meg was feeling bad about the way she'd treated Eve, and sad that they couldn't be friends. It was awkward them being in the same ward. Meg would be glad when she was out of here and didn't have to see her.

Eve had been very quiet since visiting time, she noticed. She hadn't joined in the ward chatter at all. Probably got a touch of post-natal blues, she thought.

Seeing her get out of bed and hurry out of the ward on the verge of tears, Meg felt compelled to go after her.

'I thought you might be needing these,' she said, handing Eve a wad of tissues.

'Thanks.' Eve was touched by the gesture, if wary of Meg's variable behaviour towards her. She washed her hands. 'I came over so depressed I couldn't hold it back.'

'I came out here for a weep myself yesterday,' confessed Meg.

'Hormones, I suppose,' suggested Eve.

Meg nodded. 'And all those doting dads pouring into the ward at visiting time doesn't help when you're on your own,' she said.

Back in the ward, Meg sat on the edge of Eve's bed with her cocoa, both babies in the nursery for the night. Several of the women were chatting among themselves.

'I wondered if it was something I'd said,' Eve blurted out impulsively. 'When you wouldn't take my calls.'

'Sorry about that,' said Meg, eyes lowered, pale cheeks brightly suffused. 'I, er . . . I always seemed to be busy when you called.' She hurriedly changed the subject. 'Have you decided what you're going to call your baby?'

'Josie.'

'That's pretty.'

'Have you chosen a name yet?' Eve enquired.

'Rebecca, shortened to Becky.'

'Nice.'

Sipping her cocoa, Eve said, 'I can't help thinking that Ken . . . that we should have been choosing a name for her together.'

Meg looked at the floor. 'It's those sort of things that really get to you when you're on your own,' she said.

'Mm.' Eve finished her cocoa and put the cup down on her locker. 'Are your parents pleased with their granddaughter?'

'My father's tickled to bits,' said Meg. 'Mum's doing her best, but she obviously finds the whole thing most embarrassing.' She stared into her mug. 'If I was a widow she'd be the most doting granny in London. But having an unmarried mother as a daughter is completely beyond the pale.'

'She's not that bad, surely?' said Eve.

'She isn't bad,' corrected Meg. 'Just very conventional.' The atmosphere between them seemed to have regained its former ease and Eve felt her gloom dissolve. It was obvious that Meg didn't feel that any further explanation for her odd behaviour was necessary, so Eve said no more about it.

'Who was that gorgeous man who came to visit you this evening?' Meg asked lightly.

'Gorgeous man?' Eve was puzzled. 'I don't think I know any of those.'

'Tall, dark and dishy,' she said. 'He was with your parents.'

'Oh . . . that's my brother, George,' Eve informed her.

'I guessed he was a relative of some sort because of the likeness,' said Meg.

'I've never thought of my brother as being particularly dishy,' Eve remarked.

'That's because you look at him with a sister's eye,' said Meg.

'George, dishy,' said Eve, smiling. 'Is he really?'

'Very,' said Meg.

'I must tell him,' grinned Eve. 'He'll be thrilled to bits.'

'As long as he doesn't get a swollen head,' remarked Meg, sipping her cocoa.

'George wouldn't know how,' Eve told her.

'Is he married?' Meg enquired chattily.

'No . . . well, only to his business,' she said, and went on to explain the basic details of George's situation and how he was a confirmed bachelor. 'Mind you, the right woman could probably change all that. So, shall I tell him you're interested?'

'No fear,' laughed Meg. 'I was making an observation, not setting myself up for a relationship. I'm right off men at the moment. A classic clase of once bitten, twice shy.'

'I can imagine,' said Eve.

Meg changed the subject. 'I'm going home tomorrow,' she said. 'All being well with Becky, that is.'

'I'm absolutely dying to go home,' said Eve, 'but I have to wait a few more days, as I came in after you.'

'Most of the first-time mums are dying to get out of here,' said Meg. 'Those who already have children are enjoying the rest.'

As they talked, Eve sensed the bond between them growing. She was feeling a lot less gloomy by the time she settled down for the night, having got back on to her old footing with Meg. She was now certain she hadn't imagined a friendship in the making between them.

But the next day, when Eve said goodbye to her when she left the hospital, Meg seemed to draw back again. When Eve suggested they might get together sometime, Meg was noticeably reluctant to commit herself.

Oh well, if she's going to be as inconsistent as that, I'm better off not seeing her again, thought Eve, hurt for the second time. But with the new responsibilities of motherhood to be coped with, she had more pressing matters on her mind than the peculiar moods of a casual acquaintance.

One morning about two weeks later, Meg was pacing her lounge with her daughter screaming in her arms. 'Shush, Becky, shush, darling.' Her voice was determinedly gentle as she tried not to let her own desperation show in her voice for fear it would make things worse. Why was the child crying? she asked herself for the umpteenth time. She'd fed her, winded her, cuddled her, changed her nappy. And still she shrieked. Perhaps it had been a mistake to put her on the bottle. But the doctor had insisted she do so because her lactation had been poor. And Becky didn't have any trouble feeding from the bottle. So what in heaven's name was the matter with her?

'All babies cry,' the health visitor had told Meg when she'd made her routine visit earlier that morning. Becky had been sleeping like an angel at the time, having had Meg up all night.

'What – all the time?' Meg had queried.

'She doesn't cry all the time,' corrected the other woman, looking at the sleeping child. 'She isn't crying now.'

'She cries a lot, though,' declared Meg, who was despairing because she seemed unable to make her baby content. 'You should hear her at night. I'll have complaints from the neighbours if she carries on like this.'

'She'll soon settle down,' the health visitor had said, 'and so will you.'

Meg was wondering if she would ever settle to this new and different way of life. She felt as though she'd been plucked from the comfortable world she knew into a nightmare of anxiety and new emotions, the sweet ache of loving Becky overshadowed by the crushing weight of responsibility produced by that love. She wanted so much to be a good mother and seemed to be failing dismally.

The telephone rang. With Becky sobbing into her shoulder, she went to the hall to answer it. It was Tricia from the shop, asking when Meg would be coming in, because there were queries piling up that needed her attention.

'The way I feel at the moment, I don't think I'll ever get into the shop again,' she snapped, choking back the tears and adding in a more professional manner, 'I can't talk now. I'll ring you back later.'

She put the phone down. 'I have to pay attention to my business, Becky,' she muttered thickly to her daughter as she walked the floor with her, her own cheeks wet with tears. 'It's what keeps us. And I can't do anything if you won't stop crying.'

Becky's reply was a snuffly sob.

The morning didn't improve. Meg managed to get the baby to sleep for long enough to put some nappies into the washing machine, but by the time she'd washed the dishes that had collected in the sink, Becky was screaming the place down again. Walking the floor with her, Meg noticed her own reflection in the mirror above the fireplace. Good grief! Is that dishevelled wreck of a woman really me? she asked herself.

This wasn't how she'd imagined motherhood would be. Up till now, she'd always been in charge. Although her disastrous love life had been out of her control recently, she'd been in total command of everything else. She'd thought that juggling motherhood with a career would be just a matter of good organisation. She hadn't realised that the baby would take over her life completely.

Prior to Becky's arrival, Meg's apprehensions about single motherhood had mostly been about the stigma for the baby. She'd not envisaged the effect on herself of the huge responsibility to be shouldered alone. Apart from her daughter's health and well-being, she also had to provide for her, and she'd done nothing yet about childcare arrangements so that she could attend to the business which was to feed them. She couldn't even think about it while Becky was still so unsettled.

By lunchtime, or what would have been lunchtime in the days before eating and sleeping had become such luxuries, Meg was beside herself with worry. It was as though there was only her and the shrieking Becky in the whole of the world. She just didn't know what to do.

She'd vowed not to bother her mother, but desperation drove her to the telephone only to find that Bea wasn't at home. Feeling oddly deserted, Meg replaced the receiver.

Still Becky cried. How in heaven's name was she going to stop her? She'd have to ring the health visitor for advice. But in her heart she knew that Social Services couldn't give her what she really needed – a friend who would understand how she was feeling. She'd give a lot to talk to Eve, but knew it would be a mistake.

Back in the armchair, nursing the baby, the crying abated slightly. Meg kissed her daughter's face, her skin damp and warm against her own. She cradled her in her arms, looking at her, so helpless and beautiful and so totally reliant on her mother. Meg's feeling of inadequacy was all-consuming.

Much against her better judgement she went to the telephone, knowing that if she made this call she would be setting something in motion that she must not draw back from again. Holding her baby in one arm, she found the number and nervously dialled it.

'Hello. Is that Eve? 'Meg could hear a baby yelling in the background, which immediately made her feel less alone.

'Speaking.'

'This is Meg . . . Meg Myers.'

'Oh.' There was a lengthy pause before Eve said in an even tone, 'Hi. How's it going?'

'Terrible,' she admitted. 'This baby of mine just won't stop crying.'

'Snap,' said Eve, sounding surprisingly calm, Meg thought, considering the racket that was going on in the background. 'I'm having a bad morning with Josie too. She's being a real little misery-guts. I don't know why.'

'I was wondering if I could possibly see you,' said Meg, far too desperate to put on a front. 'I'm feeling a bit cut off . . . I could really do with some company.'

There was a long silence. 'Sure,' said Eve at last. 'But you're the one with a car. It'll be easier for you to come to me.'

'When?'

'Whenever you like,' said Eve casually.

'Could I come now?'

'Sure,' said Eve, and Meg could detect no sign of pique in her voice. 'Mum and I are just about to have a late lunch, if you'd like to join us.'

'Thank you,' said Meg, who couldn't remember ever feeling this grateful to anyone before.

'See you soon then,' said Eve.

When she replaced the receiver, having obtained Eve's address, Meg was the one who was crying, not her baby. She was weeping with gratitude for Eve's warmth and unquestioning friendliness. After the way Meg had treated her, it was a wonder she'd managed to be civil, let alone invite Meg to lunch. Given the opportunity, Eve would be a true friend, Meg was certain of that. And she wanted that friendship, so much!

* * *

'What a pair of little angels,' said Dot, looking at the babies sleeping side by side in their carrycots while Eve, Dot and Meg sat at the table eating scrambled eggs on toast.

'You wouldn't be saying that if you'd heard Becky earlier,' said Meg, who felt much better now that she was here with Eve and her warm-hearted mother. They were such a calming influence, Meg was feeling almost human again. 'I thought I'd go mad.'

'It can be a bit wearing when they cry like that at first,' said Dot.

'I was a nervous wreck at the flat on my own with her,' said Meg.

'It gets easier with time,' said Dot. 'You get more confident and they settle down. And they grow so fast, she'll be giving you her first smile in a matter of weeks.'

'I thought I was losing my mind this morning when she wouldn't stop crying,' Meg told them.

'Don't ever get yourself into a state like that again,' said Eve, who could barely recognise this fraught, untidy woman as the smart, self-assured Meg she was used to. 'If you're feeling a bit lonely, just give us a ring.'

'I really appreciate that. I'm finding motherhood rather frightening,' confessed Meg, who wouldn't have admitted it to another living soul apart from Eve and her mother. 'I think I must be some sort of a freak.'

'Why would you think a daft thing like that?' wondered Dot.

'Well, no one else seems bothered by it,' she explained. 'None of the other mums in the maternity ward said anything about it.'

'They all have husbands to share the responsibility,' Eve reminded her. 'Anyway, you don't know what they're feeling like inside.'

'True.' Meg finished her lunch, the first proper food she'd tasted since she'd been home from hospital. 'I've never been afraid of responsibility before.'

'You've never had a responsibility like this one before,' Dot pointed out. 'You're bound to be anxious in the early days. It's a huge emotional upheaval becoming a mother for the first time, and not everyone can take it in their stride right away.'

'You don't seem to be having any trouble with it, Eve,' Meg observed.

This was true. Eve herself was surprised at how easily she'd adjusted. Since she'd been home from the hospital, she'd been happy for the first time since before the accident. She was still missing Ken, but Josie filled her life to such an extent she didn't have time to brood. 'I'm not. But I do have my own personal support system,' said Eve, smiling towards her mother. 'I don't know if I'd be so calm without her.'

'What about your mother, Meg?' enquired Dot. 'Can't she give you a hand?'

'She's busy.'

'Goes out to work, does she?' said Dot in an understanding manner.

'Not exactly . . . she does do some charity work but she doesn't have a job as such,' explained Meg. 'She has a lot of women friends, they visit each other, that sort of thing. She'd come if I asked her to, I expect. But she was out when I phoned her this morning. I can't expect her to alter her arrangements just because I've had a baby.'

'No, of course you can't,' agreed the good-humoured Dot. 'It's different for me. I had too much time on my hands before Josie came along. She's given me a new lease of life.' She grinned. 'When her mother goes back to work, I shall spoil her rotten.'

After lunch Eve and Meg fed the babies together while Dot washed the dishes.

'It must be nice, having your mum on hand while the baby's still so new.'

'It is,' said Eve.

'Still wanting to get your own place, though?' enquired Meg.

'That's a priority,' said Eve.

'Still hoping to get a council flat?' enquired Meg, though she was a stranger to such things as corporation housing lists.

'Actually, there's been a development as regards that,' said Eve, her voice lifting.

'Oh?'

'I might be able to put a deposit on a little place of my own and have a mortgage instead of paying rent,' she explained.

'Really?' said Meg. 'How come?'

'Apparently I'm due for some compensation from the railway for losing my husband in the train crash,' she said.

'That's brilliant,' said Meg, who sounded unsure about how she should react. 'Did it just come out of the blue?'

'Not really,' Eve said, and went on to explain how the family had encouraged her to make a claim. 'I didn't want to do it, but now that supporting Josie is a reality, I'm glad I did.'

'Mm.'

'The solicitor is very cagey about it,' she said. 'He says they can't guarantee it, but they think that I might get as much as a few hundred pounds, so I'm hoping I'll have enough for the deposit on a house.'

'Brilliant.' Meg finished giving Becky her bottle and lifted her on to her shoulder, gently patting her back. 'But isn't it taking rather a long time?'

'I'll say,' agreed Eve. 'The accident was more than nine months ago. It takes ages, apparently because of all the other claims and the legal work involved. It'll still be a while before it's finally settled.'

'Let's hope it's worth waiting for,' said Meg, a little flatly.

They moved on to other things. 'So, what's happening to the boutique while you're being a full-time mum?' asked Eve.

'The staff are coping as best they can,' she said, settling

Becky into the crook of her arm. 'Her ladyship is taking all my time and energy at the moment, but I shall have to apply my mind to business soon, or I might find myself without a boutique to go back to.'

'Have you found someone to look after Becky while you're at work?' enquired Eve.

Meg shook her head. 'I've done nothing about it at all,' she confessed. 'I shall have to buck my ideas up about that.'

'Still, at least you've got a manageress looking after things,' said Eve.

'Mm,' Meg confirmed. 'Tricia does a good job. But it is *just* a job to her. She can't be expected to have the same interest as the owner.'

'I suppose not.'

'A business partner would be the ideal solution for me now that I have other calls on my time besides the shop,' said Meg, thinking aloud. 'Someone to share the responsibility and workload as well as the profits.'

'Sounds sensible,' said Eve.

'It's just an idea for the future,' she said. 'Meanwhile I have to start looking for someone I can trust to look after Becky.'

The conversation came to an end because Dot appeared, suggesting a walk in the park. Meg couldn't join them because the folding wheels she had for the carrycot were at home.

'I didn't think to bring them,' she said. 'I'm still not used to taking everything but the kitchen sink with me when I go out anywhere.'

'Next time you come, make sure you bring 'em,' said Dot, implying an open invitation. 'We usually take Josie for a walk in the afternoon.'

'I'll remember that,' said Meg, feeling much more like her old self. 'Thanks for the company. I feel heaps better.'

'Any time,' said Eve, deliberately keeping things casual.

*　　*　　*

'What did you think of Meg?' Eve asked her mother as they headed towards the park in the spring sunshine with Josie asleep in the pram.

'I liked her,' said Dot. 'Not really our sort, though, with her posh accent and rich parents.'

'No airs and graces, though,' Eve pointed out.

'None at all,' agreed Dot.

'I took an instant liking to her too when I first met her at the antenatal clinic,' said Eve. 'She turned funny with me for a while and I never did find out why. She made some excuse about being busy when I phoned.'

'Probably had something else on her mind,' suggested her mother.

'That's what I thought,' said Eve. 'Anyway, I'm not gonna bring it up. Not unless she does it again, then I shall have it out with her.'

'It's best forgotten,' agreed Dot.

'When I first met Meg,' Eve went on thoughtfully, 'she seemed ultra-confident, as though nothing would faze her. But when you get to know her, she isn't quite so sure of herself.'

Dot nodded in agreement. 'She seems to think a lot of you,' she said. 'Needs you somehow.'

'Yes, I felt that too,' agreed Eve. 'I think we'll probably be seeing a lot more of her in the future.'

Eve was right. Meg came to the house in Marshall Gardens most afternoons with Becky. Eve looked forward to it. They took the babies to the park or the shops unless the weather was bad, when they stayed in and chatted, never seeming to run out of things to talk about. Dot enjoyed it too, and made a great fuss of both babies.

'What a life,' said Eve one afternoon on the way back from the park. 'Afternoon walks, long discussions over tea and biscuits . . . I'll miss all this when I'm back at work.'

'Don't remind me about work,' said Meg, making a face. 'I feel really out of touch with mine.'

'Once you've found someone to look after Becky, you'll soon get back into the swing,' said Eve.

'I think I'll go into central London tomorrow to see what's about in the boutiques up there,' Meg said thoughtfully. 'It might start me thinking fashion instead of Farley's rusks.'

Eve and Dot both smiled.

'Do you fancy coming?' she asked, looking from one to the other.

'Clothes aren't my thing,' said Dot with a wry grin, waving her hand towards the baggy grey cardigan and navy skirt she was wearing. 'But you go with her, Eve. You've always been interested in that sort of thing.'

'Do come, Eve,' urged Meg. 'We can take the babies with us.'

'You don't want to drag the little ones around London with you,' said Dot. 'Why not leave them here with me?'

'Both of them?' the two young women chorused.

'That's right,' said Dot. 'A break will do you both good.'

'I couldn't possibly impose on you, Mrs Granger,' said Meg.

'Call me Dot, and you wouldn't be imposing,' she assured her.

'Well . . .' Meg was tempted but didn't want to take advantage of the other woman's good nature.

'I'm quite capable of looking after two babies at the same time, you know,' asserted Dot, misunderstanding Meg's hesitancy.

'I know that,' Meg was quick to assure her. 'I was thinking of you.'

'There's no need. Go on, give yourself a treat and have a couple of hours off.' Dot looked from Eve to Meg. 'Just leave me their bottles and some nappies and they'll be fine.'

'In that case,' said Eve, smiling at Meg, 'King's Road, Chelsea, here we come.'

Chapter Six

In the early afternoon of the following day, George and his father left the house in Marshall Gardens to go back to work in George's car, replete with Dot's home cooking. Their usual lunchtime pie and a pint at the pub had been given the go-by today because Dot had put on a family meal so that George could spend some time with his little niece.

'The nipper's coming on a treat,' remarked George, opening the car door.

'She's a little cracker,' agreed Ned. 'Eve's doing a good job.'

'Motherhood suits her. It seems to have brought her out of her grief for Ken,' said George as they settled into their seats. 'I haven't seen her looking so cheerful in ages.'

'You can still see the pain in her eyes, so I don't think she's over it,' said Ned. 'But, yeah, having the baby does seem to have cheered her up.'

George started the engine, his thoughts turning to business. 'I'm hoping to close the sale on that Austin Cambridge this afternoon,' he said, preparing to drive away.

'You reckon the punter will come back and do the business then?'

'Sure of it,' said George. 'He's playing it cool . . . taking his time in the hope that we'll drop the price again.'

'And will you?'

'Not by much,' said George. 'It's a fair price we're asking. We'll never be able to afford to get the showrooms built if we give the stock away.'

'Not much chance of your doing that,' chuckled Ned.

It was common knowledge that his son was a shrewd businessman.

'I'm running a business, not a charity,' he pointed out. 'But my prices are fair, I'd never rip anyone off.'

'I wouldn't be working with you if I wasn't sure about that,' said his father.

Although George was hungry for success, he was scrupulously honest in all his dealings. He didn't live extravagantly either, seeing no point in robbing the profits for his own use at this early stage. He and his father were of one mind about building the business into something substantial before reaping the benefits.

'I'm going to the car auctions at Acton tomorrow morning, Dad,' said George. 'So you'll be holding the fort.'

'No problem,' said Ned.

'You'll clear the stock while I'm out, will you?' joked George.

'I'll do my best.' Ned was always pleased if he closed a sale when he was left in charge. It was a standing joke between them.

As they turned the corner out of Marshall Gardens, George had to swerve suddenly to avoid an estate car coming the other way.

'Bloody maniac,' he said, pulling into the side of the road, shaken by the near miss, which in turn made him angry.

He leapt out of his vehicle and marched towards the estate car, which had also drawn into the kerb, around the corner. A woman had got out and was storming towards him. Before he had a chance to give vent to his own fury, she roared, 'What the hell do you think you're playing at, you bloody lunatic? I've got a small baby in my car . . . you could have killed us both.'

'It was your fault,' was his gravel-voiced reply. 'You turned the corner too wide.'

'I certainly did not,' she yelled, her voice shrill with temper. 'You're the one who was wide. You were all over the road.'

'Rubbish,' he fumed. 'You shouldn't be driving a car with just yourself inside, let alone a poor defenceless child.'

'You're the one not fit to be driving,' she said, blue eyes flashing. 'I've a good mind to report you for dangerous driving.'

'Don't make me laugh. If anyone needs to be reported, it's you.' He stared at her, eyes hot with rage, the fact that she was extremely attractive infuriating him even more and adding fuel to his argument. 'Tell me, what did you do to pass the driving test, sleep with the instructor?'

'How dare you . . .'

Ned, who had got out of George's car and was standing nearby listening, made a stern intervention. 'That's enough, son,' he admonished. 'There's no call for that sort of talk. I think an apology is in order.'

George knew his father was right about *that*, anyway, and had the decency to admit it. 'Okay,' he conceded, looking at the woman coldly, 'I shouldn't have said that and I apologise. But that doesn't alter the fact that you nearly caused an accident with your reckless driving. If I hadn't managed to swerve . . .'

Ned moved swiftly between them, his hands raised. 'Now calm down, the pair of you,' he commanded. 'I saw what happened and I think you both took the corner a bit too wide.'

'Keep out of it, Dad,' said George.

Before Ned could reply, the woman spoke directly to George. 'I can't imagine how an arrogant pig like you can be related to someone as nice as Eve.'

'You know my sister?' asked George, his manner more subdued.

'I wouldn't mention her if I didn't, would I?' she snapped.

'All right, there's no need to adopt that tone,' George retorted. 'I haven't seen you around here before, that's all.'

'I haven't known Eve long,' she explained crisply. 'We were in the maternity ward together. I remember seeing you visiting her there.'

'You must be Meg. Eve's mentioned you,' intervened Ned, smiling warmly at her.' Any friend of Eve's is a friend of ours. Isn't that right, George?'

'Dunno about that,' mumbled George, still in a state of simmering umbrage.

Ned looked from one to the other. 'Why don't you admit that you were both to blame and be glad that no harm was done?'

'I still say that she . . .' began Goerge.

'And I say it was you,' countered the woman. 'But I don't have any more time to waste arguing with you about it.' She looked directly at Ned and managed a smile. 'Nice to meet *you* anyway,' she said, and walked briskly back to her car.

George watched her go, slim hips swinging in her short skirt. Much to his annoyance, he found himself admiring her.

'I had a bit of a set-to with your brother on the way to your place this afternoon,' Meg told Eve as they headed for Chelsea through the dense central London traffic.

'Really?'

'Yes, I didn't mention it in front of your mother in case she banned me from the house.'

'Mum isn't quite as daft as that over her son,' said Eve lightly.

'You never know how far people will take family solidarity.'

'That's true,' agreed Eve. 'But what happened, anyway?'

Meg told her.

'That doesn't sound like George at all.' Eve was thoughtful. 'My brother is usually the most easy-going of men.'

'That wasn't my impression.'

'Strange,' pondered Eve. 'He must have been convinced that he was in the right.'

'He wasn't, though . . .'

Finding herself on dangerous ground, Eve said quickly,

'As I'm not in a position to give an opinion, I think we'd better change the subject.'

'Okay.'

'So . . . how did you feel about leaving Becky for the first time?' Eve enquired.

'Guilty as hell,' Meg told her.

There's no need,' Eve assured her. 'Becky will be fine with Mum.'

'That's what's keeping me calm,' she said. 'Heaven knows what I'll be like when I go back to work and have to leave her with a stranger.'

'I can imagine,' remarked Eve. 'Makes me realise how lucky I am to have Mum to look after Josie when I go back to work.'

'When is that?'

'I'm hoping to be fixed up with a job by early May,' Eve told her. 'I can't afford to stay at home any longer than that.'

The traffic in Chelsea was heavy, but they eventually managed to find a parking space in a side street and joined the throngs of people in the King's Road. Everyone seemed to be carrying boutique bags, Eve noticed. The women's skirts here were shorter than anything she'd seen in the suburbs. No wonder the term mini-skirt was beginning to be used. The easy-to-manage, Vidal Sassoon style of haircut seemed to be as much in evidence as the ubiquitous beehive, too.

A young woman in a startling mid-thigh dress made entirely of a Union Jack caught the attention of them both.

'Patriotic dresses are really "in", aren't they?' remarked Eve, who had noticed the Union Jack on T-shirts, jackets, dresses, mugs and posters in the shop windows.

'Us Brits have something to be proud of now,' said Meg. 'Britain is swinging and London is putting Paris's nose out of joint as far as fashion is concerned. Several British designers are at the forefront.'

'There are certainly plenty of boutiques here,' remarked Eve.

'Every time I come, more seem to have opened,' said Meg. 'And it all started with Mary Quant back in the mid-1950s.'

The vibrant atmosphere permeated everything, the pale spring sunshine spreading its light across the lively cosmopolitan crowds. Eve and Meg ambled in and out of the boutiques, all different but oddly alike, most of them throbbing with pop music and verdant with pot plants. Clothes hung informally on garment rails – dresses, separates, skinny-rib tops.

'Today's cheap expendable fashion is much more youth-orientated than couture fashion, isn't it?' observed Eve as they took a rest in a coffee bar which was resonating to the Beatles' 'I Want to Hold Your Hand'. 'It makes you wonder what we're gonna wear when we hit thirty.'

'Not all the boutiques cater only for beanpole teenagers like Twiggy, you know,' Meg reminded her. 'Mine certainly doesn't.'

'True,' agreed Eve.

'Anyway, women of all ages are getting more relaxed about what they wear these days,' Meg went on. 'The way hem lines are rising across the age-range is evidence of that.'

Eve sipped her coffee and looked at Meg. 'Well, do you feel a bit more in the swing of things now?'

'I do,' she said, her eyes shining. 'I'm quite looking forward to getting back to work. How about you? Are you looking forward to going back?'

'Not likely.' Eve laughed. 'The sort of job I'll be doing isn't something you look forward to. It's merely a source of income.'

'Why not find something you *can* look forward to then?' suggested Meg.

'Beggars can't be choosers,' said Eve. 'I'll probably go into a factory because it pays well.'

'There must be something more inspiring around for a bright spark like you,' said Meg.

'I've never given it much thought,' Eve told her. 'When Ken was alive I saw my job as a temporary thing, something I would only do until I left work to have a family. My wages subsidised his income and helped towards our savings for the deposit on a house. Now I need the money to support Josie, I have to have a steady income.'

'Having to go to a job you don't enjoy every day isn't much fun, though,' said Meg.

'How many people have a job they really enjoy?' It was a rhetorical question. 'Most of us are too dominated by the need for a regular wage to consider whether or not the work is fulfilling and enjoyable.'

'All except for spoilt rich kids like me whose daddy set them up in business.'

'That wasn't what I meant,' said Eve with a half-smile. 'But you are more fortunate than most.'

'I know.'

'I probably wouldn't have gone back to work if Ken had lived,' said Eve. 'I always intended to have more than one child, and close together so they would be company for each other.' She combed her fringe back from her brow with her fingers. 'I still miss him. I don't think I'll ever get over him.'

'I'm sure you will eventually,' said Meg reassuringly.

'It isn't that easy when you really loved someone,' said Eve.

Meg lowered her eyes and stared into her coffee. 'It was just words, Eve,' she said, looking up. 'I didn't mean anything.'

'Sorry.' Eve reached out and touched her hand. 'I'm still a bit touchy.'

'I expect you'll meet someone else eventually,' suggested Meg.

'Not me,' said Eve. 'I'll never get married again – *not ever.*'

'You can't know that for certain,' said Meg. 'You're still young. It's impossible to tell how you'll feel later on.'

'No one else could ever match up to Ken in my eyes,' Eve told her.

Meg swiftly changed the subject. 'Well,' she said, smiling, 'now that I've had this little break, I'm dying to get back to my daughter. So perhaps I'm not such a bad mother after all.'

'You're not a bad mother at all, you just expect too much of yourself,' said Eve. 'And Becky is in very good hands. My mother is one of those people who can make a meal, see to a baby and vacuum the living room all at the same time.' She paused, smiling. 'Maybe not in that order, but she is a housewife and mother extraordinaire.'

Back at the house in Marshall Gardens, Dot was having a wonderful time. She thrived on feeling needed. Being busy and purposeful had made her feel fully alive again. It reminded her of her happiest years, when her own children had been little.

The babies had kept her busy, of course, but Dot loved it. It was like having twins, something she'd always fancied.

Now that they were both sleeping, she was peeling the potatoes for the evening meal and mulling over an idea she hadn't been able to get out of her mind all afternoon. She made a decision. Yes, she was definitely going to pursue it.

When Eve returned from Chelsea, she felt completely revitalised. Meg was such fun, and the brief insight into fashion from a boutique owner's point of view had been interesting.

Her mother seemed in particularly good form, she noticed, happy and sort of excited. After Meg and Becky had gone, Dot sprang a surprise on her daughter.

'You know that Meg's been talking about finding someone to look after Becky when she goes back to work . . .' she began.

'Yeah,' said Eve, making a face. 'She's absolutely dreading it. It makes me realise just how lucky I am to have you.'

'Er, well . . . the thing is, Eve,' said Dot uncertainly, 'I was wondering if you'd have any objection to my offering to look after Becky for her.'

Eve looked at her in astonishment. 'You mean – look after both babies?'

'That's right,' she said.

'Oh, Mum,' said Eve worriedly, 'have you thought what you would be taking on?'

'I won't do it if you'd rather I didn't,' Dot quickly pointed out. 'If you feel that Josie might not get her share of my attention if I were to have the two of them.'

'That's the last thing on my mind,' Eve assured her. 'Because I know how capable you are. In fact, I think it would probably be a good thing for both the children, especially as they get older and need company. But are you sure you want two of them to look after?'

'While I'm having one I might as well have the other,' she said firmly. 'And at least Meg could go to work with an easy mind.'

'Are you sure it won't be too much for you?' Eve was concerned.

'I'm forty-eight, not eighty-eight,' Dot reminded her.

'I wasn't thinking about your age,' Eve told her. 'I'm only twenty-seven, and I think I'd find looking after two babies at the same time a bit of a handful.'

'If it was for twenty-four hours a day, I probably would find it too much. But it would only be during the daytime,' Dot reminded her. 'And Meg doesn't open the shop on Mondays, so I'd have Sunday and Monday off.'

'What about Dad?'

'It wouldn't affect him,' she said. 'He'll be out at work.'

'I meant in that he's never wanted you to work,' Eve reminded her.

'He's never wanted me to *go out* to work,' Dot said. 'I wouldn't be going anywhere to do this.'

'Meg would pay you, though, and he's always been a bit funny about being the bread-winner,' Eve pointed out.

'I shall talk to him about it, of course,' Dot assured her. 'But I don't see how he can object to my having a bit of extra pocket money of my own.' She looked very determined suddenly. 'I really want to do this, Eve.'

'In that case, go ahead and talk to Meg about it,' said Eve.

'There's one thing I will need if she agrees to it, though . . .'

'A prescription for tranquillisers,' Eve laughingly suggested.

'No, you daft cat,' Dot grinned. 'A double buggy so that I can take the babies out.'

'I'm sure Meg will be only too happy to supply you with one of those,' said Eve.

'I could kiss you, I'm so happy and relieved,' was Meg's response to Dot's proposition the next day when she came visiting. 'I can go back to the boutique with an easy mind now.'

'I'm so glad you're pleased,' said Dot, flushed and happy.

'We'd better talk terms and times then, hadn't we?' suggested Meg.

With everything agreed, the three women had a cup of tea and a chat. Meg was thinking what a blessing it was she'd decided to pursue a friendship with Eve after all. It was of immense value to her. The Grangers were a terrific family, so warm and friendly – except for the ghastly George, of course.

Having an open invitation to the house in Marshall Gardens was proving to be something of a lifeline to Meg. She didn't feel isolated and afraid of motherhood any more. Thank goodness she had decided to put her complicated emotions behind her and telephone Eve that day.

* * *

Meg was already back at work and the time was drawing near for Eve to do the same. She'd fixed herself up with a job in a canned food factory in Acton and had become increasingly gloomy about it. Being on an assembly line all day was going to seem hellish after being at home with her daughter. Because of her responsibilities to Josie, she had decided not to take Meg's advice and look for something more interesting. She would see how she felt when she was actually doing the job.

But the week before she was due to start at the factory, she received a telephone call that changed everything.

'Eve, it's Meg.'

'Hi, Meg. Before you ask, your daughter is fine,' she said, because Meg called several times a day to check on Becky.

'Good. But Becky isn't the reason for my call, not this time.'

'No?'

'No. Listen. Do you want a job?'

'I've got one.'

'I mean, working for me here at the boutique,' she explained.

'I thought you didn't have any vacancies,' Eve reminded her.

'My manageress has just told me she's leaving, and I need a replacement.'

'Manageress!' exclaimed Eve. 'I'm not qualified to run a boutique.'

'You'd soon learn the job,' Meg said. 'I'd teach you myself.'

'But surely you'd be better off promoting one of your existing staff?' Eve suggested.

'There's no one I could trust with the responsibility,' Meg said. 'They wouldn't want it, anyway. My full-timer is only eighteen and has no interest beyond serving behind the counter. The others are all part-time.'

'I'm flattered to be asked, of course, Meg, but I honestly

don't think I'm up to it,' said Eve, wanting to be perfectly honest even though the idea excited her. 'How can I be when I've no experience in that line of work?'

'You're interested in clothes and you're fed up with your present job,' was Meg's answer to that. 'I want someone with the right sort of personality to deal with customers, and someone who I get on well with. Those things are far more important to me than experience, which you'll soon gain on the job anyway.'

'Well . . .'

'Do say yes. Whatever they've offered you at the factory, I'll match it with the promise of a increase when you've learnt the job,' she said. 'And you wouldn't have to travel so far to work, so your fares would be less and you could have longer with Josie in the mornings.'

The idea was irresistible to Eve. It was the first time a job had really interested her. She'd grown up believing that paid employment was merely a bridge between school and motherhood. She knew, instinctively, that she could make a success of this.

'So, what do you think?' asked Meg.

'What makes you so sure I could do the job?' Eve asked.

'Call it a gut feeling,' explained Meg. 'Your general attitude towards things is the same as my own. That day in the King's Road when you were so interested in everything, I knew you'd be right for my boutique. But I didn't have a job to offer you then.'

'What about working hours?' Eve asked.

'You'd have to work Saturdays, but you wouldn't have to work Mondays so it would still only be a five-day week,' she said.

'All right,' said Eve decisively. 'You've talked me into it. I'll ring the factory and tell them I won't be starting.'

A whoop of delight came down the phone.

'It looks lovely on you,' said Eve to a customer who was

trying on a short scarlet dress with a lurex thread running through it. She worked in the offices at Ealing Film Studios, apparently, and was a regular customer at Trend. Her quest today was something for a party, and Eve was with her outside the changing rooms, where she was looking at herself from a distance in the full-length mirror.

'You don't think it's too short, do you?' asked the woman.

'Not at all,' said Eve, who was wearing a black mini-skirt with a crisp white blouse which was perfect for her dark colouring. 'People are wearing them a lot shorter than that.'

'Yes, I've noticed,' said the customer. She was about thirty and quite ordinary to look at, but slim and smart, with very well-cut hair.

'You can carry that length off,' said Eve, looking at her approvingly.

'Do you think so?'

'Oh, yes,' said Eve enthusiastically.

'I'd rather you were honest with me,' said the customer. 'I don't want to look ridiculous.'

'I wouldn't let you leave here looking ridiculous,' said Eve. 'It would be bad for business, because you'd never come back.'

'There is that.' She studied herself from different angles.

'You look terrific, I promise you,' said Eve. 'The colour is gorgeous on you. Just the thing for an autumn party.'

The customer eventually purchased the dress and left the shop smiling. Eve then served a crowd of office workers – shopping in their lunch hour – with various small items: T-shirts, belts, tights. One of them bought a skinny-rib sweater.

Eve had been working at Trend for four months. For the first time in her life, her work was a joy to her, something she looked forward to every morning. Leaving Josie wasn't easy, especially now that she was doing new things almost every day. But she was thriving in her grandmother's care.

At six months she was dark-eyed like her mother, had apple cheeks and could sit up on her own.

After serving a few more customers, Eve looked at her watch. She was waiting for Meg to come back so that she herself could go to lunch. Meg had gone to buy stock from a factory in Hackney and was calling on a couple of wholesalers on the way back. Eve was the only member of staff on duty. The junior had gone to lunch and the afternoon part-timer hadn't come in yet.

Situated in a busy shopping parade near the station, overlooking the fine trees and grassland of Haven Green, Trend was open plan, with polished wooden floors and modern fittings. The front of the shop was stocked with casual wear, the back with smart suits, coats and dresses.

Just inside the door was a bargain rail. Anything that was particularly slow-moving was put on here. They couldn't afford to have stock around for long in these times of fast-changing fashion.

'Hi,' said Meg, sweeping in looking elegant in a scarlet suit with a short skirt, and long white boots. 'Are you dying of hunger?'

'I could do with something to eat.' She and Meg had agreed that Eve mustn't be afraid to speak her mind during working hours. It was the only way their friendship could survive under the strain of a working environment, where minor irritations could become major resentments if left to simmer. Eve was determined that that wouldn't happen. Their friendship was important to her. She had never had a friend with whom she felt so much in tune. 'But it's all right, I'm not about to pass out or anything.'

'Sorry I'm late back, I got caught in the traffic,' Meg said.

'Not to worry.'

'I've got some terrific stuff in the car,' she added. 'You'll love it.'

'Ooh, that's good,' said Eve, who took a keen overall interest in the boutique. 'I can't wait to see it.'

'Go and have your lunch while I get it out of the car,' said Meg, considerate of her employee. 'I didn't stop to unload because I didn't want to keep you from your break any longer.' She paused thoughtfully. 'I suppose we really ought to shut the shop over the lunch period so that we both get our break at a regular time.'

'We'd miss out on a lot of good business if we did that,' Eve pointed out. 'Quite a few people come in their lunch hour.'

'That's a point.'

'I think we should carry on as we are,' suggested Eve. 'I don't mind what time I go to lunch. As long as I can leave dead on time in the evening.'

'We're of the same mind about that,' smiled Meg. They were both eager to get back to their daughters after work. 'That's the only drawback of having a career, you miss out on being with your offspring.'

They had discussed this on several occasions before and agreed that it was a problem to which there appeared to be no solution, since no one could be in two places at once.

'Go and have your lunch, Eve.'

'In a minute.' Eve couldn't resist knowing what she had to look forward to. 'What sort of things did you get?'

'Some gorgeous sweaters and some deliciously short skirts.'

'Sounds good.'

'I got a few trouser suits too,' Meg said. 'I thought we'd give them a try. The wholesaler reckons they're going to be really big sellers this winter as an alternative for women who don't like wearing mini-skirts. We'll have a look at the stuff together this afternoon and get it priced up.'

'Have you had lunch?' asked Eve.

Meg nodded. 'I had a sandwich with the wholesaler. I've known him for years.'

'I'll go to the staff room and eat my sandwiches then.' She paused. 'Can I use the phone in the office first, though?'

'Course you can, I've told you there's no need to ask.'

'Thanks,' said Eve, ever mindful of the fact that Meg was her employer as well as her friend, even though Meg made no big thing of it.

'No prizes for guessing who you're going to be calling,' said Meg, smiling.

Eve grinned. 'I'll find out if Becky is okay while I'm at it,' she said.

They laughed. Calling Eve's mother was something they both did a lot of, because they liked to keep in regular touch.

As a friend Meg was loyal, supportive and good fun. As an employer she was in control and assertive. But she was also sympathetic to the plight of a working mother, since she was in the same situation herself. On the odd occasion when Eve had been late because of some problem with Josie, she received wholehearted co-operation from Meg. Eve knew she wouldn't have got the same sort of understanding from her previous employer, because he was a man.

Eve went into Meg's office at the back of the shop, a contemporary room littered with modern art and pot plants. She spoke to her mother and made kissing noises to Josie, which was a regular ritual.

'So everything's okay at home then, is it, Mum?' Eve said.

'Yeah,' she confirmed. 'Everything's fine. Me and the girls are going to the shops this afternoon.'

'There's a sharp breeze,' said Eve. 'Make sure you wrap up.'

'Make sure I wrap your daughter up, you mean,' Dot said with a smile in her voice.

'Sorry, it's the built-in worry button that came with Josie as part of the package,' said Eve. 'But I know she's in good hands.'

'I should think so too . . .'

'I'd better go,' said Eve, wanting to eat her lunch. 'I'll see you tonight.'

'Oh, before you go,' said Dot, remembering something.

'A letter came for you. A typed envelope. I think it's from the solicitor's office.'

'Ooh, perhaps the compensation offer has come through at last,' said Eve. 'Can you open it and tell me what it says?'

She could hear the rustle of paper as the envelope was opened.

'Yeah, it is from the solicitor's office,' confirmed Dot. 'They want you to contact them at your earliest convenience.'

'Sounds interesting,' said Eve. 'I'll give them a ring now.'

'Okay, dear,' said Dot. 'I'll see you later.'

The solicitor's secretary said she couldn't give Eve any details over the telephone and asked if she could call into the office as soon as possible. Because it was only a few minutes' walk from the shop, Eve said she would go right away. Eating a sandwich quickly to stave off hunger pangs, she put on her coat, and left the shop.

She hurried towards the Broadway, her heart pounding as she dared to hope that there might be enough compensation for the deposit on a house.

Chapter Seven

'How much did you say?' gasped Meg a short time later when a rather shaken Eve got back from the solicitor's office with astonishing news.

'Eight thousand pounds,' repeated Eve, almost reverently. 'I've been awarded eight thousand pounds in compensation.'

'Wow!'

'It's a ruddy fortune,' breathed Eve. 'Apparently, they took into consideration the fact that I lost my provider and have a child to bring up on my own.' She shook her head slowly, exhaling with a soft whistling sound. 'It's still an awful lot of money, though.'

They were in Meg's office, the rest of the staff now back on duty in the shop. Meg was sitting at her desk, her hand trembling slightly as she doodled with a biro on a jotter pad. 'You'll be able to buy a house outright now,' she said, 'never mind just having enough for the deposit on one.'

'I'll have some money left over, too, if I stay in the same property price bracket as I intended,' mentioned Eve.

Meg lowered her eyes to hide an unwanted stab of resentment. 'I hope you're not going to retire to the Bahamas,' she said, managing to keep her tone light.

'Hardly,' replied Eve. 'It's an awful lot of money to someone like me, but not enough to think about giving up work.'

'I *was* just kidding,' Meg explained.

'Course you were.' Eve tutted in self-derision and put her hands to her head, which was throbbing from all the excitement. 'Stupid of me. The shock of coming into money must have wrecked my sense of humour.'

'Don't look so worried about it,' said Meg. 'Surely this is cause for a celebration?'

'I could *never* celebrate something like this,' said Eve, and promptly burst into tears.

'Oh, Eve.' Meg went to her friend and hugged her. 'I'm sorry, I didn't mean to upset you.'

'It wasn't you, you haven't upset me,' said Eve thickly, wiping her eyes and composing herself. 'It's me. I'm doing it to myself. I'm so damned hung up about this whole thing.'

'In what way?'

'Well — and this will sound really ungrateful — but no amount of money can ever compensate me for losing Ken.' She blew her nose and sat down on a chair near the desk while Meg went back to her own seat. 'I hate the idea of having the money. I feel as though I'm cashing in on his death.'

Meg bit her lip, almost choking on a lump in her throat. 'You're not cashing in on it,' she said. 'You're only getting what's due to you . . . what you need to make a decent life for Josie. She's Ken's child after all.'

'I know all that, but . . . it's hard to explain.' She pushed her floppy dark fringe away from her damp brow, feeling very distressed. 'I know this will seem silly, but accepting the money hurts. It's an actual pain, here,' she said, pointing to her heart.

Clearing her throat, Meg said, 'I can understand it making you feel emotional. But you have to look at the situation objectively. Bringing up Josie isn't a short-term thing. You're going to have to provide a home for her and support her financially for many years to come. This money is a mere drop in the ocean to what you're going to need. But at least it means you can get your own place . . . get out from under your parents' feet, as you've been wanting to.'

'Yeah, I know,' agreed Eve. 'I'm being really stupid.'

'Come here,' said Meg, standing up and opening her arms.

'Oh, Meg, you're such a good friend,' said Eve, hugging her tight. 'Thanks for being there for me.'

'You've been there for me enough times since Becky was born,' Meg reminded her. 'I reckon it's the least I can do.'

'Us single parents have to stick together,' said Eve, feeling the bond of friendship grow inside her, warm and strong.

'We certainly do.'

'Can I use the phone again?' asked Eve. 'I feel as though I can tell my mother about the money now without bursting into tears.'

'Go ahead,' said Meg, walking across the room and turning at the door. 'When you're ready, and you've had your lunch, I'll be in the stockroom sorting through the new stuff. You can help me price it up.'

'Be with you in a jiffy,' replied Eve.

'Okay.'

Making her way straight to the stockroom without going through the shop, Meg's face was wet with tears as she shut the door behind her. Forcing them back, she wiped her eyes and carefully renewed her mascara in her handbag mirror so that Eve wouldn't know she'd been crying. It was imperative her friend didn't know how deeply affected she was by what had happened to Eve today.

That evening Becky was determined not to settle down to sleep. Bathed and adorable in a white babygrow, she was all chuckles in her mother's arms, but the minute Meg put her down in her cot, she let rip.

The doorbell rang. Meg went to answer it with the baby in her arms. Seeing her parents standing there, her heart lurched. Her mother would turn up the very night the baby was being difficult.

'She's still up then,' said her father, looking at Becky with delight. 'We *are* in luck.'

'She should be in bed and asleep at this time,' said Bea reproachfully, looking at her watch. 'It's turned eight o'clock.'

'She usually is . . .' began Meg.

'Can't be that usual, or she'd be asleep in her cot now,' cut in Bea, sweeping into Meg's lounge, looking even more pear-shaped than usual in a navy-blue twinset with a tweed pleated skirt and boat-like brogues.

'She just wouldn't go down tonight for some reason,' Meg tried to explain.

'Wouldn't go down?' questioned Bea. 'You're the child's mother, you make the rules.'

'It's game, set and match to she who shouts the loudest at the moment,' said Meg lightly, making a joke of it in an effort to defuse her mother's disapproval.

'You shouldn't give in to her,' admonished Bea.

'I can't just let her scream,' Meg pointed out. 'Even apart from the fact that it's upsetting for both of us, I live in a flat, remember. I'll have the neighbours complaining.'

'Isn't it time you moved into a house?' said Bea. 'This place isn't suitable for a baby.'

'I know that,' sighed Meg. 'But I never seem to get time to set things in motion. Moving house is always so fraught with problems.'

'That's what comes of trying to run a business when you've a baby to look after,' lectured Bea. 'You don't get time for the things that matter. A career and motherhood just don't mix, I don't care what anyone says.'

'What do you suggest I live on if I give up my career?' enquired Meg.

'You could get a job working for someone else,' Bea suggested. 'Something with shorter hours and less responsibility.'

'There's nothing I'd like more than to be able to spend more time with Becky,' said Meg, clinging to her overtried patience. 'But I couldn't manage on a part-time salary.'

'Your father would help you.' It would never occur to

Bea to consult her husband before committing him to something.

'Daddy has quite enough on his plate,' Meg pointed out. 'Anyway, I prefer to pay my own way.'

'There's just no reasoning with her,' Bea muttered to Frank as they sat down together on the sofa.

'Leave the girl alone,' he said.

Becky began to wriggle and whimper in her mother's arms.

'That child should be in a proper routine,' said Bea forcefully. 'That's what babies need. If you're going to get her out of her cot every time she cries, she'll do it all the more. You're just making a rod for your own back.'

'Let me have her,' said Frank, grinning at the baby, who gave him a dimply smile.

Meg handed his granddaughter to him and she emitted a fat chuckle.

'There you are,' said Bea to Meg. 'She's just playing you up.'

'She's gorgeous, though, aren't you?' said Frank, bouncing her on his knee.

'Don't get her excited,' warned Bea, 'or Meg will never get her to sleep.'

He settled her in the crook of his arm, kissing the top of her head. She was pink-cheeked and blue-eyed, with fair downy hair. 'Isn't she just the most adorable thing you've ever seen, Bea?' he said.

Bea's heart was actually melting at the sight of her, but outward sentimentality wasn't her way. 'Yes, she's a beautiful child.' She turned to her daughter. 'But she shouldn't still be up at this time. When you were her age I always put you to bed at six o'clock on the dot. You have to start as you mean to go on with babies, or they'll run rings around you. And it won't end there; she'll be doing just as she likes later on, if you're not careful. Children need to know who's boss.'

'She knows very well,' said Meg with a mischievous grin, 'that it's her.'

Frank was amused by that and laughed heartily. But Bea had little capacity for humour and said, 'Exactly my point. You have to have a firm hand with children.'

'Coffee?' offered Meg, so that she could escape to the kitchen away from her mother's disapproval.

They both said that that would be lovely and Meg departed thankfully.

'Give that child to me, for goodness' sake, Frank,' commanded Bea, because he was bouncing Becky on his knee again. 'You'll make her sick, jiggling her around like that.'

'She loves it,' he said, looking at the baby. 'Don't you, cuddlekins?'

'Oh, really.' Bea gave him a withering look. 'How can you expect the child to learn to speak properly if you talk gibberish to her?'

'She's six months old,' he reminded her. 'Everyone talks daft to babies.'

'That doesn't make it right,' she declared. 'You should have more sense.' She tutted and turned to him. 'Give her to me.'

He did as she asked, and Becky snuggled against her grandmother for a few moments before starting to wave her fists and whimper. 'She's dead tired,' said Bea, and there was no disguising the tenderness in her voice. 'But she just won't give in and go to sleep.'

'She doesn't want to miss anything,' said Frank, adding bravely, 'must take after you.'

But Bea wasn't listening to him. She was intent upon getting the baby to sleep, cradling her in her arms and stroking her head very softly. The child gradually became still. 'I think I'll try and get her to go down in her cot,' she said to him in a whisper.

'All right, dear.' It was a rare treat for him to see the gentle side to his wife's nature and he was heartened by it.

A few minutes later, Meg reappeared with a tray of coffee

and biscuits. He told her her mother was trying to get the baby to settle in her cot.

'She'll be lucky.' Meg put the tray down rather forcefully on a small table. 'I won't pour her coffee . . . she could be gone for hours.'

'I know your mother can be tiresome at times, dear,' said Frank, ever the peacemaker. 'But she does love you and the baby.'

'As long as we keep at a safe distance from her snobby cronies,' said Meg.

In all honesty Frank couldn't deny what Meg was saying. His wife wasn't an easy person. Sometimes she drove him to distraction with her strident opinions and constant demands – for more money, material acquisitions, prestige. She could be vain, narrow-minded and selfish. But despite all of that, he was devoted to her and fiercely loyal. 'It's difficult for her.'

'I know she can't help the way she is, Dad. You don't have to make excuses for her,' said Meg, sitting beside him and pouring the coffee.

'It's the way she was brought up,' he explained. 'She'll get over the embarrassment of your situation eventually. She's getting to love Becky more all the time.'

'I should damned well hope she is,' said Meg, setting down a cup of coffee in front of him. 'Becky *is* her grandchild.'

He touched his daughter's hand. 'Your mother and I are of a generation who find these things hard to accept,' he explained. 'Illegitimacy was considered scandalous when we were young.'

'It still is by most people, especially the older generation,' she told him. 'But I didn't get pregnant just because it's cool to be uninhibited these days, you know.'

'I'm sure you didn't, dear,' he said, his cheeks burning because it embarrassed him to discuss such things with his daughter.

'A bit later and it wouldn't have happened at all, because

the Pill is now available to women who aren't married,' she informed him. 'But I'm very glad it did happen, because I wouldn't be without my daughter for anything.'

'Of course you wouldn't, dear, none of us would,' he said, relieved she hadn't lingered on the subject of birth control. 'You'll just have to give your mother more time to get used to your . . . er, rather unusual circumstances.'

'You didn't seem to have any trouble accepting them,' she said.

'I was as upset as she was when you told us you were pregnant.'

'Only because of what it would be like for me, though,' she said. 'Not because of the scandal to yourselves.'

'I'm lucky in as much as I don't give a damn what other people think,' he said. 'It isn't like that for your mother.'

Meg sipped her coffee and nibbled a biscuit. 'Mum's right about one thing, though,' she said. 'Motherhood and business aren't the most compatible of things. I won't go so far as she does and say that they don't mix. But I am finding it hard.'

'You must be exhausted at the end of the day,' he said sympathetically. 'Coming home from work and having to see to Becky, especially if you've had a bad night with her.'

'That side of it doesn't bother me at all,' she explained. 'It's more that I don't want to miss seeing her grow up. I don't want to turn around one day and realise she's leaving home and I've missed the whole thing.'

'But you wouldn't want to give up your business even if you could afford it, would you, dear?' Frank said perceptively.

'To be perfectly honest, no, I wouldn't,' she told him. 'I enjoy my work and want to do well at it. I can see nothing wrong with that. Anyway, being in business means I can provide well for my child, and I want to go on doing that.' She sighed heavily. 'But I want to be a good mother too. It's a classic case of wanting it all, and that just isn't possible.'

'There is a way you could have more of it, though,' he said.

She turned to him. 'Is there?'

He nodded. 'If you were to take a business partner, you could share the responsibility, work fewer hours and have more time with Becky.'

'I've already thought of that, vaguely,' she said. 'But it isn't that easy. I don't know anyone who'd be interested, for a start.'

'It might be an idea to start asking around in your trade,' he said. 'Failing that, you could always advertise.'

'Oh no, I wouldn't want to go into business with someone I don't know.'

'It wouldn't be ideal, I agree,' he said. 'But you're going to have to do something. Even apart from the fact that you need more time with Becky, you might want to expand your business at some point soon, and as things are at the moment, you wouldn't be able to cope because you just don't have the time.'

'I've had similar thoughts about that myself,' she admitted.

'You'd have to be very careful who you chose as a partner, of course,' he said. 'Some partnerships end in disaster.'

'It would have to be someone I know I could trust and get on with,' she said. 'Trouble is, none of the people I know have any money to invest.'

'What about that friend of yours who works with you?' he said.

'Eve would be perfect,' said Meg.

'But she doesn't have any money going spare, I suppose.'

'She does, actually,' said Meg, her cool expression hiding the tumultuous emotions aroused by the topic. 'As from today she does have some cash.'

'There's your answer then.'

Meg shook her head. 'No. As much as I'd like her as a partner, I wouldn't ask her to invest in my business.' She was adamant. 'That would be a really insensitive thing to do. She needs that money for other things.'

'A high-flying businesswoman wouldn't worry about that,' he said, giving her an affectionate grin.

She looked at him intently. 'You're the high-flyer in the family,' she said. 'I could never use a friend to further my business interests.'

'But if it was in her interests too . . . ?'

'I still wouldn't do it.'

'It doesn't pay to be too soft in business, you know,' he said.

'Come off it, Daddy,' she replied with a knowing smile. 'You're an absolute softie when it comes down to it. You only force yourself onwards and upwards because Mummy drives you.'

'I haven't done badly for all that,' he remarked.

'No one could argue with you on that score,' she was quick to confirm. 'But I don't believe it was ever what you really wanted.' Meg had grown up knowing the truth about her father's success in business, and as she'd become more aware of things she'd begun to have views of her own about it. 'I think you'd much rather have had a quiet life with a little house somewhere, running that hardware shop your father left you.'

'Ah well, there are some things a man doesn't discuss with his daughter,' he said mysteriously. 'No matter how much he loves her.'

Meg knew he would say no more on the subject, but the conversation came to an end anyway as Bea returned to the room. 'Ah, coffee, wonderful,' she said, flopping into an armchair. 'I can certainly do with a cup after all the story-telling I've been doing.'

'Story-telling?' said Meg in astonishment. 'Becky is six months old.'

'It's the sound of the voice they find so reassuring,' Bea said. 'Anyway, it's done the trick. She's fast asleep.'

'Thanks, Mummy,' said Meg.

'No need to thank me, dear,' she said. 'I *am* her grand-mother.'

When it suits you, thought Meg, but she said wickedly, 'You've made a rod for your own back there, you know. She'll have you at it every time you come to visit now. You won't know who's boss.'

'Once in a while it doesn't hurt to give a baby a little of what it wants,' Bea said knowingly, missing the joke as usual.

'If you say so,' said Meg, smiling.

One Sunday afternoon in the spring of the following year, in a neat semi-detached house on the corner of Daisymead Avenue, Ealing, there was a small gathering in progress. Its purpose was to celebrate the fact that the refurbishment of Eve's house was now complete – three months after she'd moved in. The buffet meal was over and the guests were having coffee in the lounge.

'The place looks a picture, Eve,' said her father when she found herself standing next to him after she'd finished serving the coffee. 'You've done wonders with it.'

'I did have the odd bit of help, you know,' she reminded him, because George and her father had assisted her with the decorating as well as the hundred and one other jobs that arise when you move into a place that needs doing up.

'Just a little,' he said modestly. 'So, how does it feel to have your own place?'

'Wonderful.' She added quickly, 'Not that I didn't enjoy living with you and Mum.'

'But there's nothing like having your own place,' he said.

'That's right,' said Eve.

At first she'd missed the support and convenience of having her parents on hand. Getting to work in the mornings was more of a scramble now that she had to take Josie to her mother's in the pushchair before catching the bus to work. Hopefully this was only temporary, because she'd used some of the compensation money to buy a second-hand estate car which George was teaching her to drive.

'Knocking the wall through to the dining room was a really good idea,' her father remarked, glancing towards the arch in the centre of the room, lit with shafts of sunlight through the front bay window. 'It makes it look a lot bigger.'

'I prefer the open-plan look,' said Eve. 'It's more up to date.'

It was a traditional thirties-built house with three bed-rooms and a small garden. She'd had to settle for an older property because she wanted to stay near to her parents and there weren't many new private houses being built around here, not in her price range anyway. She'd furnished it in contemporary style – three white walls contrasting with one in bold royal blue, long, low sofas, fitted carpet, bookshelves and a glass-topped occasional table, plus plenty of mirrors and pot plants.

'I'm not one for making fancy speeches,' said Ned. 'But I'm proud of you.'

'Me?' Being rather a self-effacing person, Eve was puzzled by this. 'Why's that? I've only been able to get the house because I was given the money. I didn't earn it or anything.'

'I was referring to the way you've coped since Ken died. I know it hasn't been easy for you, but you've got on with your life and you're making a fine job of bringing up Josie.'

'I'm not really on my own, though, am I?' she said. 'I've got the family as back-up.'

'It isn't the same as having your husband beside you, though, is it?'

A wave of sadness engulfed her. 'No, Dad, it isn't the same.'

She looked into the soft dark eyes that she, George and Josie had all inherited, and a lump rose in her throat. She loved both her parents, but her father had always been especially close to her. If she had any criticism of him at all it was that he could be a bit domineering towards her mother in that he wouldn't let her go out to work. But that was more to do with his generation than his nature, because there wasn't a kinder man on the planet.

'Anyway, would you like me to go around and see if any more coffee is wanted?' he asked.

'If you like.'

'You go and talk to your guests.'

'Perhaps I'd better.' She went over to her mother, who was sitting with a group of friends from Marshall Gardens. 'Enjoying yourselves?'

'Lovely, dear, thanks,' replied Dot, and the others agreed.

Eve moved on, chatting to various friends and relatives. She found Meg sitting with the staff from the boutique.

'I've just been upstairs to check on the babies and they're both fast asleep,' she informed Eve, standing up to face her, leaving the others to chatter among themselves.

'They'll be better for a sleep.' The children – now turned a year – were having their afternoon nap.

Meg glanced around the room. 'The house looks lovely,' she said. 'I ought to start looking for a house myself. Becky is far too cooped up at the flat now that she's walking.'

At that moment George appeared at Eve's side with Josie, snuffling and grizzling, in his arms. 'I heard her crying when I was in the bathroom,' he explained. 'Thought I'd better bring her down in case she woke the other one up.'

'They were both dead to the world when I was up there a few minutes ago,' said Meg quickly, because she always felt the need to defend herself against George.

'Well, this one isn't now, is she?' said George with an edge to his voice. He and Meg were sworn enemies. Ever since that first disastrous meeting it had been all-out war between them. Matters weren't helped by the fact that their paths crossed regularly because of Meg's friendship with Eve.

'Come on then, madam,' said Eve, taking her daughter from George.

'She's woken up with a right mood on her by the look of it,' said Meg as Josie buried her face in her mother's shoulder, making little sobbing noises.

'She hasn't had her sleep out, that's why,' said Eve, kissing her daughter's head. 'I'll try to get her to go back down or she'll be grumpy all afternoon.'

'Can I do anything useful while you're upstairs, sis?' offered her brother. 'Make some more coffee or anything?'

'I'd like to do something to help too,' said Meg.

Eve thought about this, then looked from one to the other. 'Actually, there is something you can both do for me,' she said with a wicked grin.

They waited, eyeing her warily.

'I'd like the two of you to be civil to each other,' she explained. 'Just for me, for today . . . for the sake of the party.'

Neither of them said a word.

'It won't hurt either of you to make the effort just for a couple of hours,' she continued in a pleasant but firm tone. 'Tomorrow you can revert to your normal bickering selves if you must. But just for this afternoon, be nice, please.' She paused. 'I'm taking my daughter upstairs. See you later.'

Meg and George watched her go, then looked at each other.

'Bit of a tall order,' he said.

'An impossibility, I'd say,' was her opinion.

'What is it exactly that makes you think you are so superior?' he asked.

'I might ask you the same thing.'

'Unlike you, I don't consider myself to be better than everyone else,' he said.

'You could have fooled me.'

'It's all in your mind.'

'Rubbish,' she said. 'You've an ego the size of America. That was obvious to me the minute I first clapped eyes on you. I'd never come across such arrogance before.'

'*Me*, arrogant!' he exclaimed. 'That's rich, coming from you.'

'And what's that supposed to mean?'

'I've seen ten-year-old kids on the bumper cars at the fair with more road sense than you,' he told her. 'Yet you tried to make out that near miss we had was all my fault because you're too damned arrogant to admit your own failings.'

'Oh, not that again,' she said. They had been over the incident *ad nauseam*. 'You know perfectly well that you were in the wrong, but you're too full of male vanity to admit it.'

'You'd know all about vanity,' he said, 'since you could win prizes for it.'

'What right do you have to say that?' she demanded. 'You don't even know me.'

'I didn't know Marilyn Monroe but I knew that she was sexy,' he said.

There was a harsh silence. Meg stepped in front of him and looked at him directly, her cheeks brightly suffused. 'You've a right to your opinion but I'd like to know what exactly it is I do that makes you think that I'm vain.'

'It's in the way you speak, move, look.'

'I didn't ask to be sent to a private school, you know,' she said. 'What am I supposed to do, start talking rough?'

'Anything would be better than that terrible posh accent you put on.' Why was he saying this when he didn't usually give a damn how people spoke? What had happened to his 'live and let live' principle?

'I don't put it on,' she informed him brusquely. 'It's my natural way of speaking. God forbid that I ever get to talk like you.'

'You'd better stop mixing with my family then, if the way we speak isn't refined enough for you,' he suggested.

'Oh, grow up,' she said irritably. 'What does an accent matter? No one else in your family seems to have a problem with mine. It's just you and your appalling manners. Talk about a rotten apple in the barrel . . .'

His dark eyes bored into her. 'I don't usually get complaints about the way I behave.'

She couldn't argue with that. George was generally thought to be the best thing since the invention of easy-care fabrics. He was so good-natured, people said, and he'd never let you down. George just couldn't do wrong, apparently. It was only Meg who couldn't stand the sight of him.

'Okay, so you don't like the way I speak, and the way I look upsets you too,' she said. 'What's wrong with my appearance?'

Nothing was the short answer to that. Quite the opposite. She was gorgeous. Frighteningly beautiful, in fact, with her lovely face, terrific figure and legs like you wouldn't believe.

'Stop fishing for compliments.'

'I wasn't.'

'Course you were,' he said. 'Women like you can't get enough flattery. You expect it and you don't like it when it doesn't happen.'

'Women like me?'

He hesitated only for a moment. 'You know perfectly well that I mean smart, beautiful women.' He gave her a sharp look. 'Happy now you've made me say it?'

Nobody had told her she was beautiful in a very long time. Not since . . . She blotted the thought out; she wouldn't look back. She daren't . . .

'I didn't make you say anything,' she denied crisply. 'The fact of the matter is, I sell clothes for a living. I wouldn't have much of a head for business if I didn't realise that making the best of myself goes with the job.'

She could go about in a roll of mildewed wallpaper and still look stunning. But he wasn't going to pander to her ego by saying so. Being of an amiable disposition, it was disturbing for George to come up against someone to whom he reacted with such intensity, especially when his dislike of her was complicated by the fact that he fancied her. He could only put his conflicting emotions down to the fact that he was intimidated by her. He wasn't used to women from moneyed backgrounds who had their own business and a surfeit of self-assurance. The novelty in itself had an erotic element.

He wasn't in the habit of insulting people but he kept doing it to her. He became some sort of a monster whenever she was near, which in turn filled him with compunction. He really didn't need all this emotional hassle. It would be easier if he didn't have to see her at all. But ever since that first explosive meeting, she always seemed to be around.

His parents thought she was wonderful. No one else was irritated by her la-di-da accent and supercilious attitude. Animosity and desire for her grew in equal proportions with every meeting. It would be absolute madness to get involved with someone like her, but he found himself wanting to with increasing ardour. It was infuriating!

Still, as his dislike of her was obviously reciprocated, there was no likelihood of anything developing between them. The thought depressed him, and that enraged him even more. The whole thing was getting out of hand.

'And then you wonder why men want to rape you,' he heard himself say.

The instant the words were out, he was appalled by them. But it was too late. He saw her face tighten, eyes spark with fury. She looked as though she had been physically slapped, and was about to hit him. 'You're disgusting,' she said.

'I'm sorry,' he said quickly. 'I shouldn't have said that.'

She stared into his face, drawn despite herself to those deep, penetrating eyes. As much as she loathed him, he aroused feelings in her that excited but terrified her because she knew they would only lead to pain. She was wary of strong sexual attraction, having been so badly hurt because of it in the past. She wasn't prepared to risk it again. Still, as George had no time for her, she was quite safe.

Such was the perversity of her emotions, this upset her too. She was angry and confused and wished the wretched man didn't keep appearing in her life. But since she wasn't prepared to give up her friendship with Eve, she would just have to live with that.

'Don't worry about it,' she said coldly. 'It's obviously what you think. And it's just the sort of typical male arrogance I would expect from someone like you.'

'Look . . . I've said I'm sorry and I really did mean it,' he said.

'Forget it,' she replied in a brittle tone, her blue eyes ice-hard.

'But . . .'

'Your opinion is of no interest to me whatever,' she said haughtily.

'Please . . .'

'Just drop the subject.'

'At least let me apologise.'

It wasn't like Meg to be so unforgiving. But she just couldn't bring herself to accept his apology, even though she could see that he was genuinely sorry. For some reason the damned man brought out the very worst in her. 'If you'll exuse me,' she said with stinging politeness, 'I think I'll get back to the party.'

And before he could say another word, she turned and joined the conversation with her colleagues from the boutique.

George had to physically restrain himself from chasing after her. Such was his remorse, he wanted to get down on his knees and beg her forgiveness. But that was just ridiculous. He *had* apologised, there was no call for the snotty cow to be quite so lofty. It was that very attitude that had made him deliver the insult in the first place. He hadn't meant it, had just wanted to rile her because she unsettled him so much he hardly knew what he was saying.

Oh well, perhaps things were best left this way, with them at loggerheads. The thought was little comfort to him, though.

Upstairs in her daughter's bedroom, Eve was sitting by

Josie's cot waiting for her to go back to sleep. The little girl's long dark lashes curled below the delicately veined lids, her cheeks were flushed with sleep, her pink dress emphasised her dark looks. Her lightly waving black hair curled untidily around her face.

Eve couldn't help an occasional feeling of disappointment that her daughter resembled her in appearance so totally. Try as she might, Eve could see nothing of Ken in her. Maybe when she got bigger she might have some of his mannerisms, but at the moment she was all Granger.

Sitting there in the quiet bedroom with its faint scent of baby powder, the distant sound of talk and laughter drifting up from downstairs, she felt a choking tenderness for her daughter. This was followed by an aching sadness. Ken had been gone almost two years and she was still grieving.

It wasn't something she was aware of every minute of the day as she had been at first. But it was still a dominant force in her life and crept up on her when she least expected it. At work, walking along the street or just enjoying some special moment with her daughter, Ken's absence prevailed.

The sound of Josie's breathing becoming steadily even indicated that she had gone to sleep. Eve stood up carefully, enjoying the pleasure of looking at her daughter. She turned to Becky, sleeping in the small bed Eve had installed for her because she and Meg sometimes stayed overnight. Becky was as fair as Josie was dark. Eve was very fond of the little girl who was growing up so close to her own daughter.

Meg was such a part of Eve's life now, she didn't know what she'd do without her lively company and warm heart. The job at the boutique had changed Eve's attitude to work completely. After years of clock-watching, she'd never imagined that the working day could pass so quickly and enjoyably. She felt as though she had found her niche in retail fashion, and was often inspired with ideas for the boutique. Increasingly Meg seemed to value her thoughts and suggestions.

As a mere employee, though, Eve sometimes felt limited

in what she could do for the business. She knew she had a lot more to offer and would like to shoulder more responsibility. This vague ambition was completely at odds with the fact that she would also like shorter working hours so that she could spend more time with Josie.

Be content with what you have, she admonished herself. But as she went downstairs to join her guests, the beginning of an idea began to edge its way into her mind.

Chapter Eight

During that summer of 1965, the Americans had a major triumph in modern technology when the first American astronaut walked in space. Less awe-inspiring but equally momentous for British pop fans was the news that the Queen's Birthday Honours list included MBEs for all four of the Beatles. Mick Jagger was in the news too, but not quite centre-stage on this occasion; he was best man at the wedding of photographer David Bailey – the son of an East End tailor – whose exceptional talent had brought him fame and fortune in the exciting new age of meritocracy.

While taking a vague interest in all of this, Eve and Meg were busy making their own news. Eve passed her driving test and Meg sold her flat and moved into a small house near Haven Green.

Although Eve didn't have the confidence to put her thoughts into words, she was becoming increasingly pre-occupied with the notion that had first taken root on the day of the lunch party.

In the autumn something happened which made her decide that now was the perfect time to take the idea further.

'We'll have to find somewhere else for our daughters to go for their tap and ballet classes when they're old enough to get into that sort of thing,' Meg remarked casually to Eve one morning when they were in the stockroom together going through some new lines that had just come in.

'Oh? Why's that?' enquired Eve.

'The dancing school in the room upstairs is moving to

larger premises,' she explained. 'They're not going to renew their lease.'

'Really?'

Meg nodded, writing a price ticket and attaching it to a black ribbed sweater. It wasn't a good idea to store much stock in today's quick-change clothing market and one of everything was put on show in the shop as soon as it came in. The shelves and rails in the stockroom were used for duplicates. 'I don't suppose we'll miss all that thumping and bumping coming through the ceiling when the lessons are in progress,' she remarked lightly. 'But the people who run it are pleasant to have as neighbours. And, of course, having a dancing school over the shop is good for business in that it gets us noticed by all the mums collecting and delivering their little darlings. Many a sale has been made while a mother waited for class to finish.'

Eve was immersed in her own thoughts and didn't reply.

'Talk to yourself, Meg, why don't you?' Meg admonished jovially.

'Sorry.' Eve looked at her, then blurted out, 'I was thinking what a good idea it would be for us to buy the lease.'

'Us? You and me?' Meg was astonished.

'That's right. I think we should expand . . . start a children's range. If we were to take the lease on the upstairs premises we could have the kiddies' department up there. Of course, we would have to have stairs put into the shop leading directly to it, rather than use the public stairs next door.'

'But . . .'

'Some of London's top boutiques are including a children's range now,' Eve cut in, carried along by enthusiasm.

'I know that,' said Meg, taken aback. 'But what's all this "we" business about?'

Eve held her head. 'Oh God, I'm sorry. You must be thinking I've got a cheek.'

'Not a cheek exactly,' said Meg in a querying tone. 'But I would like to know what you mean.'

'I've been thinking of talking to you for ages about an idea I've had,' Eve explained. 'But I wasn't sure about it until now. The premises upstairs becoming vacant has made my mind up for me.' She put the red jersey mini-dress she'd been pricing down on the table. 'I've been wondering if you'd consider the idea of having me as a business partner. I've got some money put by from my compensation and I'd like to buy into your boutique.'

Meg's face lit up but she was cautious. 'There's nothing I'd like more,' she said.

'I sense a but . . .'

'But it's a very big step for you to take,' Meg pointed out.

'With lots of advantages for us both.'

'Plenty of those.' Meg smiled enouragingly. 'But have you thought it through properly? Are you sure you want to do this with your money?'

'I've been thinking about it for the last few months,' Eve explained, 'and I'm sure it's the right thing. It would solve problems regarding working hours. As things are at the moment, we're both tearing ourselves apart trying to combine motherhood with a career. Because we want to be good at both, we're in a state of permanent stress. If I were to buy into your business, we could run it between us, share the responsibility and the working hours. It's the perfect solution.'

'I won't argue with that.'

'We could even think about opening the shop on a Monday,' Eve suggested effusively. 'Working three days a week each.'

Meg looked thoughtful, waiting for her friend to continue. This had to be Eve's own decision. Meg didn't want to influence her in any way.

'As it is now, you couldn't expand even if you could afford it because you wouldn't be able to put in the extra time because of Becky,' Eve went on.

'True.'

'There you are then,' said Eve, her cheeks brightly suffused as enthusiasm reached fever pitch. 'With two of us running the shop, it wouldn't be a problem. And if I were to buy into the boutique, there would be more money available to pay for the expansion.'

'Right.' Meg was beaming now, because she knew there was no doubt in Eve's mind. 'Now that you've made up your own mind, I can let you into a little secret.'

Eve waited expectantly.

'I've wanted you as a partner ever since you first came to work here,' Meg confessed. 'But you didn't have the money to invest then. And when you got your compensation, I didn't suggest it because I thought you'd want to hang on to the money you had left over after you bought the house as something to fall back on.'

'I did want that. But you can't have everything, and this is too good an opportunity to miss,' Eve said. 'Obviously, we'd have to talk terms, but I presume that, as a partner rather than an employee, I'd get a higher salary and a share of the profits.'

'Of course.'

'So I'd get a return on my money and more time to spend with Josie,' she said. 'Leaving it in the bank can't give me that.'

'I have to admit that it would be better for me too,' said Meg.

'Even apart from all the practical advantages, I would enjoy actually being a part of the business,' Eve told her.

'The feeling's mutual,' said Meg. 'But we must find out how much the lease is before we do anything else. In case it's beyond our means.'

'I'd like to buy into the boutique anyway,' said Eve, 'even if the expansion doesn't go ahead.'

'Well, Eve, I'm all in favour of the idea,' Meg told her. 'But before we actually set the wheels in motion, I think you should talk to someone else about it. Get another opinion. Make quite sure it's the right thing for you to do.'

'I don't need to,' insisted Eve. 'I know it's the right thing.'

'Even so,' said Meg, who wanted Eve to be absolutely certain because there was always a risk with any business, 'I'd feel better if you had a chat with someone with a good business head on their shoulders. Talk to your brother. I should think he's wise when it comes to this sort of thing.'

Eve threw her a look. 'That can't be a compliment I'm hearing, can it?' She smiled. 'Not for your arch-enemy?'

'Whatever I feel about George personally, I respect his commercial judgement,' Meg said. 'The way he's building his car sales business is proof that he knows what he's doing. You and I are biased towards the idea because we're friends and potty about the fashion business . . . there might be some pitfall we've both overlooked that he'll spot. Do talk to him about it, Eve. I'd really value his opinion.'

'Why don't we talk to him together?' suggested Eve. 'He'll be at my parents' for dinner tonight. George and I always eat there on Thursdays. I'll give Mum a ring and tell her there'll be one extra. I know she won't mind. Stay on when you go to collect Becky. Josie's usually asleep when I take her home in the car. Becky can do the same.'

Meg smiled but shook her head. 'Thanks, but no,' she said. 'If I'm there, the occasion will turn into a battle and upset everyone.' She shrugged her shoulders. 'It's just the way it is between George and me. For some reason we're an explosive combination. I think it's best if I give it a miss.'

'Frankly, I think the two of you need your heads knocking together,' said Eve with a friendly tut. 'But, okay, I'll let you know what he thinks about it tomorrow.'

'I think it's a great idea, Eve,' said George over dinner that evening. 'Apart from the business advantages, it would be ideal for your domestic arrangements.'

'I think so too,' said her father, enjoying a large portion

of shepherd's pie. 'It's the perfect opportunity to use your money to build something for the future.'

'Your dough won't be as safe as having it in the bank, though,' warned George, introducing a cautionary note. 'There's always an element of risk when you buy into any business. You could lose the lot if things go wrong.'

'I've thought about that,' Eve assured him. 'But Trend isn't some fly-by-night operation like some of the boutiques that are opening to cash in on today's quick-change fashion market. Meg's built a good solid business over a number of years.'

'I know,' he agreed wholeheartedly. 'And you won't go far wrong with her as a partner.'

Eve was as astonished as she had been when Meg had spoken well of George. 'I thought you couldn't stand the sight of her,' she said.

'I can't,' he confirmed. 'But she's a damned good businesswoman. She must be to run a classy operation like hers.'

'That's funny,' said Eve. 'She said more or less the same thing about you.'

'Blimey, had she been smoking dope or something?' said George jokingly.

'I could hardly believe my ears when she suggested I talk to you about it before we went ahead,' remarked Eve.

'You mean . . . it was her idea?' he said incredulously.

'That's right. She seems very keen for me to do the right thing with my money,' she explained. 'And she thinks you're the best person to advise me.'

'You don't mean she actually credits me with having any brains?' he said.

'She does, apparently,' said Eve. 'You'd never guess from the way the two of you are always at each other's throats, though.'

'They're like a couple o' daft school kids,' said Ned. 'They declared war the minute they clapped eyes on each other. I was there, I saw it happen.'

Eve looked from one to the other of her parents with a serious expression. 'Getting back to the partnership – you both agree with George that it's a good idea, yeah?'

Ned nodded, forking a piece of carrot.

'There's only one disadvantage as far as I can see,' said Dot.

'Oh?' Eve looked worried.

'As you'll be sharing the hours, I won't get to look after the children together any more,' said Dot, smiling.

'Surely that will make things easier for you, won't it?' said Eve.

'I must be a glutton for punishment,' Dot said lightly, 'but I really enjoy having them at the same time. Now that they're toddlers they amuse each other. They're very sweet together.'

'You'll be seeing plenty of them together, don't worry,' Eve assured her. 'Because I'll be bringing Josie round here to see her granny on my days off. And you won't have the responsibility for them both while I'm here.'

'There is that,' said Dot.

'So we're all agreed I should tell Meg to get the legalities underway, then?' asked Eve.

George grinned. 'You'd have done that anyway, whatever we thought of the idea.'

'You'd have to have had a really solid objection to put me off, I must admit,' she said with a wry grin. 'I've got a good feeling about this.'

As though to add her approval, Josie let out a loud chuckle from her high-chair.

'There you are,' said George. 'Even your daughter approves.'

The partnership went ahead without delay. The expansion took longer. By the time the purchase of the lease was legally finalised and Eve and Meg had agreed on the plans for the stairs, found a builder to do the job and got the new children's department decorated, stocked and ready to open with an additional assistant, a period of six months had elapsed.

The new department was accessed by way of a wide polished wooden staircase at the side of the shop. It catered for children of both sexes and, like most modern fashion establishments, easy care and washability were their most important sales features. Man-made fibres were very much in demand.

As was happening increasingly in adult fashion, where sweaters were swapped by brother and sister and husband and wife, many of the clothes for children were unisex too. Trousers, dungarees and jerkin tops in brightly coloured knitted fabrics were suitable for both boys and girls. Age boundaries had been widened too, in that many of the children's styles were similar to those in the adult range. Shift dresses worn over ribbed sweaters and matching ribbed tights were suitable for both mother and daughter.

Eve and Meg decided to have a social gathering after the shop closed on the evening before the new department was due to open, to mark the occasion and publicise the event. To add a personal touch to the party, they invited their families; the rest of the guest list was made up of staff, neighbouring shopkeepers, a reporter and photographer from the local paper and some of the manufacturers and wholesalers they dealt with on a regular basis.

Drinks and canapés were on offer in the new department on a table at the top of the stairs, which were decorated with pink and blue balloons tied with ribbons to add an air of gaiety.

Although Meg knew Eve's family quite well and Eve had met Meg's parents briefly on odd occasions since they'd been working together, the two families had not met until the party.

'Haven't they done well?' said Dot, making an effort to be friendly to Bea Myers because she was so fond of Meg. But Eve had warned her that Bea wasn't easy to get on with. 'It looks a picture with all the balloons and everything.'

'Yes, it does look nice.' Bea sipped her sherry, casting a critical eye over Dot's navy-blue crimplene suit. As usual Bea was expensively dowdy, this time in a brown woollen suit. 'I don't see the necessity for a party, though.'

'I think it's because they need the publicity,' suggested Dot, helping herself to a morsel of toast with anchovy. 'A write-up and picture in the paper will be worth more than any amount of advertising.'

'They could have got that without putting on a party,' responded Bea.

Dot was no expert on the subject so didn't argue. She was only trying to make conversation with this difficult woman because she was the mother of her daughter's business partner. 'It's wonderful what the girls have done, don't you think?' she persisted, glancing around the new department with its eye-catching tableaux of children in various different situations to illustrate the flexibility of the clothes for sale.

'They've made a good job of the new department,' said Bea without enthusiasm. 'But it isn't what they should be doing with their time, is it?'

'No?' wondered Dot.

'Of course not,' asserted Bea, tight-lipped and truculent. 'They should be at home looking after their babies.'

'Ideally, yes,' agreed Dot, 'but since neither of them is in a position to do that, their partnership is making things a whole lot easier for everyone, the children included.'

'My daughter doesn't have to work, you know,' proclaimed Bea in a strident manner. 'My husband and I can well afford to support her and Becky.'

'Children worth their salt don't want to sponge on their parents once they are of an age to make their own way, do they?' said Dot, gritting her teeth and adding, with a touch of inverted snobbery, 'just as well in Eve's case, 'cause she'd be out of luck if she was expecting financial assistance from us.'

Bea raised her eyebrows without comment.

'Anyway, I take my hat off to them for having the gumption to do something like this,' said Dot.

'All their energy should be going into those children,' persisted Bea.

'The kiddies aren't suffering,' Dot was keen to point out. 'Since I look after them, I can personally vouch for that.'

'Their place is at home,' insisted Bea. 'I would never have left my child with someone else while I pursued a career.'

'Neither would I, but women didn't have the opportunity in our day, did they?' Dot reminded her.

'Because people knew what was right, that's why,' opined Bea.

'Times are changing,' said Dot. 'Women are beginning to see themselves as more than just homemakers, and I think that's something we're going to see a lot more of in the future.'

'Heaven knows where it will all end,' sighed Bea.

'Be proud of your daughter,' said Dot. 'I know I'm very proud of Eve. It can't be easy bringing up a child without a husband.'

Bea winced. 'My daughter could have got married, you know,' she said.

'I don't doubt it,' said Dot, who had had quite enough of this ghastly woman's attitude. 'A lovely young woman like Meg wouldn't be short on offers of marriage. But not from the father of her child, I suspect.'

'What makes you say that?'

'He walked out on her, didn't he?'

'She told you that?' Bea was aghast.

'No. But it doesn't take a genius to work out that that's what happened,' said Dot. 'She's still smarting from it if you ask me, the poor dear. You can see the hurt in her eyes sometimes. And don't imagine I think any the less of her because of her situation, because I don't. I think she's smashing and I'm proud to have her as a family friend.'

Dot's attention was diverted by a tugging at her skirt. 'I wanna balloon, please, Gran,' requested Josie, Becky by her side. They were two years old now and very cute in their Trend outfits, Josie in a red pinafore dress over a white sweater, Becky in a tartan dress with a velvet collar. 'I wanna balloon.'

'You'll have to ask Mummy, pet,' said Dot. 'I think she wants the balloons to stay where they are until later. You can have one to take home.'

'Me want a balloon too, Gran,' said Becky, blue eyes focused persuasively on Dot.

'Go and ask your mothers,' instructed Dot kindly, pointing across the room. 'They're just over there, look.'

Holding hands, the little girls trotted off, leaving Dot smiling and Bea scowling.

'May I remind you that you are not Becky's grandmother.'

'Of course not,' said Dot, puzzled. 'Whatever makes you say that?'

'She called you Gran.'

'So she did, bless her,' said Dot, smiling as she remembered. 'She was just copying Josie. They're proper little mimics at that age.'

'You haven't encouraged her to call you Gran, then?'

'Of course I haven't,' said Dot, deeply affronted. 'Why on earth would I try to steal your granddaughter when I have one of my own?'

'I suppose you wouldn't,' said Bea, having the grace to look sheepish.

'If you're worried about getting left behind in the granny department, why don't you get more involved with Becky?' suggested Dot boldly.

'I see her on a regular basis,' said Bea defensively.

'But do you have fun with her?' asked Dot.

'It isn't my place to have fun with her,' Bea stated categorically. 'A grandparent's role is an authoritative one.'

'It might have been years ago,' said Dot. 'My grandmother was a fierce old lady who I dreaded going to see. I don't want any grandchild of mine to feel like that about me. You have to be firm with 'em, of course, but that doesn't mean you can't play with them and make them laugh.'

'That might be your way of doing things,' said Bea haughtily, 'but it certainly isn't mine.'

'Don't blame me if she doesn't enjoy coming to visit, then,' said Dot.

'I wouldn't dream of blaming you for anything,' said Bea, who felt oddly disconcerted by Dot and hoped she never had the misfortune to encounter her again. 'And I'll thank you to mind your own business.'

'Sure,' agreed Dot, keeping her temper.

'Good,' said Bea.

Having already had more than she could take of Bea's company, Dot moved away and wandered over to her daughter, who was cutting balloons from the bunch and handing them to the children. Meg was on the other side of the room, talking to the people from the local paper.

'Phew, what a pain in the arse Meg's mother is,' Dot said to Eve, who looked stunning in a scarlet trouser suit with a black velvet collar. 'Not a bit like that lovely daughter of hers.'

'Bea is a bit daunting,' agreed Eve.

'Talk about delusions of grandeur,' said Dot. 'I've met some snobs in my time but she just about takes the biscuit.'

Eve gave each child a balloon, then turned to her mother. 'There's probably something lacking in her,' said Eve, who usually tried to see the best in people. 'That sort of blatant uppishness is often a defence mechanism.'

'It's a wonder Meg is so nice, being brought up under her influence.'

'Meg takes after her father, and he's a lovely man,' said Eve.

'He must be a saint to put up with a wife like that,' cackled Dot.

Spotting Meg beckoning to her from across the room, Eve said, 'Can you keep hold of these two for me, Mum? I'm wanted over there.'

'Course I can, love,' agreed Dot, taking each of the toddlers by the hand. Within minutes she was chatting to some of the other guests and swelling with pride as they admired her charges.

'Your line of business is something I've always fancied,' Frank Myers was saying to George and Ned, with whom he'd felt an instant rapport. 'I'm interested in cars. I reckon I'd make a good car salesman.'

'Why didn't you go into it then?' enquired George with interest.

'Security, I suppose,' said Frank. 'I was born into the hardware trade, albeit on the retail side, and I stayed with it. A case of the devil you know. You can't risk a change of direction when you're married and have responsibilities.'

'Which is why I don't intend to get tied down,' said George. 'Not until my business is where I want it to be, anyway.'

'It looked as though it was doing pretty well when I passed there the other day,' remarked Frank, who had learnt earlier in the conversation where George's car lot was.

'He won't rest till he's got showrooms,' Ned informed Frank. 'It's his ambition to open proper showrooms for good quality used cars.'

'*Our* ambition,' corrected George. 'We work together, remember.'

'It's *your* business, though, son.'

'Yes, it is,' agreed George. 'But you're my right-hand man.'

'Trade's good at the moment, then?' asked Frank conversationally.

'We've no complaints,' said George. 'Everybody wants to get mobile, fortunately.'

'More cars on the road every second, according to the papers,' remarked Frank. 'Women are adding to the numbers . . . taking to the road in droves.'

137

'Not half,' said Ned. 'The two-car family isn't the novelty it was a few years ago.'

'What's the competition like in the car trade?' enquired Frank.

'Pretty hot.' George sipped his beer. 'Someone comes in, has a look at a motor, tries to screw us into the ground on the price then says he'll think about it and goes straight down the road to see if he can do better. Some you win, some you lose. It's all fair competition.'

'That sort of healthy competition I could cope with,' said Frank, his brow furrowing. 'At least you're not under threat from the supermarkets with their cut-price goods that the small man can't hope to match.'

George gave him a questioning look. 'How does that affect a large wholesale outfit like yours?' he was interested to know.

'By introducing a range of hardware and kitchenware into their stores, the supermarkets take business from the small hardware shops, who in turn cut down on their orders to me,' he explained. 'And this is only the beginning.'

'They shouldn't be allowed to stick their fingers into other people's pies,' said George. 'It's bad enough that small grocery shops are being put out of business by them. The least they could do is have the decency to stick to food.'

'That's progress for you. Even more worrying are rumours in the trade of big hardware chains opening, sort of DIY centres,' said Frank. 'If that happens, it'll put the small hardware shops out of business altogether and me along with them, since they're my bread and butter.'

'We all know that competition is a good thing for the consumer,' said George, 'but it's the consumers who'll suffer when they can't find a hardware shop within walking distance.'

'Still, it's early days . . . might not come to that,' said Frank.

They chatted about other things – sport, the government,

the new breath test for drivers that was being debated in Parliament.

'I bet the publicans are worried it'll go through,' said George.

'People will still drink as much,' said Frank. 'They'll just have to get used to leaving their cars at home.'

'Talking of pubs, mate,' said Ned, looking at Frank, who he had taken a real liking to, 'you'll have to come out for a drink with me and George one night.'

'I'd like that,' said Frank.

'I reckon our daughters being in partnership makes us practically related,' said Ned jokingly. 'So we ought to get better acquainted.'

They were all smiling at this when Bea appeared at her husband's side.

'We're leaving,' she informed him brusquely.

'Leaving? But why, dear?' he said. 'The party's only just begun.'

She threw him a look. 'I said we are leaving,' she repeated meaningfully.

'But Meg will be very hurt if we go now, dear,' he pointed out.

'I can't help that. We are going – *now*,' she announced through clenched teeth.

'But why?' he asked again.

She replied in a whisper which was loud enough to be heard by the others. 'It isn't our sort of thing,' she hissed. 'Not our sort of people.'

George wanted to put the old witch in her place. But a scene would embarrass Frank, who didn't deserve it. It would also spoil the party for his sister, and her partner. Whatever his personal feelings for Meg, there was no denying the fact that she had worked hard with Eve to organise this party, which was important to them both. With supreme self-control, he pretended he hadn't heard the derogatory comments.

Winking at his father, a wicked glint in his eye, he said to

Bea, 'We were just saying that Eve and Meg being partners makes us practically related.'

'I hardly think so,' she said in a manner indicating that she'd sooner gargle with broken glass than have even the most tenuous link with the Grangers.

'Just a joke, love,' said George.

'Don't call me love,' she rebuked. 'I don't care for that sort of familiarity.'

Determined not to get rattled, George said simply, 'Okay.'

'Come along, Frank,' Bea commanded.

'You can't leave now,' said George impulsively. Meg would be hurt by her parents' early departure and it was suddenly imperative to him that he stopped this happening.

'Oh, do mind your own business,' Bea said as though he was a difficult child.

Now he really did want to strangle her but managed to keep his head. 'I'm just about to say a few words to wish the girls well in their new venture,' he said. This was purely a delaying tactic; he'd had no intention of doing any such thing. 'It wouldn't be polite to leave just as someone is about to speak, would it? So I'm sure you can manage to hang on for a bit longer.' He stared defiantly at Bea. 'I can't imagine a cultured lady like yourself behaving in a way that isn't polite.'

Bea saw the challenge in his eyes. 'Since you're making such a fuss about it for some reason,' she said with seething impatience, 'we'll stay a bit longer.'

'In that case I'd better go and get on with it,' he said.

From the look Bea gave him, George knew he had made a second enemy in the Myers family. But he really didn't care.

Standing in the centre of the gathering and calling for silence, he said, 'I know you'll all be relieved to hear that I'm not going to make a long speech.'

This was greeted with cheers.

'But I couldn't let the occasion pass without saying a few words about my sister Eve and her partner, Meg,' he continued. 'Eve hasn't had things easy these last few years, but anyone who doesn't know her well wouldn't realise that, because she always manages to keep smiling.' He paused, looking at Eve, who turned pink and gave him an embarrassed grin. 'When she came to me and asked what I thought about going into partnership with Meg, I didn't hesitate in giving the idea my wholehearted support.' He looked across at Meg for a few lingering seconds. 'If it had been anyone else she was about to team up with, I might have had a few reservations, especially as Eve didn't have any experience in that line. But I was confident that Meg was a safe bet for anyone to go into business with. She's really quite something, and her parents must be as proud of her as we are of Eve.'

There was a ripple of applause and agreement. Meg was looking at the floor.

'So, let's all join together in wishing them well with their partnership and every success with their new children's department.' He raised his glass. 'To Eve and Meg.'

As glasses were raised, he looked across the room at Meg, who was smiling at him. Their eyes met and happiness washed over him. At that moment something happened to him. He wasn't sure what it was, but he knew he would never be the same again.

'So what was all that about the other night?' Eve asked her brother one afternoon a few days later. They were driving into central London in George's car, having left Josie in Dot's care. 'I couldn't believe it when you said all those nice things about Meg. Anyone would think that you're falling for her.'

'Don't be ridiculous.' He was a little too quick to deny it. 'I was just trying to make a point to that terrible mother of hers, that's all. What a cow! She was threatening to spoil the party for you both by walking out.'

'She is awful, I know.'

'Must be dreadful for Meg having a mother like her,' he said. 'I feel sorry for her.'

'You'd better watch yourself, Georgie boy,' Eve joshed. 'First you're saying nice things about her, then you're feeling sorry for her. You'll be asking her to go out with you next.'

'Do leave off . . .'

'Isn't too strong a protest supposed to be a sign of something . . . ?'

'Shut up and think about the job in hand,' he said, because Eve was going with George to help him choose a new suit in an effort to bring him up to date. Her idea, not his.

'Okay.'

'Where shall I head for first?' he asked.

'Carnaby Street,' she said.

'You're joking . . .'

'No, I'm not. Carnaby Street is to modern men's fashion what the King's Road is to women's, so that's where we're going.'

'But I want a new suit for work, not a pair of pink hipsters,' he said.

'And a suit for work you shall have,' she said lightly. 'But something a bit more hip than the boring ones you usually wear.'

He tutted. 'Just because you've gone into the fashion business doesn't mean we all have to dress like pop stars, you know.'

'They don't sell only hipster jeans and Beatles suits in Carnaby Street,' she informed him mildly.

'What's wrong with the men's outfitters in Ealing Broadway where I usually get my clothes?' he wanted to know. 'It's always suited me well enough up until now.'

'Nothing's wrong with it,' she said. 'I just think you ought to broaden your horizons and be a bit less traditional.'

'All right, don't go on,' admonished George. 'I'll have a look. But I'm promising nothing more than that.'

He managed to find a parking space in a side street and they joined the hordes of people in the narrow Soho lane.

'Plenty of tourists about,' remarked George, listening to the multilingual babble around them.

'Makes you proud, doesn't it?' said Eve. 'To think they've come all this way to see what us Brits have to offer.'

'Yeah,' he said.

As they ambled on, Eve noticed young men with shoulder-length hair and girls in mini-skirts reaching new heights, some dazzlingly clad in bright red or black PVC. The excitement in the atmosphere was so vibrant Eve felt quite buffeted by it. There was almost a sense of community on these dusty pavements. It was like being at some special event.

She finally managed to get George inside one of the less 'way-out' shops, where he bought a charcoal-grey slimline suit.

'It isn't too flash for me, is it?' he asked doubtfully as they left the shop with the suit safely in the bag.

'No, it's just right,' said Eve, who thought her brother looked terrific in it. 'You need a smart suit when you're selling cars.'

'I must say I felt good in it, but I don't want to look like some ageing mod.'

'You poor old man,' she teased him. 'People will definitely look at you and wonder what a pensioner is doing in a suit like that.'

'I'm serious.'

'You'll impress Meg in it,' said Eve, laughing. 'She likes men to be trendy.'

'How many more times must I tell you,' he said emphatically, 'I'm not interested in impressing Meg Myers.'

'Not much,' she said.

'Eve . . .'

'Now let's get you some shirts, then we'll go over to Chelsea so that I can cast my beady little business eye over the boutiques in the King's Road,' she interrupted.

'Oh no,' he wailed.

'Don't worry, I won't drag you around the shops for long,' she promised. 'I'll only be looking, not buying. I just want to see what other boutique owners are stocking.'

'You'd be daft to buy somewhere else when you have a shop of you own,' he said.

'Only part of a shop, George,' she corrected jovially.

'Same thing,' he said.

Making their way back to the car in the spring sunshine through the jostling crowds, Eve watched people dive out of vans with loaded garment rails draped in protective linen covers. Shoppers emerged from boutiques laden with bags, and taxis were doing a roaring trade. Eve felt very much a part of the fashion scene and was proud to be a part-owner of a boutique.

Chapter Nine

Bart Baxter had been shopping in Carnaby Street that afternoon too. On his way home he called at a flat on the ground floor of a block in Acton to see his mother. 'So, what do you think of the new whistle and flute, eh, Mum?' he asked. He twirled, grinning, teeth gleaming whitely against his outdoor complexion. 'Is this a smart piece o' gear, or what?'

'It looks smashing on you.' Lil Baxter was awash with pride for her handsome son, his lean athletic build perfectly suited to the slim lines of his new Italian-style suit in a pale shade of grey. Wincing slightly as she moved, she leaned over to put her crochet work down on the sofa, then rolled her wheelchair towards him so that she could feel the fabric of the jacket between her finger and thumb. 'Lovely material, son, and a nice modern style too. I've seen young fellas on the telly wearing suits like this.'

'I'd be a fool not to keep up to date for my stage work, wouldn't I?' he said.

'You would,' she agreed.

Looking at the top half of himself in the mirror above the fireplace, a moment of doubt flickered across his greenish-grey eyes. 'The important thing is, will the suit go down well with the audience?'

'Course it will,' she assured him without a moment's hesitation. 'You'll have the women throwing their under-wear at you.'

'I should be so lucky,' laughed Bart, combing his fingers through his wavy brown hair, its untidiness giving him a boyish look. 'The sort of dives I perform in, I'm lucky to get their attention, never mind their knickers.'

Lil's much-loved black cat, Marbles, stalked into the room and sprang on to her lap, the enormous green eyes from which he took his name half closing with pleasure as she fondled his head affectionately. 'It won't always be that way, son,' she encouraged, her brown eyes glowing with warmth. 'You'll get your break one day.'

'I hope so,' he said.

According to the sign-writing on his van, Bart was a window-cleaner. In his heart and his spare time he was a professional entertainer – a club singer who incorporated jokes and anecdotes into his act to give it a wider appeal.

His mother, a chubby fifty-year-old who kept herself immaculate and was rarely seen without lipstick because it was good for her morale, wheeled herself and the cat across the living room towards the door, unaided by her son, who knew better than to encroach upon the limited independence that was so important to her. 'Hey, Nora,' Lil shouted down the hall towards the kitchen, 'come in here and have a dekko at my boy. He looks a picture.'

A large, energetic woman of about Lil's age with a frizzy ginger perm came bounding into the room wearing a pink nylon overall. 'Oh my word, there's a sight for sore eyes,' she said, smiling broadly to reveal enormous teeth as she cast an approving eye over Bart. 'If I were twenty years younger . . .'

'I told him he'll have all the women after him in that outfit,' said Lil. 'Elvis Presley had better watch out.'

'He will an' all,' agreed Nora, who was Lil's resident carer-cum-companion-cum-housekeeper.

'Thanks for your kind words, ladies. But that's enough poncing about for one day,' announced Bart with a purposeful air. 'I must get changed and go and do some work.'

'You've got time for a cuppa tea, though?' said Nora persuasively.

'I'll make time for a quick one, thanks, love,' he told

her. 'I'll take this new gear off while you make it, though. I don't wanna spill anything on it before it's even had its first outing.'

While Nora went to make the tea with Marbles at her heels, Bart slipped into his mother's bedroom and changed into the casual shirt and jeans he wore for work. Back in the living room, ensconced in an armchair, he enquired casually, 'So, how's everything with you, Mum?'

'Pretty much the same as it was yesterday when you were here,' she said, because Bart called to see her every day. 'What's new with you?'

'I've got a few more bookings lined up,' he told her brightly.

'That's what I like to hear,' she enthused. 'Anything special?'

'No . . . the same old pubs and downmarket clubs I usually work in, but they're firm bookings so I'm not complaining,' he said. 'One of the gigs is a "men only" do.'

She laughed. 'I'm glad I won't be in the audience that night.' If Bart had a local booking, he would sometimes arrange for his mother and Nora to come and see his act. He valued his mother's judgement and listened to her criticism.

'It wouldn't half cramp my style if you were,' he said. 'The material I use at that sort of do isn't suitable for a mother's ears.'

'I bet it isn't,' she said. 'But tell me . . . how's the day job?'

'Mustn't grumble,' he said. 'I'm going to try to expand my round.'

'Oh yeah?'

'Mm. I think I'll branch out to Ealing,' he explained. 'Try to get in with some of the shop people there. Most of 'em will be fixed up with a regular window-cleaner, but there might be some who aren't satisfied with the service they're getting.'

'I wish you could give the window-cleaning up,' she said wistfully.

'Not possible at the moment,' he replied. 'But it isn't a problem, because cleaning windows suits me fine. I'm my own boss. I can work hours to suit myself so that I get time for other things.' He meant singing lessons and working on his act.

'But entertaining is what you should be doing full time,' she pointed out, frowning. 'It's what you were born to do. You're not getting the chance to make full use of your talent.'

'I wouldn't say that, Mum. I get regular stage work. All right, so they're low-class venues, but it's all good practice,' he said in his usual optimistic manner. Only in his most desperate moments did he allow himself to wonder if, at thirty, he had missed the boat. But he would never voice these occasional doubts to his mother, because she – unnecessarily in his opinion – held herself responsible for the fact that he hadn't been able to pursue a career in showbusiness. 'I'll be on the telly one of these days, don't worry.'

'But I do worry.' She studied her hands, then looked up at him. 'I really appreciate everything you do for me, son.'

'And I appreciate everything you've done for me over the years,' he replied.

'Look . . . you don't have to employ Nora,' she continued. 'I could have somebody come in for a few hours every day instead. You wouldn't have to earn so much money if you didn't have to pay Nora, so you could spend less time window-cleaning and more time working on your career.'

'We've been into all this many times before, Mum. A daily help just wouldn't be enough for us, because we need someone here all the time.' He paused, looking troubled. 'It upsets me to hear you talk like this. Let's change the subject.'

'But Bart . . .'

'I've told you how I feel about this,' he said, leaning towards her, his expression gentle but serious. 'I don't have the power to make you better, but I can make sure that you get decent care. I *need* to feel I'm doing something to help. Please don't try to take that away from me.'

His father had died of TB when Bart was four, and Lil had raised him on her own, cleaning shops and offices to keep them. Although life must have been hard for her, he couldn't remember her ever being miserable, though he realised now that there must have been times when she had been. It wasn't her way to be gloomy, which was probably where his own cheerful personality came from. She was a terrific woman: warm, kind-hearted and funny. She was also his most dedicated fan.

He'd been stage-struck for as long as he could remember. As a child he used to put on shows in the living room here at the flat. He would make his mates do a party piece and get all the kids in the street to come and watch. Naturally he gave himself top billing, telling jokes and acting the fool. His mother had entered into these occasions with gusto. As well as making toffee to encourage the kids to come, she used to introduce the acts. She'd given him something money couldn't buy – a childhood he'd remember with pleasure for the rest of his life.

National Service had given him the opportunity to use his talent in a more challenging way. Posted to Malaya, he'd joined an entertainments group that had put on regular variety shows. Singing – mostly pop songs and ballads – became the main part of his act. His voice was powerful, with a slight huskiness, and he could really belt them out. By the end of his service he had a serious love of showbusiness and planned to try and make it as a professional when he got back into civvy street.

But his plans had been wrecked by an unexpected deterioration in his mother's health soon after he'd got back. She'd developed a crippling condition of the spine, and mobility had become difficult for her. They were told she must prepare herself for life in a wheelchair.

Because it was so important to her that he have a life of his own and she didn't become a burden to him, he'd stayed on in his own flat. It was only a few streets away but it gave them both the independence that was so vital to any adult relationship. To solve the practical difficulties, he'd employed Nora, which enabled his mother to retain her dignity as well as continue to live in her own place.

Nora was one of those selfless spinsters who'd devoted her life to looking after her elderly parents. When they'd died, she'd found it hard to manage the rent, so a residential job was perfect for her. Bart did his old bedroom up so that she could have somewhere to retreat to when she felt the need for privacy. He paid her a salary on top of the accommodation and food that came with the job.

It proved to be the ideal solution. His mother had care and companionship with the added security of knowing that he was only a few minutes away if he was needed. But the special care he was determined Lil would have had to be paid for, which meant that Bart couldn't be without a steady income. So his dreams of a full-time career in showbusiness could not be pursued seriously. With a living to earn, he didn't have time to visit West End theatrical agents and try to persuade them to take him on to their books, or attend auditions that came up.

Rather than be limited by a job in a factory, however, he'd set up as a window-cleaner so that he could be flexible with his working hours. Although he was disappointed at the way things had turned out, he accepted his fate with a good heart and would never jeopardise his mother's way of life for the sake of his career.

Nora came in with the tea. 'Oh, by the way, Bart, I forgot to tell you . . . Rudy Kemp has been trying to get hold of you.' She glanced towards Lil and explained, 'He rang up while you were having a nap.'

Bart's eyes lit up with interest. 'Did he say what it was about?'

'No, he just said to tell you to contact him right away if you called in here,' she said. 'Otherwise he'll catch you at your own place later on.'

'Sounds like he's got a job for you,' said Lil, her voice lifting optimistically.

'Yeah, it does,' said Bart. 'I'll pop round to the café to see him when I've finished my tea.'

Rudy Kemp was the proprietor of a working men's café in a busy shopping parade in Acton. He also ran a theatrical agency. The latter was very small, just a hobby really, though he was listed in the official showbusiness reference books, and hoped for success in this field.

He didn't have any clients who made a full living treading the boards. They were all part-time performers like Bart, working in the hinterland of entertainment. Rudy didn't move in the sort of social circles that produced useful theatrical contacts. The people he dealt with were pub landlords and the managers of working men's clubs. Very occasionally he managed to produce a booking at some private function at a hotel or community hall.

'I suppose I'd better buy a cuppa tea even though I've just had one, or you'll accuse me of taking up space that could be used by a paying customer,' said Bart, joking across the counter to Rudy. They were very good pals.

'Have it on the house,' said Rudy, pouring the tea into a mug from a large white enamel teapot.

'Cheers, mate,' said Bart. 'I got your message . . . is it about a job?'

'I'll say it's about a job,' said Rudy, putting the mug of tea on the counter in front of Bart. 'Something really classy this time.'

'Sounds interesting.'

'You go and sit down with your tea and I'll join you in a minute to give you the details,' said Rudy, who was a small, emotional man of middle years with thinning dark hair, a swarthy complexion and a neat moustache.

Bart sat down near the window at a table covered with a plastic cloth bearing gaudy images of fruit and vegetables. A collection of condiments adorned the centre, with a tomato-shaped ketchup container standing next to a bottle of brown sauce. The other tables were all occupied by men, most of them eating fried food in some form or other. The air was thick with steam, the smell of frying and cigarette smoke.

Having cleared the queue at the counter, Rudy joined Bart with a cup of tea for himself. He was wearing a blue and white striped plastic apron over a white shirt and a rather incongruous red bow tie which he sported because it made him feel theatrical.

'Come on then, mate, tell me about this job,' urged Bart eagerly. 'I've got windows to clean . . . a crust to earn.'

Rudy's small brown eyes gleamed with excitement, for he was passionate about his sideline. A breakthrough for one of his clients could lead the way to the big time for Rudy himself. 'This one's a bit special, mate, it could be the break you've been waiting for.'

Bart sipped his tea thoughtfully, observing Rudy, whose idea of a significant booking wasn't quite the same as Bart's. According to Rudy, every engagement was the one that was going to get Bart noticed. He was almost as keen for Bart's career to take off as Bart was himself, partly because it would be a feather in his own cap but mostly, Bart believed, because he was firmly convinced of Bart's potential. 'Tell me about it then,' he said.

'I've only got you the cabaret spot at a motor traders' annual dinner dance, that's all,' Rudy announced triumphantly.

'Oh.'

'It'll be a good do,' said Rudy eagerly, sensing Bart's disappointment. 'A posh venue.'

It wasn't the sort of thing that was going to get Bart spotted by some powerful impresario, but at least it was an improvement on his usual bookings. 'Where is this upmarket venue?' he asked.

'A big hotel out Ruislip way,' Rudy informed him. 'In the ballroom.'

'Sounds all right,' said Bart.

'It's a smart place,' said Rudy, 'and you'll be working with a decent band.'

'Really?'

'Yeah,' confirmed Rudy. 'I'll get you a contact number so you can arrange to go through your numbers with them beforehand.'

Bart could just picture the scene. His audience half cut by the time he came on stage, and him struggling to make himself heard above the clamour and rattle of conversation and crockery. Still, it *was* a professional engagement, and slightly better than the places he usually worked in.

'I'd appreciate that,' said Bart, who couldn't help but feel a thrill every time he got a booking, no matter how seedy the venue. 'When is it?'

'At the end of May,' Rudy informed him. 'So you'll have plenty of time to work out what material you're gonna use.'

'Good.'

'It's a Friday night, too,' said Rudy, 'which leaves you free on the Saturday if anything else of interest comes up.'

'How much?'

'Ten quid,' said Rudy. 'Less my commission, of course.'

'O' course,' said Bart, with a grin. He suspected it was the kudos of being entitled to commission from a professional engagement that excited Rudy more than the actual money.

Bart was very fond of Rudy. They were two of a kind, drawn together by a mutual dream. Their business association had come about in the most unlikely way when Bart called at the café for breakfast one day soon after Rudy's wife had died. Feeling sorry for him, Bart had engaged him in conversation, chatting about his own showbusiness aspirations in order to divert the other man's mind from his own grief.

Rudy hadn't any experience at all as an agent at that time, but his interest was immediately aroused. He was friendly with several local publicans who put on live entertainment in their pubs on a regular basis. Seeing an opening for Bart in that field, he'd lost no time in arranging a booking for him. Their partnership had started there. As Bart had got to be well known on the pub and club circuit, he'd begun to get regular work but didn't earn enough to give up his day job.

'So, can I tell them that you'll accept the job then?' Rudy asked now.

'Yeah, go ahead,' said Bart.

'I think we'd better go in my car on that night as it's a posh do,' suggested Rudy. 'It won't look professional for the cabaret act to turn up in a window-cleaner's van.'

'One of these days we'll go in a Rolls Royce,' said Bart in a jokey manner.

What Rudy lacked in contacts he made up for in enthusiasm, and his faith in Bart never faltered. 'You'll get there, son,' he'd tell him. 'You'll do it, believe me.'

'In the mean time,' said Bart now, glancing across the café, 'There's a queue at the counter.'

The other man emitted an eloquent sigh, spreading his hands. 'Inside here,' he said, pointing to his heart, 'I'm a theatrical agent. But still I have to stand behind the counter of a greasy-spoon café.'

'It's your living, mate, the same as cleaning windows is mine.'

'I know.'

'The difference between us is that you actually enjoy your proper job,' said Bart.

'Maybe I do,' admitted Rudy with a rueful grin. 'But that doesn't stop me having dreams.'

'Me too, Rudy, me too,' said Bart, smiling and putting his head at an expressive angle. 'But being alive is an expensive business and the bills have to be paid.'

'You're telling me.'

'Anyway, we'd all be lost without you behind that counter,' said Bart, because this was a well-known local meeting place.

'You would?'

'Too true,' affirmed Bart. 'You provide your customers with a lot more than just a fry-up.'

Rudy stood up, looking pleased. 'That's nice to hear,' he said. 'But I won't be so popular if I don't go and pay attention to them.'

Bart watched him at the counter, talking to a couple of market traders. He was a popular man, but a sad and lonely character somehow. Bart suspected that his part-time 'little earner' helped take his mind off how much he still missed his wife.

Finishing his tea, Bart turned his mind to his own 'proper job' and worked out his plan for the next day. He would find the time to spend a couple of hours in Ealing looking for new business.

Eve was about to rush off to a fashion show at a wholesaler's in Wimbledon when a man called at the shop, offering his services as a window-cleaner.

'You must be a mind-reader,' she said.

It was a blessing that *she* wasn't, thought Bart, since his thoughts of her were almost entirely carnal. He'd been brought up to respect women and not to leer at them, but he couldn't take his eyes off this one. She was gorgeous in a natural sort of way – shiny dark hair, tall and slim, and he'd never seen anyone with such big velvety eyes.

'Is anything the matter?' asked Eve, who was wearing a green suit with a short skirt, her hair worn in a simple bob.

'No . . . no,' he said, realising he was still staring at her. 'You were saying that I must be a mind-reader. Why's that?'

She smiled and he was mesmerised. She had neat white teeth, and a dimple in her cheek. He loved the way her eyes lit up. 'I was saying to my partner only the other day that we'd have to find someone more reliable to clean the windows.' She looked towards the shop window. 'I had to do the job myself the other day. They get thick with dust being on a busy road like this.'

'You don't have anyone to clean them regular, then?' he surmised.

'He's supposed to be regular, but he comes when he feels like it,' she said, rummaging in her handbag and taking out some keys. 'These windows need doing twice a month, at least, and he left us for three months last time.'

'That isn't good enough, is it?' Bart said, mentally thanking the other window-cleaner for his unreliability. 'Not for a smart shop like this one.'

'The window is our showpiece and we like it to sparkle.' She paused, noticing him frowning, and asked again, 'Is something wrong?'

Yes, something *was* wrong as it happened, *very* wrong. He'd just noticed that she was wearing a wedding ring. Dammit. So that was that. He should have known that she'd be attached. A woman like her wouldn't be on her own.

'No . . . nothing at all,' he lied.

'That's all right then, er . . .' She looked at the card he'd handed to her when he first came in. 'Mr Baxter.'

'I'm usually known as Bart.'

'Oh. Okay . . . er, Bart, so when can you do our windows?'

'Would right now suit you?'

'That would be brilliant.' She looked at her watch. 'I have to go out now, though, so let me pay you before I go and leave you to it.'

'It'll be two shillings, please,' he said. 'And have you somewhere I can fill my bucket?'

She took the money out of the till and handed it to him, showed him where the kitchen was and said, 'Can you come every two weeks in future?'

'Sure,' he said. 'But you haven't seen what sort of a job I'll make of the windows yet.'

'Don't worry,' she said with a grin. 'If I'm not happy with the job, you won't get paid to do it a second time.'

156

As she headed for the door, rattling her keys, he said, 'You're not thinking of using that blue estate car that's parked outside, are you?'

She turned. 'Well, yes, I am as a matter of fact. Why?'

'One of the front tyres is flat,' he informed her. 'Very flat . . . looks like a puncture to me.'

'Oh no,' she wailed, her brow knitting into a frown. 'How did that happen? I didn't notice anything when I came to work this morning.'

'Probably a slow puncture,' he suggested. 'You must have gone over a nail or a piece of glass or something without noticing it.'

'It would have to happen today, when I'm in a hurry,' she said. 'Oh well, it can't be helped. I'll just have to change the wheel.'

'I'll do it for you if you like,' he offered obligingly.

'I can't expect you to do that,' she said, though she hoped he would insist, because she'd never changed a wheel before.

'It won't take me a minute,' he told her. 'You don't want to spoil your smart clothes by getting them dirty, do you?'

There was a time and place to insist upon women's equality and this, in Eve's opinion, was neither. 'I won't argue with that.' She looked at him, noticing the attractive green tones in his eyes. 'If you're sure you really don't mind.'

'I wouldn't have offered if I did,' he said cheerfully. 'Give me your keys and I'll have it done in no time.'

She watched him from the window as he strode across the crowded pavement to the car, a tall, slim figure in jeans and a checked shirt. While he was changing the wheel she made herself useful by helping a customer decide on the dress she had tried on, assuring her that hem-lines were rising for every age group and not just the under twenty-fives.

'Have you finished already?' she asked when Bart came back into the shop.

'Yep, all done.'

'How much do I owe you?'

'Leave off,' he said, grinning. 'It's all part of the service.'

'That's very kind of you,' she said.

'No trouble at all,' he said, handing her back her car keys. 'I'll fill my bucket and get cracking on the windows now.'

Having answered a couple of last-minute queries from the staff, and left them the telephone number where she could be reached in an emergency, Eve went out on to the noisy, bustling street. A sudden surge of people indicated that a train had just arrived at the station. 'See you in a couple of weeks then,' she shouted up to Bart, who was cleaning the windows of the upper floor.

'You can count on it,' he said, smiling down at her from his ladder.

'I hope I can,' she said, turning to get into her car.

He watched her vehicle join the stream of traffic and move slowly past the row of taxis lined up on the edge of the green. What a lovely woman, he thought, polishing the glass with a damp shammy leather. And what a pity she was married.

What a very attractive man he was, thought Eve, as she drove past the station towards the Broadway, smiling quietly to herself.

Meg thought he was terrific, too, and Meg being Meg, she came right out and said so.

'Where did that gorgeous hunk of a man spring from?' she asked when Bart came to clean the windows one morning two weeks later. She and Eve were in the office, having both come into the shop for their weekly business meeting, one of the rare times they were at the shop together.

'From Acton, according to his card,' Eve informed her.

'I mean, how come we've got him cleaning our windows instead of that miserable old bugger who usually does them?' Meg wanted to know.

'He came looking for business so I booked him to do the windows regularly,' explained Eve.

'Who wouldn't have?' said Meg, glancing towards Bart,

who was passing their window on his way up the ladder to the upstairs windows. 'It's worth paying just to see him go up and down the ladders.'

'Honestly, Meg,' tutted Eve with a smile in her voice.

'What's wrong with that?' queried Meg lightly. 'Men don't have the monopoly on lust, you know. Anyway, don't try to pretend that you haven't noticed how gorgeous he is.'

Eve couldn't deny that Bart Baxter was rather special. 'He does seem nice,' she said.

'Nice!' snorted Meg. 'He's the sexiest thing I've seen in ages.'

'I meant that he has a nice way with him,' said Eve. 'Very pleasant and obliging.'

'I'm not bothered about his personality,' said Meg in her light-hearted, bantering way. 'I'm just enjoying the view.'

'Give him a look and he might ask you out,' suggested Eve.

'I'm quite happy to admire him from afar, thank you very much,' said Meg. 'Which is just as well, as it's you he fancies.'

'Me?'

'Oh, come on, don't make out you haven't seen him looking at you,' grinned Meg. 'He nearly fell off his ladder just now, he was so busy peering through the window at you with adoring eyes.'

'Don't be so daft.'

'It's true,' insisted Meg. 'He's got eyes for no one but you.'

'You and your vivid imagination,' said Eve, but in truth she had noticed the admiring glances of Bart Baxter and, surprisingly enough, enjoyed the attention. He was the first man she'd responded to in that way since Ken, and she'd forgotten how good it felt.

'It isn't my imagination, insisted Meg.

'Well, be that as it may,' said Eve dismissively, 'let's get started on the meeting.'

159

'Okay.'

They discussed the week's turnover for both departments, various staff matters, and the trade in general: how much it was influenced by pop stars and how incredibly short skirt lengths were getting for women of all ages.

'It'll go the other way eventually, I suppose,' said Meg.

'It's almost certain to, I should think,' agreed Eve.

'Some designer will probably start a trend by bringing in skirts down to our ankles.'

'I hope not,' said Eve emphatically. 'But you can never tell what's going to happen in today's fast-changing market.'

'Change is the essence of our business,'Meg reminded her. 'But I must admit, it's changing exceptionally fast at the moment.'

Their business complete, they had a cup of coffee and a general chat, then Eve prepared to leave because it wasn't her afternoon for duty. 'Oh, by the way,' she said, getting her car keys out of her bag, 'Mum and Dad and I are going with George to a dinner dance at a hotel in Ruislip two weeks on Friday. There's a spare ticket up for grabs if you fancy coming with us . . . if you can get a sitter for Becky.'

'Who's going to be looking after Josie if your mum is going?' wondered Meg.

'My neighbour has agreed to sit with her,' Eve explained.

'I see.' Meg was thoughtful. 'What's the do in aid of?'

'It's the annual social get-together for the members of some motor traders' association that George belongs to,' Eve explained.' I expect we'll have to sit through some boring speeches but the meal should be all right and the dancing might be fun. It would be great if you could come.'

'Does George know that you've asked me?' Meg wanted to know.

'No, I haven't mentioned it to him yet because I didn't think of it until last night,' she explained. 'I thought I might as well wait until I'd spoken to you about it.'

'Oh.' Meg sounded uncertain.

'I just thought it would be a break for you,' said Eve. 'After all, neither of us has much of a social life, do we? Because of the children.'

Meg looked doubtful. 'I could probably persuade my parents to sit with Becky, but frankly, Eve . . . I wouldn't want to spoil George's evening by being there,' she said. 'I'm not exactly flavour of the month with him, am I?'

'I wouldn't be too sure about that,' was Eve's opinion.

'Come off it,' said Meg. 'He can't stand the sight of me.'

'That's probably just a front,' said Eve. 'Anyway, I'd like you to come, and Mum and Dad would enjoy your company because they're very fond of you. So do say you'll think about it.'

'Okay . . . provided my parents will sit with Becky, I'll come.'

'Fabulous,' said Eve, smiling.

Chapter Ten

The dinner was at the coffee stage and the president of the association was on his feet making his annual speech. A rotund man of middle years, with balding hair and a bright-red face, he didn't tend much towards brevity. But as the wine had been flowing steadily throughout the meal, most people were benignly receptive to his lengthy discourse.

'A social revolution is what we're living through now,' he was saying, his booming voice reaching all corners of the room. 'A time of changing attitudes and values. Things are certainly different to when I was young.'

There was a rumble of agreement.

'My teenage daughter tells me that I'm behind the times . . . "uncool" as she puts it,' he continued. 'Because I won't let her do exactly as she likes, come in late and whatnot.' A pause while he consulted his notes. 'There are certain aspects of these modern times that I am very much in favour of, though. People being rewarded for what they can do rather than who they are, for instance.'

Another murmur of assent.

'Something else about the present day that I'm all in favour of – and I know you will be too . . .' he grinned broadly, hesitating for a moment to sharpen their interest, 'is the fact that this is a time of great prosperity in the motor trade.'

Cheers and whistles filled the room.

'But even though our society in general is becoming more relaxed, and old traditions are being dispensed with,' he continued, 'I urge all our members not to do away with good old-fashioned courtesy and service to customers. It's up to us to raise the image of our profession as car traders, a reputation which has been damaged to the point of ridicule over the years by a few unscrupulous members of our trade.' He took a sip of water. 'Second-hand car dealers are generally thought to be shysters who'd sell a dodgy car to their granny for twice what it's worth. By being honest and fair in our dealings we can help people realise that the majority of us are not like that.'

A ripple of general approval.

'Anyway, that's enough from me until next year,' he said finally. 'All that remains is for me to thank you all for coming and hope you'll let your hair down and enjoy the cabaret, which will be followed by dancing.'

'Cor blimey, I thought he'd never stop,' complained Ned.

'What he said made sense, though,' remarked Dot, looking smart in a matronly sort of way in a navy-blue crêpe de Chine dress bought specially for the occasion from one of the more traditional dress shops in the high street. 'I thought he was quite good, actually.'

'He does ramble on a bit,' said George. 'But it's only once a year.'

'I thought he captured the mood of the times very well,' said Meg, attractive in a red dress with billowing chiffon sleeves.

'Me too,' said Eve, who was stunning in emerald-green satin.

'The important question is,' said Meg with a wicked look in her eye, 'what are we going to do about the dancing, since there are only two men and three women in our party.'

'We don't need a man to dance with if we do it disco style,' Eve pointed out. 'The two of us can dance together.'

'I've got a better idea,' said Dot, who'd had a few drinks and was determined to enjoy herself since she didn't get

a night out very often. 'You can borrow my old man.'
She paused, grinning. 'But I warn you, he doesn't come
cheap.'

The three women were in the mood for fun, and cackled
with laughter.

'What about George?' joked Meg, because she'd also
had a few drinks and fancied a spot of devilment. 'Is he
up for grabs?'

'You'd better ask *him* that,' said Dot, who was becoming
more flushed and giggly with every sip from her wine glass.
'I stopped speaking for him a long time ago.'

'So how about it, George?' said Meg, deliberately pro-
voking him.

'Dancing isn't my strong point,' he told her evenly.

'Eve and I will take a chance on that,' she giggled. 'We're
not fussy.'

This produced a burst of hilarity from the women, who
were ready to laugh at anything. The men took the order for
drinks and departed to the bar, which was at the opposite
end of the room to the stage, the tables set around the dance
floor between them.

'They could have got the waitress to bring the drinks,'
remarked Dot.

'Course they could,' agreed Eve. 'They just wanted an
excuse to get away because they feel threatened by us
women kidding 'em on.'

'Poor George is scared to death we're gonna drag him on
to the dance floor,' hooted Meg.

When George and Ned returned with the drinks, they were
all so busy chattering they didn't pay any attention to the
four-piece band coming on to the stage.

'And so, ladies and gentlemen,' said the leader of the
group, who was also the compère of the cabaret, 'please
put your hands together for someone who is no stranger to
pub and club audiences in and around London. He's got a
terrific singing voice and no one can put a story over quite
like him. Will you please welcome . . . Bart Baxter!'

Eve and Meg were laughing about something else and missed most of this.

'Shush, you two,' said George. 'Give the man a chance.'

They composed themselves and turned their attention to the show.

'Wow!' cried Meg, nudging Eve excitedly. 'Look who it is.'

'Good God,' gasped Eve, staring at the stage, where Bart had launched into some humorous dialogue about car dealers.

'What's he doing cleaning windows when he has talent like that?' Meg whispered to Eve after a while. 'He's really good.'

Eve nodded, observing the way people warmed to his relaxed, easy-going humour.

'He looks even more gorgeous out of his window-cleaning gear,' remarked Meg.

He certainly did, thought Eve. His lightly tanned complexion was enhanced by the white of his shirt, and his hair was gleaming. After a few more stories, he sang the Frank Sinatra hit of a few years ago, 'All the Way'. There wasn't a sound in the hall, not a clink of glass or a whisper of conversation. Eve positively melted.

'Well, fancy that,' said Meg when the song ended to loud applause. 'Who would have thought he could do something like that?'

'You know him, then?' assumed Dot.

'He's our window-cleaner at the shop,' Meg told her.

'Well, I'll be blowed.'

Bart sang a few more numbers, and finished his act with the Seekers' smash hit of the previous year, 'The Carnival is Over'.

'This party isn't over though, ladies and gentlemen,' he said when the applause finally subsided. 'The dancing is about to begin, so enjoy yourselves and thanks for listening.' He waved his hand and left the stage.

'What a smasher,' said Dot. 'He should be on the telly.'

When Eve spotted Bart heading for the bar with a small, dark-haired man, she got up and went over to them.

'Remember me?' she asked.

'I certainly do,' Bart said, looking delighted. 'I didn't realise you were here.'

'And I didn't realise you had such hidden talents,' she said.

He spread his hands, grinning broadly and putting his head on one side saucily. 'Mr Versatility, that's me.'

'So I've noticed,' she said. 'Anyway, I just had to come over to tell you how all of us at our table enjoyed your performance.'

'Thank you,' he beamed. 'I can take any amount of that sort of talk.'

'I'm only saying it because it's true,' she told him ardently. 'My friend thinks you were terrific, and my mum thinks you should be on the telly.'

'She should speak to my agent about that,' he said, and introduced Rudy to Eve.

'If it was only a question of talent, Bart would have had his name in lights long ago,' Rudy told her lightly. 'Unfortunately, you have to have that special bit of luck as well. It's a very competitive business.'

'I can imagine,' said Eve. 'I've always had the impression that it's hard to make it to the top in showbusiness.'

'Never mind the top, I'd settle for just a few rungs up the ladder.' Bart gave a wry grin. 'If you'll pardon the pun.'

She smiled, looking from one to the other, her gaze finally resting on Bart. 'I wonder if you'd do me a small favour?'

'If I can, certainly,' he said.

'Would you come over to our table and have a drink with us,' she requested. 'It would make my mother's evening.'

'Sure.' He looked at Rudy as though about to excuse himself.

'Both of you,' she added.

At the table they were given a hearty welcome, and after the introductions had been made, George got them each a chair. Bart sat next to Eve, so that Rudy was beside Dot. Ned went to the bar to get them both a drink.

'Enjoyed your act, mate,' George said to Bart. 'It was really good.'

'Good?' scorned Dot. 'It was bloomin' marvellous.' She looked at Bart. 'I've only one criticism . . .'

He frowned, looking at her uncertainly. 'And what's that?'

'It wasn't long enough.'

Bart laughed. 'You had me worried there,' he said. 'I thought you were going to tell me I was singing out of tune or something.'

'No chance . . . pure velvet, your voice,' she smiled.

Meg was sitting on the other side of Eve. 'I think we're going to lose our window-cleaner before very long, don't you, Eve?' she said. 'He'll be too busy signing autographs to come round with his bucket and ladder.'

'I think so too,' agreed Eve.

'It's a nice thought, but I wouldn't count on it,' said Bart.

The atmosphere was warm and friendly. Dot told Rudy it must be very exciting being a theatrical agent, and he told her he wasn't really an agent but the owner of a greasy-spoon café; she said it was still an interesting thing to do even if it wasn't his real job. Ned came back with the drinks and everybody drank to Bart's success.

As the conversation became general, Bart asked Eve to dance.

'It's about time someone started the ball rolling in that direction,' said Meg.

Facing each other on the dance floor and moving to the beat of a Beatles number, Bart said, 'Your husband isn't here, then?'

Her expression changed dramatically and she didn't answer right away. She still found it painful to actually say the words. 'My husband died nearly three years ago,' she said at last.

'I'm sorry,' he said solemnly. 'I had no idea. I didn't mean to pry.'

'That's all right,' she said, lowering her eyes to hide her pain.

'You don't expect . . .'

'People to die at my sort of age,' she finished for him. 'You're quite right, you don't. He was killed in a train crash.'

'What a terrible thing,' he said with genuine feeling.

'Yes, it was,' she said sadly. 'And still is, if the truth be told. I miss him so much, even after all this time.'

'Any children?'

'Yes, I have a daughter,' she said, the softness returning to her voice. 'She's just turned two now and very sweet.'

Bart noticed the difference in her since he'd mentioned her husband. She seemed almost like another person, as though all the energy had been physically drained from her. The last thing he'd expected was for her to be a widow. He should have been pleased, because it left the way clear for him. But there was such sadness about her as she was reminded of her tragic loss that his heart ached for her. Odd to feel so strongly for someone he didn't even know. He remembered that her initial impact on him, that day at her shop, had been intense, though he'd put that down to sheer physical attraction.

'Does she look like you?' he asked chattily.

'So people tell me,' she said.

'She must be lovely then.'

She accepted the compliment graciously, smiling at him and seeming to return to her normal self. 'You've got the gift of the gab off stage too, then?' she remarked.

'No, not really,' he said. 'I'm just saying what I see.'

Eve knew somehow that he meant what he said and it wasn't just a cheap chat-up line. She sensed that she could trust Bart Baxter with a lot more than just the cleanliness of the boutique windows. 'Thank you very much, 'she said gracefully. 'Flattery will get you everywhere.'

* * *

Rudy hit it off with Dot and Ned right away and they became engrossed in conversation immediately after Eve and Bart left the table to go to the dance floor. This left Meg and George rather out of things, and obliged to be sociable towards each other.

'Fancy a dance?' he asked casually.

'Don't overdo the courtesy,' she riposted.

'I'll try again then,' he said with a slow smile. 'Would you like to dance?'

'Better,' she said, 'but I thought dancing wasn't your thing.'

'It isn't,' he said. 'But I'll give it my best shot.'

'In that case, I'd love to.'

'Let's go then,' he said, taking her arm and guiding her towards the floor.

Facing him as they danced, she felt the strong pull of physical attraction. Smiling, she asked, 'So, what's going on?'

'Come again?' he said, looking puzzled.

'We've been in the same company all evening and you haven't insulted me once,' she pointed out.

'I could say the same thing about you,' he said.

'You haven't given me cause to insult you,' she mentioned.

'I must be slipping.'

She laughed, and his hostility towards her crumbled. When she was in this mood he found her adorable.

'Yes, I think you must be,' she agreed.

The music was loud and catchy. They swayed in time to the beat, not touching but wanting to.

'We ought to go out together one evening,' he heard himself say in a sudden desire to be with her alone, to get to know her better. 'We could go for a meal. We can't talk properly with this music blaring.'

'Us, go out?' She was doubtful but excited despite herself. When he wasn't being arrogant, he was wonderful.

'Yeah,' he confirmed. 'It would be interesting to see

if we can get through a whole evening without an argument.'

'You and me together on our own for a whole evening sounds like a recipe for disaster,' she said, keeping her tone light to hide how acutely vulnerable she felt suddenly. This was her legacy from Becky's father; he'd made her afraid to get involved with any man.

'Look at it as an experiment if it makes you feel better,' he said. 'Anyway, we've managed to be civilised to each other this evening.'

'Only because we've been with other people and we haven't wanted to spoil things for them,' she pointed out. 'But a whole evening on our own . . . 'She drew in her breath, shaking her head. 'We'll probably come to blows.'

'I'm prepared to risk it if you are,' he said with a lazy grin.

'Okay,' she found herself saying. 'Providing I can get a babysitter, of course. When did you have in mind?'

'How about next week . . . Saturday night, perhaps?' he suggested.

'I'll see what I can do about a babysitter and let you know,' she said.

'Have you always wanted to be an entertainer?' Eve enquired of Bart. It was the following Friday evening and they were in an Italian restaurant in Ealing having coffee after a delicious pasta dish followed by tiramisu. Bart had invited her out last week on the dance floor and there hadn't seemed any sensible reason to refuse, even though she wasn't looking for any sort of romantic involvement.

'For as far back as I can remember,' he said with a wholesome enthusiasm Eve found appealing.

'You really do want to make it big, don't you?' she suggested.

'Every performer wants to make their name,' he said 'But it's more that I'd like to earn enough to have performing as a full-time career instead of a spare-time job.'

'I'm sure your time will come.'

'I hope I don't have to wait much longer,' he said. 'I'm thirty now.'

'You poor old thing,' she smiled, adding, 'you're in your prime.'

'I need that break while I'm still relatively young, though,' he said.

'It must be hard cleaning windows when you've got your heart set on doing something completely different,' she remarked.

'It brings in the dough,' he said.

'Entertainers do all sorts of jobs when they're trying to get established, don't they?' she said. 'I remember reading about it somewhere. Some of the big stars waited on tables and worked in bars in the early days.'

'Some have worked in shops, on the bins, anything,' he said.

'What about holiday camps?' she suggested. 'Some showbiz people get started that way, and at least you get the chance to perform.'

'It's seasonal work,' he said. 'Once the summer season's over you're out of a job.'

'You could always find some other kind of work for the winter.'

'No. I can't be as casual as that,' he said with a serious expression. 'I have to have a steady income all year round because I have responsibilities.'

'Oh, I see.'

She knew he wasn't married and wondered if he had children from a previous marriage to support. But to ask would be intrusive.

'What about you?' he asked. 'Are you doing a job you enjoy?'

'I am now,' she told him. 'I didn't realise work could be such fun until Meg gave me a job.'

She ran through a brief account of how she'd come to be in partnership with Meg.

'She's not been a lifelong friend then?' he said, taking a friendly interest.

'No, not at all, but I get on better with her than women friends of much longer standing. In fact, I've never felt so close to anyone outside of the family. We tell each other everything,' she said. 'She changed my life and I trust her completely.'

'I feel much the same way about Rudy,' he confided. 'I only got to know him a few years ago, but he's a true mate. He might not be the most well-connected theatrical agent in the business, but he believes in me and I'd trust him with anything.'

'He seems very nice,' she said. 'But if he isn't a particularly good agent, might you not do better to get another?'

'I wouldn't do that,' said Bart. 'Rudy does the best he can for me. He gets me regular bookings . . . they're low-profile and don't pay much, but it's work . . . all good practice. I get a real buzz when I connect with the audience.'

'You certainly did that the other night, I can promise you that.'

'Not all audiences are so appreciative,' he told her with a wry grin. 'In some of the rough clubs I work in, they actually get a kick out of making sure you die on stage.'

There was an inherent niceness in Bart, a kind of determined cheerfulness, she thought. 'What about the artistic temperament we hear so much about?' she teased him mildly. 'I thought you showbiz people were all supposed to be riddled with it.'

He roared with laughter. 'Maybe they are in showbiz proper, but you wouldn't get far if you showed any sign of artistic temperament in the sort of places I work in.' He paused thoughtfully. 'I've met one or two difficult types on the pub and club circuit. But most of them are smashing people. There's a great sense of camaraderie among performers when we're doing a show, a feeling of us against the rest of the world. I know it's a cliché, but it is lonely up there on stage.'

'You don't seem the temperamental type,' she said conversationally.

'I don't think I am,' he said. 'But if you want an honest opinion about that, my mother's the person to ask.'

'Mums are usually biased towards their children,' she smiled.

'Yeah, I suppose they are,' he said. 'But mine is very honest. She and I are great pals.'

'Have you ever been married?' Eve wondered, sipping her coffee.

'No.' He pondered the question. 'I've come close to it a few times, but it just wasn't to be. I'm probably too single-minded for any woman to put up with in the long term.'

'I don't believe that.'

'It's true,' he said. 'I'm very focused on my stage work and most of my spare time is taken up with that. A man who is obsessed with a stage career and out doing gigs at the weekends isn't much of a prospect as a husband.'

'I suppose not.'

They drank their coffee in a comfortable silence for a while.

'I'm really enjoying your company, Eve,' he said suddenly.

'Likewise,' she said.

'Can we do this again?'

'That would be lovely. But I'm not free to go out just when I like. Not with a young daughter to look after.'

'I understand that.' He paused, putting his cup down on the saucer. 'I was wondering . . . would you and your little girl like to come with me to my mother's for lunch on Sunday?'

She immediately panicked and felt the need to slow things down. 'Oh, Bart,' she said, biting her lip, 'it's really kind of you to ask me and I'm enjoying this evening enormously. But I don't think I'm quite ready for anything as serious as Sunday lunch with your mother.'

He grinned. 'Not as heavy as it sounds,' he assured her. 'I'm not about to propose to you or anything.'

'I didn't think you were, but . . .'

'But I would like to see you again,' he cut in. 'And I've got bookings on Saturday and Sunday night this weekend so I'm not free then. As I always go to Mum's for Sunday lunch and that sort of arrangement would save you having to get a babysitter, I thought it would be a nice idea. That's all, no ulterior motive. It would be a real treat for my mother to have a kiddie in the house, too.'

'Well . . .'

'No strings, I promise you,' he said. 'Just Sunday lunch.'

Still uncertain, she didn't reply.

'You've probably got other plans anyway,' he suggested, looking disappointed.

'My daughter and I do usually go to my parents' for Sunday lunch, actually,' she said.

'It doesn't matter then,' he assured her. 'It was only a thought.'

Much to her surprise, she found herself wanting to accept his invitation. 'Going to my parents' is quite a casual arrangement,' she said. 'They don't mind if something else comes up and I don't go.'

His eyes lit up and his eagerness was frighteningly obvious to her. 'Can I take that as a yes then?' he said.

'I wouldn't want to give you the wrong impression, though,' she said. 'I mean, well . . . this might sound silly but I still feel married.'

'Didn't you say it had been nearly three years since your husband died?' he remarked.

'That's right.' She sipped her coffee. 'But as I said, I still feel married to him. I think I always will.'

'Are you trying to tell me that there could never be anything between us?' he asked.

'I'm saying that I don't feel as if there could be anything serious between me and any man,' she tried to explain.

'I see.' He leaned forward, looking at her. 'You can't be sure of that, though.'

'No, I can't be sure,' she said. 'It's just something I feel inside. And I want to be fair to you about it from the start.'

'Who knows what might happen if you'll give yourself a chance to get to know someone better?' he asked her.

'Who knows indeed?' She raked her fingers anxiously through her dark hair. 'I'm sorry. I'm not making a very good job of this, am I?' she said. 'You're the first man I've been out with since Ken died . . . I'm out of the habit of this sort of thing. The truth is, I suppose I'm a little scared.'

'Of me?'

'Of getting into something out of my depth,' she confessed, looking at him.

He sat back and finished his coffee. 'As I've said, it was only a casual invitation, and if you feel I'm rushing things or putting pressure on you, please don't come on Sunday. I've no intention of trying to talk you into anything you'd rather not do.' He pushed his hair back from his brow absently. 'But neither do I want to give up. I like you and I think you like me. That's all there is to it at the moment, a mutual attraction. But I think that's a good enough reason for us to see each other again, don't you?'

'Put that way, yes,' she said. 'As long as you understand how I feel about any sort of serious relationship.'

'I understand that, and I promise to respect it,' he said.

'In that case, I'd love to come with you to your mother's on Sunday.'

'Wonderful,' he said.

His obvious pleasure warmed her heart and aroused something wonderful deep inside her. But she was frightened, too, because she sensed that she had just reached a watershed in her life, a turning point she didn't want.

It was Meg's turn to work Saturday at the boutique the next

day. Eve called in to see her in the morning with Josie, after shopping in Sainsbury's in the Broadway.

'Well . . . you obviously had a good time last night,' said Meg as they went through to the office, where Josie immediately began amusing herself by clambering on and off a chair.

'What makes you say that?' enquired Eve.

'The beaming smile is a bit of a giveaway,' grinned Meg.

'I don't know what you mean,' Eve protested lightly.

'Don't give me that,' joshed Meg. 'You're positively glowing.'

Eve laughed. 'I did enjoy myself, I must admit,' she said.

'Good company, was he?' Meg enquired, smiling. 'As well as being the sexiest thing this side of the river?'

'Bart's a really nice bloke.' She looked at Meg. 'But the reason I popped in was to say I hope all goes well for you tonight.'

Meg gave a wry grin. 'George and me, out on a date. Can you imagine it?'

'I can, as it happens.'

'God knows why I agreed,' Meg said, shaking her head in disbelief 'Must have been all the wine I'd had during dinner.'

'I've got a feeling you'll both have a smashing time,' said Eve.

'That's a joke,' grinned Meg. 'We'll probably be at each other's throats before the starter has even been served.'

'It's all that stifled passion,' said Eve, teasing her. 'You obviously fancy each other like mad.'

'Don't make me laugh,' Meg said, not very convincingly.

The conversation was interrupted by one of the staff with a query.

'Be a love and make some coffee while I go and sort things out in the shop,' Meg said to Eve. 'There's biscuits in the tin if Josie wants one.'

'Sure,' said Eve.

'Well, you certainly do things in style, George,' said Meg, looking at him across the table as they came to the end of dinner in a classy West End restaurant. They had managed to get through the entire meal without a cross word.

'Nothing but the best for someone like you,' said George, who had used a large chunk of his salary to impress her. Lord knows why he was going to all this trouble. But – much against his better judgement – he wanted to please her so that tonight wouldn't just be a one-off.

'You think you have to splash out because a posh bird like me will expect it of you . . . am I right?' she asked.

'Not to put too fine a point on it, yes,' he admitted.

'You've got the wrong idea about me, you know, George,' she told him with a slight shake of the head. 'I don't have an exalted lifestyle with a hectic social whirl. I'm just a working mum trying to do her best for her child. I rarely go out of an evening these days.'

'Only because circumstances force you to stay at home,' he said.

'No, not really,' she said. 'I was never one to go out every night of the week even before Becky was born . . . well, not after my teens and early twenties anyway. I enjoy a night out now and again, sure, a few drinks and some laughs.' She waved a hand around the restaurant, which was lush with soft lighting, expensive carpeting, silver cutlery and tribes of well-trained waiters hovering to meet their every need. 'Don't get me wrong, I'm enjoying all of this immensely, but it wouldn't bother me if I didn't have it. I would have been just as happy if we'd gone to the new Italian that's opened in Ealing Broadway.'

'Now she tells me,' he grinned.

She reached out and put her hand on his, keen to reassure him. 'Don't get me wrong, George, this evening's been lovely and I appreciate your going to the trouble and expense on my account, but it isn't essential to me.'

The touch of her hand on his sent shock waves through him. God, he wanted her *so much*. 'You've got such panache,' he said, composing himself. 'And posh places go with that sort of image.'

'That panache is simply a result of the fact that I have a way with clothes,' she said, removing her hand from his. 'I'd be in the wrong line of business if I didn't have it. I enjoy looking good, I always have. But that doesn't mean I want to go to the best places all the time.'

'You were brought up to have the best of everything, though,' he said.

'Yes, I admit I was an advantaged child,' she said evenly. 'And those things are still important to my mother.'

'Not your father?'

She emitted a tinkling laugh. 'He's just the poor guy who pays all the bills.'

'He seemed like a nice bloke when I met him at the party you gave at the shop,' he said.

'He is,' she said with sincerity. 'And very special to me.'

'Sounds as though you don't get on so well with your mother, though?' At one time he'd thought that Meg was cast in the same mould as Bea Myers. But that clearly wasn't the case.

'Unfortunately I don't,' she confessed. 'I'm fond of her, of course, but I don't like the sort of person she is.'

'Mm.' He was careful not to comment about this.

'Still, at least she's stopped making quite such a fuss about my being an unmarried mother,' she continued. 'In fact, she's beginning to dote on Becky. I have to stop her from spoiling her. It's just as well she doesn't look after her while I'm at work. She'd ruin her.'

'She doesn't want to take the job away from my mother, then?' he said.

Meg gave a wry grin. 'She isn't devoted enough to give up her well-ordered life,' she said. 'And why should she, just because I'm a working mother?'

He was thoughtful. 'It's hard, bringing up a kid on your own, isn't it?' he said. 'Eve's situation has made me realise that.'

'There are times when you wish you had someone to share it all with,' she confessed. 'The joy as well as the worrying bits.'

'I can imagine.'

'But I manage well enough, and when it's all getting on top of me, I turn to Eve,' she told him. 'Having her as a friend has been a life-saver.'

'I think she feels pretty much the same about you,' he said.

'I hope so.' She gave him one of her slow smiles which made him want to take this self-assured, independent woman in his arms and protect her from all of life's adversities.

'I get the impression you'd rather not talk about Becky's father,' he ventured.

She flinched as though from a physical blow, her eyes losing their sparkle. 'And you'd be dead right,' she said.

'No hesitation there, then . . .'

'I can see no point in dragging up the past,' she said, in a tone that didn't invite persuasion.

'Sounds to me as though you were hurt.'

'I was, very badly,' she said. 'Which is why I don't like to even think about it.'

'Okay, I'll not say another word,' he told her.

'Thank you,' she said with emphasis. 'I'd appreciate that.'

Tension had crept into the atmosphere. To ease an awkward moment George ordered more coffee. For a few brief moments he'd seen a different side to Meg, a sad, vulnerable woman who seemed damaged by life. Now she reverted to the capable, self-assured woman he knew her to be.

'How about you?' she said, light-hearted again. 'A good-looking bloke like you hasn't led the life of a monk, I bet.'

'I've had my moments,' he admitted, his eyes twinkling.

'And the rest . . .'

'But there's been no one serious these past few years because I've put all my energy into the business,' he explained.

'I'm the same,' she told him. 'My daughter and my business fill my life.'

Tension defused, the conversation began to flow easily again. He told her of his plans for the future, and how he was hoping to have showrooms built on the land he now rented as a car lot if he could persuade the owner of the land to sell to him at a price he could afford.

She told him that introducing a children's range had proved to be an excellent idea and that the two departments complemented each other perfectly. Mothers out shopping for their offspring very often left the boutique with something for themselves too, and vice versa.

It was getting late. Meg said it was time she went home to relieve her parents of their babysitting duties. He said he'd get the bill.

'Can I see you again?' he asked while they were waiting.

She hesitated. 'Do you think that's wise?' she asked, smiling.

He gave her a quizzical look, his eyes narrowing slightly.

'I mean, we've managed to get through one night without arguing, but it might be asking too much to expect it a second time,' she explained.

'I think it's definitely worth a try,' he said, giving her a crooked smile that made her heart leap.

'On one condition, then,' she said, her expression becoming serious.

'What's that?'

'That we don't ask about each other's past,' she said. 'We're not kids. We've both been around the block, let's leave it at that.'

'Fair enough,' he said.

'In that case, the only thing that stands between you

181

and me and another night out is the availability of a babysitter'

'Great,' he said, and meant it.

She felt warm inside. For all that her trust in men had been shattered, the thought of getting to know this one better made her feel happier than she'd been in ages.

Chapter Eleven

The nature of the responsibilities Bart had mentioned became clear to Eve when she visited his mother's home and guessed that he was footing the bill in that household. Even though he was little more than a stranger to Eve, she found herself expecting nothing less of the sort of man she perceived him to be.

She took an instant liking to Lil and admired the positive way she coped with her disability. Physical pain was sometimes noticeable when she moved, but if she was miserable about being in a wheelchair, she certainly didn't show it. Eve had rarely been in a home so infused with life and laughter. Her own spirits lifted as soon as she stepped inside the door.

It was easy to see why Bart had such a cheerful disposition. He and his mother really sparked each other off.

'Been doing wheelies up the high street in your chair, Ma?' he joshed as they sat down for lunch at the table in the living room.

'I thought I'd have a change this week, son,' she laughed. 'I've been burning rubber around the park instead.'

Nora grinned at Eve. 'Take no notice of 'em, love,' she advised her. 'There's no stopping those two when they're in one of their daft moods . . . they're both barmy.'

Lil and Nora both made a great fuss of Josie. Lil told her how pretty she looked in her pink dress, presented her with a red felt elephant which she'd made for her, and gave her a bag of Dolly Mixtures 'for after dinner'.

Josie enjoyed the attention but was somewhat distracted by Marbles, the cat, who made a hasty retreat behind the sofa after some rather boisterous affection from the two-year-old.

'This is delicious,' said Eve, tucking into roast lamb and mint sauce.

'We've Nora to thank for that,' said Lil, smiling at her companion. 'She's a whizz in the kitchen, aren't you, ducks?'

'I do my best,' said Nora.

'There's something to be said for being in this chair – at least it gets me out of the cooking,' grinned Lil with an astonishing lack of self-pity. 'It never was my strong point.'

'You can say that again,' agreed Bart. 'It's a wonder I lived to be an adult considering the stuff she gave me to eat.' He looked at his mother, his eyes twinkling. 'We were the only family in the street who had to eat their gravy with a knife and fork.'

Enjoying the joke even though it was against herself, Lil chuckled. 'I don't know where I went wrong. I used all the right ingredients but somehow they never came together properly for me.' She paused thoughtfully, looking at Bart. 'Remember my suet dumplings?'

'Can I ever forget?' He sucked in his breath, shaking his head. 'The best that can be said about them is that me and my mates were never short of spare cricket balls.'

They all laughed, including Josie, who didn't understand the joke but was infected by the jovial atmosphere.

'You don't look too bad on it, anyway, Bart,' commented Eve.

'There was always bread and cheese to fall back on,' he said.

'I couldn't go far wrong with that,' giggled Lil.

'You made lovely toffee, though, didn't you, Mum?' he said.

She smiled wistfully. 'Yeah, somehow I managed to get the hang of that. God knows how. I used to make a great batch of it to give to the kids who came to Bart's shows.' She looked at Eve and continued, in an explanatory manner, 'He was forever organising entertainment, here in this living room, would you believe?' She tutted, her face softening. 'I dunno how we used to pack everyone in, but we did.' Her eyes were misty when she rested them on Eve. 'Oh, happy days. We used to have such a lot of fun when Bart was growing up.'

'I can imagine,' she said.

The conversation moved on and Eve noticed what a lively interest Lil took in the world around her. She obviously read the papers and was fascinated by people. She seemed intrigued by Eve's business and wanted to know all about her family. Naturally the subject got around to how Eve and Bart had met.

'You can imagine my surprise when I looked at the stage and saw our window-cleaner up there,' said Eve. 'All dressed up and doing his stuff like a seasoned professional.'

His mother's expression darkened and she said in a subdued manner, 'Yeah, that's what he should be making his mark as, a performer, not a window-cleaner.'

A look passed between mother and son. Tension drew tight in the air and Eve knew she was in the crossfire of emotional conflict.

'Don't start that again, Mum,' he said in mild admonishment. 'You know I don't mind doing the job.' He winked at Eve. 'It keeps me fit. And I get to meet the most interesting people.'

The slight feeling of discord melted away and the chatter flowed freely again. Lil was very up to date with the news and they touched on various topics, including the recent sentencing of the Moors Murderers, Ian Brady and Myra Hindley, to life imprisonment. They also got on to the subject of the first episode of a controversial new television comedy series called *Till Death Us Do Part*, which had raised a few establishment eyebrows but made a great many people laugh.

When the meal was finished, Bart and Nora set about clearing the table, refusing offers of help from Eve.

'You sit down with Mum and keep Josie amused,' said Bart, waving his hand towards the sofa on which Marbles, now out of hiding, was snoozing. 'Move that damned cat. He hogs the sofa.'

Not having the heart to disturb the cat, Eve was about to squeeze herself in beside him when she found herself almost sitting on some crochet work.

'Nearly had my crochet hook in your bum, didn't you, love? Sorry about that,' Lil apologised. 'I was working on it while I was waiting for you to arrive. Careless of me to leave it there.'

Lifting the work up to pass it to her, Eve remarked, 'You did this?'

She nodded.

'It's beautiful,' said Eve, studying the lacy pattern in pale-blue silky thread.

'It's just a little top for my neighbour's daughter,' explained Lil.

'Do you do much of this sort of thing?' enquired Eve with interest.

'I do, as it happens,' replied Lil. 'I knit and sew too, but crocheting is my favourite.'

'She's always at it,' said Nora, stacking dishes at the table.

'You need something to do when you're sitting about all day,' explained Lil. 'I have to have something to do with my hands or I get really edgy.'

'She even has her crochet hook going while she's watching the telly of an evening,' remarked Nora before departing to the kitchen carrying a tray of dirty dishes.

'I couldn't just stare at the box with nothing to do,' said Lil. 'It would drive me mad.'

'It's a very high standard of work,' commented Eve, looking more closely at it.

'I've had enough practice over all the years I've been doing it,' said Lil.

'What else do you make?' enquired Eve, an idea beginning to form.

'I've done all sorts in my time . . . dressing table mats, shawls, jumpers, fancy table covers. I've been doing a lot of the little tops that are so popular with young girls lately,' she said. 'And just recently I made a mini-dress for the girl upstairs.'

'Do you charge much?'

'I don't charge anything,' Lil informed her brightly. 'I only do it for friends, people who live here in the flats mostly.'

'There's an awful lot of work in it, though,' said Eve.

'That's true, but I enjoy it and it keeps me occupied,' she said. 'People sometimes give me a box of chocolates or a bottle of something from the off-licence to show their appreciation. I'm quite happy with that.' She gave Eve a shrewd look. 'But I have to be supplied with the materials if anyone wants something made.'

'I should think so too.'

'Do you want me to make something for you?' asked Lil. 'Is that it?'

Eve lifted Josie on to her lap, cuddling her and kissing the top of her head; she gave her a sweet from the bag. 'Well, not for me personally, but you've given me an idea,' she blurted out excitedly.

'I have?'

'Yeah. I was wondering if you might be interested in the idea of making some money out of your hobby.'

The other woman shook her head. 'I wouldn't charge friends.'

'That isn't what I meant,' Eve explained. 'I was thinking more in terms of your making crocheted garments for us to sell at the boutique on a regular basis.'

'Oh, I see.' Lil was thoughtful.

'Anything crocheted is in great demand at the moment – tops, dresses, jackets,' said Eve. 'There's always a market for crocheted wear, of course, but it's a bit of a craze just now.'

'Your idea sounds interesting,' said Lil. 'But how would it actually work?'

'We'd supply you with everything you need and pay you by the garment,' said Eve. 'The fact that they would be hand-made would mean we could charge the customer accordingly and this would be reflected in the price we would pay you. This is high-quality work and we'd respect that. I'm not saying you'd make a fortune, but you would be fairly paid.'

'Well . . . I've never thought of going commercial,' was Lil's response. 'I just do it for the pleasure of it.'

'No harm in being paid for something you enjoy doing, though, is there?' Eve pointed out. 'I do it all the time.'

Lil's eyes were shining. 'It would mean I'd always have something definite to work on,' she said, 'which would be lovely.'

'Oh, yes,' confirmed Eve. 'We'll sell them as fast as you can make them.' She paused, her gaze resting on the other woman. 'So, what do you say?'

She hesitated for a moment, then said, 'I think I'd like to give it a try.'

'I'll have to talk it over with my business partner, of course,' Eve told her, 'but I'm pretty certain she'll be in favour of the idea. Once I've cleared it with her, it'll just be a question of working out the costings with you so that we all have our fair share.'

'Sounds like you've got yourself a job then, Mum,' remarked Bart, who had come back into the living room from the kitchen and had been listening to the conversation.

'It does, doesn't it?' she said, smiling. 'Isn't it exciting?'

'If you want to do it, then good luck to you,' he said.

'As long as you only do it for pocket money, and don't put yourself under pressure.'

'Don't worry, son, I wouldn't be able to turn out enough garments to make a living from it,' she told him, because she knew how important it was to Bart that he support her.

'That's all right then.' He looked at Josie. 'Right, now that that's all settled, does anyone fancy a trip to the park . . . to feed the ducks and have a go on the swings?'

'Yes, please,' said the little girl, taking his hand and jumping up and down excitedly.

Nora didn't go with them to the park. She said she was going to have a nap.

'She'll be wanting some time on her own, I expect,' Lil remarked to Eve, who was pushing her chair, Bart having gone ahead with Josie to the duckpond with a bag of bread.

'The two of you seem to get on very well together, though,' said Eve.

'We do,' Lil confirmed. 'Mainly because we respect each other's privacy.'

'I suppose you have to be extra careful about that sort of thing when you're with someone so much,' said Eve.

'Not half,' said Lil. 'I know that Nora needs time on her own, and she respects the fact that I don't want her fussing over me every minute of the day, even though I have to be reliant on her in so many ways.'

'It's good that you have that sort of understanding,' said Eve.

'Oh, yes. Sometimes of an evening she'll stay in her room to watch the telly instead of watching it with me in the living room,' Lil went on. 'I leave her alone because she needs a break from me. I know she's a paid companion, but I like to think we're good friends, despite that.'

'I'm sure that's how she sees it too,' said Eve. 'She seems very contented.'

'I'd hate it if she got fed up and left,' said Lil. 'It's hell having to be reliant on anyone, but I'm used to her.'

'Are you in much pain?' asked Eve.

'It comes and goes,' she said. 'But I've got painkillers for it, and some days are better then others.'

'Must be awful.'

'You get used to it, and it isn't there all the time,' Lil explained.

After they'd spent some time with the ducks, they went to the playground area. Eve sat on a bench next to Lil and they watched Bart pushing Josie on the swing, his face wreathed in smiles.

'I don't know who's enjoying themself more, Josie or Bart,' said Eve.

'Me neither,' Lil agreed, looking at her son. 'He's very good with kids.'

'I can see that.'

'He might have had some of his own by now if he hadn't been so busy trying to make it as a performer,' she said.

'Maybe,' agreed Eve.

'He's a good son to me.'

'I can imagine,' said Eve, oddly moved by this indomitable woman, who would be a tragic figure if it wasn't for her spirit.

The afternoon passed all too quickly. When Josie tired of the playground, Eve and Bart played chase with her on the grass for a while. They went back to Lil's for tea, and chatted until Bart said it was time he went home to get ready for the gig he was doing in south London that evening.

Eve thanked Lil for a lovely afternoon, said she would be in touch with her about the crochet work soon, and left with Bart, quietly confident that she'd made a new friend in Lil.

Having driven Eve and Josie home in his van, Bart gave Josie a big hug at Eve's front door. 'See you soon, I hope, sweetheart,' he said.

'Okay, Uncle Bart.'

'But it all depends on what your mother has to say about that.'

'Her mother thinks that would be a really nice idea,' said Eve.

'I'll give you a ring in the next couple of days to fix something up then, yeah?' he said.

'I'll look forward to it,' she said, feeling happier and more exhilarated than she had in years.

As soon as Bea Myers realised that George Granger was the reason her daughter needed a babysitter so regularly in the evenings, it was all-out war between them. Bea didn't like George and made damned sure she reminded him at every opportunity, making snide remarks when the couple returned to Meg's flat after an evening out.

'You've been to some terrible pub, I suppose,' she said one night.

Being no pushover, and disliking Bea Myers every bit as much as she disliked him, George said, 'A pub! Leave off, Mrs Myers. A pub's too expensive for me. We've been down the fish and chip shop.'

'Fish and chips . . .'

'Not fish, that was too pricey for me. We had a portion of chips between us and ate them from the paper outside the shop.'

'That's really disgusting,' snorted the humourless Bea.

'He's pulling your leg, Mum,' said Meg, stifling a giggle. 'Actually, we've been to a restaurant in the West End.'

'Oh . . . oh, I see. Well, I hope you showed him which cutlery to use,' she said in a spectacular display of rudeness.

'Cutlery?' said George, fired up and full of devilment. 'Was that what those silver things were? I thought they were table decorations.' He turned to Meg. 'You should have told me and I wouldn't have used my fingers.'

'George, stop it,' admonished Meg. 'You're making things worse.

Although George was a match for Bea Myers, he didn't

like her attitude. One night when he called for Meg and was given a particularly cutting dose of Bea's superiority, he decided it was time he made his position clear.

He confronted her in Meg's living room while Meg was upstairs saying goodnight to Becky, Bea and Frank were settled in armchairs by the television. 'I think it's time you and I had a little chat, Mrs Myers.'

'I've nothing to say to you,' she said.

'In that case, I'll talk and you'll listen,' he said in such a commanding tone that she stood up and faced him, looking startled.

'I'll do no such thing,' she said, turning to leave the room.

'Stay where you are and listen to me, woman,' he ordered.

She turned back to him, looking worried, then appealed to her husband for support. 'Are you just going to sit there and let him speak to me like that, Frank?' she rebuked.

'I think you should listen to what he has to say,' said Frank, who was very embarrassed by the way she treated George.

'Thanks, mate,' said George, while Bea turned red then white with fury.

'I know you don't approve of my seeing your daughter . . .' he began.

'Full marks for observation,' she interrupted acidly.

'Fortunately Meg is an adult and doesn't need your approval,' he continued, undeterred by the fact that Meg had entered the room.

'How dare you . . .' began Bea.

'So,' he cut in, determined to make his point, 'for as long as she still wants to see me, I shall be around. You can insult me until you're blue in the face and it will make no difference. I do think that you are probably embarrassing both your daughter and your husband by displaying the manners of a moron, though.'

While Bea stared at him, lost for words, he turned to Meg. 'Are you ready then?'

She nodded and they left the house together.

'I can't believe I just heard you call my mother a moron,' said Meg when they got into the car.

'I didn't call her a moron,' he corrected. 'I just said she was using the manners of one.'

'Even so, not many people would dare to do that,' she told him.

'Sorry, Meg, but I've had enough.'

'Don't apologise,' she said. 'I'm glad you spoke out. I've begged her to be civil to you but it's like talking to the wall. Maybe now she'll realise that she's met her match and start showing some courtesy. I don't know how you've stood it this long, quite frankly. It's a wonder you want to carry on seeing me.'

'It would take more than your mother's sharp tongue to make me want to stop doing that,' said George, who could hardly believe how strongly he felt for a woman he had once thought was cold and arrogant and now knew to be warm and caring. 'In fact I can't think of anything that would do that.'

'I'm glad,' she said, leaning over and kissing him on the lips.

'Maybe we could stay at home sometimes,' he suggested. 'You won't need to ask your mother to babysit then.'

'Suits me,' she said happily.

As soon as the door closed behind Meg and George, Bea turned on her husband.

'I'm disgusted with you,' she told him tearfully. 'Fancy just sitting there letting that awful lout insult me.'

'George isn't a lout,' said Frank.

'So you're taking his side.'

'I'm just trying to be fair. You've been asking for what happened tonight, the way you've been treating him,' he pointed out in a quiet but firm tone. 'I've warned you about it before.'

'So . . . let me get this straight,' she said through clenched teeth. 'You don't mind your only daughter going out with that . . . that ruffian.'

'George is a decent chap,' said Frank. 'He isn't the ruffian you make him out to be.'

'He's a second-hand car salesman with the manners of a barrow boy.'

'He's a well-established businessman,' Frank corrected. 'And I've always found him to be perfectly polite.' He paused. 'With respect, dear, you're the one whose manners haven't been what they should be recently.'

'That's a terrible thing to say to your wife.'

'I'm sorry if it upsets you, but it's true,' he told her.

'Well, really,' she said, her voice quivering. 'I never thought I'd live to see the day my own husband turned against me.'

'I haven't turned against you,' he said patiently. 'But you really have misjudged George.'

'Oh, give me strength,' she said, her small blue eyes hot with angry tears.

'George is a good man and he seems genuinely keen on Meg,' Frank continued. 'After all, it isn't every man who wants to take up with a woman who's had another man's child, is it? But he seems to be genuinely fond of Becky.'

'Take up with her?' she echoed. The phrase had a frighteningly permanent ring to it. 'You don't think it will get really serious, do you?'

'It might,' he said.

'God forbid!'

'You've been wanting her to find a husband for Becky's sake,' he reminded her. 'I think she stands a good chance with George.'

'I want her to find a husband, yes,' Bea said, 'but a professional man, someone with a bit of class, not riff-raff like George Granger.'

'I wish you wouldn't speak like that about him,' Frank said.

'I shall say whatever I like about him,' she declared.

'He is the brother of Meg's business partner, remember.'

'He's common.'

'I don't think it matters that he's a bit rough around the edges if his heart's in the right place,' said Frank.

'You would say that,' she pronounced, 'because you've never had any class yourself.'

He flinched. She still had the power to hurt him even though he'd been on the receiving end of her cruel tongue for so long. 'That hasn't stopped me keeping you in grand style all these years, though, has it?' he said.

'No, but that's beside the point,' she said dimissively, her mind still full of the altercation with George.

'Anyway, it's entirely up to Meg who she goes out with. We don't have the right to interfere in her life,' he pointed out, brushing aside his wife's careless insult to him, something he'd become an expert at over the years.

'There must be something we can do to stop her seeing him,' she said.

'There isn't,' he said. 'Nothing at all. She's long past the stage where we had any influence over her opinions about anything.'

'We're still her parents.'

'She's grown-up, Bea, old enough to live her own life and choose her own friends.' Observing his wife's deathly pallor and trembling lips, he went on, 'You only upset yourself with this disapproval of anyone who isn't in the same social group as yourself.'

'It's George Granger who's upset me.'

'You know you've shown yourself up, that's why you're so distressed,' he said.

'That's right, blame the whole thing on me,' she retorted.

'Try to calm down,' he advised her. 'Let things go over your head. Live and let live. You'll find life a lot easier that way.'

'I can't just let things go over my head,' she told him. 'Especially George Granger.'

He shook his head and said in a warning tone, 'Well, Bea, you'll be the loser if you carry on towards George as you have been doing, because your daughter will stay away from you altogether. And how will you feel then, if you can't see Becky?'

'Meg wouldn't do that.'

'She might if you make things too uncomfortable for her and George,' he said.

'I don't agree.' She appeared to become bored with the subject. 'Meg's an intelligent woman, she's bound to get fed up with him before too long.' She threw her husband a defiant look. 'I shall not give the matter any more thought. I shall go shopping for clothes tomorrow to cheer myself up.'

'Is that really necessary?' he asked, frowning darkly.

'Since when has buying new clothes had to be necessary?'

'The thing is, Bea . . .'

'Oh, and while we're on the subject of shopping,' she butted in, 'I've been meaning to ask you to fix me up with one of these new cards that Barclays Bank have just brought out . . . it's called a credit card, or something.'

'No.'

'What?'

'No,' he repeated. 'I'd rather not get you one of those.'

'No?' she echoed incredulously. 'What on earth are you talking about?'

'I'm saying I won't get you one, or me, for that matter,' he stated categorically.

She stared at him, dumbfounded. 'I don't understand,' she said at last.

'My business isn't doing as well as it was, dear,' he explained. 'We need to slow down on the spending . . . for a while at least.'

'We can't possibly do that,' she declared, seeming not to notice that her husband was under strain. 'We have certain standards to maintain.'

'Be that as it may, we need to make some economies,' he said. 'The market in my line of business is changing and becoming frighteningly competitive. With all these cash-and-carry warehouses opening up for retailers to use, as well as the supermarkets stocking various items of hardware, it's becoming increasingly difficult for wholesalers like myself to make a profit.'

'There's always been strong competition,' she said, 'no matter what line of business you're in.'

'Not like it is at the moment,' he replied, trying to make her understand.

'It'll only be a temporary thing,' she suggested.

'I can't be sure of that,' he told her. 'Times are changing. It's out of my control.'

'All businesses have their highs and lows,' she said, determined not to have her comfortable lifestyle upset. 'You're too negative, that's always been your trouble.'

He sighed. 'I'm just being realistic,' he informed her.

'Oh well,' she said impatiently, 'you're the bread-winner, it's up to you to sort it out. I shall expect you to provide me with a credit card as soon as possible.'

'I'd rather not run up any more bills,' he told her.

'Then you'll have to pay it off every month so that it doesn't accumulate, won't you?' she informed him.

'But . . .'

'Just do it, Frank,' she commanded. 'But right now I'm going upstairs to check on Becky.'

As she stood up to leave the room, he stared into space, mulling things over. Bea might well be right about his being negative and lacking in class. But his biggest failing was being too soft with his wife, especially when it came to her spending habits. If he'd kept a tighter control on their finances from the beginning and not let her indulge her extravagant tastes quite so freely, he'd have had money to fall back on when things weren't so good. Why did he allow her to trample all over him? Because he couldn't bear to disappoint her by not being the high achiever she expected him to be, that was the answer to that.

'All right, dear, I'll get you a credit card,' he said with a sigh of resignation as she crossed the room to the door.

'Thank you,' she said.

Frank knew that Bea had no idea how stressful business was these days, and how much worry was involved, so much so that it made him feel quite ill at times.

The summer of 1966 passed in a blur of happiness for Eve. The mood in London generally was vibrant and exciting. There seemed to be a special kind of energy about as skirts got ever shorter and men's hair longer. The sense of optimism that was so palpable on the streets as British fashion and pop music led the world and England's footballers won the World Cup reflected Eve's own mood.

And for very good reason. Her daughter was thriving, her business was flourishing, her friendship with Meg was unwavering, and she and Bart had a lot of fun together. Because of Josie, they didn't exactly paint the town red of an evening. Sometimes Eve would get a sitter and they would go to a restaurant or a club; occasionally Eve went with him to a gig. But mostly they stayed home at Eve's. He was great with Josie, who adored him. On Sundays the three of them would go out to the park or the zoo or the river. If the weather was nice, they'd take a picnic to Runnymede.

His mother was a good friend to Eve too, and their business connection was a huge success. As Eve had known they would be, Lil's crocheted garments proved to be excellent sellers, and she kept the boutique regularly supplied.

'How are the long-sleeved tops Lil's making for our autumn and winter range coming on?' Meg enquired of Eve at their weekly business meeting one morning in the late summer.

'She's got our order almost complete, I think,' said Eve. 'But she knows we don't need it until we've cleared the summer stock.'

'We'll want them soon, though,' said Meg. 'It's nearly time to display our new stuff.'

'I'll ask her on Sunday,' said Eve. 'Bart and I will be going there for lunch.'

'Lunch with his mother, supper together at your parents' . . . you and Bart are really going strong then,' remarked Meg lightly.

'Yeah, he's great,' she said with enthusiasm. 'I like him a lot.'

'Only like?'

'No, more than just like. I enjoy being with him and he's very special to me, but . . .' Eve trailed off, not sure how to answer the question fully.

'You're not in love with him?'

Eve pondered on this, her expression darkening. She still had nightmares about the train crash and vivid dreams about Ken in which she relived her feelings for him. All the emotions she had experienced when he was alive were there in the dream – love, passion, desire. When she awoke to the awful truth that he was dead, she felt desolate. He was still a huge influence on her life. Her feelings for Bart didn't come close to what she'd felt for Ken, but she did feel something very special for him and would hate to lose him as a friend. 'I don't think I have it in me to love any other man in the way I loved Ken,' she said now.

'That doesn't mean you can't let yourself fall in love again,' said Meg. 'Even if it isn't at such an intense level.'

'It isn't a question of not letting myself, or not wanting to move on,' she said, meeting Meg's clear blue eyes. 'But it isn't something I can make happen. What Ken and I had was so special, I really don't think it can be repeated.'

'Does Bart know how you feel?'

'He knows that I would never consider the idea of getting married again. I made that clear at the start.'

'How does he feel about that?'

'He seems quite happy with the way things are between us,' she said thoughtfully. 'As far as I know, it suits him.

He's too busy trying to get established in showbusiness to want to be tied down with a wife and child.'

'That's what George used to say, that he was too busy getting his business established to want a regular relationship.'

'And then you came along.'

'That's right,' said Meg, smiling mistily. 'And then I came along.'

'And . . . ?'

A cryptic smile was Meg's reply.

'Come on, don't go all mysterious on me,' urged Eve, grinning. 'You asked me about me and Bart and I told you.'

Meg's expression became deadly serious. Eve had never seen her so solemn. 'I can't believe what's happened to me these past few months,' she said gravely. 'I couldn't stand the sight of George . . . well, you know what we were like.'

'Don't remind me,' said Eve with a wry grin. 'The pair of you were a real pain.'

'Now . . . well, now I love him so much it hurts,' she said, tears filling her eyes.

'Oh, Meg . . .'

'Yeah, I'm desperate about him,' she admitted. 'Completely helpless.'

'And him?'

'He hasn't said so but I think he feels the same,' she said.

'It looks that way to me,' said Eve. 'From seeing you together.'

'But I don't want to rush things and scare him off,' confessed Meg.

'From what I've seen of the two of you together, there's no chance of that,' said Eve.

'I hope not.'

'You've nothing to worry about,' Eve assured her in a positive manner. 'My brother obviously adores you. I think he always did, even when you were arch-enemies.'

'I don't know what I'll do if he doesn't ask me to marry him.'

'Give him time and I'm sure it will happen, because the two of you are so right for each other,' said Eve. George and Meg were now accepted by the Grangers as a couple.

'I think we are too,' said Meg. 'We're so different yet so alike, too, in a lot of our views. We have a great time together.'

'Funny how things work out, isn't it?' pondered Eve.

'Mm.' Meg thought back to the first time she'd ever set eyes on George, when he'd visited Eve in the maternity ward. Even from a distance he'd made an impression. She could admit to herself now that she'd hated him because she'd been in thrall to him from the start and it had been a scary feeling. All she wanted now was to be with him – to touch him, to feel him beside her, hear his voice, see his smile. She wanted to wake up beside him and have him as the father to her adored daughter. She'd thought she could never love a man again after Becky's father. But what she felt for George surpassed anything that had gone before. 'I'd do anything for him, Eve, anything at all.'

'He's a lucky man,' said Eve.

'I'm the lucky one,' corrected Meg, 'having George as a boyfriend.'

'Wouldn't it be terrific if we were to become sisters-in-law?' said Eve.

Meg leaned forward and rested her hand lightly on Eve's. 'If that doesn't happen, you're gonna have one very miserable friend and business partner on your hands.'

'I'll have to keep my fingers crossed very tightly then, won't I?' said Eve. She was worried by the depth of her friend's feelings for George because it made Meg so vulnerable.

Chapter Twelve

Meg got her wish and married George in the early summer of the following year. Eve was so happy for them.

Bea Myers – conveniently forgetting her strict adherence to the traditional view that it wasn't 'quite the thing' for a woman in Meg's situation to have a church wedding – used the opportunity to repair the damage Meg had done to the family reputation by putting on a wedding to outshine all others in the neighbourhood. She insisted that Meg have bridesmaids, church bells, the lot.

The scene outside the church after the ceremony made an impressive tableau, with Meg in white, and George and the other male participants in top hat and tails. The sun shone from a blue sky dotted with wispy white clouds, and Josie and Becky were so pretty as bridesmaids, they almost stole the show. But not quite, because Meg was a stunning bride, her face almost ethereal beneath a billowing veil, her blonde hair swept back into a chignon.

'Well, the Myers have certainly made sure their daughter got married in style,' said Dot at the lavish reception at a hotel in Ealing.

'I'll say,' agreed Ned.

The meal and speeches were over and the guests were mingling in this interim period until the evening party began. Eve and Bart had been sitting at the top table because Bart was best man, Eve matron of honour and Josie a bridesmaid. Now that the formalities were over, they had come to join Eve's parents, who were sitting at a table with Lil Baxter and Nora, whom Meg had invited because of Lil's connection with the boutique. Rudy had been invited too, having got to know the bride and groom through Bart.

'Meg and George seem to be enjoying themselves even though they would have preferred a much smaller wedding,' remarked Eve, who was sitting next to her mother.

'They're so pleased to be married, I think they'd be happy whatever the size of the wedding,' said Dot. 'But I know they both wanted to keep it small.'

'Meg's mother wasn't having that,' said Eve. 'She's a very determined woman.'

'This must have set Frank back a bit,' remarked Dot. 'Our contribution was relatively small; Bea wouldn't hear of us paying for anything other than what's customary for the groom's parents. She made it very plain that this was their show. Just as well, really, 'cause we couldn't afford a fraction of what this must have cost 'em.'

'They can afford it,' said Eve.

'I'm not so sure about that,' commented Ned. 'I don't think Frank's business is quite the thriving concern it used to be.'

'Really?' said Bart, who had Josie sitting on his lap. 'What makes you say that?'

'He mentioned something about it at George's stag night when he'd had a few drinks,' said Ned. 'I get the impression the poor bloke's struggling.'

'Things can't be that bad if they can put on a do like this,' Lil pointed out.

'True,' agreed Nora.

'That doesn't necessarily follow,' said Dot. 'People like the Myers could get a bank loan if they didn't have the ready cash.'

'I'm not saying they're on their uppers or anything as drastic as that,' Ned explained. 'But I don't think business is as good as it used to be for Frank. He seems like a worried man to me.'

'I'd be permanently worried if I was married to Bea,' laughed Bart.

'Poor old George, having her as a mother-in-law,' added Ned.

'Don't worry about George,' Eve cut in. 'From what I can gather, he can handle her. He doesn't put up with any of her nonsense.'

'It's a wonder she allowed her husband to go to George's stag night,' said Dot. 'I shouldn't think it's their sort of thing.'

'Frank must have put his foot down,' was Ned's opinion. 'And I'm very glad he did. He's a nice bloke . . . and thinks the world of George.'

'Which is more than she does, the stuck-up cow,' said Dot.

'Shush, Mum,' whispered Eve, glancing at Josie. 'She repeats everything.'

'Maybe it would do Bea Myers good to know what we're saying about her,' Dot replied in a hushed tone. 'She needs taking down a peg or two.'

'That wouldn't take her down, it would probably make her even more superior,' suggested Eve. 'She'd say that that sort of talk is only to be expected from peasants like us.'

There was a murmur of agreement, and the conversation became general until the bride and groom came over.

'Are you all enjoying yourselves?' enquired Meg, looking radiant.

Everybody said they were. Meg moved over to talk to Lil and Nora while George sat down between his mother and sister.

'Well, son,' said Dot, 'how do you feel now that you've actually taken the plunge?'

There were no words to describe how George was feeling at this moment. Ecstatic seemed hopelessly inadequate. Since Meg had become a part of his life he'd found a depth of feeling he hadn't known he was capable of and certainly couldn't articulate. Ordinary things he'd always taken for granted had begun to register with vivid clarity – the warmth of the sunshine, the smell of rain. He'd never thought of himself as an emotional man, but sometimes he wanted to cry with the sheer joy of being with Meg. Now was one such moment.

He could still hardly believe that someone as beautiful and independent as Meg would give him a second glance, let alone be in love him. But she was. He was in no doubt about that and it was a great feeling. With her beside him, the future was a glorious prospect. How wrong he'd been to think that involvement with a woman would hold him back. Meg's encouragement helped him to move forward.

After their honeymoon they would start life together properly in a house in Ealing not far from where Meg had been living. He'd sold his flat and she'd sold her house so that they could share the home they had chosen together. If someone had told him a few years ago that he would marry a woman who had had another man's child, he wouldn't have believed them. But Becky had become as much a part of his life as Meg and he couldn't have loved her more if she was his own child.

Everything was so perfect, it scared him. How could something this good last? He dismissed such thoughts and answered his mother's question. 'I feel wonderful, Mum, absolutely marvellous!'

The party was in full swing and everyone seemed to be having a good time. The bride and groom had gone to get ready to leave, Bea was fussing around her cronies, Ned and Frank were jigging about on the dance floor with their respective granddaughters, Dot was dancing with Rudy, Lil and Nora were getting quietly sozzled at the table, and Eve was dancing with Bart.

It was a slow, smoochy number and they were dancing close. Bart had been particularly affectionate towards her all day.

'Enjoying yourself?' he asked.

'It's been a lovely day,' she said. 'You?'

'Oh yeah,' he said. 'I'm having a great time.'

'You did a good job as best man.'

'And you were a lovely matron of honour,' he said. 'I fancied you rotten.'

'You're not supposed to be fancying people during a wedding ceremony,' she admonished. 'It's a solemn occasion.'

'Being in church doesn't bring nature to a halt,' he laughed. 'I bet George could think of nothing else while he was taking his vows.'

Eve drew back and looked down at her long pale-lemon taffeta dress. 'I should have got changed but Josie said she wanted me to stay in my pretty wedding clothes a bit longer.' She grinned. 'Never let it be said that I give in to my daughter.'

'You don't to any serious degree,' he said. 'I've seen you in action, so I know. If it's important that you don't give in to her, you stand your ground no matter how much she tries to wear you down.'

'Fearsome, am I?'

'Determined is the word.'

'So is my daughter.'

'You're telling me,' he agreed. 'I don't know who's worse, you or her.'

She looked into his clean-cut face, his eyes exuding their special warmth. Because he spent a lot of time with her and Josie in their home environment, he'd become closer to her than if she'd been free to go out every time they saw each other. 'You're getting to know me too well.'

'Well enough to know that I want to marry you,' he said impulsively.

'Oh, Bart,' she said, taken aback, 'you're not being serious?'

'Never more so,' he said tenderly. 'I'm in love with you and I want to marry you.'

She didn't move, just stood there staring at him while the dancing went on around them. She felt buffeted by real life after a year of fun and laughter with Bart, and she couldn't hide her feelings.

'I've obviously said the wrong thing,' he said, looking crushed.

'Please don't be upset,' she replied, feeling terrible. 'I told you when we first got together that I didn't want to get married again. I thought that suited you because you didn't want to get tied down with a wife and child. You said you wanted to concentrate on your career.'

'That was then,' he said in a soft voice. 'Things change.'

'Look . . . can we talk about this later?' she suggested as swaying bodies moved around them. The situation couldn't have been less conducive to a serious discussion.

'We can forget about it altogether if you'd rather,' he said brusquely, and she knew he must be deeply hurt because it wasn't in his nature to take offence.

She pulled him closer to her and looked into his eyes. 'Don't be like that, Bart, please,' she said persuasively. 'Let's talk about it later on, after Josie's in bed.'

'Okay,' he agreed, but he didn't look happy.

A shadow had fallen over the day and the rest of the party seemed interminable. Eve longed for the time to pass so that she could be alone with Bart, to put things right, to take that wounded look out of his eyes and explain that she did care for him, a lot.

Soon after the bride and groom left for their honeymoon, Josie became tired and fretful, so Eve took her home. Bart had to stay on because, as best man, he had certain responsibilities. He said he would join her as soon as he could.

It was almost midnight when he arrived.

'Look, let's not make a big thing of this,' he said, and she could tell that he felt awkward as they sat down in her lounge with a cup of coffee. 'I obviously misjudged your feelings for me.'

'You didn't,' she said. 'I think the world of you . . .'

'But you don't love me.'

'Yes, I do . . .'

'But not enough to marry me.'

'It isn't a question of degrees, of whether it is or isn't enough,' she tried to explain.

'What is it a question of, then?'

'It's about my not wanting to get married again,' she said. 'That's all.'

'So what have we been doing this last year, then, Eve?' he wanted to know.

'Spending time together and being happy,' she said.

'We've been a couple.'

'We still are,' she said. 'Just because I don't want to get married doesn't mean I don't want you in my life.' She sipped her coffee, looking at him over the rim of the cup. 'Though, of course, I'll understand if you'd rather find someone who's prepared to make the full commitment.'

'I don't want anyone else,' he said irritably. 'That's just the point.'

'You're making me feel as though I'm committing some sort of crime because I don't want to get married again,' she said.

'Sorry.' He raked his thick brown hair from his brow in an agitated manner. 'I know it's cool not to bother to get married these days, but I'm old-fashioned. I want to make it legal.'

'My not wanting to get married has nothing to do with any current trend, neither has it anything to do with my feelings for you,' she told him.

He pondered on this for a while. 'I suppose it's all to do with your late husband,' he said.

'Yes, it is,' she told him frankly and without apology.

'But he's been dead for four years, Eve,' he pointed out with strong emphasis. 'You can't stay married to a ghost forever.'

His words hit home with a bruising sensation. 'You don't understand . . .'

'Look, I know you had a good marriage, and no other man can ever mean the same to you as he did, but that doesn't mean you can't have a happy marriage with someone else.'

'Please don't try and force me into something I don't want, Bart,' she urged him.

'Oh, Eve!' He was shocked, his voice quivering. 'That's the last thing I would ever do. I want to make you happy, not miserable.'

'I know that, and I'm sorry.' She put her cup down on a small table, her hand trembling slightly. This new development had thrown her into turmoil. 'Could we just give it some more time and see how it goes? I don't think I could bear to stop seeing you.'

'I don't want that either.'

'Can't we just carry on as we are then?' she suggested. 'Though obviously I don't expect you to hang around on the offchance that I'll want to get married at some point.'

'I know that.'

'Let's stay as we are,' she urged him. 'But if you want out at any time then you must tell me. It's important that we're honest with each other, as we have been tonight.'

He stood up and opened his arms to her, his voice husky with emotion. 'All right, Eve, we'll do it your way.'

'Thank God for that,' she said, slipping her arms around him, a hot rush of relief physically weakening her.

One Saturday afternoon in the autumn of that year, when it was Eve's turn for duty at the boutique, she popped down to the Broadway in her lunch hour for some shopping. While she was in Bentall's she happened to meet Ann and Joan, two of her ex-colleagues from the mail-order company.

'It's been years,' she said, delighted to see the two women. 'How are you both?'

They said they were fine and asked if she had time for a cup of tea to catch up with all the news. She decided she could manage a quick one, so they all trooped into the cafeteria.

'We've wondered how you were getting on,' said Joan,

a redhead of about Eve's age. 'We haven't heard from you since you sent a card announcing the birth of your daughter.'

'Sorry about that,' she said, making a face. 'I meant to keep in touch, but you know how it is . . . you're busy and never get around to it.'

They both agreed that this often did happen when someone left the firm.

'We heard you'd gone into business,' said Joan. 'A boutique, someone said.'

'That's right.' She gave them some details about Trend and they said they'd look it up when they had more time.

'Well, you certainly look well, Eve,' said Ann, a bottle-blonde with a beehive hairstyle. 'Positively blooming, in fact.'

'A darned sight better than when we last saw you.' Joan coloured up. 'I didn't mean that quite how it sounded,' she explained. 'You were still in shock from the train crash when you left to have your baby and you weren't on top form. No offence intended.'

'None taken,' said Eve lightly, but her stomach had knotted at the memory of those terrible days. 'I must have looked awful . . . I felt terrible for a long time after the accident.'

'You're over it now, though, I expect,' suggested Ann.

'Oh, yeah, I'm fine now,' said Eve, and moved hastily on to other subjects because thoughts of the accident still upset her. She enquired about various people she'd known at the firm and asked to be remembered to them.

Because she had to get back to work, Eve left the two other women finishing their tea and departed, making a few purchases in the store and calling at the Ladies' on her way out. While she was inside one of the cubicles, she heard movement outside and recognised the voices of Ann and Joan. She was about to join them when, to her horror, they began discussing her. Natural curiosity made her stay where she was, almost despite herself, listening to what was being said.

211

'Eve looks terrific now, don't you think?' remarked Ann.

'Yeah, she looks really well,' agreed Joan. 'And talk about smart . . .'

'I noticed that,' said Ann. 'You can tell she's in the fashion business.'

'I'm glad things are going well for her now,' said Joan. 'She deserves some luck, after what she's been through.'

'It must be terrible to lose your husband so young,' said Ann.

'Do you reckon she knew what he'd been up to before he died?'

'Dunno,' said the other woman. 'But surely she must have. There must have been signs. I reckon I'd know if my husband was seeing someone else.'

Seeing someone else? Eve's heart was thudding, her breath coming fast. The sound of running water and the heavy click of the roller towel stabbed at her sensitised nerves as she listened, dreading what she might hear next.

'I'm not so sure about that,' said Joan. 'They say the wife's always the last to know when her old man's having an affair.'

'Mm, there is that. Let's hope she didn't get to know about it,' said Ann. 'What she doesn't know can't hurt her.'

'That's the way I look at it an' all,' said Joan. 'It's all past history anyway, with him being six foot under.'

Although she would have liked to burst out of the cubicle and confront them, Eve was so overcome with weakness from the shock of what she'd heard that she had to sit on the lid of the toilet. She was shaking violently. By the time she'd recovered sufficiently to leave the cubicle, the two women had gone.

Feeling sick and shaky, she left the store and walked back to the boutique across Haven Green, oblivious to the warm autumn sunshine on her face, the riot of colours on the trees, the carpet of leaves on the grass. The overheard conversation beat into her brain over and over again. Things that had happened in her marriage that she hadn't queried at the time now rushed into her mind with a new significance. All those nights Ken had been out working, his unreliability and preoccupation.

No, the idea was preposterous. Ken wouldn't have had an affair. Everybody knew how devoted he had been to his wife. There had obviously been some sort of a misunderstanding.

She tried to put it out of her mind. After all, Ken was dead, so what difference did it make now if it was true, which it wasn't? But the pain and uncertainty just wouldn't go away. It shouldn't matter, but it did. *A lot!* How could it be otherwise when her faith in something of such value was at stake?

After a torturous weekend thinking about it until her head ached, she telephoned Joan at the mail-order firm and arranged to meet her after work. She *had* to know the truth.

'You didn't know about it then, Eve?' said Joan that evening. They were sitting in a coffee bar in Acton near to where Joan worked. As Eve had obviously heard everything that had been said, Joan saw no point in denying it.

'Of course I didn't know about, it because it didn't happen,' said Eve. The truth was just too painful to accept. 'And I want to know who's been spreading such malicious gossip.'

Joan drew hard on a cigarette, looking at Eve. 'One of the girls at the firm saw your husband with a woman,' she said evenly.

'That doesn't prove anything,' Eve pointed out hotly. 'She could have been a customer . . . someone he was doing a job for.'

'Yeah, sure,' said Joan diplomatically.

'So why did everyone assume the worst?' she wanted to know.

Joan stirred her coffee, reluctant to hurt Eve with what

she knew. 'What does it matter now?' she said gently. 'The man is dead. You'd be better off letting things be.'

'I *have* to know,' insisted Eve through dry lips. 'As I was obviously the subject of gossip, I think I've a right to know why.'

'All right.' Joan inhaled on her cigarette again, looking at Eve. 'Ken and this woman were wrapped around each other when they were seen. Very lovey-dovey, apparently. They were in a pub somewhere. I can't remember which one, it's all such a long time ago. They were seen in his builder's van together too. 'She paused, lowering her gaze. 'They were in . . . I think they call it a compromising situation.'

Eve visibly flinched, the blood draining from her face.

'I'm sorry,' said Joan, 'but you did ask. I told you it was best left alone.'

'Would you leave it alone if you were in my position?' asked Eve.

'I don't know the answer to that,' said Joan, shaking her head. 'But there doesn't seem much point in dwelling on it and upsetting yourself.'

'Who was it who saw them together?' Eve felt compelled to ask.

'Sheila Willis, I don't know if you remember her,' said Joan.

'Small ginger woman with plenty to say for herself?' said Eve, casting her mind back.

'That's the one.'

'I'll ring her at work, arrange a meeting,' said Eve.

'She left the firm a couple of years ago to emigrate to Australia,' Joan informed her. 'She hasn't kept in touch.'

Eve brushed her damp brow with the back of her hand, feeling desperate. 'But I *have* to contact her.'

'I don't see how you can, since no one has her address,' said Joan, sipping her coffee. 'Anyway, what good would it do?'

'I have to know for sure,' said Eve.

'I think you do know for sure, don't you, Eve?' said Joan.

214

'I don't know anything except that Sheila saw something and put her own interpretation on it,' replied Eve miserably. 'Did she say anything about this supposed woman?'

'Not that I can remember,' said Joan. 'I don't expect she was able to study her.'

'If Ken was having an affair,' said Eve, still trying to convince herself that it wasn't true, 'surely he wouldn't have been stupid enough to be seen with her in a public place?'

'People get careless when they're in that sort of a situation, I should think,' suggested Joan. 'They get carried away, throw caution to the winds.'

As the truth became impossible to deny, Eve felt bitterly disillusioned. She'd already lost Ken; now her treasured memories of him were to be tainted too. The fact that it was all a long time ago didn't make her feel any less humiliated and rejected. 'Yeah, I suppose they might,' she agreed.

'I'm really sorry to be the one to tell you,' Joan apologised. 'I feel awful about it.'

'There's no need for you to feel bad.' Eve swallowed her coffee without tasting it just to moisten her parched mouth. 'Thanks for taking the time to meet me.'

'No problem,' she said. 'I just wish the circumstances had been happier.'

'Me too.'

Joan reached across and put her hand on Eve's. 'I should forget all about it if I were you,' she advised her. 'Pretend you never heard that conversation on Saturday.'

If only it was that easy, thought Eve, too distressed to speak.

For weeks the truth about her marriage festered inside Eve, plaguing her by day and keeping her awake at night. She confided in no one and kept up a front despite the pain gnawing away inside her.

Although she made a supreme effort to behave as if nothing was wrong, Meg saw through the façade.

'It's true what they say about a trouble shared, you know,'

she said one evening when she called at Eve's home for a chat. 'And don't say there's nothing wrong, because I won't believe you.

'That obvious, is it?'

'Only to me,' Meg assured her. 'So if you feel like talking, I've got the time. George is at home with Becky.'

Although Eve hadn't been able to bear the thought of confiding in anyone, out it all came in a tide of anguish.

'I feel so dreadfully betrayed,' she said, her dark eyes heavy and shadowed.

'I can imagine.' Meg looked very pale.

'I'm angry, hurt, humiliated,' Eve continued. 'I don't know what to do to make the pain go away. It isn't as though I can confront him with it, hear his side of the story, take my anger out on him.'

'So there's only one thing you can do,' advised Meg. 'Forget all about it.'

'Easy for you to say,' Eve told her. 'But I can't get it off my mind. It's enough to make you lose all faith in human nature.'

'You mustn't do that, Eve.' Meg was adamant. 'These things sometimes happen, you mustn't let it make you cynical.'

Eve shook her head, as though still bewildered by the facts. 'I know it must be true because Joan had no reason to lie about it. But in my heart I still can't believe that Ken would have had an affair.' Her expression became hard. 'I hate him for it and I can't even punish him.' She paused, looking at Meg intently. 'It's an odd feeling to find out that you never really knew the man you loved and shared everything with. It's as though a large chunk of my life has been taken away from me.'

'There's not a damned thing you can do about that,' said Meg. 'But you mustn't let it ruin your life now. You've the future to think of, yours and Josie's. Ken's the past. Forget him and think of Bart. Bart is a man you really can trust.'

'How can I ever trust any man again?' Eve asked her.

216

'I would have staked my life on Ken being faithful.' She looked into space. 'We had something so special . . . how could he have cheated on me like that?'

Meg studied her hands for a moment. 'I don't know, Eve,' she said in a tone of resignation. 'You'll just have to put it down to the frailty of human nature. It doesn't mean Bart will do the same thing.'

'I want to know who she is, Meg,' Eve said. 'I have to talk to her, find out if she was in love with him . . . if it was serious between them.'

'And hurt yourself even more?'

'I can't hurt more than I do already, thinking about it over and over.'

'But you can't find out who she was, can you?' Meg reminded her. 'Not if the woman who saw them together has gone abroad and no one knows where she is. Anyway, from what you've said, she didn't know anything about the woman.'

'That's the infuriating thing,' Eve told her. 'But I just can't get it off my mind. I keep going over my life with Ken, wondering where I went wrong, what he was doing when he wasn't with me. I keep imagining them making love, wondering where they were doing it, when they were doing it. Was he in love with her, or was she just his bit on the side?'

'For heaven's sake, let it go, Eve,' Meg advised her urgently. 'That time has gone, Ken has gone. You can't let this disrupt your life and spoil things for you just when everything is going so well. You went through enough when he died.'

Eve sighed. 'Everything you say is true. But you can't just switch pain off, can you?'

'No, you can't,' agreed Meg, 'but you can discipline yourself not to let the thoughts take hold and destroy you.'

'You're right,' said Eve, feeling suddenly more positive than she had since she'd found out the truth. 'I've a lot going for me, and a daughter to raise. I'm blowed if I'm going to let myself be destroyed by something I can do nothing about.'

'That's the spirit!'

'Oh, and by the way,' added Eve, 'I think it's probably best if we keep this to ourselves. It'll only upset the family.'

'No one will hear about it from me, I promise you,' Meg assured her.

As the misty golden days of autumn darkened into the frosts of winter, the hippy and flower-power style of dress increased in popularity. Trend catered modestly for this fashion by stocking embroidered shirts and overblouses in cheesecloth, and loose-flowing kaftans. Mini-skirts and dresses were still as popular as ever for the majority of customers and were now often worn with the new long coats inspired by the film *Dr Zhivago* to protect exposed legs from the bitter winter weather.

Immersed in a busy lifestyle, combining a career with motherhood and continually striving to be good at both, Eve had little time to brood on the past. But still unwanted thoughts and imaginings haunted her; her shattered illusions were always at the back of her mind.

Christmas passed pleasantly enough. She and Josie went to her parents' for Christmas Day and Eve invited everybody, including Lil and Nora, to her place for Boxing Day. But even while being a busy hostess, Eve's troublesome thoughts persisted.

'If only I could talk to Ken's lover,' she confided to Meg, who was helping her get the tea ready in the kitchen.

'I still don't see how that would help you,' said Meg.

'I think I could put it behind me for good then,' Eve tried to explain. 'Once I knew how things stood for them. How she felt about him . . . was he planning to leave me and have a future with her?'

'We've been through this before,' said Meg. Eve had

mentioned the same thing several times over the past few months.

'Sorry, am I being a pain?' she asked, putting some cold meats on a serving dish.

'No,' said Meg, arranging mince pies on a plate. 'I just wish you would forget all about it, for your own sake.'

'I can't, and you're the only one I can talk to about it,' said Eve.

'Yes, I know,' said Meg.

'I didn't mean to mention it again,' said Eve. 'It just sort of slipped out.'

'It doesn't matter,' Meg assured her.

'The reason I keep going on about it to you is probably because it's always on my mind, no matter what I'm doing.' She forced a smile. 'Anyway, this isn't the time to talk about it, so let's get the food on the table. Can you take the Christmas cake into the other room for me when you've done the mince pies?'

'Sure,' said Meg.

'Is anything the matter, love?' George asked Meg a couple of days later over their evening meal. Becky was fast asleep in bed.

'No.'

'You've been a bit quiet these last few days,' he said.

'I'm okay, George.'

'You don't look it,' he said, giving her a studious look. 'You definitely look peaky.'

'I'm fine, really,' she fibbed. 'It's probably just the make-up I'm wearing. The pale look is really in at the moment.'

'You'd tell me if you weren't feeling well, wouldn't you?' he asked.

'Course I would,' she said. 'Why on earth wouldn't I?'

'You never know with you independent women,' he said, teasing her.

'Don't worry, you'd soon know about it if I was ill,'

she said with false brightness. 'I'd have you running about after me, bringing me meals in bed and plumping up my pillows.'

'Willingly would I do it,' he smiled.

She could have wept with love for him. He was so kind, so caring, such good company and so right for her. He never tried to be a dominant husband, jealous of her career and wanting her to give it up now that she was married. He was proud of her success and interested in her business, as she was in his. She talked about the boutique to him, he talked cars to her, welcoming her ideas and opinions about the showrooms he was still hoping to have built if he could ever persuade the landowner to sell the land to him at the right price.

But she wasn't being honest with him when she said there was nothing wrong. There was something troubling her very badly, something she didn't think she could live with for another moment.

In a sudden moment of decision, she vowed she wouldn't let the New Year come in without doing what could no longer be avoided, however dreadful the consequences.

Chapter Thirteen

Eve was delighted to receive an unexpected visit from Meg on Saturday evening, the day before New Year's Eve.

'I can do with some company,' she said, ushering her inside. 'I'm not seeing Bart tonight . . . he's out on a gig.'

'Yes, I remembered you saying he was working tonight,' said Meg, keeping her tone light, as though this was just an ordinary visit. 'So I knew you'd be on your own.'

'Is George at home with Becky?' enquired Eve chattily.

Meg nodded. 'But she was in bed and asleep when I came out so he'll be able to relax and watch the box in peace.'

'Fancy a drink?' offered Eve. 'I've got some booze left over from Christmas.'

'Just something soft for me, please,' Meg replied. 'I'm driving.'

'I think I'll be a devil and have a gin and tonic,' said Eve.

'Why not?' said Meg, forcing a smile.

The two women sat by the fire with a glass-topped coffee table between them, the flickering glow of the flames adding cosiness to the sleek modern décor. Meg stared into her glass, wishing it contained gin instead of orange squash, because she was badly in need of Dutch courage. Her mouth was dry, her heartbeat horribly erratic.

'Isn't this nice, just the two of us for a change?' remarked Eve. 'Peace and quiet without the kids wanting this and that.'

'Actually,' Meg said, nervously clearing her throat, 'this isn't just a social visit.'

'No?'

'No. I've come because I have something to tell you,' she explained.

'You *are* being dramatic,' said Eve lightly.

'There's no easy way of saying this, Eve . . .' Meg began.

'Ooh, I don't like the sound of that,' said Eve, becoming serious. 'A harbinger of doom if ever I heard one.'

'It isn't good news.'

Now Eve looked really worried. 'You're not ill, are you?' she said in a rapid staccato tone, one hand flying to her throat.

'No, no . . .'

'Is it George or Becky then?'

'No one is ill,' Meg assured her. 'It's nothing like that.'

'Oh well,' said Eve, her voice warm with relief, 'if nobody's ill, it can't be that bad. But get on with it, for goodness' sake.'

Meg swallowed her drink and forced the words out. 'You've been saying that you think you'd feel better if you could meet the other woman in Ken's life . . . that if you knew the truth about what happened between them you could put it behind you . . .'

'Yes, I have been saying that,' said Eve, with a questioning look, her voice rising. 'Why? Have you found out who she is?'

'I've known all along who she is.' Meg lowered her gaze for a moment, then looked up, taking a deep breath and forcing herself to meet her friend's eyes. 'You're looking at her.'

'What!' It was so absurd, Eve thought she must have misheard.

'It's me, Eve,' said Meg through trembling lips. 'I'm the woman who was having an affair with your husband!'

The silence was agonising.

'You're having me on,' said Eve at last, in a shaky voice.

'I wish I was, believe me,' sighed Meg with a slow shake of her head.

'But you must be. I mean, you didn't even know Ken.' Eve was so confused, she couldn't make sense of anything. 'You knew nothing about him except what I told you.'

The other woman stared into her lap. 'I'm afraid I did,' she said.

Disgust rose in Eve's throat; she felt physically sick as the awful truth sank in. 'You already knew Ken before you got to know me?' she said. 'Is that what you're saying?'

Meg nodded. 'But when I met you at the antenatal clinic that day, I had no idea who you were. As far as I was concerned you were just another mum-to-be who I got on really well with,' she explained. 'We only used to talk about pregnancy at the beginning and I didn't get to know your surname because I always went in to be examined before you so didn't hear your name called out.'

'So when *did* you find out who I was?' enquired Eve, needing to know the details but dreading every word Meg uttered.

'When you came to my flat. As soon as you told me about the train crash, I realised you must be Ken's wife. I was as devastated then as you are now, and for both our sakes I tried to stop the friendship developing. I drew back, didn't take your calls when you phoned.'

'I wondered about that at the time,' said Eve miserably.

'Knowing who you were, hearing you talk about Ken and your happy marriage was too much for me,' Meg told her.

'Oh, Meg, I could bear anything, anything at all except this,' said Eve, her voice breaking. 'Tell me it isn't true.'

'I can't, because it is,' Meg made herself say.

'God, I'm so bewildered,' said Eve, putting her hand to her head. 'I can't think straight.'

'I felt like that when I first discovered who you were,' Meg said. 'I was shattered when I realised that we couldn't be friends.'

'But we *did* become friends, didn't we?' Eve pointed out.

'At your instigation, as I remember. Having dropped me like a hot brick, you called me one day right out of the blue.'

'Yes. I was feeling so wretched that day that what had happened in the past didn't seem important compared to the huge responsibility of facing motherhood alone,' she explained.

'So you used me . . .'

'I didn't see it that way,' Meg told her. 'I was so desperate for the company of someone I could relate to, I just picked up the phone and to hell with the consequences. Your friendship was a lifeline to me when Becky was so new and everything seemed so frightening. I thought, why shouldn't we be friends? Ken's dead so he can't come between us. Anyway, we were both victims of his deceit, even though you didn't realise it then. So I just let the friendship continue along its natural course, hoping you'd never find out.'

'You must have been having a good laugh at how naïve I'd been,' said Eve in a small voice.

'Of course I wasn't.' Meg was shocked at the suggestion. 'You must know that's the last thing I would ever do.'

'I don't know anything about you any more,' Eve told her with candour. 'For all I know, you stayed friendly with me just so that you could find out about your lover's other life . . . the one you weren't a part of.'

'No, I swear that wasn't the reason,' Meg denied most adamantly. 'Learning about Ken from your point of view was very painful for me because I'd been given a completely different version of your marriage from him. But I continued to see you because I wanted you as a friend.'

'All these years our friendship has been based on deceit,' said Eve.

'No, our friendship has been based on mutual liking and respect for each other,' insisted Meg. 'It exists because we like each other, as people. It has nothing to do with Ken.'

'But all this time you were lying to me by omission,' said Eve.

'Yes, I was,' admitted Meg. 'But would it have been right

224

to tell you the truth as soon as I knew who you were? Would it have made your life happier? I don't think so.'

'That isn't the point . . .'

'If you hadn't happened to hear those women gossiping you'd have lived your life in blissful ignorance,' Meg went on, desperately afraid of losing Eve's friendship. 'The truth has only come out now because you've been upsetting yourself so much, wanting to know what sort of relationship Ken had with the other woman in his life, I had to tell you. I couldn't let you go on torturing yourself about it any longer.'

'When I think of all the things I've told you, personal things, thinking you were a true friend . . .' began Eve.

'I was a true friend, and I still am,' Meg cut in. 'What do you think it was like for me to hear you talking about your wonderful marriage when I knew different? I knew that Ken was a liar and a cheat. He'd been deceiving us both.'

'Did you know he was married when you started the affair?'

'Yes, I knew he was married,' Meg confessed, meeting Eve's eyes. 'But he didn't paint quite the same picture as you.' She chewed her bottom lip, frowning. 'You can't imagine how I felt when I realised it was his baby you were having. He'd sworn to me that he hadn't been near you in that way for years. He said his marriage was over in all but name. I'd never have got involved with him if I'd known he was lying about that.' She paused, fiddling with her fingernails. 'Stupid of me to be taken in when everyone knows that married men always say their marriage is over when they're trying to get another woman into bed.'

It was as though a series of physical blows were being hammered into Eve's chest. She looked at Meg. 'Don't tell me Becky is . . .'

Meg nodded. 'Yes, she's Ken's child, Josie's half-sister.'

The shock took the breath from Eve and stunned her into silence. 'So he must have been . . . ?' she said in a whisper.

'Exactly,' said Meg. 'The fact that there are three days between the girls speaks for itself.'

'This is getting worse by the second,' muttered Eve.

'It isn't exactly happy families,' agreed Meg.

'So . . .' began Eve, clearing her throat and forcing herself to ask the question burning inside her, 'did you love him?'

'Oh yes,' said Meg. 'I loved him all right, or thought I did at the time. I was besotted with him, in fact.'

'And him?'

She hesitated for a moment. 'I thought he was in love with me. He said he was, made me feel as though I was the only woman in the world for him. He was so convincing I didn't doubt him for a second,' she said, her breathing ragged and uneven. 'But since getting to know you and hearing about your life with him, I realise it was all just a game to him.'

'Did he talk about leaving me?' asked Eve.

Meg didn't reply; she just stared fixedly into her drink.

'Don't be coy about it,' said Eve bitterly. 'You've shattered my illusions this far, you might as well do the job properly.'

'Yes, he did say he was going to leave you,' she blurted out. 'According to him he was going to tell you about me while you were on holiday, and move in with me when he got back from Torquay. He said it was just a formality, that you would be as relieved as he was to end the marriage.'

'Oh, I see.' Eve's voice was little more than a whisper.

'I can't believe I was gullible enough to believe him when it was obvious he was just stringing me along,' Meg continued. 'He wouldn't have left you, not in a million years. I don't think he had any intention of it. We'll never know for sure, of course, but my guess is that if he'd lived to come back from Torquay he'd have made up some excuse for me as to why he couldn't leave you. He was having his cake and eating it, it's as simple as that.'

'How long had it been going on?' Eve made herself enquire.

'For several months before he died,' Meg admitted frankly.

'And all that time I didn't have a clue,' said Eve, almost to herself.

'Didn't you suspect anything when he was out so much?'

'No. I thought he was working. It was incredibly stupid of me, I know, but I trusted him,' she said simply.

'You and me both,' said Meg.

Eve stared into the fire. 'How did you meet him?' she wondered.

'He fitted the cupboards in my kitchen at the flat,' Meg informed her. 'I got hold of him through the local paper . . . saw his advertisement and rang him to arrange for him to come and give me an estimate.'

'And invited him into your bed,' accused Eve vehemently.

'It might make you feel better to believe that I made all the running,' was Meg's reply to that, 'but it was him, Eve. He came on strong to me.'

'And you fought him off like mad, of course,' Eve said acidly.

'Yes, I did at first, as it happens,' Meg told her. 'Contrary to what you might think, I'm not a home-breaker. I don't make a habit of sleeping with married men. But when he convinced me that his marriage was over . . .' She sighed, looking shamefaced. 'I'm afraid I eventually just caved in. I don't have to tell you how persuasive Ken could be when he wanted his own way about something.'

At this moment Eve couldn't bear to remember the man or the marriage she had once thought of so fondly. 'You knew he was married, that should have been enough.' It was as much as Eve could do to stop herself physically attacking Meg. 'You should have done the decent thing and stayed away from him.'

'Do you think I don't know that?' said Meg. 'I'm not proud of what happened.'

'I should damned well hope not.'

'It was a serious mistake, and if I could turn the clock back I would,' she said with sincerity. 'But I can't, so now that it's out in the open, you and I both have to deal with it as best we can.'

'To think that I trusted you all this time,' said Eve. 'I've told you things I'd never tell another living soul.'

'And have I ever broken a confidence or let you down?'

'That isn't the point,' said Eve. 'I bared my soul to you.'

'The things you told me about your marriage tore me to shreds inside, because they were telling me that the man I loved was a liar,' Meg cut in. 'Okay, so you're the victim in all this, but there were times in the early days of our friendship when *I* felt like the victim, times when I felt as though I *hated you* . . . hated you for having something I never could.'

'Why didn't you stop me talking about it if it was so painful for you?' Eve said, with a hard edge to her voice.

'You needed to talk about him . . . it was helping you to work through your grief,' Meg replied. 'So it was my penance to listen. My punishment for having an affair with a married man was to listen to the details of his married life and realise how little I mattered to him. There were times when I almost blurted out the truth, when you were talking about how good it had been. But I managed to stop myself. Even apart from the fact that I didn't want to risk losing you as a friend, I didn't want to inflict pain on you when it wasn't necessary. What would have been the point when the man was dead?'

'I can't take all this in,' said Eve, pressing her fingers to her throbbing temples.

'We've both been badly hurt,' Meg pointed out. 'I was knocked sideways by his death too, you know. And because I was just the "other woman", I wasn't even able to say goodbye to him at his funeral. I found out from the newspaper that he'd died. "Local man killed in train crash", it said, and there was a photo. I was completely shattered.'

'I hope you're not expecting me to feel sorry for you,' Eve said.

'I'm just trying to make you see that we've both been through the same experience. We've both grieved for him, both suffered through his deceit,' said Meg. 'This should bring us closer together, not drive us apart.'

'I was his wife,' said Eve. 'You can't compare the two.'

'People don't hurt less because they don't have an official piece of paper, you know,' said Meg.

'Probably not.' Eve was too full of her own pain to sympathise.

'He hurt me too, Eve,' Meg reminded her. 'He was cheating on us both.'

'Yes, but I'm the victim of *your* deceit as well,' Eve reminded her. 'And that's what *really* hurts.' She shook her head sadly. 'All this time I've thought you were being so open about everything. I trusted you with my secrets, I would have trusted you with my life. And all the time you weren't being honest with me.'

Meg put her empty glass on the table and leaned forward as though to help make her point. 'Can you try to understand how this bizarre situation came about?' she implored her. 'When I first found out who you were, you were still grieving for Ken and heavily pregnant. The last thing you needed then was the truth. As time passed and our friendship became more important to me, my affair with Ken mattered less. After a while I hardly ever thought about it, and almost never once I got together with George. It was as though it had never happened. It only came back to mind recently because you became obsessed with it after hearing that gossip. For your sake I knew I'd have to put our friendship to the test and tell you the truth.'

'Our friendship,' said Eve in a brittle tone. 'That's a joke.'

'Ken's long gone, Eve,' said Meg. 'We mustn't let the past destroy what we have now.'

'This isn't about you and Ken,' proclaimed Eve. 'It's

about you and me, about you being someone I don't know, someone I never knew . . . only thought I did.' She stared at Meg, then lowered her eyes. 'It's the fact that you've deceived me for so long that hurts, can't you see that?'

'I know, and I'm sorry.'

'You've become a stranger.'

'No I haven't,' Meg cried out emotionally. 'Nothing's changed except that you know something about me that you didn't know before.'

'It's much more than that,' said Eve, 'and you know it.'

'Yes . . . yes, I suppose so,' Meg admitted ruefully. 'But I've explained why I deceived you. And I'm still the same person I always was.'

'You might be the same person,' said Eve, 'but my perception of you has changed.'

'You know about a mistake I made, something I deeply regret, that's all,' insisted Meg. 'You found out that I'm not perfect. Who is?'

Eve's shoulders ached with tension as she sat stiffly in the chair. She felt very tired suddenly, and needed to be alone to gather her jumbled thoughts. 'I'm sure you can justify to yourself what you did a thousand times over, but at this moment I feel as though I never want to see you again.'

'Oh, Eve, no . . .'

'I'm sorry,' said Eve wearily. 'I just can't handle this. Please leave.' She stared at her hands in her lap. 'Just get out!'

Meg got up and left without another word.

After Meg had gone, Eve sat staring into the fire, bewildered and bruised by this massive emotional upheaval.

She felt as though she'd lost the best friend she'd ever had, and it was almost as painful as losing Ken had been. Meg had become so dear to her, she could never have imagined that such a dark secret lay between them.

If nothing else, this whole miserable business had banished any lingering illusions about Ken she'd been harbouring after hearing the gossip. The man she had worshipped had been an accomplished liar to whom the sanctity of marriage had meant nothing. She felt such a failure, and such a damned fool.

How she hadn't realised that Ken wasn't serious about their marriage was beyond her. In retrospect, it had been obvious. He hadn't wanted to build something solid, as she had, with a home of their own and a family, and had only been going along with what she wanted for the sake of domestic harmony. He hadn't wanted that sort of commitment.

However, Ken wasn't the issue now. Meg was. Eve felt at once violently resentful towards her, yet desolate at the thought of losing her friendship. Obviously it couldn't continue as it had been: the loss of trust was too great, the humiliation too painful. Could any friendship survive such a blow?

A total split would have far-reaching effects, since they were sisters-in-law and business partners. Eve wasn't a vindictive person. Despite everything she'd said to Meg in anger, she could understand the other woman's dilemma when she'd realised who Eve was. She could also see that both she and Meg were victims.

But this didn't lessen the feeling of betrayal, or alter the fact that Eve's perception of Meg had changed completely. Eve felt robbed of dignity by the fact that she and Meg shared intimate knowledge of a man Eve had thought her own. What a mess, she thought, going over to the sideboard and pouring herself another drink, a large one this time.

Driving home through a blur of tears, Meg admonished herself for being pathetic. What had she expected? Had she seriously believed that Eve would simply brush aside the fact that her best friend had been sleeping with her husband and tell her not to worry about it?

Meg brooded on the fact that she had made two big mistakes. The first was having the affair with Ken; the

second was becoming friends with Eve after she'd realised
that she was Ken's widow. The affair she deeply regretted,
but she could feel no remorse for her friendship with Eve,
because it had meant so much to them both. There was
no point in deluding herself. Eve would never feel the
same about her again. Would you, she asked herself, in
her position?

She thought back to the cause of all the trouble – Ken
Peters – and reflected on how their relationship had come
about.

He'd pursued her from their very first meeeting, even
though she'd constantly rejected him on account of his being
married. But she'd been attracted to him despite herself and
he'd been the most determined suitor. A fatal combination.
She remembered how he would wait for her outside the
boutique when she finished work of an evening; when she
ignored him he would follow her home and ring her doorbell
persistently until she'd had to let him in.

When he'd finally convinced her that his marriage was
over, she'd fallen for him in a very big way, had become
almost manic about him, in fact. This was why she'd been
careless enough to be seen with him in public, and also
the reason she'd become pregnant, the latter being the only
good thing to come out of the whole sordid affair.

Besotted with him, she'd stayed at home of an evening
waiting for his calls and cried herself to sleep when he didn't
ring. She'd lost weight because she was always too hyped
up with longing to eat properly; she'd even lost interest in
her business for a while. Permanently charged with sexual
energy, she had lived on her nerves, never sure when she
would be seeing him again.

Compared to what she now felt for George, her feelings
for Ken seemed insignificant. As overwhelming as her
passion for him had been at the time, she could see now that
it had been nothing more than an extreme case of physical
attraction. She could hardly bear to remember how much in
thrall she'd been to Ken. But she wasn't going to be allowed

to forget it now that their relationship had emerged from the past to come between herself and Eve.

In some small corner of her heart, Meg was relieved that it was out in the open. It had been a lonely feeling, with not another living soul knowing who the father of her child was. The truth would have to come out at some point anyway. Because when Becky was old enough, she had the right to know who her father had been. The time for that was later on. But as the secret was out between her and Eve, there was someone else she must tell, without delay. Before he had the chance to hear about it from anyone else.

After a sleepless night, Eve could hardly drag herself out of bed the next morning. The last thing she felt like being was sociable. But Lil was expecting her and Josie for Sunday lunch with Bart, and she wouldn't let her down, especially not on New Year's Eve. So she got herself and Josie ready and prepared to put on a cheerful face.

'I supposed you two young things are going out celebrating tonight . . . to see the new year in?' said Lil as Eve struggled through a roast beef meal, forcing herself to eat so as not to offend Bart's mother.

'Yeah, we're going to Eve's parents' place for a bit of a knees-up,' replied Bart.

'You can join us if you like,' said Eve. 'Mum and Dad would be delighted, and I'll come and collect you in the car.'

'It's nice of you to offer, love, but I prefer to see the new year in at home,' the older woman explained. 'Me and Nora will have a drop o' something at midnight, though, eh, Nora?'

'That's right.' Nora waved her hand towards the dish of roast potatoes. 'Any more, anyone?'

Bart helped himself, but Eve shook her head.

'So, who's gonna be at your party then?' enquired Lil conversationally.

'Just the family and some of Mum and Dad's friends and neighbours, I expect,' said Eve.

'Sounds like the perfect recipe for tomorrow's hangover,' chuckled Lil. 'And having Meg and George there means you've got some company of your own age.'

Eve's stomach knotted at the thought of having to socialise with Meg. She didn't know how she was going to get through it. But she said, 'Yes, I should think we'll have a good time.'

When they'd finished eating, Bart suggested that he and Eve go for a walk because he needed to stretch his legs.

'It's too cold for you, Mum, and for Josie, so can she stay here with you and Nora for half an hour?' he asked.

'Certainly, son.' Lil was happy to agree. 'We'll be glad to have her to ourselves.'

As soon as they had shut the front door behind them, Bart said, 'I only suggested we go for a walk so I can talk to you on your own. I want to know what the matter is.'

'Nothing,' she lied.

'Do me a favour,' he said, turning to her and holding her gently by the arms. 'You may have convinced Mum and Nora with your award-winning performance, but I know better.'

She sighed. 'I should have known you'd see right through me.'

They walked down the concrete path out of the flats towards the street. The cold penetrated right through to the bone, angry dark skies making everything look even greyer in this tightly packed industrial suburb once nicknamed 'The Washtub of London'. That had been in the nineteenth century, when Acton's country estates were sold for cheap housing – attracting large numbers of workers to the area for employment in the town's many laundries.

As they were both shivering violently, they took shelter in Bart's van, which was parked in the road, and she told him what had happened.

'Meg – having an affair with your husband!' he exclaimed when she'd finished. 'Bloody hell. No wonder you're upset.'

'I feel so betrayed, Bart,' she said, tears streaming down her face. 'Meg and I have been closer than sisters. Now I feel that I've never really known her at all.'

He held her close while she sobbed. 'You're bound to feel gutted after a shock like that,' he said, taking a clean handkerchief out of his pocket and handing it to her. 'Anyone would be.'

'I can still hardly believe it,' she said into the handkerchief.

'Still, it isn't as though you were best mates when she was actually involved with Ken, is it?' he pointed out on a more positive note. 'That really would have been a betrayal.'

'She still deceived me, though, didn't she?' Eve reminded him.

'Yeah, she did, no one can deny that,' he agreed. 'But I suppose she felt she didn't have any choice if she wanted to stay friends with you.'

'I feel as though I don't want to have anything more to do with her,' Eve told him. 'And that breaks my heart too.'

'It'll be very awkward if you split with her completely, won't it?' he asked.

'Because we're related and in business together?' she said.

'Yeah.'

'You're right, it will,' she agreed, wiping her eyes. 'I just don't know what to do. At the moment I can't bear the thought of even being in the same room as her. The last thing I want to do is go to the party tonight.'

'Is it worth losing a good friend because of something that happened a long time ago, before you even knew her?' he wondered aloud. 'Something that's irrelevant to your life now?'

'I've thought of nothing else since last night and I just don't see how we can stay friends,' she told him. 'I mean, how can you come back from something like this?'

Bart pondered the question. 'I don't know if it's possible for you to get back on to your old footing with her,' he said, 'but you can't cut her out of your life completely, not without making things uncomfortable for the rest of the family. And you can't run a business successfully with someone you're not on speaking terms with.'

'I can't work with her, not after this.' Eve was very distressed.

'You could try,' he suggested. 'You enjoy your work; why upset everything because of an emotional issue like this?'

'I could ask her to buy me out of the business, I suppose,' she suggested. 'The shop's done well so she can afford it.'

'I don't think that would be a good idea,' he responded instinctively.

'No?'

'No. Not while it's all still so fresh in your mind,' he said. 'You might feel different later on when you're over the shock. It won't be easy working with her, but the alternative could be worse.'

'I must admit, I don't want to leave the partnership,' she said.

'Then don't,' he advised her. 'Not yet, anyway. See how it goes.'

'Mm. The more immediate problem is facing her tonight at the party,' she confessed. 'New Year's Eve is supposed to be a celebration, a time of warmth and love towards your fellow kind. I feel more like murdering her than being nice.'

'New Year is also a time for looking forward and making resolutions,' he said pointedly.

'But I can't just sweep it under the carpet and pretend nothing's changed,' she told him emphatically.

'Course you can't,' he agreed. 'You'll have to bluff it out for the sake of the family, though, at least for tonight. And I'll be with you to give you moral support.' He grinned. 'I'll make sure you don't lose control and scratch her eyes out.'

'Oh, Bart,' she said, her eyes still wet with tears, 'you're such a tonic.'

'All part of the service,' he said, kissing her on the lips.

'We'd better get back,' she said, drawing away 'The others will be wondering where we've got to.' She shivered. 'It's freezing out here too. I'm like a block of ice.'

'We can nip round to my place for half an hour to get warmed up, if you like,' he joked, brows raised saucily. 'Take your mind off things.'

'Trust you to turn this into an opportunity,' she said, but her rebuke was affectionate.

'Just trying to cheer you up.' He put his hand on her face and turned it to his. 'And it's worked. I can see the beginnings of a smile.'

Her self-esteem had taken a knock after learning about Ken and Meg. The fact that it had been a long time ago didn't mean she wasn't left with a sense of rejection. Bart's light-hearted lustfulness helped her to feel normal again. 'We're in the middle of visiting your mother, remember,' she said, opening her door.

'Oh well, it was a nice idea,' he said.

'Yes, it was, Bart,' she agreed softly, and they walked back to his mother's arm in arm.

When they got back to the flat, Lil and Nora were helping Josie to dress her doll in the new outfit Lil had crocheted for it, happily hindered by Marbles, who was stretched out across Lil's lap, purring loudly, paws dangling.

Nora greeted Bart with the news that Rudy had been on the phone and wanted him to return the call as soon as he got back. Bart went to the telephone in the hall while Eve chatted to the others in the living room.

'Watcha, Rudy,' greeted Bart. 'I understand you wanted to talk to me.'

'I'll say I wanna talk to you,' said Rudy, his voice high with excitement.

'Why, what's on?'

'Have I got a gem of a job for you, Bartie boy?' he told him. 'You're really on your way this time, mate. This is the big break.'

'Tell me about it, then.'

'It's only a booking at Peaches Club,' Rudy informed him triumphantly. 'What do you think about that?'

'Not *the* Peaches . . . in the West End?'

'The very one.'

'Blimey!'

'My thoughts exactly.'

'How did that come about?'

'The singer they had booked for the cabaret has been taken ill suddenly and they need someone to fill in for him at short notice,' Rudy explained. 'The manager has been ringing round all the agents to try to find a replacement, but all the suitable acts are booked up, this being New Year's Eve. So he gave me a bell . . . only as a last resort, but it doesn't matter about that as long as it gets you out there, gets you noticed by people who matter.'

'Oh, it's tonight,' said Bart, with a sickening thud of disappointment.

'I realise it doesn't give you much time. But whatever plans you've made, cancel 'em,' commanded Rudy. 'This is big – the break we've been waiting for.'

For once Rudy's optimism was justified. Peaches Club was a classy nightclub much used by showbiz types. The mere thought of appearing there made Bart catch his breath. He stood the chance of being seen by people who had influence in the business. And even if there was no one special in the audience tonight, the mere fact that he had appeared at Peaches would help to bring in decent class bookings in the future. He wanted to do this job – *so much*. It would be professional suicide to let the chance pass him by. But still he said, 'I can't do it, Rudy, sorry.'

'What?'

'I can't do it,' repeated Bart.

'Can't do it?' Rudy shouted into the phone. 'Have you gone raving mad?'

'Sorry, mate, but I've made other arrangements for tonight,' he explained.

There was a short silence followed by an explosion down the line. 'I'm talking about Peaches Club in the West End, not some grotty back-street pub.'

'I know that.'

'So, what's all this nonsense about your not doing it?' Rudy demanded.

'There's something else I have to do.'

'Nothing can be more important than a chance like this,' insisted Rudy. 'Not for a struggling performer like yourself.'

Bart had a mental image of himself on stage at Peaches Club; felt the songs pouring out of him, could hear the applause. 'That's where you're wrong, Rudy,' he told him. 'There is something more important, and that's what I shall do.'

'If it's something you're doing with Eve, she'll understand why you have to cancel when you tell her about the gig,' said Rudy. 'She wouldn't want you to miss a chance like this, not Eve. She wants you to get on.'

'I'm not going to tell her, and neither are you,' said Bart firmly. 'She needs me with her tonight and that's where I'll be.'

'You can't do this to me,' said Rudy. 'I've more or less committed you.'

'Then you shouldn't have,' Bart admonished. 'Not without checking with me first.'

'You might never get another chance like this one.'

'I realise that. It's just one of those things.' Turning this job down was almost a physical pain. 'As much as I'd love to do it, it just isn't possible . . . not tonight.'

'Bart, please, just think it over.' Rudy was pleading now.

'Sorry, mate.' He had to speak quickly and bring the

matter to a close in case temptation proved too great for him. 'You'll just have to tell them to find someone else.'

'But . . .'

'Thanks for thinking of me. Cheers,' said Bart, and put the receiver down.

He stayed where he was for a few moments, trying to come to terms with his disappointment and compose himself.

When he eventually went back into the living room, Eve looked up and asked, 'Everything all right?'

'Fine.'

'Did Rudy have a job for you?'

'Yeah.'

'Anything interesting?'

'Just a run-of-the-mill booking for next month,' he fibbed, because if Eve knew the truth she would insist on him taking the booking. But she was in a state of trauma, and tonight his place was with her.

'Is everything all right, Eve?' enquired her father. They met on the landing; she'd been to check on Josie, who was asleep in her parents' spare bed, and he'd just come out of the bathroom. The raucous sound of New Year celebrations drifted up from downstairs, excitement growing as midnight approached. Pop music could be heard above the talk and laughter, and there was some rather tuneless singing from the party guests. 'You seem a bit quiet.'

'Everything's fine,' she replied. 'Josie's fast asleep.'

'I'm not talking about Josie,' he said. 'I'm talking about you, you don't seem yourself.'

'I'm absolutely fine.' She still hadn't spoken to Meg, because every time she looked at her she wanted to hit her for not being the open and honest person Eve had thought she was. She wanted to make her suffer for wrecking their friendship.

'I thought perhaps you'd got something on your mind,' he said.

'Nothing special,' she replied.

'Well, I've always been a good listener,' he said. 'And no one would miss us for ten minutes while we have a chat up here.'

Her father had always been ultra-perceptive to her moods, for as far back as she could remember. She could fool everyone else, even her mother, but she couldn't fool him. There was nothing she would like more at this moment than to bare her soul to him and have the benefit of his advice. But this was a party, a time for fun and laughter, not emotional problems. Anyway, Meg was his daughter-in-law, and both Eve's parents were fond of her.

If Meg's secret came out, it wouldn't be Eve's doing. Meg would probably decide to make it common knowledge eventually, since one day she would have to tell Becky who her father was. But that would be Meg's decision. No one would hear about it from Eve.

She smiled at her father. The fact that he was there for her made her feel better; it always had. 'Honestly, I'm fine,' she said.

'Well, you know where I am if you need me,' he told her.

'Thanks, Dad.'

'There must be something in the air tonight,' he said. 'Meg looks as if she's got the worries of the world on her shoulders as well.'

'Does she?'

'She's trying to hide it, but you can tell something's upset her.'

Reminded of what a close-knit family they were and how any ripples on the family pond would be felt by everyone, Eve made a firm decision on her course of action.

'You and your extra-sensory perception,' she teased him lightly. 'Come on, let's go downstairs and join the party.'

Meg was standing next to George when Eve went into the

crowded living room. Eve beckoned to her to come outside into the hallway.

'Look,' began Eve when they were out of earshot of the others, 'you and I are going to have to meet at family occasions like this all the time, and run our business together, so the only sensible thing to do is to try and put what happened behind us and get on with things.'

Meg smiled uncertainly. 'Well, yes, that's fine with me.'

It would be, wouldn't it, you bitch? thought Eve with a vehemence that made her want to weep with fury. You're the one who's in the wrong. It's your fault I feel bitter and twisted. But she bit back her rage because that sort of attitude wasn't going to help either of them. 'It'll make things difficult for everybody if we're at loggerheads,' she said.

'You're right.'

'So . . . let's be very adult about it and try to carry on regardless.'

'Oh, that would be great, Eve.' Meg's voice was warm with relief and she moved towards her friend with her arms outstretched.

Highly charged with emotion, Eve shrank back. She could just about manage polite conversation, but anything more than that was out of the question. 'So, who's looking after your daughter tonight?' she asked to help pass an awkward moment.

'My neighbour,' said Meg. 'I was lucky to get anyone on New Year's Eve. My parents have gone to a dinner dance.'

'You could have brought Becky with you and put her to bed with Josie if you were stuck,' said Eve in a stilted tone.

'I would have if I hadn't been able to get anyone,' was Meg's reply.

Eve nodded. The atmosphere was dreadful, as though a wall stood between them. She and Meg weren't used to conversations punctuated with awkward silences, and it came hard.

'Well, we'd better go in the other room and join the party,' suggested Eve because she felt so uncomfortable. 'Bart will be wondering where I am.'

Meg nodded and they went to join the others. Eve was trembling all over.

The small room was crowded with people at various stages of inebriation. The Christmas decorations had lost their relevance and seemed stale, curtains of cigarette smoke hanging around the paper chains. Eve knew this would be one New Year's Eve she would always remember but want to forget, the year her illusions had been brutally shattered.

But when everyone linked hands in a circle for 'Auld Lang Syne', she made a resolution. She couldn't forget what had happened but she could make every effort to push it to the back of her mind and get things back to how they had once been between herself and Meg.

If tonight was anything to go by, it wasn't going to be easy. But perhaps with the passing of time her feeling of alienation towards Meg would lessen.

She turned to Bart next to her and smiled. He winked and grinned back. Thank God he'd been with her tonight, she thought, through a mist of tears. New Year always made her emotional. This year she wanted to sob her heart out. But she opened her mouth and joined in the singing with brio.

Opposite his sister in the circle, next to his wife, George was also making a resolution. All day he'd been trying to come to terms with the bombshell Meg had dropped on him last night when she'd got home from Eve's.

Meg and Ken Peters, he could still hardly believe it. His dead brother-in-law was the father of his own stepdaughter. It took some getting used to. He'd never quite trusted Ken, but Meg was the last person he would have expected to have an affair with a married man. The fact that it had been his own sister's husband somehow made it seem worse.

But it *shouldn't* matter to him. As Meg had so rightly pointed out, the affair had happened before either he or Eve had known her. Why should she be punished for a mistake she'd made before she'd ever set eyes on them? He reminded himself that he had taken her for better or worse, and he'd taken her child unconditionally.

His intellect told him she was right. But his emotions were more difficult to deal with. He didn't want to be angry with Meg for hurting his sister, but he couldn't help it. He was also disappointed to have his own illusions about Meg destroyed. To make things worse, he knew he was being unreasonable. Meg hadn't been some innocent young girl when their relationship had begun. He'd known she'd been around. *The woman had a child, for God's sake*. But Meg and Ken Peters – it was so damned sleazy!

This reaction was unfair, he was aware of that. After all, he was no saint himself. He hadn't lived the pure life before he'd met Meg. He *had* drawn the line at married women, though.

Whatever happened between Eve and Meg, he was determined not to let this blast from the past affect his marriage. Meg was the best thing that had ever happened to him, and he loved her deeply.

He sang heartily, vowing to put the whole thing where it belonged – in the past – and look forward to a happy new year of 1968.

Chapter Fourteen

The fashion trend known as the Romantic Look, which had been so strong during 1967, continued into the following year. Velvet was ubiquitous. Jackets with wide floppy collars and revers, frilly blouses, and shirts with high cravat necklines and lace ruffles were popular with both sexes.

One of Britain's most exciting new designers, Zandra Rhodes – who had originally trained as a textile designer – created unusual combinations of prints and fabrics which she made into billowing kaftan-style dresses. Mini-skirts were still hugely popular with the majority of women, though, even though mid-calf-length skirts and dresses were pushed on to the market by designers anxious for a new proportion for their clothes.

'The midi is so ageing to women, don't you think?' Meg said to Eve at one of their weekly boutique meetings towards the end of the winter.

'Positively matronly,' agreed Eve.

'I can't see it catching on.'

'Me neither,' said Eve. 'But you never know with fashion.'

'You're right about that. If a thing becomes "the look", we all start wearing it and think it looks terrific, no matter how much we hated it at first,' Meg pointed out. 'It's just a question of getting used to it.'

'You get used to anything in time,' remarked Eve casually.

Meg's mood changed instantly. Tormented by compunction about her affair with Ken, she saw accusation where none was intended. 'Meaning that you've had to get used to a certain fact, I suppose.' The words came out as though of their own volition. 'If you've got something to say, I wish you'd come right out and say it instead of hinting.'

'I wasn't hinting at anything,' denied Eve truthfully. 'Must you misunderstand everything I say?'

'How can I help it when you keep coming out with snide remarks?' she said.

Eve wanted to say, 'Let's be friends again and stop this sniping that's tearing us apart.' But instead she said, 'It isn't my fault your guilty conscience is making you hear things that aren't there.'

Meg tried to say, 'This friction is killing me, please let's stop before it drives a permanent wedge between us.' What she actually said was, 'You'd better speak up, I can't hear you properly from where you are up there on the moral high ground.'

'Oh, for heaven's sake . . .'

This was how it was between them. Fuelled by unwanted resentment on Eve's part and guilt on Meg's, hostility flared at the slightest provocation. In this tense climate, the most innocent comment could lead to a full-scale row.

The bickering went on for month after month through a year that saw violent anti-Vietnam War demonstrations in London, an upsurge in cults and Eastern religions, and the mini-skirt become so brief as to be charged by the inch at the dry cleaner's.

Although Eve desperately wanted everything to be as before between herself and Meg, and continually strived to make it happen, she just couldn't do it. Dialogue consisted of stilted conversation with bitter undertones. The chit-chat and laughter they had once taken for granted was a thing of the past. As well as being thoroughly unpleasant at a personal level, acrimony between business partners was not commercially expedient. Judgements were impaired by the constant presence of raw emotion.

Things finally came to a head one day in the autumn of

that year after their weekly meeting; they were trying to be sociable by discussing the new hit musical *Hair*, which extolled the joys of hippie life and was thought by some people to be quite shocking, with its nudity and use of the four-letter word. Neither of them had seen the show, but much had been written about it in the newspapers. Apparently thirteen members of the cast had appeared on stage naked at the première, the day after stage censorhip was abolished.

'I wouldn't have the nerve to stand up in front of an audience with nothing on,' observed Eve.

'Nudity is nothing to be ashamed of,' said Meg sharply, glaring at Eve across the desk.

'I didn't say it was,' Eve defended, her hackles rising. 'I was only saying that I, *personally*, wouldn't have the courage to bare myself to an audience on a stage. Would you?'

'If I was an actress and it was necessary to the part I was playing, yes, I'd do it,' said Meg in a belligerent manner.

'It takes a lot of guts, even for an experienced actress,' said Eve.

'We're not in the dark ages now, you know,' Meg reminded her. 'Anything goes these days. That's why stage censorship was abolished, so that the theatre can give a broader aspect to its themes and be in tune with the times.'

'Some of us are more uninhibited than others, I suppose,' said Eve.

Meg stared at her, tight-lipped and furious. 'Oh God, here we go again,' she said accusingly. 'I suppose you're implying that I'm some sort of moral degenerate?'

'I wasn't suggesting any such thing.' Eve could feel the situation moving out of control, and there seemed nothing she could do to stop it. The bad feeling was too strong.

'Yes you were,' retorted Meg. 'Perhaps if you'd been less inhibited, your husband might not have turned to me.'

This was the first time the affair, as such, had been mentioned outright since the time of the confession. Up until now it had been all strong innunendo. Now they were both going for the jugular, thought Eve miserably. 'And if you'd been a little less eager, maybe he wouldn't have.'

'He was the eager one,' said Meg nastily. 'I can assure you of that.'

'I suppose you couldn't get a man of your own?' Eve was appalled at what she was saying but couldn't stem the flow of words, her eyes filling with hot, angry tears. 'So you had to take someone else's.'

'It wasn't like that,' Meg protested, her eyes also bright and wet. 'You were probably so cold, he was glad of some warmth and comfort. I bet you would only do it in the dark.'

Now Meg had gone too far. Eve had to keep her hands tightly clasped to stop herself from slapping her. 'How dare you?'

'I bet it's true,' said Meg, hating herself but unable to stop.

'At least I don't drop my knickers for the first man who asks me, regardless of whether or not he's married,' said Eve.

'I don't suppose anyone ever asks you to.' Meg couldn't believe she'd said that.

'You spoilt bitch,' accused Eve. 'You've always had everything you want, that's why you're so greedy. I suppose it gives you a real buzz to take something that belongs to someone else.'

'Ken didn't belong to you,' Meg said. 'No one belongs to anyone.'

'True,' agreed Eve, 'but how would you feel if some other woman did with George what you did with Ken? You just ask yourself that.'

Meg winced at such an unbearable thought. Whilst making her even more painfully aware of what Eve must have suffered over the affair, she still couldn't stop the argument.

'I'd hate it, of course I would,' she admitted. 'But I still say that I don't own George any more than you owned Ken.'

'No, but as his wife, you have the right to his fidelity.'

'You're just playing with words,' said Meg. 'Isn't it time you grew up?'

There was a brief hiatus while Eve came to a sudden decision. 'Yeah, you're right, it is time I grew up, and I think I just have. At least, I've become adult enough to accept the fact that it isn't working between us any more. It's high time I broke away from you and the boutique.'

'Oh?' Meg stared at her, blue eyes wide with fear.

'I want out, Meg.'

'What!' Her voice was high-pitched with shock and anxiety.

'I want you to buy my share of the business – dissolve our partnership,' said Eve.

'But, you can't leave . . .'

'I have to,' said Eve. 'And I hope you'll co-operate.'

They were both whey-faced and trembling. Neither of them wanted this. But although Eve had spoken on impulse, she knew it was the only way forward, and she suspected that Meg realised it too. You couldn't run a business efficiently when you were constantly at war with your partner.

'If that's what you want, then good riddance,' snapped Meg, but she didn't mean it.

Every word Eve uttered was torn from her heart. 'We'd better put it in the hands of a solicitor right away, then,' she said shakily. 'Because I don't want to stay on here for a minute longer than I have to.'

'There's no need for you to wait for it to go through legally,' Meg told her. 'You can collect your things and leave right away.'

'Good idea,' said Eve, rising abruptly, her legs like jelly. 'I'll come back to discuss the details another time when we're both feeling calmer.'

And she left on the verge of tears.

'Are you sure you've not been too hasty?' queried Bart over a glass of wine with Eve that evening when Josie was in bed. 'You've walked out of a good business and a friendship that's meant so much to you.'

'I know. But what else could I do?' she asked, raising her hands in a helpless gesture. 'Meg and I couldn't go on as we have been. It was destroying us both.'

'Mm, I can understand that,' he said. 'What will you do now?'

'I've decided to open a boutique of my own,' she informed him. 'I'll use the money from the partnership, and get a loan against the house to make up the difference.'

'That's very brave of you.'

She made a face. 'It's a bit daunting, I must admit,' she told him, 'setting up from scratch. But I don't see what else I can do, except get a job working for someone else.'

'That would be easier,' he suggested.

'But not the right thing for me.'

'Perhaps not.' He seemed rather preoccupied.

'Not after running a business,' she went on. 'Anyway, being my own boss means I can be flexible about hours.'

'That side of things will be more difficult for you, though, without Meg to share the hours and the work load,' he said.

'I'll just have to make definite provision for the times I can't be at the shop,' she told him.

'Yeah.'

Noticing an air of excitement about him and realising that he had other things on his mind apart from her problems, she gave him a close look and asked, 'Has something happened?'

'Well, yeah.' He smiled sheepishly. 'It has, actually.'

'Why didn't you say?' she said in a tone of gentle admonition. 'Letting me ramble on when you've got things to tell me.'

'You were upset,' he said, 'so I thought I'd wait until we'd finished discussing your news before we got to mine.'

'It's something nice, isn't it?' she said, managing to smile.

He nodded.

'Well, tell me then, before I die of curiosity,' she urged him.

'I've been offered some regular stage work,' he told her. 'Resident compère and singer in a really classy club. The money's good and it'll be steady all-year-round employment.'

'Oh, well done, Bart.' She went over to his chair and hugged him. 'I'm *so* pleased for you.'

'I'm chuffed to bits myself,' he confessed.

'I should think so too, it's marvellous news, and very well deserved.' She perched next to him with her arm around his shoulder. 'How did it come about?'

'The manager of this upmarket club was out on a stag-night pub crawl last weekend and happened to call in at the place where I was working while I was doing my act. They were slumming it, as blokes do on a stag night,' he explained. 'Anyway, he came to see me after the show. It turns out he's looking for someone to compère the show at his club and thought I was the man for the job.'

'What does the job actually entail, though?' she wondered.

'More or less the same as I do now . . . I'll sing a few songs, tell a few gags,' he explained. 'But I'll introduce the other acts as well, and open and close the show.'

'Sounds great.' She looked at him. 'This happened *last* weekend,' she said. 'All that time and you didn't tell me?'

'I wasn't sure if he was serious,' he explained. 'But he got on the blower to me today, and the job's mine if I want it.'

'Does this mean you can give up your window-cleaning round?'

He gave her an odd look. 'Oh yeah,' he said. 'I'd give that up.'

She rose and went back to her own armchair, looking at him studiously. 'There's some sort of drawback, isn't there?' she said.

251

There was a pause; he cleared his throat. 'The job is in Spain,' he blurted out.

'Spain?'

'Yeah, a big hotel with a nightclub attached that caters for British expats as well as holidaymakers and stays open all the year round,' he informed her. 'This manager geezer is back in the UK for a break after the summer season, before all the pre-Christmas parties get underway.'

'I see.'

'There's another reason why I didn't say anything to you about it,' he explained.

'Oh?'

'I'm still not sure whether or not to take the job,' he informed her.

'Your mother?' she surmised. 'You're worried about leaving her.'

'No, it isn't that. Mum will be fine with Nora to look after her,' he said. 'And as I'll be earning steady money, I won't have any trouble paying Nora's wages. I haven't told Mum yet, but she'll be keen for me to take the job. You know how much she wants me to be a full-time entertainer.'

'I certainly do.' Eve was trying not to show how devastated she was about the prospect of his going away, because she didn't want to spoil it for him.

'You're the reason I've been so uncertain,' he told her frankly. 'I couldn't bear the thought of leaving you. But now that you're going to end your partnership with Meg and make a new start, you could come with me.'

'You're asking me to go with you to live in Spain?' she exclaimed.

'That's right,' he said eagerly. 'I didn't say anything before now because I wasn't sure if you were serious about leaving the partnership and I didn't want to put pressure on you.' He paused, looking at her tenderly. 'But as you've made your mind up about that, marry me, Eve, and come to Spain?'

There was nothing in the world she would rather do. The

idea of being with Bart, away from this whole sorry mess, was extremely tempting. But she had responsibilities here. 'We both know that isn't possible,' she said.

'Why not?' he asked. 'You're at a crossroads in your life, about to start something new. You could open a shop in Spain. I understand there are plenty of opportunities out there.'

'And what about Josie?'

'She'd love it . . . the three of us together, it would be great.'

'She starts school next year.'

'There's bound to be an English school she can go to nearby,' he said. 'There are lots of British people living there.

'It isn't just the schooling, Bart,' she said. 'There are other things too.'

'Like the fact that you don't want to marry me,' he said, twisting her heart with his look of disappointment.

'It isn't that. 'She sighed. 'I can't take Josie away from the people she loves here, her grandparents, my brother . . . it wouldn't be fair.'

'Oh.' He was obviously hurt. 'But she'd have us, and she'd soon make friends. Our relatives could come out to visit.'

'I know the job is regular as far as anything in showbusiness can be,' she went on, 'but it might not be a long-term thing. It could be that Josie just gets settled and we'd have to uproot her again. My daughter has the right to stability and it's my job to provide it.'

'Showbusiness always involves travel once you do it for real,' he pointed out. 'You have to go where the work is.'

'But if you were based in England, at least Josie and I could stay put while you went away to work,' she said. 'We wouldn't have to relocate at the end of every contract.'

'I may not be able to give her stability, but I can give her love.'

'I know that, Bart . . . I'm sorry.'

'I accept the fact that Josie must come first, but I think you're using her as an excuse,' he said.

'Oh, Bart, don't say things like that,' she begged him.

'I think you're still clinging to the memory of your dead husband,' he said. 'That's what this is all about, not Josie.'

'Bart, don't . . .'

'If you were over him, you wouldn't let something that happened years ago ruin your friendship with Meg,' he declared.

'Ken isn't the reason for my split with Meg,' she denied, her voice quivering 'I've made it clear that that happened because of a loss of trust for Meg.'

'Okay, okay, I'm sorry, I shouldn't have said that,' he said with genuine contrition. 'But Ken still lives on inside you, stops you fully committing yourself to anyone else.'

'Perhaps he does still matter,' she admitted, impatient because she was feeling so wretched. 'I was married to the man, for heaven's sake, and I loved him, regardless of the fact that he obviously didn't feel the same about me.'

'It's past, Eve.'

'Look, Bart, I'm so damned confused I hardly know what I feel,' she said, her voice rising. 'This morning I had a massive row with someone who used to be my closest friend and I was forced to end my partnership with her, which not only leaves me without my friend but without my income too, with a daughter to support. While I'm still trying to recover from that, you ask me to up sticks and go to Spain with you. Don't you think I have enough on my mind?'

'You needn't have any of those worries,' he told her. 'I'll take care of everything. You know me, Eve, if it doesn't work out for me in showbusiness in Spain, I'll always find a way of earning a living.'

'It would be all too easy for me to say yes, and let you take the worries off my shoulders,' she said. 'But that isn't my way. Anyway, you need to concentrate on yourself. Not to be worrying about whether or not Josie and I are settling in, whether or not you can feed us and pay the rent.'

'But I want to do it, because I love you,' he said simply.

She swallowed hard on a lump in her throat, tears welling beneath her lids. 'Can't you see, Bart, I don't want to turn to you because it would easier,' she tried to explain. 'You're worth more to me than that. I have to finish what I started when I went into business with Meg. I have to prove that I can stand on my own two feet.'

'I take it that's a definite no, then,' he said, his voice hardening.

Life without him was a bleak prospect indeed, but her circumstances didn't offer a viable alternative. 'It has to be, I'm afraid,' she said sadly, biting her lip. 'Because I'm simply not in a position to get married and go abroad.'

'I see.' He stared broodingly into his glass for what seemed like forever. She'd never seen him so solemn. 'Okay,' he said with chilling finality, 'I understand what you're saying, and I won't ask you again, I can promise you that.'

She knew he meant forever, and it hurt. 'I wouldn't expect you to,' she said.

'I know that.'

Tension pulled tight between them. 'At least this way you can go to Spain and give the job all you've got,' she said, hoping to ease the atmosphere.

'I still haven't actually accepted,' he said, a hint of uncertainty creeping into his resolute manner.

At that moment she knew she only had to ask him not to go to Spain and he would stay here with her, under any terms she cared to name. She had never needed him more than she did at this difficult time in her life. But she said, 'You *must* take the job, Bart. You've made provision for your mother, so there's nothing to hold you back. If you don't go, you'll be letting her down as well as yourself. This way she can stop feeling guilty about your having to clean windows to support her.'

He pondered on this, then his eyes gleamed with determination and she knew that his final decision had been made. 'Yeah, you're right. I'd be a fool to turn it down.'

'When do they want you to start?' she enquired, dreading his reply.

'As soon as possible,' he said. 'Their current man has agreed to stay until they find a replacement but is keen to go because he's got another job. There's quite a bit of work for entertainers on the Costa del Sol, apparently, some of it all year round. I wouldn't have taken this job if it had been seasonal, though, not with Mum to think of.'

'I'll miss you, Bart,' she said from the bottom of her heart.

'I'll miss you too.' He looked at her lingeringly but made no attempt to embrace her as he normally would have done at such an emotional moment.

With a sinking heart, she realised how serious the situation between them was. Coming on the same day as the break-up with Meg, it was almost too much to bear.

Meg, too, was in a state of emotional turmoil that same evening, after another blazing row with George over supper. Ever since the confession at the end of the previous year, their life together had degenerated into a battleground. He'd tried to be mature about her affair with Ken, had sworn it would make no difference to their own relationship. But it had nudged its way into their lives despite all his good intentions.

The parlous state of their marriage wasn't all his fault, Meg admitted that. Her strained relations with Eve these past months had made her edgy at home and quick to take offence. A discussion with George over something as indisputable as the weather could escalate into a major slanging match with the emphasis always shifting on to that wretched affair. This latest altercation had flared up when she'd told him what had happened between her and Eve that day.

'You'll find it hard to manage without her, won't you?' he said with genuine concern.

'I'm quite capable of running a business on my own,' she pointed out in a curt manner, because she was worried and upset.

'I know that,' he was quick to assure her. He had always admired her business acumen.

'It doesn't sound much like it.'

'I meant from the point of view that you've got used to sharing the hours and the responsibility,' he explained.

'I managed before Eve came into the business,' she said.

'You found it easier when she joined, though,' he reminded her. 'You told me it was hard managing on your own once Becky came along.'

'There is that,' she was forced to admit.

'Is there nothing you can do to patch things up?' he enquired.

'Nothing,' she said determinedly. 'We can't hope to get along because Eve is eaten up with resentment about that blasted thing I had with Ken.'

'I suppose it's understandable,' he said. 'He *was* her husband.'

'I might have known you'd take her side,' she accused.

'I'm not taking sides . . .'

'Why do you always come out in her favour then?' she demanded.

'I don't mean to,' he told her honestly. 'If I can see her side of the argument, it's probably because she's my sister.'

'Your first loyalty is to your wife,' she heard herself say, and thought with horror that she was beginning to sound like her mother.

'If you hadn't played around with a married man, none of this would have happened,' he said, hearing the words as though some narrow-minded stranger had uttered them.

They stared at each other, she wounded, he full of remorse.

'Meg, I'm sorry,' he said. 'That was a horrible thing to say.'

'It's obviously what you were thinking, though,' she snapped.

'I'm only human,' said George, who had done his best to get the past out of his mind these last few months. 'Ever since that bloody affair came to light, there's been nothing but trouble, for you and me, as well as between you and Eve.'

'Am I to be punished for that one mistake for the rest of my life?' she asked.

'No one's punishing you,' he said. 'Not intentionally, anyway.'

'Then let it go.'

'I'm trying to, but it keeps coming back to haunt us,' he said. 'Even to the point of wrecking your business partnership.'

She abandoned her meal and got up, her face blotchy, eyes filled with tears. 'I'm sick to death of the subject and I really don't want to talk about it any more, George.'

She looked exhausted, pale and heavy-eyed. 'I love you, Meg,' he said.

And she loved him, desperately. 'If that's true, then don't let the thing with Ken wreck our marriage,' she urged him.

'We *mustn't* let that happen,' he said. 'Come and sit down and finish your meal, love.'

'I don't want any more.' She was too upset to eat and too emotional to try to put things right with George. 'I need to get out of here for an hour or so to calm down. Will you listen for Becky while I pop round to see my parents.'

'Of course I will,' he said, feeling helpless against the ugliness that had come between them. 'When have I ever refused?'

'You're well rid of her,' was Bea's reaction to the news

of her daughter's dissolved partnership. 'You managed perfectly well on your own.'

Frank didn't agree. 'You took a partner because you were finding the business too much after you had Becky,' he reminded her.

'I'll just have to get used to being on my own again, won't I?' said Meg.

'But you have a husband to consider now, as well as a daughter,' her father pointed out. 'Wouldn't it be worth trying to put things right between you and Eve, just for the sake of an easier life?'

Neither Meg's nor Eve's parents knew about 'the affair'. Keeping it from them was one thing she and Eve had agreed about. One day Meg would tell them who Becky's father was. But right now she had quite enough problems without adding her mother's shock and disapproval to the list. As far as her parents knew, the partnership was ending because of differences of opinion about business. 'No, Daddy, it just isn't working between us any more,' she told him.

'Perhaps you should look for another business partner,' he suggested.

'No.' She was adamant about that.

'But you'll find it very hard running the boutique on your own now that you have family responsibilities,' he reminded her. 'You don't want to miss Becky's childhood because you're tied to the business every hour God sends.'

'I'll have to find an assistant I can trust to stand in for me when I'm not there,' she said firmly. 'Because I'm not taking another partner.'

'Once bitten, twice shy, eh?' he said.

'Something like that,' she replied. She didn't feel like talking about the fact that no one could ever replace Eve, as a partner or a friend.

'You'll be better off without her,' Bea stated categorically. 'She's always lowered the tone of the boutique.'

'That really isn't fair, Bea,' admonished Frank. 'I've always found Eve to be a most charming young woman.'

'You would,' said Bea, 'because you've no class either.'

Meg had thought she was completely drained of emotion after the day she'd had. But a surge of fury towards her mother lashed through her. 'Daddy has plenty of class, and so has Eve. Just because someone doesn't have middle-class vowels doesn't mean they don't have class,' she said, glaring at her mother. 'Eve was the best thing that ever happened to my business and I won't have you saying bad things about her.'

'But you've fallen out with her yourself,' said Bea, who was puzzled by this attack.

'Just because Eve and I don't see eye to eye doesn't mean that I've stopped admiring and respecting her as a person,' Meg informed her.

'I was only speaking as I find,' said Bea.

'You couldn't have been, because you wouldn't be able to say such things about Eve if you had,' said Meg. 'You were just being spiteful. And rememember, it's my in-laws you're insulting . . . *my husband's family*. I suggest you don't do it again in my hearing or you and I will seriously fall out.'

'Well!' said Bea. 'You're in a funny mood tonight and that's a fact.'

'Let's all calm down and have another cup of coffee, shall we?' said the peaceable Frank. 'I'll go and put the kettle on.'

The following morning, George took time off work to call on his sister. He wanted to know what her plans were now that the partnership with Meg had ended.

'Blimey, Eve,' he exclaimed when she told him, over a cup of coffee. 'Wouldn't it be easier for you to get a job?'

'Yes, it would be easier, but that isn't what I'm going to do.'

'But setting up in business on your own . . . . ?'

'You did it.'

'Yeah, but . . .'

'You're a man,' she finished for him.

'No. That isn't what I was going to say,' he corrected firmly. 'I was going to say that I didn't have any responsibilities when I first started.'

'I see your point, George,' she said reasonably. 'But I think I'll be better able to cope working for myself rather than someone else. Shop girls aren't exactly well paid, and there'd be no question of flexible working hours to fit in with Josie.'

'Mm. There is that,' he agreed, but he still seemed doubtful.

She threw him an enquiring look. 'You were all for my going into business when I went into partnership with Meg.'

'Because you were going to be sharing the responsibility and the work,' he said. 'Doing it all on your own will be hard going.'

'Nothing worthwhile is ever easy.'

'True.' He sighed. 'If only you and Meg could work something out between you, there'd be no need for any of this.'

'We can't, so it isn't an option,' she said in an uncompromising manner.

'Yeah, I got that impression from Meg,' he said. 'She was in a right old mood last night.'

'That's understandable after what happened during the day,' said Eve, perversely defensive towards her estranged friend. 'I wasn't in the best frame of mind myself.'

'We ended up having a flaming row,' he said. 'She went off in a huff to her parents', left me looking after Becky.'

'That didn't hurt you,' she said briskly.

'I didn't say I minded . . .' he began.

'I should hope not,' she cut in. 'Meg's the best thing that ever happened to you, and the least you can do is look after her daughter on the odd occasion that she asks you.'

'I quite agree,' he said, astonished to find himself under attack.

'As long as you appreciate a good thing when you have it.'

'I do,' he said. 'But I'm at a loss to know why you've turned on me.'

'I haven't turned on you,' she said, irritable because she was still hurting from the events of yesterday and worried about the future. 'I just think you might have been a little more understanding, that's all. Your wife probably wouldn't have felt the need to go to her parents if you had been.'

He was baffled by her attitude. 'I thought you and Meg had had a major falling-out?'

'We have,' she confirmed.

'So why are you getting hot under the collar in her defence?'

'I've fallen out with her, not stopped caring about her,' she said.

'Don't the two things usually go together?' he queried.

She tutted. 'Of course not,' she said, raising her eyes. 'Why is it that men always see everything in black and white?'

'Maybe we don't function at such a deep emotional level as women,' he said.

'Surely you can see that something as delicate as human relations is never simple?'

'Yeah, I do realise that,' he said. 'I suppose I just hadn't thought it through properly.'

Women were complicated creatures and George would never claim to understand them. But knowing that his sister still cared for his wife gave him a warm glow of hope. He might be less emotionally intense than the female of the species, but he did know how much Meg was suffering because of the way things had turned sour with Eve.

Chapter Fifteen

Eve opened a boutique in West Ealing the following February, just in time for the spring range. She called it New Range. Smaller than Trend, it was very well situated, in a busy shopping area which already had some dress shops and a couple of trendy hairdressing salons that drew people from other parts of west London. Being a fair distance from Trend, it wasn't a threat to Meg.

Oddly enough, now that their break-up was an established fact, Eve found it easier to be civil when she and Meg were forced into each other's company at family occasions. During their period of enmity, they had developed a conversational technique that never went beyond polite superficiality but wasn't embarrassing for the people around them. This was important with regard to their daughters, who enjoyed being together.

The winding-up of the partnership had been achieved without conflict. Eve had received her initial investment back, plus a percentage of the increased value of the business in recognition of her contribution to its growth.

It had been a harrowing few months for her as she'd searched for suitable shop premises, negotiated a loan on her house to add to her partnership money and striven to get everything swiftly finalised so that she could start earning again. And all without Bart's warm-hearted presence to sustain her.

Most difficult of all was finding the right person to employ as her assistant; she needed someone smart, efficient and experienced in fashion retail, whom she could trust to stand in for her at the shop on a regular basis. Those applicants mature enough to be trusted with Eve's business when she wasn't there were mostly married with children and wanted either part-time hours or a job without responsibility because they had quite enough of that at home.

The answer came in Theresa, a divorcee in her late twenties with no ties, a smart appearance and a passion for clothes, which looked good on her slim figure.

'I need someone who can run the shop when I'm not here and take over at short notice if, for instance, something comes up with my daughter and I have to leave suddenly,' explained Eve at the interview. 'She's at full-time school now, but if she's ill or on holiday, I won't be here much at all, so you'll have to take charge and do the cashing-up and the banking. There'll be times, too, when I have to go out on business.'

'That'll be no problem to me,' announced Theresa, a confident redhead with heavily made-up green eyes, beehived hair and a friendly disposition. 'I used to practically run things at my other place.'

'Where was that?' enquired Eve.

'A shop in Oxford Street,' she said.

'Why did you leave?'

'Wanted something nearer to home,' she explained. 'Got fed up with being squashed on the tube every day.'

Having checked her references, Eve took Theresa on as senior sales assistant, with a junior working under her. Theresa was a diligent worker and trade gathered momentum nicely. Life fell into a pleasant working routine again for Eve, but she frequently found herself remembering those halcyon days working with Meg at Trend before things had gone wrong. No matter how loyal and efficient the staff, by the very nature of things they couldn't have the same depth of interest in the shop as the owner.

It wasn't just the business side of their partnership that Eve missed. She was nostalgic for Meg's entertaining company, her delicious outrageousness, her sense of fun and the moral support they had once given each other in such abundance.

Losing Bart had been more of a wrench than she'd believed possible. She would never forget the night he'd come to say goodbye.

'When are you off?' she'd asked.

'Tomorrow.'

'We'll keep in touch,' she suggested.

'I don't think that's a good idea,' he said coolly.

'Not even an occasional letter?' she asked, thinking her heart would break.

His mouth was set in a determined line. 'There's no point in dragging things out. A clean break is best as there's obviously no future for us together.'

'But surely, after all we've been to each other . . .' she began, because she couldn't bear the thought of what he was suggesting.

'You can't have it both ways, Eve,' he cut in abruptly, face grimly set, eyes smouldering with emotion. 'You've made it clear where you stand, so now we have to get on with our lives.'

She wanted to be with him so much she didn't think she could let him go. But what was she to do? Abandon her plans here and drag her daughter off to a foreign country, away from a way of life she knew and relatives who loved her? Or ask him not to go to Spain and lose the chance of a breakthrough in his career. No. Her original decision must stand, no matter how painful. She simply wasn't in a position to make the commitment he wanted from her. 'I suppose you're right,' she said sadly.

'Give Josie a kiss for me,' he said, his voice slightly distorted.

'She's asleep or you could do it yourself,' she told him.

'It's probably best this way,' he said. 'Saying goodbye might have upset her.'

'She'll miss you,' she said, struggling not to break down.

'I'll miss her too.' It was obvious from the quiver in his voice that he was finding it hard to stay in control.

They stood facing each other in Eve's living room with nothing left to say. Suddenly they were hugging each other, their tears mingling in a last heart-rending embrace. Then he was gone from her house and her life. She still couldn't remember that night without wanting to weep.

He was doing well in Spain, according to his mother, from whom Eve received regular bulletins. She visited her whether she had work to collect or not, because Lil was a friend.

'I'm kept really busy now that you and Meg have split up and I have two shops to supply,' said Lil one afternoon that spring when Eve called to see her about work.

'You must let us know if it's getting too much for you,' said Eve.

'I will, don't worry,' Lil assured her, idly fondling the cat, who was curled up on her lap. 'But I can't see that happening.'

'No?'

'Definitely not,' she confirmed. 'I'm happier than I've been in years. And why wouldn't I be when I'm being paid for something I enjoy and would be doing anyway?'

'As long as you're happy with the arrangement,' said Eve, sipping her tea.

'You changed my life, Eve, and I'll always be grateful to you for it,' said Lil, nibbling a biscuit. 'You can't imagine what it's like to be earning a little money of my own. It's made me feel like a useful human being again.'

'I'm so glad,' said Eve.

'It's a pity you didn't change my life even more by becoming my daughter-in-law,' said Lil, her shrewd gaze resting on Eve.

'Yeah, well . . . that just wasn't to be,' Eve said, lowering her eyes.

Realising that further comment would be intrusive, Lil hastily changed the subject.

'I see in the paper that Paul McCartney's got married,' she mentioned.

Eve nodded. 'I bet there'll be a few broken hearts among his fans about that,' she said. 'Some of them will take a dim view of having their heart-throb snapped up by Linda Eastman.'

'The two of them look right together, I thought,' said Lil. 'I hope it lasts.'

'Me too,' said Eve. 'But not many of these showbiz marriages do.'

'True enough,' agreed Lil. 'Let's hope this one does.'

Eve went to Marshall Gardens to watch the moon landing, since such a momentous occasion was better enjoyed in company. Josie slept upstairs while Eve, Dot and Ned sat glued to the box in the early hours of that incredible Monday morning in July.

When they saw American astronaut Neil Armstrong step off the ladder of the lunar module to become the first person ever to set foot on the moon, Eve got goose pimples all over and both she and her mother shed tears.

'It's nothing short of a miracle,' said Ned, his eyes fixed on the screen.

'Amazing,' agreed Dot.

'It's an astounding achievement for the Americans,' commented Eve, who found the whole thing humbling.

'A giant leap for mankind, according to the astronaut,' said Ned. 'And the whole world should congratulate the Yanks.'

'I couldn't agree more.' Eve giggled. 'Hip, hip, hooray, to the USA.'

A week later the Grangers had cause for congratulations of a more personal nature when George's landlord at the car lot finally agreed to sell him the land so that he could go ahead and build showrooms. To mark the occasion, he took his wife, sister and parents out for a meal on the Sunday evening.

As it was a warm summer's evening he drove them out to the country, to an olde-worlde pub with a restaurant, near Denham.

'This is lovely, George,' said Eve, sipping wine with her fillet steak and glancing at the oak beams around the walls. 'And it's very generous of you to take us all out for a slap-up meal.'

'I've waited long enough for the geezer to sell me the land,' he said. 'I reckon it warrants a celebration.'

'You can go ahead and get some plans drawn up now, can't you?' said Meg. Although she and George still didn't get along well in private, they always made an effort in public.

'Don't worry,' he said, beaming at them all, 'I've got an appointment with an architect for first thing tomorrow morning.'

'No sooner the word than the deed, eh, son?' said Ned.

'I'm certainly not gonna hang about, having waited so long,' replied George.

'You've worked really hard,' said Dot. 'You deserve to get on.'

'I haven't done it on my own, you know,' George pointed out, looking at his father. 'Dad's been grafting too.'

'I only work for you,' Ned pointed out, modest as ever. 'I don't run the place.'

'Don't listen to him,' George told the others. 'He's my right-hand man.'

The atmosphere was extremely jolly and Eve was enjoying herself, especially as she rarely had an evening out now that Bart wasn't around. Being in Meg's company was easier than usual, too, with the wine flowing and the conversation of a general nature.

When they'd all finished eating, Eve proposed a toast to George and her father and the success of the long-awaited showrooms. All too soon it was time to leave. Eve and Meg both had to get back to release their babysitters, in Meg's case her parents, in Eve's her neighbour.

'We should have gone somewhere local and had a taxi,

George,' said Eve as her brother drove through the narrow
country lanes leading to the main road back to Ealing,
Meg in the front with George, Eve in the back with her
parents. 'Then you needn't have had to watch how much
you drank.'

'It won't do me any harm to cut down on the booze for
once,' commented George, who enjoyed a drink.

'I'll second that,' said Eve, because George occasionally
enjoyed a drop too much.

Because they were so busy chatting, it seemed no time at
all before they were back in Ealing. As they passed the car lot
on their way home, George slowed down almost to a halt and
looked across at the rows of cars visible in the street lighting,
coloured bunting flapping in the breeze around them. 'Just
think, folks,' he said happily, 'this time next year, there'll
be pukka showrooms here, and proper offices instead of the
Portakabin.'

'How long do you reckon the whole thing will take?'
wondered Ned.

'It could take as long as a year by the time we get the
plans passed and the building work done . . .' George was
distracted suddenly by something he saw. 'Hello . . . what's
going on over there?' he muttered, pulling in to the kerb.

'What's up?' asked Ned.

'I thought I saw something move over there.' He peered
ahead. 'I did an' all. There's someone in the Rover,' he said,
his voice rising angrily. 'Some bugger's trying to nick it.'

'Bloody hell,' said Ned. 'There's a lot of money tied up
in that motor.'

George leapt out of the car and tore towards the car lot
with his father on his tail.

'You two stay here,' Eve said to her mother and Meg as
she too got out of the car. 'I'll go and see what's going on.'

With her heart beating wildly, she followed the two men.

Realising there were two people involved in the attempted
theft of the Rover – one man outside the vehicle keeping

watch, the other inside trying to get the engine started by tampering with the wires beneath the dashboard – George told his father to go back to his car and wait there. Then he went into the Portakabin and rang the police.

Back outside, he was shocked to see his father fighting with one of the intruders, and hurried to his assistance. On the edge of George's vision he spotted Eve running towards him.

'Go back to the car and stay with Mum and Meg,' he told her. 'I'll deal with this.'

'I'll help you . . .'

'No . . . you keep out o' the way. This is no job for a woman.' He turned away from her and ran to his father's aid. 'Get off him,' he said, lunging towards the affray and dragging the would-be robber away from Ned.

'You'll regret this,' said the man gruffly.

'Go back to the car, Dad, I'll take care of this,' George managed to utter as he struggled to get free from the man, who had shifted his attention from Ned to George. His opponent was a tough bruiser and George had difficulty holding his ground. But with a supreme effort, he managed to force the man down over the bonnet of the car, only to find himself pulled back by the villain's partner, who took him unawares and shoved him to the ground.

Momentarily stunned as his head hit the tarmac, George lay still, unable to move. When he did eventually struggle to his feet, one of the men was brandishing a knife at him while the other got back inside the car.

'We need a motor and we're gonna take this one,' the knife-holder informed George in gravelly tones. 'So it ain't no use your trying to stop us.'

As the intrepid George moved towards the man, he saw the silver gleam of the blade in the glow of the streetlight. His breath caught fearfully in his throat but he managed not to show it. 'You won't scare me with that thing,' he bluffed.

'Keep back or I'll let you have it,' threatened the man.

He moved closer, with the blade pointing directly at George, whose heart was hammering against his ribs.

'Leave my son alone, you thug,' intervened Ned, stepping forward.

'I thought I told you to go back to the car, Dad,' admonished George.

'And leave you here with this load o' scum, not likely,' was Ned's reply.

'Get out of the way, Dad,' yelled George as his father deliberately placed himself between his son and the robber. 'For Christ's sake, do as I say.'

But his father was not easily deterred when his son's safety was at stake. 'Give me the knife,' he demanded of the man.

'You want it, Grandad,' replied the thug, 'so I'll give it to you.'

As George pushed his father out of the way, the man went after him and thrust the knife towards Ned's chest.

Concerned for her father and brother, Eve hadn't gone back to the car but had stayed nearby in case she was needed. Horrified by what she saw, she rushed to her father as he fell to the ground. On her knees by his side, she could see in the glow from the street lighting that his eyes were closed. Blood was seeping through his shirt. 'Dad,' she cried brokenly. 'Oh my God, no . . .'

The arrival of the police, who sent for an ambulance and arrested the men, barely registered with Eve as she stayed on her knees on the ground by her unconscious father.

Her mother pushing past the policemen, followed by Meg, brought her to her senses and she instinctively became strong. 'He'll be all right, Mum,' she said, managing to sound reassuring. 'The ambulance is on its way.'

But lying in a pool of blood in a shabby car lot, surrounded by the people who loved him and a handful of policemen, Ned Granger died before the ambulance even got there.

While his wife held Ned's hand, uttering unheard words

of comfort, a stupefied Eve watched her beloved father slip away.

Afterwards Eve never knew how she got through the rest of that night. But somehow she managed to distance herself from her own emotions and do what had to be done. She telephoned her neighbour from the Portakabin to explain what had happened and ask if she could stay the night with Josie because she herself needed to be with her mother. Then she went home to Marshall Gardens with the others, haunted by images of her father in the hospital mortuary.

Meg said she had to go home because of Becky, but insisted that George stay with his mother and sister. Although dazed and in a state of shock, Eve realised this was an act of kindness on Meg's part, because she could easily have telephoned her parents and asked them to stay the night with Becky. She was acknowledging the fact that his mother needed George more than Meg did tonight and giving the three of them a few hours alone together while their grief was still so fresh. Meg had been fond of her father-in-law but her sorrow couldn't possibly go as deep as theirs. Eve was touched by her thoughtfulness.

The three of them sat around in stunned bewilderment, drinking tea and talking. Eve and her mother wept. George – who considered tears to be strictly a woman's prerogative – sat stiffly in a chair or paced the room, trying not to break down. He was deathly white.

'They'd better lock that murderer up and throw away the key,' he said. 'Because if they don't, I'll find him and I'll kill him, I swear.'

'That sort of talk won't help anybody,' said Dot, her voice thick with emotion.

'Mum's right. You don't solve violence with violence,' agreed Eve, but she knew how George felt; she herself was seething with rage at the senseless destruction of the life of a good man.

'If only I'd made sure Dad had gone back to the car, he'd

still be alive now,' said George, who'd been chain-smoking ever since they got home.

'How could you have made him do anything when you had those villains to deal with?' Eve pointed out.

'I should have left 'em to get on with it and forced him out of danger,' insisted George. 'He saved my life and lost his own. It should be me in the mortuary, not him.'

'There's no call for that sort of talk either,' reproached Dot.

'It's my fault,' he said.

'Don't be so silly, George,' Eve admonished, but her tone was gentle because she could see the extent of his distress. 'The person to blame is in police custody.'

'Why didn't I drive straight past the car lot?' he muttered, torturing himself. 'Then I wouldn't have known anything about it and the thugs could have had the car and no one would have got hurt. A heap of metal isn't worth dying for.'

'Your father didn't die for a car,' said Dot. 'He died because he is . . .' She swallowed hard. 'He *was* a decent man who wouldn't stand by and see wrong being done.'

'I'll never forgive myself,' George went on, completely inconsolable.

'You've nothing to forgive yourself for,' Eve insisted.

'Oh yes I have,' he said, his face grey and twisted with pain. 'And no one will convince me otherwise.'

Eve put her arms around him and held him. His strong, muscular body trembled but he still didn't cry.

It was almost dawn before Eve managed to persuade her mother to go upstairs for a rest. Eve and George dozed in armchairs in the living room for a while, but Eve was anxious to get home to Josie. Neither of them wanted to leave their mother in the house alone, so George agreed to stay with her while Eve went home to release the babysitter. George said he would go home for a change of clothes when she got back.

While she was at home, Eve also made the necessary arrangements for her business. She telephoned Theresa before she left for work to explain what had happened and to tell her that she wouldn't be at the shop at all today and probably not for the rest of the week.

Theresa was most sympathetic and co-operative. She told Eve not to worry at all, that she would look after things in her absence for as long as she needed her to. Because it was part of her job to stand in for Eve when necessary, she had a set of shop keys, which meant she could open and close the boutique without any problem.

Eve went back to her mother's with Josie, prepared to stay for as long as she was needed, confident in the knowledge that her business interests were being well looked after.

Meg came to the house in Marshall Gardens that morning to say that George was trying to get some sleep and would be over later on. She had Becky with her – this being the school holidays – and offered to take both the children out for the rest of the day so that Eve and Dot didn't have to worry about keeping Josie amused.

'As the weather's nice I'll take them to Runnymede,' she said. 'I've brought a spare swimsuit with me that Josie can use to save you going home to get one for her.'

'That's kind of you, thanks,' said Eve.

'Once the funeral's over I'll be able to have the kids whenever you need me to,' said Dot, who still looked after Becky and Josie in the school holidays on the days their mothers had to go into work. 'I'll be wanting something to keep me occupied then.'

'Don't worry about that now,' said Meg. 'I've arranged not to go into the shop today anyway. And I can always get my mother to have Becky if I'm really stuck. Now that the baby stage is over, she doesn't mind filling in as long as it isn't likely to be permanent.'

Eve went out into the street with Meg to see them off. 'Thanks for taking Josie off our hands for a few hours,' she said. 'This isn't a good atmosphere for a child. Poor Mum's being very brave but she's in a hell of a state.'

'Who wouldn't be?' Meg stared at her feet before looking up and meeting Eve's eyes. 'I'm *really* sorry about your Dad, Eve.'

'Thanks.' She gritted her teeth to stop the tears flowing. 'Don't sympathise with me too much or I'll start howling. Anyway, you can't be feeling any too grand. You and Dad always got on well.'

'It's knocked me sideways actually,' Meg admitted. 'But it must be much worse for you. I don't know what I'd do if I lost my father.'

'I don't know what I'm going to do either,' confessed Eve, her face working as she fought to stay in control. She wanted to put her arms around Meg and cry on her shoulder as she once would have done. 'But I can't let go because of Mum. She needs me to be strong right now.'

'It must be hard for you, especially as you've already . . .'

'Lost Ken,' Eve finished for her. 'Well, we both know what that felt like, don't we?'

Eve hadn't meant anything by it. She was so distracted by grief, she wasn't being careful enough with her words. Seeing the remark hit home, she said quickly, 'That wasn't meant in any snide way. I just wasn't thinking.'

'It's all right.'

Every road leads back to Ken, thought Eve. Even at a time like this, when he's the last person on our minds, he's still there between us, causing tension and making it impossible for us to get back to our old footing.

The children were already in the car, giggling and shouting out of the window, too young to be deeply affected by what had happened. Both women looked at them.

'I'd better get going before they're too overexcited,' said Meg.

'Thanks again for keeping Josie occupied,' said Eve. 'It's the most useful thing you can do around here right now.'

'I know,' Meg said, opening the car door. 'See you later.'

'Yeah.'

Waving until the car turned the corner, Eve felt her eyes fill with tears at the memory of happier times between them, all the more poignant in this present time of grief.

'You mustn't feel you have to stay here with me,' said Dot when Eve went back inside. 'You shouldn't neglect your business.'

'I'm certainly not going to leave you here on your own,' declared Eve.

'It's something I've got to get used to, isn't it?' said Dot, her voice breaking. 'Because I *am* on my own now.'

'You're not on your own, Mum,' said Eve, putting her arms around her. 'You've got me . . . you've got George.'

'Yeah, I know, love, and I'm very grateful for it,' she said, hugging her daughter. 'But it isn't the same as having your dad around. We'd been together a long time.'

Her mother seemed to have become elderly and frail overnight, Eve noticed. Her face was pale and drawn, her greying hair dishevelled. She even seemed to look thinner, though she couldn't possibly have lost enough weight to be noticeable in such a short time. Eve couldn't imagine her mother without her father; they'd been like one person to her.

She held Dot close. 'Oh, Mum, what are we gonna do without him?'

'I don't know, Eve,' said Dot through a fresh flood of tears, 'I really don't. But we'll manage somehow. We don't have a choice.' She wasn't as confident as she sounded. She simply couldn't envisage life without Ned. 'We'll get by, don't worry.'

The sound of George coming in the back door drew them apart.

'We didn't expect you back so soon,' remarked Eve.

'Thought you'd be having a sleep,' added Dot.

'You're joking,' he said, his voice harsh with grief. 'I don't feel as though I'll ever be able to sleep again.'

276

'We all feel like that at the moment,' his mother told him. 'But you must have your rest.'

'Don't worry about me.' He put his arm around her. 'How are you feeling, Mum?'

'I'm bearing up, son. I've just been telling Eve she mustn't feel she has to stay here with me if she needs to go to work,' she said. 'And that applies to you too.'

'You've no need to worry about that as far as I'm concerned,' he informed her. 'I'm not going near the car lot ever again.'

'But you'll have to,' said his mother, wiping her eyes and moving forward and turning to face him. 'It's your living.'

'Not any more,' he said.

Eve and her mother stared at him, shocked. 'What ever do you mean by that?' asked Dot.

'I'm packing it in,' he announced. 'I'll sell the stock and clear out of there.'

'But the showrooms . . . ?' began Eve.

'That was something Dad and I were going to do together,' he reminded her. 'I'm not going ahead now.'

'But George . . .' began Dot.

'It's nothing for you to worry about, Mum,' he said in a kindly tone, putting an arm around her shoulders again. 'Everything will be just fine. I'll get it sorted.'

Dot looked worried and Eve was appalled at the change in her brother. His face was bloodless, his eyes black with shadows. This certainly wasn't the right moment to discuss his business plans for the future.

'In the mean time, I suppose we ought to start thinking about the . . .' He paused, his face working, and Eve thought he was going to collapse into tears, but he composed himself and finished, 'The funeral.'

At that moment the front doorbell rang and Eve went to open the door to the first of a stream of well-wishers come to offer their condolences.

People lined the streets for the funeral procession. The brutal nature of Ned's death added to the fact that he had been a popular member of the community brought them out in hordes despite the rain, which was heavy and persistent.

There was a sea of umbrellas at the cemetery too. Friends, neighbours, shopkeepers, people who only knew him by sight came and stood in the wet to pay their last respects. The rain became torrential at the graveside, beating on the umbrellas and soaking the mourners' shoes as it splashed to the ground, making it muddy underfoot. Eve and George stood either side of their mother as they went through this final agony, barely aware of the weather and the dampness seeping into their black clothes.

When the ordeal was over and the crowds began to disperse, George escorted his mother back to the car while Eve stayed for a few quiet moments alone by her adored father's grave. She felt years older than she had a week ago.

Sensing someone beside her, she turned, her mouth falling open. 'Bart!' she gasped. 'How on earth did you get here?'

'By plane . . .'

'You know what I mean.'

'Mum phoned me to tell me what had happened,' he explained. 'I flew in yesterday. I'm going back tonight.'

'All that way for such a short time,' she said warmly. 'That's what I call a magnificent effort.'

'It was worth it,' he said.

'I really appreciate your coming.'

'Ned was a good bloke . . . I liked him. 'He gave her a wry grin. 'And after all, he could have been my father-in-law.'

'He might well have been,' she said, 'if the circumstances had been different.'

The atmosphere was suddenly fragile, fraught with tension and emotion. He cleared his throat nervously. 'It must have been a terrible blow for you all,' he said. 'I couldn't believe it when Mum told me. I'm *so* sorry.'

'Oh, Bart.' She put her arms around him, tears falling, the joy of seeing him blotting out the misery of their last meeting and dissolving any awkwardness. 'I'm *so* pleased to see you.'

278

'Likewise,' he said, holding her to him.

She drew back, wiping her eyes. 'Does my mother know you're here?'

'I don't think she noticed me, there was such a crowd.'

'You'll come back to the house for a bite to eat?' she suggested hopefully. 'She'll be so glad you came.'

'I'd like that.' He looked doubtful. 'Rudy's with me, though. He brought me in his car. I don't have wheels of my own in the UK now.'

'Bring him with you,' she said. 'Mum will be touched that you're both here.'

'Okay then, we'll see you back at the house,' he told her, smiling.

'So, how's the job going?' Eve asked a bit later. She'd found a seat next to Bart, who was having a ham sandwich and a glass of beer in Dot's crowded living room.

'Fine,' he said.

'You're certainly looking well,' she remarked, because he was tanned and his hair was several shades lighter.

'Thanks . . . I'm feeling great.'

'Has it come up to your expectations, being a real professional at last?' she asked.

'It certainly beats window-cleaning,' he said, cocking his head and grinning in a way that made her heart melt.

'I'm sure.'

'It's a different way of life altogether,' he told her.

'So, now that you're one of these nocturnal showbiz types, what do you do during the day?' she asked.

'Sleep, work on my act. Now that it's my only means of support, I have to keep it fresh by working out new comedy material, trying new songs,' he explained. 'And I'm working at the club till the small hours, so I don't get up until late.'

'Sounds positively luxurious.'

'Compared to doing the two jobs, it is,' he said. 'I'm really enjoying it, but I have to work hard for my money.

I put everything into it now that I'm not burdened with window-cleaning.'

'I'm so glad it's working out for you,' she said. 'You deserve to do well.'

'Thanks.' He sipped his beer. 'And thanks for going to see Mum so often. She told me that you're a regular visitor.'

'She's a friend,' Eve pointed out. 'I enjoy going to see her.'

He asked how things were going in general, then enquired after Josie and they chatted about her for a while.

'You've no regrets about going to Spain, then?' Eve asked later.

He didn't reply, and she thought she perceived a certain wistfulness in his expression. 'Regrets are pointless,' he said, his voice hardening. 'We only get one shot at life and you have to take your chances when they come. The job just happened to be in Spain, so that's where I had to go. Had it been in the UK, I'd have stayed here.'

'Yes, I know.'

Their conversation was interrupted by George, whose complexion since their father's death was permanently the colour of porridge, despite the sunny weather they'd been having until today's rain. 'Good to see you, mate,' he said, shaking Bart's hand. 'I appreciate your making the effort. All the way from sunny Spain to see Dad off . . . he would have been tickled.'

Eve slipped away to mingle with the other guests, leaving the two men to chat. As numbed by grief as she was for her father, she was still stirred by Bart and saddened that he was no longer in her life.

But she'd had her chance with him and rejected it. The time for her and Bart had passed. She must accept that. But seeing him again made it very hard.

Dot made a point of having a chat with Rudy, since he'd taken the time and trouble to attend her husband's funeral.

'It was so good of you to come,' she said, finding him sitting alone eating a sandwich while Bart chatted to George.

'Bart wouldn't have missed it for the world, so I offered to drive him over to save him hiring a car,' Rudy said.

'I expect he was glad of the company,' she remarked.

He nodded. 'I should think so. I was glad of the chance to pay my respects, anyway. I only met your husband a few times, as you know, but I liked him.'

'Most people did,' she said.

He looked at her gravely, his little brown eyes full of compassion. 'I can't tell you how sorry I am about what happened, my dear.'

'Thank you,' she said with a sigh. 'It's a sad business.'

'It's bad enough losing him,' he said, 'but under such shocking circumstances . . .'

'It's hard to come to terms with, I won't deny that,' she said.

'I can imagine.'

She met his eyes and found herself confiding in him in a way she never would to her children because she didn't want to add to their own grief or have them worrying about her.

'To be quite honest with you,' she confessed, 'I don't know how to get out of bed in the morning at the moment.'

'You keep on doing it, though, don't you, when all you really want to do is put your head under the covers and shut out the world,' he said. 'That's the important thing.'

'Part of me wants to shut out the world,' she told him. 'The other part is frightened of being alone.'

'Oh, yeah,' he said, nodding his head thoughtfully. 'I remember the feeling well.'

'I don't know which is worse, the fear of being a burden to my children or the fear of being alone,' she said.

'When I lost my wife, I didn't have the first of those things to worry about, because I don't have any children, but I did fear the overwhelming loneliness,' he said.

'It's awful,' she agreed.

'The café helped me a lot,' he said. 'Working kept me

281

sane.' He looked at her. 'At first, though, the sadness doesn't go away whatever you're doing. It's something you have to actually experience to know what it's like.'

'Mm.'

'But life does begin to fall into a new pattern, eventually,' he said. 'You do learn to cope.'

She managed a weak smile. 'Yeah, I'm sure I will.' She shrugged her shoulders. 'It's a case of having to, isn't it?'

'I'm afraid it is,' he said sagely. 'But if you ever need someone to talk to, just give me a ring or come over to the café and we'll have a chat over a cuppa tea.'

She didn't seriously intend to take him up on his offer, but the fact that he had made it gave her a surprising amount of solace. Knowing that he had been through what she was going through now made her feel somehow slightly less alone.

'That's kind of you, Rudy,' she said. 'You must give me the address and phone number of the café before you go.'

'I will.'

She stood up purposefully. 'Meanwhile I'd better make sure the other guests are being looked after properly.'

'Yeah, o' course.'

'See you later.'

'Sure.'

Struggling to be brave in the face of adversity, she went among the gathering with a determined show of mettle. But she actually felt lost and bewildered and wondered for the umpteenth time how the hell she was going to manage without Ned.

Chapter Sixteen

'Don't you think you should go back to work, George?' Meg gently suggested one warm, humid morning in August. Becky had gone to play with a friend at a neighbour's house and the couple were alone together. 'It's more than two weeks since the funeral. Time the car lot was open for business again.'

'How many more times must I tell you?' he snapped. 'I will *not* be opening the car lot again, *ever*. The business is up for sale and the agent is dealing with all enquiries.'

'You ought to keep things ticking over, though, or you'll lose the goodwill and that'll affect the asking price.' She hated having to nag him when he was so obviously tormented. But she couldn't sit back and do nothing while he sank deeper into depression and self-castigation, believing himself to be responsible for his father's death. 'Anyway, if the place gets too run-down, you'll have difficulty finding a buyer for it. Neglected property is a magnet to vandals.'

It was one of those oppressive August days, heavy and airless, with wasps and bluebottles buzzing into the house at the first sign of food. Meg's clothes felt damp against her skin despite the fact that she was wearing only a sun dress. They were sitting at the kitchen table, drinking coffee amid a pall of smoke, cigarettes having become George's staple diet since the tragedy. He'd lost a dramatic amount of weight and his ghastly pallor was emphasised by a growth of dark stubble.

Meg was at her wits' end about him. Once so industrious and cheerful, her husband had become idle and morose. When he did manage to drag himself out of bed, he sat about the house smoking and hardly saying a word. He was still in his dressing gown now, and it was almost noon. He didn't eat, he wasn't sleeping properly and he wouldn't go out.

In reply to her comments, he shrugged his shoulders as though he couldn't care less. 'If I can't find a buyer, I'll sell the stock and the Portakabin as they stand. The lease runs out soon anyway, and I won't renew it. I hadn't finalised the purchase of the land, so I'm not left with that on my hands. 'He sighed heavily. 'What does any of it matter anyway?'

'It matters a lot,' she told him emphatically. 'We're talking about a business you worked hard to build into something worthwhile.'

'A business in which I no longer have any interest,' he amended.

She took a deep breath in an effort to calm herself, because his attitude was deeply distressing to her. 'You won't get much for the cars if they're left standing without being cleaned or checked over,' she pointed out.

'So what?' he said gruffly, his voice hoarse from heavy smoking. 'It isn't the end of the world. All I want is to get rid . . .'

'That sort of defeatist attitude isn't worthy of you,' she cut in. 'You shouldn't even consider selling the business, in my opinion.'

'If I want your opinion, I'll ask for it,' he snapped.

She was angry now but kept her temper because she knew he wasn't himself. 'So . . . after finally getting the freeholder to agree to sell you the land, after years of relentless persuasion, you're just going to abandon your plans -- throw away the best opportunity you've ever had?'

His hostility towards her was a palpable force in the room as he stared at her across the table, eyes bloodshot and sunken in his haggard face. 'You know the reason why I'm not going ahead, so stop going on about it.'

'Your father would have wanted you to continue,' she persisted.

'My father isn't here to give an opinion, is he?' was

his brusque reply. 'If he was, we wouldn't be having this conversation.'

'You can't just give up, George . . .'

'I can do whatever I damn well like,' was his answer to that. 'I've told you, the showrooms were something Dad and I were planning together. Without him, I'm not going ahead.'

'Have you considered what you're going to do about an income?' she enquired, hoping that a reminder of reality might force him out of the trough he was in. 'When the cash from the sale has been frittered away and you've nothing left to buy another business?'

'Who says it'll be frittered away.'

'That happens if you don't keep working,' she said. 'Sitting around here all day isn't only bad for your health, it's bad for your bank balance too.'

'When the money's gone I'll get a job,' he told her dully.

'I can't imagine you wanting to work for someone else after being your own boss for all these years,' she opined. 'And you'll hate it if I'm the sole bread-winner.'

'Don't worry, I've no intention of sponging off you,' he said bitterly.

'That wasn't what I meant.' She felt hurt, and tears sprang to her eyes. 'You know I'm happy to keep us. But if I were to do it for any length of time, you'd go all macho on me and accuse me of taking away your manhood.'

'What makes you such an expert on the subject?' he asked curtly.

'You don't have to be an expert to know that that's what would happen. It's the way men are, men of your type at least,' she said. 'Anyway, I'm not prepared let you wreck your life. I can't do anything about the fact that you lost your father but I can try and stop you losing your business, something you'll regret later on when you're feeling better and able to see things in a different light.'

He didn't reply, just stared moodily into space, drawing hard on his cigarette.

Suddenly it was all too much for Meg. 'Stop shutting

me out, George,' she begged ardently, leaning forward and looking into his face. 'For God's sake, stop shutting me out.'

'Dunno what you're talking about.' His eyes were dull and lifeless.

'I think you do,' she said, her voice quivering with emotion. 'I know things weren't good between us before your dad died, but since his death you've gone away from me altogether. You've become a stranger, a bad-tempered one at that.'

'Don't keep on . . .'

'I want to help, George,' she said, her voice rising with passion. 'Don't push me away.'

'I don't want any help,' he said. 'I know exactly what I'm doing.'

'If you carry on like this, you'll lose everything you care about.'

'Just leave me alone, woman,' he ordered, sounding wretched. 'You're always on at me, nag, nag, nag. It's driving me round the bend.'

She stood up, wounded but not defeated. 'I have to start getting lunch now,' she said evenly, 'and this afternoon I'll be going to work. I'll drop Becky off at your mother's place on the way.'

'You can leave Becky here with me,' he offered. 'I'm not going anywhere.'

'Your mother looks forward to having her while I'm at work,' she told him. 'Looking after her and Josie is keeping her sane at the moment.' She paused, looking at him, her mouth set in a grim line. 'Anyway, while you're in this frame of mind, you're not fit to look after a child.'

Later, after Meg and Becky had left the house, George sat smoking, feeling deeply ashamed. He no longer seemed to be in control of his actions. Imbued with emotions with which he couldn't cope, words flowed out of him of their own volition, words he didn't mean and which hurt him to utter. He was in a state of darkest lethargy from which he could not find the will to escape. The need to punish himself for his father's death was constant, but somehow it was Meg who was taking the punishment instead of him.

Why was he hurting her? Why couldn't he stop? He felt very strange – agitated but exhausted – and the confusion in his mind was frightening. He had lost his concentration to the point where he couldn't even read the newspaper properly.

He did have sufficient clarity of thought, though, to know that he was in a hideous mess.

One day, a couple of weeks later, Eve was busy catching up on paperwork at her desk in the office at the back of her shop. It was a small room which she'd brightened up with pot plants, pictures, and family photographs, many of them of her daughter at various stages of development. The one in a silver frame in the centre of the desk, of Josie on her fifth birthday – looking rather serious for the camera – never failed to warm her heart.

In the aftermath of her father's death, Eve had been forced to let things slip at the boutique. Between the death and the funeral she hadn't been to work at all, and since then she had put in fewer hours than normal because she'd needed to spend time with her brave but grief-stricken mother. Eve's own grief for her father had changed from utter devastation to a kind of resigned sadness. It was constant and all-consuming, but – unlike her poor brother, who seemed on the verge of a breakdown – she wasn't incapacitated by it.

Applying herself to her work, Eve thought what a godsend Theresa had been these past few weeks. The woman had shouldered extra work and responsibility without a word of complaint. But it was now the end of August, more than a month since the stabbing, and Eve knew she must get back into the swing of things herself. Theresa was brilliant at running the shop but couldn't be expected to keep the books in order too.

Eve was beginning to think the recent trauma must have addled her own brain, because she couldn't seem to make the figures add up. The takings didn't tally with the amount of stock that had gone out of the shop. She went over them again and again, but they remained stubbornly unbalanced. Finally – with a sinking feeling in the pit of her stomach – she faced the fact that it was the figures that were at fault, not her own mathematical ability.

There were two possible reasons for this. Either there had been a massive increase in shoplifting while she'd been away, or someone had been helping themselves from the till.

The first wasn't a serious option, so she ruled it out and concentrated on the second. To steal money regularly from the daily takings would be a complicated matter. The most common method of theft by shop staff – of pocketing the money and not putting the sale through the till – wouldn't work at the boutique because customers always wanted a sales receipt in case they needed to return the purchased garment for any reason. So any removal of cash would show up on the daily print-out from the cash register.

This particular discrepancy was a matter of the money banked not matching the amount of stock that had been bought and, apparently, sold. So if it wasn't cash that was being taken, it must be stock.

Eve leaned back in her seat, tapping her chin with a biro. This was going to need further investigation and delicate handling. She would have to take her time and not make any rash accusations.

Meg took Becky to school and went straight to work, glad she had time to compose herself before the staff arrived, because she was on the verge of tears again.

George was becoming more unbearable with every day that passed, and the atmosphere at home was really dragging Meg down. Thank God the school holidays were over. At least Becky was out of his way for most of the day, and Meg was at the shop. That poor child must be wondering what had happened to her adoring stepfather, who was now so grumpy and unapproachable.

She made a cup of strong coffee and sat at her desk in the

office, biting back the tears. She was still smarting from the blazing row they had had last night when she'd tried to bring him back from the depths by suggesting he get out of the house, even if only for a walk.

They couldn't go on like this. Heaven knows what it was doing to Becky, and it was making Meg feel ill. But what was she to do? Any suggestion of medical help sent George into a rage. Anyway, medication alone wasn't the answer. Pills could help to a degree, but the real solution lay elsewhere, she was sure of it. She would do anything to help him find the way back, *anything at all*.

The telephone rang on her desk. It was the husband of Gloria, her senior assistant-cum-manageress, to say that Gloria wasn't well and wouldn't be coming in to work today.

'Terrific,' Meg muttered to herself with irony as she replaced the receiver, having sympathetically assured Gloria's husband that she mustn't even think of coming back to work until she was feeling well enough. As if she didn't have enough troubles; now she was going to be short-staffed, which would make it difficult when she went to collect Becky from school this afternoon.

She'd finished her coffee and was putting the float into the till just minutes before opening time when the children's-wear assistant and the junior, who worked wherever she was most needed, arrived.

Their first customer of the day appeared soon afterwards, and Meg was helping her choose a casual jacket when the telephone rang again. Excusing herself and taking the call on the extension on the counter, she heard a muffled voice at the other end.

'Meg . . . it's me.' George's voice was barely recognisable. If she didn't know better she might have thought he was crying.

'George . . . what is it?'

'Can you come home?' He sounded desperate.

'Why, what's happened?'

There was a lot of snuffling and noisy breathing down the

line. 'I need you, Meg,' he spluttered. 'I know it's asking a lot of you . . . and you've got your business to see to . . . but I think I'm going mad and I just can't handle it.'

'I'm on my way,' she said without a moment's hesitation.

Apologising to the customer, and asking her depleted staff to manage as best as they could until she got back, she grabbed her coat, hurried out to her car and drove across Haven Green as though her life depended on it.

She found George sitting at the kitchen table in his dressing gown, with his head in his hands. He was sobbing uncontrollably.

'George . . . darling, what is it?' she said, slipping her arms around him, her face close to the back of his head. 'Whatever's the matter?'

He couldn't speak for a while. When he was able to articulate a few words, he said, 'I'm sorry you've had to come home from work.'

'It doesn't matter,' she soothed. 'You're more important than work.'

'God, I'm pathetic,' he said through his sobs. 'What's happening to me?'

'Shush,' she said softly. 'You're giving in to your feelings at last, that's all . . . it's the best thing that could have happened.'

'I shouldn't have bothered you with it,' he mumbled thickly.

'Nonsense. I'm your wife,' she said softly. 'Your problems are mine too.'

'I never thought the day would come when I'd let my wife see me cry,' he wept.

'You don't have to be tough every second of your life, you know,' she told him. 'There are times when you just have to give in and be like everyone else. We're all just frail human beings . . . we each have our breaking point.'

'Sorry.'

'Stop apologising,' she admonished firmly. 'We're gonna get through this together. Let's go into the other room.'

He allowed himself to be led into the lounge and they sat close together on the sofa. Meg encouraged him to talk to her about how he was feeling.

'I can't believe I'm doing this,' he said, his body still shuddering. 'I've not cried since I was about five years old; now I can't stop.'

'It really doesn't matter, you know, George,' she said. 'It's quite normal.'

'For women maybe . . .'

'For men too,' she soothed.

'Not in the world that I move in,' he said.

'All this talk about crying being a sign of weakness is a load of rubbish,' she said. 'It's nature's safety valve. Bottling things up never did anyone any good.'

'If you say so.'

'I do.'

'I'm sorry for how I've been lately,' he said with genuine remorse. 'I've been feeling so wretched. I know you've taken the brunt of my bad temper but I just couldn't help it.'

'Stop worrying,' she said, smoothing his damp hair back from his brow, 'and tell me about it.'

'I've not been sleeping.'

'I know that,' she said. 'I lie by your side every night.'

'Every time I close my eyes I see that knife,' he confided. 'I watch my father die instead of me, over and over again.'

'He didn't die instead of you, George,' Meg said. 'He died because it was meant to happen that way. He chose to protect you . . . did it of his own free will. You can't be responsible for someone else's actions, and you have to accept that.'

'Is that really the way you see it?' He seemed slightly calmer.

'Yes, honestly.' She was adamant. 'It was a terrible tragedy, but it happened and you have to live with it and stop torturing yourself about the reasons why. Leave the guilt to your father's murderer.'

'Scum like him wouldn't have a conscience,' he said, wiping his eyes with a handkerchief and sounding stronger.

'Maybe not, but at least he's going to pay for what he did,' she pointed out. 'So you must stop punishing yourself for his crime. It's the last thing your father would want.'

'Yeah, I know.'

'I've been so worried about you.' Meg knew instinctively that George had come back to her and that this wasn't just a temporary thing. 'Well, we all have . . . your mother, your sister.'

'I'm so ashamed.' He looked at her sheepishly. 'I know I've been hell to live with.'

'I won't deny that.'

'I thought I was so strong,' he went on. 'But making your wife come home from work because you've gone to pieces is a pretty feeble thing to do.'

'Nonsense,' she said. 'We're a team, you and me. In the bad times as well as the good.'

'I didn't mean all those things I've been saying lately.'

'If I hadn't already worked that out for myself, I wouldn't still be around.'

'No, I don't suppose you would.'

She gave him a close look. 'What happened this morning to bring things to a head?' she wondered.

'I'm not sure what triggered it off,' he confessed. 'I was feeling too agitated to stay in bed, so I got up and came downstairs.' He pressed his hands to his head, remembering. 'The emptiness of the house seemed to close in on me. I felt lost and alone.' He paused again, thinking back. 'I remember feeling a kind of explosion inside of me and I lost control.' He shook his head. 'I just couldn't stop crying. I needed you so much, I just couldn't bear it.'

She wrapped her arms around him and held him tight, feeling his body against her so much skinnier than the last time she'd held him. 'That's what I've wanted . . . to be needed,' she said. 'It was awful when you turned away from me.'

'I don't deserve you,' he continued. 'It was my fault things

292

got bad between us before Dad died. I let the affair with Ken affect me when it has absolutely nothing to do with what you and I have.'

'Nothing at all,' she confirmed.

He still looked grim but she could see life in his eyes again. 'It seems like nothing at all compared to Dad's death.'

'It seemed like nothing at all to me as soon as I met you,' she said.

'Can you forgive me?'

'On one condition,' she replied, managing a watery smile.

'What's that?'

'That you think again about selling the business.'

'I don't want to sell it,' he confessed.

'Then don't.'

'Obviously it won't be the same, working without Dad, but I think I feel able to go ahead with the plans for the showrooms now,' he told her. 'I never actually wanted to give the idea up. But I just didn't have the heart to go on. I wanted to hurt myself.'

'Losing the business was a way of punishing yourself,' she suggested.

'I suppose so,' he admitted. 'I've been really stupid, haven't I?'

'Just a little,' she said with a small grin.

'It'll hurt, having to do the showrooms without Dad.'

'There's always the thought that he would have wanted the plans carried through,' she pointed out.

'Yeah, I suppose you're right,' he agreed. 'No matter what anyone says, I'll always feel responsible for his death, but there's no point in brooding on it. I have to get on with life now.' He paused, looking puzzled. 'I can't believe I just said that.'

'I can't either, but you did and it's great,' she told him.

'I feel better, Meg,' he said.

'Yes, I can see that. It's probably because you've let it all out.'

'That awful fog in my mind seems to have cleared a bit,' he

said. 'I feel almost human again . . . I feel as though I want to go to work.'

'Thank God for that.' Her voice was warm with relief. 'The first thing you must do is call the agent and withdraw the car lot from sale.'

'You're right.' He turned to her with a tender look. 'Thanks for everything, love, you've been an absolute diamond.'

'It was nothing.'

'It was everything,' he corrected. 'You've been here for me, putting up with my bad temper and self-pity. You were here for me this morning when I needed you most of all.'

'You'll be all right, George,' she said. 'Now that you've let nature take its course.'

'Will *we* be all right, too?' he asked.

'Course we will.'

'I've been a pig, letting your past come between us,' he reminded her.

'There were times when I wanted to throttle you,' she admitted. 'But I'll forgive you.' She gave him a wicked grin. 'As long as you have a shave and smarten yourself up.'

'I'll do that right away,' he said, kissing her for the first time in ages.

Many times since she'd been in business for herself Eve had wished she was still in partnership with Meg. But never more so than one autumn evening, when she was sitting in George's car parked in a side street opposite New Range with a good view of the shop. Were she and Meg still together, the odious problem she found herself with wouldn't have been nearly so agonising, because they would have tackled it together.

She'd borrowed George's car for fear her own would be recognised even though dusk was beginning to fall. It was vital she wasn't seen until she was ready. God, this was awful – she felt like some gumshoe in a third-rate movie – but it had to be done if she was to confirm her suspicions and get the matter sorted once and for all. Having kept a close eye on the books and the stock since becoming aware that something was seriously amiss, she had discovered that she was being steadily robbed.

The weather was cold, with mist rising in a smoky haze around the street and shop lights. She shivered and pulled her red anorak closer around her. The street was beginning to empty of shoppers as the stores began to close. On the dot of half past five, the queue at the bus stop was joined by the junior from New Range. The traffic built up as people poured out of shops and offices. Quarter to six and still no sign of Theresa. At least she couldn't be accused of slipping off early when the boss wasn't around, thought Eve.

With a tight knot of apprehension in her stomach, Eve kept her eyes fixed on the shop doorway, even now hoping that she was wrong and that there was some other explanation for the books not balancing. Her heart hammered nervously against her ribs when she saw Theresa come out and turn towards the door to lock up, putting the bag she was carrying down on the ground.

Eve was out of the car like a shot and across the road, darting through the traffic, which was almost at a standstill.

'Hello, Theresa,' she said to the other woman's back as she concentrated on locking the door.

'Eve.' She swung around and was visibly startled, because Eve had deliberately led her to believe she wouldn't be anywhere near the shop today. 'I didn't expect to see you.'

'Obviously not,' said Eve, looking meaningfully at the bag.

Theresa's gaze followed Eve's towards the bag. 'I'm staying at my boyfriend's place tonight,' she explained feebly. 'I've got my overnight things in there.'

'I think we'd better go inside, don't you?' suggested Eve. 'Just so there are no misunderstandings.'

Theresa tried to make a run for it, but Eve blocked her way and pushed her back towards the door, grabbing the bag. 'Wouldn't you rather we sorted this out between us in the shop than at the police station?' she said.

The other woman pushed her bright-red hair back from

her face, staring sullenly at Eve, who had firm hold of the bag.

'Open the door, please, Theresa,' commanded Eve.

With great reluctance she did as she was asked, and they went inside.

'Not a bad haul for one day . . . two sweaters, two pairs of trousers, two mini-skirts,' said Eve, pulling the items out of the bag. 'It adds up to quite a lot over the course of a week.'

'It's the first time I've ever taken anything,' lied Theresa, her big green eyes full of pique, almost as though she believed it herself.

'Don't give me that. You're at it every time I'm not around,' said Eve. 'You've been robbing me blind for months.'

Changing tack because she knew the game was up, Theresa shrugged her shoulders with an air of nonchalance. 'If you leave your business to someone else to look after, what else do you expect?'

'I certainly didn't expect this,' exclaimed Eve. 'I trusted you, Theresa, I really did.'

'More fool you,' the woman mocked. 'Everybody's on the take, given the right opportunity.'

'What a wonderful attitude,' said Eve bitterly.

'It may not be very nice, but it's the way things are.'

'Not by most people's standards,' insisted Eve.

'By all the people I know . . .'

'You should find some new friends,' proclaimed Eve. 'But be that as it may . . . are you selling the clothes you steal? They're different sizes, so they can't all be for you.'

Theresa stared at her feet.

'You might as well tell me,' said Eve, 'because I intend to find out anyway.'

'My boyfriend's got a market stall,' Theresa explained, meeting Eve's eyes defiantly.

'Oh, now I understand,' said Eve. 'So you've been working this scam together?'

'It wasn't a scam,' the other woman argued. 'You're making it sound like some big crime.'

'It is a big crime as far as I'm concerned,' Eve informed her frankly.

'Okay, so I've been taking some things and giving them to him,' Theresa said cheekily. 'Hardly the crime of the century.'

'*Giving* them to him?' queried Eve. 'You mean he doesn't pay you?'

'Of course not,' Theresa said.

'That's rather an odd arrangement, isn't it?' remarked Eve. 'You take all the risk and he gets the dosh?'

'That isn't how it is,' Theresa protested. 'He takes me out and gives me a good time. I don't want more than that from him.'

'He must be very special if you're prepared to steal for him,' said Eve.

'He is.'

'No man worth his salt would have you risk your job and put yourself in court,' said Eve.

'Court?' exclaimed Theresa, showing the first signs of concern. 'You're gonna take it that far?'

This was a tricky situation for Eve. If she took Theresa to court, it would cost time and money and she didn't stand a chance of getting back what she'd lost, because Theresa didn't have anything beyond what she earned each week, while the boyfriend would probably deny all knowledge and leave her to take the blame.

But Eve couldn't let her get away with it. It was Eve's public duty to report it to the police if only because it might stop Theresa from doing the some thing to someone else.

'Yes, I am,' she told her, going over to the telephone on the counter.

Later, when the police officers and Theresa had gone, Eve went into her office and sat down at the desk. She needed time to recover before she went to collect Josie from her mother's. She felt buffeted and physically sick, her faith in human nature shaken yet again. What sort of a world was it where a decent man like her father was mindlessly stabbed to death and she was robbed because she couldn't spend every working moment checking up on her staff?

She felt very alone suddenly, hot tears rushing into her eyes. The constant strain of combining motherhood with a career, and all the guilt and emotional baggage that entailed, sometimes got too much, especially at times like this, when she realised she couldn't even trust the people she employed.

Oh well, it's another day tomorrow, she thought, getting up and slipping into her coat, her mood brightening at the thought of seeing her beloved little daughter.

When Eve got to her mother's, Josie was eager to show her a picture she'd painted at school. 'Do you like it?' she asked eagerly.

'It's lovely, darling, well done,' praised Eve, staring at bright splodges of colour that she perceived to be a house with a spiky yellow sun sitting on the roof and some figures standing outside. 'Who are the people?'

'You and me and Uncle Bart,' she said, her dark eyes bright with the excitement of her achievement.

'So it is,' said Eve, unbearably moved by the fact that her daughter had remembered him. He'd been gone for over a year but had sent Josie presents at Christmas and her birthday.

'She's got a good memory for such a little 'un,' remarked Dot affectionately.

'Yes, she has.' It was a poignant moment for Eve, and she felt her eyes moisten. 'You're a clever girl,' she said, giving Josie a hug.

Chapter Seventeen

Eve's sprits were almost as low as hem lines as autumn turned to winter, and long coats and skirts – which had had a minority following up until now – suddenly became all the rage.

Her mood of melancholy was mostly due to the lingering effects of her father's murder, but the incident with Theresa had left its scar too. In the end, Eve had decided not to press charges. She thought the scare was enough of a lesson for Theresa. Having had her trust so blatantly betrayed, Eve was wary about leaving the boutique under staff supervision, which meant she was constantly on edge because it just wasn't possible for her to be there herself all the time. Her frail trust was placed rather cautiously in a new assistant called Caroline.

'I'm afraid to turn my back,' Eve confided to Lil one morning in November when she called at her flat to collect some work. 'If Theresa taught me anything it was to be less trusting.'

'You were just unlucky,' was Lil's opinion. 'You mustn't let one bad experience colour your judgement about everyone.'

'I suppose you're right. But coming so soon after Dad's murder, it's bound to have shaken my faith in human nature. She saw no point in dragging up the past by adding that both her husband and her best friend had deceived her too, especially as Lil had regular dealings with Meg.

'I can understand your feelings up to a point,' said Lil, drinking coffee made for them by Nora before she'd gone out to get the groceries. 'But there are still plenty of decent people about. You can't go through life not trusting anyone.'

'I'm not that twisted that I don't trust anyone,' Eve explained. 'But I do feel uneasy leaving my staff with the opportunity to nurture any inclination towards sticky fingers. Still, if I keep a close eye on both the takings and the stock, I can nip anything dodgy in the bud.'

'It makes sense to keep a eye on things, o' course,' agreed Lil. 'But to be constantly suspicious will make your life a misery. As a working mother you *have* to delegate responsibility. And if you're gonna worry about what's going on behind your back every time you're away from the shop, you'll drive yourself bonkers.'

Eve sighed. 'I know. But it isn't easy to forget what Theresa did.'

'Learn by it but don't let it rule your life,' advised Lil. 'I mean . . . where would I be if I didn't put my trust in Nora? Being in this chair makes me more vulnerable than the rest of you. But I trust Nora with everything from confidentiality to our domestic budget. I have nothing but my instincts to go on but I *know* she wouldn't cheat me out of so much as a penny piece or repeat a word that's uttered in this household.'

What Lil said was heartening but Eve still had doubts. 'I felt that way about Theresa, though,' she mentioned.

'As I've said, you were just unlucky,' Lil insisted. 'Trust people until they prove themselves unworthy, that's my motto.'

'You're right.' Lil's positive attitude was beginning to have an effect. 'Being cynical is no way to live.'

'Course it isn't.'

They turned their minds to business and Eve was full of praise for the beautiful lacy hats and scarves Lil had made.

'They're gorgeous,' she said, fingering the garments, which were in red, black and emerald green. 'They'll sell like hot cakes. They're perfect to go with the long coats people are wearing.'

'They were a dream to make,' said Lil. 'They weren't too complicated.'

'I'll probably be back to you for more,' Eve remarked. 'But in the mean time, could you do me a few more of the little waistcoats you made for us earlier in the season? They're going like a storm because they look good with long skirts.'

'Meg's doing well with those too,' Lil mentioned casually.

Eve reeled from a piercing stab of nostalgia at the sudden memory of how she and Meg had once shared the enjoyment of a really successful line. Work had been such fun then. 'Is she?' she said.

'Yeah, she's ordered more too.'

'Between the two of us, we'll make sure you don't have time on your hands,' Eve said, keeping her tone light and dismissing thoughts of the past. 'I've got a special order for you, too . . . and I need it really fast.' Eve made a face. 'Like . . . yesterday.'

'Oh?' Lil stroked her chin thoughtfully. 'Depends what it is as to how soon I can get it done.'

'You know the crocheted bikinis you did last summer that were so popular?'

'Yeah.'

'One of my customers liked hers so much she wants another,' she explained. 'She's off to the Canary Islands in a couple of weeks.'

'I think I can manage that,' said Lil with a grin. 'Bikinis don't take long, being there's hardly anything of 'em.'

Eve finished her coffee and looked at her watch. 'Well . . . I'd better get the materials you'll be needing out of the car, then get back to the shop.'

Lil gave her a studious look. 'You're looking very tired lately, Eve,' she remarked.

'Am I?' said Eve. 'It's probably because I'm always rushing about.'

'You should go out and have some fun now and again,' suggested the older woman.

'Chance would be a fine thing,' Eve said, smiling. 'But I'm quite content with my life the way it is. Even if I am permanently trying to be in two places at once.'

'I know that young Josie is the most important thing in your life, and that's how it should be,' Lil continued, 'but an occasional night out without her would do you the world of good.'

Something in Lil's manner made Eve sense a definite reason for her sudden concern about Eve's social life. 'Have you heard from Bart lately?' she asked.

'Yeah, I have, as a matter of fact,' Lil said. 'I had a letter the other day.'

'How is he?'

'Fine.'

Eve studied her hands for a moment then met Lil's eyes. 'Is he seeing someone else?' she asked. 'Is that it?'

Lil nodded, scratching her cheek, obviously feeling awkward. 'He mentions someone called Ann.'

'Oh!' Eve felt as though she'd been physically struck, but tried not to show it, aware of the fact that she had no right to feel jealous. 'He was bound to meet someone else eventually.'

'Mm.'

'And you think I should go out and find a man now that there's no hope of Bart and me getting back together?' suggested Eve.

'I won't deny that Bart's having a new woman in his life brought it to mind,' Lil admitted. 'But I didn't mean it in quite the way you describe. It's just that you work so hard and I never hear you mention any sort of social events.'

'There haven't been many since Bart went away,' said Eve.

'It's hard bringing a kiddie up on your own,' Lil pondered. 'I know that only too well. It would be nice if you had someone to share it with.'

'I must admit, I do sometimes feel like the odd one out in a society that's so couple-orientated,' Eve told her.

'I know the feeling,' said Lil. 'And you're too young to be alone.'

'I manage,' said Eve, wanting to end this conversation because she didn't want to discuss the idea of her finding a man, just any man. 'Anyway, I'll get the stuff you'll be needing from the car. Be back in a minute.'

'All right, dear.'

Collecting a large package of wool and cotton yarns from the car, Eve was thinking of Bart, recalling the fun they'd had together and feeling the ache of remembered intimacy. She tried to be happy for him with his new love, but failed dismally.

The show was over and Bart was having a drink at the bar with the comedian who suffered terribly from stage-fright and had to be well ginned up before he could get on to the stage.

'Dunno why I do it,' said the man, knocking back a large gin to celebrate the fact that his ordeal was over for tonight.

'The same reason any of us do it, I suppose,' replied Bart. 'Because we're not happy doing any other kind of job.'

'You'd think it would get easier, though, wouldn't you?' said the comedian, who was short and fat, with a florid complexion and bloodshot eyes of the most vivid blue. 'But it never does. Twenty-odd years I've earned my living telling gags, and I'm still shit-scared every time.'

'Showbusiness is so insecure, that's the trouble,' said Bart.

'You're not kidding.'

'We put ourselves on the line every time we go out on stage because performing can never be an exact science,' remarked Bart, looking smart in a maroon dinner jacket, crisp white shirt and and bow tie. 'I mean, you learn with experience and get better at it . . . you can perfect your timing and work on your material so that it stays fresh.

303

You can improve your act. But you never know how it'll go on the night.'

'Exactly.'

'I reckon you need to be nervous to get the adrenalin going,' said Bart.

'Not to the extent that I get nervous, though,' said the man.

'Maybe your stage-fright is a bit extreme.' Bart sipped a brandy, looking at him. 'You do the business, though, don't you, mate?' he pointed out. 'Never mind that you're three sheets to the wind when you go on stage. You still get the laughs . . . still get regular bookings.'

'There is that, I suppose,' agreed the man, dragging on a cigarette and gazing through an alcoholic mist into space.

Bart himself made it a rule never to drink before he went on stage, but always headed straight for the bar after the show because he was so hyped up and needed a settler.

The club – which was all marble and mirrors, plush velvet seating and soft lighting – was packed to capacity tonight and the show had gone well. Despite his torturous self-doubt, the comedian had brought the house down, as had the female singer, a busty blonde who was terrific on stage but full of attitude when she came off.

Since he'd been in full-time showbusiness, Bart had come across quite a bit of egomania, bitchiness and delusions of grandeur. But there was also a great deal of warmth and camaraderie among the performers. And the verve and excitement of being in a show was absolute magic.

Tonight he'd held the audience in the palm of his hand, and it was a good feeling. His current closing number was the Sinatra hit 'My Way', which usually went down well with the punters, especially when they'd had a few to drink. The tune was haunting, but the lyrics, though emotional, were in Bart's opinion not true to life, because very few people were able to do things their way. Unless you were rich, selfish or without responsibilities, you had to grab your chances and accept life's limitations.

But he wasn't unhappy with his life. He had a good standard of living, a comfortable flat, a reasonable wage and he was earning it in the way he knew was right for him. He'd much rather be doing it in the UK, but you couldn't have everything.

The telephone rang on the bar and the Spanish barman who answered it told Bart in English that it was for him.

'Hello,' said Bart into the receiver.

'Hi, lover,' said a female voice. 'It's Ann.'

'How are you doing, Ann?' he asked.

'Fine. You just winding down after the show?' she enquired.

'That's right.'

'How did it go tonight?'

'Quite well, I think,' he told her modestly.

'Good . . . Look, I was wondering if you fancy calling in at my place when you've finished there?'

'Isn't it a bit late?'

'It doesn't matter about that,' she said. 'I'm on late shift tomorrow so I don't have to go into work until mid-afternoon.'

'I'm feeling a bit shattered, to tell you the truth,' he told her.

'I'll soon put new life into you,' she offered blatantly.

He laughed. 'I think perhaps I'll go home,' he said, because she tended to push things and it sometimes made him feel trapped.

'Don't be an old misery, Bart,' she said in a wheedling tone. 'Come round to my place. You'll be pleased you did, I promise you.'

'I'm sure I would, but . . .'

'Come on . . .'

He'd been seeing Ann on a regular basis for the last couple of months. She was an attractive woman in her late twenties who worked as a receptionist here at the hotel. She'd come to Spain from England to make a new start after a broken marriage, and had been here several years.

She was entirely different to Eve. Ann had no hankering for independence and only worked at the hotel as a means of keeping herself until she could find a man to do it for her. She had no complicated emotions or lingering feelings for her ex-husband. No child to claim her attention. Her physical appearance was in contrast to Eve's too. Whereas Eve was tall, willowy and darkly beautiful, Ann was small, blonde and sexy, with a look of Barbara Windsor about her.

His relationship with her had come about because of loneliness. But he liked her and enjoyed her company, even though her relentless pursuit of him was a bit off-putting.

'I dunno, Ann,' he said now.

'I hope you haven't got someone else lined up,' she said accusingly.

He didn't reply immediately. 'Nothing like that,' he said eventually, keeping his tone light, even though he was irritated by her proprietorial attitude towards him.

'Why prop up the bar when you can come round to my place and have a decent drink in *real* comfort?' she persisted.

'I like drinking at the bar,' he said.

'Yeah, I know you do,' she said. 'You men are all the same.'

In the mirror behind the optics he could see the opulence of his Mediterranean surroundings: glass chandeliers, gilt-edged bar counter, glamorous women in white showing off year-round tans, men in dinner jackets. He'd come a long way from the shabby bars in London's back streets, but he was suddenly homesick for them, and imbued with a dragging sense of loneliness.

Why was he trying to avoid commitment with Ann? He couldn't have the woman he loved, so why not try to make a go of things with someone who really wanted him? 'I'll finish this drink and get a taxi to your place, Ann.'

'Fabulous,' she said.

Christmas was difficult that year for Eve, the first without her father. Her mother spent Christmas Day with her and Josie, and Eve also invited Lil and Nora, as Bart couldn't get home for the holiday to be with them. Meg and George always went to the Myers' for Christmas dinner but came to Eve's for tea. Ned's absence hung over the celebrations, but they all made a huge effort for the sake of the children, whose exuberant joy in everything helped the adults through this agonising festive season.

There was one very bad moment, when they took their places at the table for tea and Josie asked, 'Why isn't there a place for Grandad?'

The silence was breathtaking. Eve saw her mother's eyes glisten with tears. 'You know why, darling,' said Eve. 'I've told you.'

'I know he's in heaven. But isn't he even allowed to come home for Christmas tea?' enquired the child, her eyes like dark moons in her small face.

'Course not, silly,' Becky piped up before Eve had a chance to reply. 'They have their own things to do.'

'Do they have Christmas cake there?' Josie enquired of her friend.

''Spect so,' said Becky in a matter-of-fact tone.

Josie pondered on this for a moment. 'Oh, that's all right then,' she said.

The children soon became involved in a dispute over a Christmas cracker, and there was a tangible sense of relief among the adults as the awkward moment passed. Eve couldn't wait to see the back of the holiday. Next Christmas might be easier, but at the moment the grief was still too new for any of them to enjoy the spirit of the season.

The new decade got off to a bad start for a lot of people, because Hong Kong flu swept the country, claiming nearly three thousand lives in one week. Eve was forced to close the boutique when she and all her staff fell victim.

She felt like death for several days and was still below

par when she went back to work. She'd been back for just a couple of days when she had to take more leave to look after her mother and Josie, who went down with it at the same time. The only way Eve could be sure her mother got proper care was to have her to stay, and Dot was feeling too ill to argue. So Eve had both patients in bed at her place, something they both enjoyed when they were feeling a little better and could keep each other company.

At the end of the month the case against Eve's father's murderer went to trial. As witnesses, Eve and George had to appear in court, which was a traumatic experience for them both. Eve feared the distress might tip George back into depression, but he coped very well, seeming relieved to see justice done at last. The man who actually did the stabbing received a life sentence; his accomplice got eight years.

In March George opened his showrooms and began dealing in a better class of used car. The new building was sleek and modern, with offices at the back. Eve was proud of him.

Things took an unexpected turn for Eve in the spring of 1970 when she became involved in a romance with a rep from one of the garment manufacturers she did regular business with. It wasn't love, but there was mutual attraction, and a need on Eve's part for some male company of the non-brotherly sort. It was fun for a while, and they went out to restaurants and shows. But it ended on a sour note one night when Eve couldn't get a babysitter. He made it obvious that a child was a nuisance he wasn't prepared to tolerate, and Eve saw no point in seeing him again.

It had been a pleasant interlude which had given her a much-needed reminder that she was a woman as well as a mother. But casual affairs weren't for her. It wasn't in her nature to be emotionally uninvolved. She wanted someone she could get to know and share things with. Someone like Bart. Dear Bart. She still missed his uplifting presence in her life.

* * *

Dot finished washing the dishes after her lunch and looked at the kitchen clock. One fifteen. How could it still be so early? She'd done all her housework, been to the shops, made and eaten cheese on toast, prepared the vegetables and made a meat pie for her evening meal, and there was still a huge expanse of the day left to endure.

It would be a year next month since she'd lost Ned. Eve and George were wonderful, visiting her regularly and making their homes open house to her, but they had their own lives. It wasn't right to rely on them for company.

Somehow she had to rebuild her life. How, though? That was the question. She didn't have the courage to look for a job, and thought she was probably too old anyway, especially as she didn't have any marketable skills. Without Ned there didn't seem any point to anything. Now that he'd gone, the days were endless deserts of time to be filled.

She hadn't said anything to Eve because she didn't want to worry her, but every morning Dot woke up before five with her nerves jangling at the thought of another day to be lived through. Since she was too agitated to lie in bed, she was forced to get up, which made the day even longer.

It wasn't as if Ned had been at home during the day, except on Sundays. But he'd been the centre of her world, the pattern around which she'd structured her time, built her life. She'd loved keeping the house nice for them to enjoy together, making wholesome, interesting meals for him to come home to. She'd looked forward to his coming in of an evening.

Now there was only herself, she had to force herself to cook anything at all, since she didn't have much of an appetite these days. She'd had too much time on her hands before he'd died. Now the situation was unbearable.

Reminding herself of her blessings, she reflected on the fact that at least she had sufficient money to live and pay the rent, thanks to Ned having taken out some life insurance. There wasn't enough for treats, but she could manage. It was just this grinding loneliness and lack of purpose to the day that she found so difficult to cope with.

The days when she looked after the children were better. But now that they were at school she wasn't needed much except in the holidays. And Meg's mother often had Becky.

There was the radio. She enjoyed listening to *The Archers*, and sometimes there was a play on in the afternoon that helped to pass the time until the evening, when she could watch the television. But today she just couldn't face the thought of staying within these four walls on her own until bedtime.

She could walk round to Eve's shop for a chat, or go and see George at the showrooms. If she went now they would probably both be on their lunch break and might have time to talk. Then she could do some window-shopping. Yes, that was what she'd do to help her through another purposeless day.

Tidying her hair in the mirror on the wall above the fireplace, she thought what a fright she looked, so pale and gaunt, her hair almost white now. She went upstairs and put some lipstick on, something she rarely bothered to do these days because there didn't seem to be any point.

Looking at herself in the wardrobe mirror, she noticed that her summer dress was hanging loosely on her. Eve was always nagging her about not eating properly. She said she ought to get some new clothes in a smaller size. But Dot had neither the heart nor the interest.

Back downstairs in the kitchen, she took her shopping bag out of the kitchen cupboard. She didn't have any purchases to make but a bag made her feel as though there was a purpose to her going out. She felt more confident clutching a shopping bag, somehow.

The streets were flooded with June sunlight, the air smelling of summer, the sky blue and cloudless. The glorious weather made her want to cry. Bright days like this emphasised her sadness. But she mustn't let it show, she thought, lifting her chin and starting off down the street towards the main road and George's showrooms.

Election posters still adorned some of the windows in the houses, she noticed, more red than blue around here, this neighbourhood being staunchly working-class. The Tories had been voted back into power at last week's general election, with Edward Heath as prime minister. The result had been totally unexpected. Nearly all the opinion polls had predicted an easy Labour victory. It didn't matter one way or the other to Dot, who had other things on her mind as she reached the main road.

'Wotcha, Mum,' said George, excusing himself from a customer and going over to his mother as soon as she entered the showrooms. 'Anything wrong?'

'No. I was just passing and thought I'd pop in,' she said.

He looked relieved that all was well. 'If you go into my office and make yourself comfortable, I'll be with you as soon as I can.'

'You see to your business, son,' she said. 'Don't worry about me. I'm in no hurry.'

She went to the office area, where Joan the secretary was busy at the typewriter in a room outside George's office. 'Hello, Mrs Granger,' she said, peering at Dot through her spectacles and smiling rather absently. 'How are you keeping these days?'

'Fine, dear, thanks.'

'Would you like a cuppa tea or coffee while you're waiting for George?' offered Joan, a homely woman of middle years who had returned to work after her children left home.

'Not for me, thanks,' Dot said. 'I've just had my lunch.'

'Out shopping, are you?' Joan enquired chattily.

'That's right,' fibbed Dot, because it seemed feeble to admit the truth.

'If you'd like to go through to George's office, I'm sure

he won't be long,' said Joan, and turned her attention back to her typewriter.

Dot went into her son's office and sat down on a chair near his desk. George always seemed to keep this door open, so she didn't close it, which meant she could see through into the outer office.

Glancing around the room, she thought it would be smart if it wasn't so untidy. She had to clench her fists to stop herself tidying the papers that littered the big leather-topped desk. The filing cabinet was open, the top strewn with papers. This was the workplace of a busy man.

Through the open door she saw George come into the outer office, followed by the customer. He began talking to Joan about a hire-purchase agreement. The salesman appeared at George's side, and at the same moment the telephone rang. Joan answered it and said something to George, who came rushing into his own office to take the call. 'Be with you in a minute, Mum,' he said, embarking on a conversation while signalling to the salesman who was waiting by the door that he wouldn't be long.

Dot stood up. George put his hand over the mouthpiece. 'Two minutes, Mum, I promise.'

'You get on with your business,' she said, blowing him a kiss. 'I'll see you later.'

And she left.

Eve was with a customer when Dot arrived at the boutique. The woman had just bought a trouser suit and Eve was completing the sale. Eve asked her mother if all was well and was assured that it was and that Dot had just called in for a chat.

'Lovely,' said Eve. 'Take a pew and I'll be with you in a minute.'

Dot sat down and waited while Eve put the purchase into a bag and the money through the till, chatting to the customer as she worked. Someone else came in as the first customer went out.

'Sorry to keep you waiting, Mum,' Eve apologised. 'The staff are out at lunch, which is why I'm on my own. Caroline will be back in a minute. As soon as I've got some cover, I'll put the kettle on and we'll have a cup of something in the office.'

Dot was about to offer to make the tea, then changed her mind. Since Ned had died, everywhere she went she felt like an appendage. 'Don't worry, love,' she said, rising purposefully. 'I've just remembered something I have to do.'

Eve's brow furrowed. She knew her mother was feeling wretched, no matter how hard she tried to conceal it, and it twisted Eve's heart. She would do anything at all to help her, but she knew there was only so much anyone could do to fill the void left by Ned. 'Don't go, please,' she urged. 'The girls will be back soon and we can talk while I eat my sandwiches.'

'I'll see you later, love,' said Dot with false but, hopefully, convincing cheerfulness. 'I've got some shopping to do.'

'Are you all right?' Eve looked worried.

'I'm absolutely fine, love . . . don't you worry about me,' she said, and left her daughter to attend to her customers without interruption.

Walking back along the crowded main road, Dot stopped to gaze unseeingly into the windows of Rowse's drapery store and the Dolcis shoe shop next door. She felt shaky and ashamed for bothering her children in the middle of a working day just because she was feeling lonely. It was pathetic!

Biting back the tears, she walked on past Marks and Spencer towards the side turning that led to Marshall Gardens. But as she passed the bus stop, she stopped, pondered on something for a few moments, then joined the queue.

The café was crowded with people and thick with smoke and steam. A roar of noise buffeted Dot as she opened the door: the vociferous clamour of people talking, the clatter of crockery and metallic scrape of knife against plate, spoon

313

against dish. The instant Dot stepped inside, she regretted her impulsive action and was about to make a hasty retreat when a voice boomed across the room.

'Dot . . . Dot Granger.' Rudy had spotted her as he took a meal to a table. He delivered the food and came over to where she was standing uncertainly just inside the door. 'Well, there's a sight for sore eyes. Hang on a minute and I'll find you somewhere to sit.'

Her face was scalding with embarrassment, her heart pounding. The place was packed with people eating cooked meals, this being the lunch period, and the most she could possibly manage was a cup of coffee. This was what happened to you when you led a solitary existence: you lost track of time and forgot about other people's commitments. People were busy working during the day and didn't have time to talk to some lonely housewife with too much time on her hands.

Now she really was in a quandary. She could hardly take up table space at this busy time for the price of a cup of coffee, and if she ordered a meal she couldn't eat, Rudy might take it as a criticism. There was only one thing for it.

'I only came for a chat . . . you said to call in if I fancied some company any time,' she confessed, feeling foolish for the third time that day. 'But I can see I've chosen a bad time. You're still in the middle of the lunchtime rush.'

'There's a table for two over by the window,' he told her in a tone so warm and welcoming she could feel its healing properties reaching her battered self-esteem. 'You go and sit down and I'll join you as soon as I get clear.'

'Another time, perhaps,' she said, still afraid she was imposing.

'No, don't go . . . please.' He seemed genuinely glad to see her. 'Once this rush is over, things will probably quieten down for a while. And I'd enjoy a chat.' He glanced towards the counter, where the queue was snaking towards the door, and tutted. 'My assistant left unexpectedly a couple of days ago and I haven't managed to find a replacement yet. That's why I'm so pushed. It's a damned nuisance.' He ushered her over to the table. 'Can I get you something to drink while you're waiting?'

'A cuppa tea would be nice.' She pulled her purse from her bag, only to have him wave his hand dismissively.

'One tea on the house coming up,' he said.

'Thank you.'

He weaved his way through the tables, a dapper, speedy figure, the bald patch on the back of his head gleaming within a rug of greying dark hair. He brought her cup of tea over almost at once, obviously giving her priority over the waiting customers, then hurried back behind the counter. She watched him taking the orders and handing them through a hatch to the kitchen, pouring cups of tea and coffee at the counter, taking meals to tables.

Dot couldn't believe she had come to this. First she'd tried to force her company on to her children in the middle of their working day; now she was sitting in a café in a neighbourhood right off her own manor, waiting to talk to a man she hardly knew, just because he had once casually offered her a listening ear.

Watching Rudy darting between the tables and the counter, she had an unexpected idea. She rubbed her chin thoughtfully, wondering if she dared take it further. Then, in a sudden burst of bravery, she got up and went over to Rudy, who was taking an order, the queue just as long as it had been when she'd first walked in.

'Why don't I give you a hand?' she heard herself suggest.

'Don't be daft,' he said. 'You haven't come here to work.'

'True,' she agreed. 'But as I'm sitting about doing nothing while you're rushed off your feet, it makes sense for me to help. It'll give me something to do while I'm waiting.'

'Well . . . if you're sure,' he said, but he still looked doubtful.

Carried along by a growing tide of courage which had begun the minute she'd boarded the bus to Acton, she lifted the flap and went behind the counter. 'Got an apron I can borrow?' she asked.

'I'll soon find you one,' said a bemused Rudy. When he came back with a white laundered apron, Dot was already pouring tea from a large metal pot.

Having not worked outside the home for many years, having to cope with a queue of working men was terrifying. Her hands were shaking so much she could hardly hold the teapot steady. But somehow she managed to pour the tea without spilling too much, and as she worked she felt the beginnings of a kind of peace, something she hadn't experienced in a long time.

She didn't know the price of anything, or how to work the cash register, but she could pour tea and coffee and take food to the tables, leaving Rudy free to deal with the orders and the money. The customers were a bit rough and ready but a friendly crowd. Judging by the light-hearted banter, they were all regulars and obviously thought a lot of Rudy.

'You on a go-slow today, mate?' came a good-humoured crack from one of the tables.

'When I asked for egg and bacon, I didn't realise I'd have to wait while you went to the farm to get the ingredients,' said another.

It was all said in fun, and Rudy took it in good part.

'I haven't enjoyed anything so much in ages,' Dot told him later when the rush was over and they sat down together for a cup of tea and a sticky bun.

'Really?' He sounded amazed.

'Yes, really,' she said. 'At least I feel as though I've been doing something useful with my time instead of sitting about at home feeling sorry for myself.'

'Been a bit down in the dumps, have you?' he enquired in a friendly manner.

She nodded. 'I know I'm luckier than a lot of people. I've got a couple of good kids and two lovely granddaughters.'

316

She considered Becky to be her granddaughter even though there was no biological tie. 'But some days that doesn't seem to help. Today I just couldn't stay in that house on my own any longer.' She told him about her visits to Eve and George. 'I was just about to go home when I remembered what you said and I hopped on the bus before I had a chance to change my mind. I've thought of coming to see you before but never quite found the courage. Losing Ned did terrible things to my confidence.'

'Losing your partner does that,' Rudy said wisely. 'That's why the café was such a godsend to me when I lost my wife. Even though the last thing I wanted to do was get out of bed to open up for the breakfast trade, I had no choice, and it was the best thing I could have done. It forced me out of the house and made me talk to people.'

'It's certainly done wonders for me this afternoon,' Dot said.

'Now you've broken the ice, I hope you'll come again,' he said.

'You can bet on it.'

Their conversation was constantly interrupted because Rudy had to get up to attend to his customers.

'You're a busy man,' she remarked lightly.

'I like to be busy but it's a bit too hectic without a counter assistant,' he told her.

'So I can see.' She paused thoughtfully. 'How on earth do you manage to fit your theatrical agency work in?'

'I don't, not any more,' he told her. 'But I used to do it at quiet times and evenings when I'd closed the café.'

'You've given it up altogether then?' she said enquiringly.

'Yeah. It was never really going anywhere, even though I tried to convince myself otherwise,' he explained. 'It was just a hobby really. Once Bart went abroad, I lost interest.'

'I know nothing about these things,' confessed Dot, 'but don't you get a percentage of what Bart earns even though he is living abroad?'

317

'No . . . I didn't get that job for him,' he said. 'He was approached direct and negotiated the contract himself, so I'm not involved.'

'Do you miss it?'

'Sometimes,' he said. 'But I didn't have the time to give to it because this place keeps me fully occupied.' He waved a hand towards the room. 'I know it's only a greasy-spoon café, but it's a good business and I love the place. I think of my regulars as mates.'

'They obviously feel the same way about you,' she told him.

'I hope so,' he said. 'I've got customers who've been coming here for years . . . shift workers, van drivers, people who live in bedsits and can't be bothered to cook for themselves.' He paused, looking round. 'Hard men, shady characters some of 'em, I get all sorts in here.'

Someone came in and went over to the counter. 'I'll see to it,' Dot offered, amazing herself. 'You stay there and finish your tea.'

Too taken aback to argue, Rudy let her carry on. It was an easy order, just tea and a doughnut, which she was able to deal with herself at the counter rather than having to pass the order through to the cook in the kitchen. She was even able to work out the price from the list on the wall but had to call on Rudy for instructions on how to use the cash register.

Back at the table, Rudy said, 'Well, you've soon got the hang of things.'

'I surprised myself,' she admitted.

'If you're not very careful I might be tempted to offer you a job,' he smiled, only half joking.

'If you do, I shall certainly give it serious thought,' she told him, smiling properly for the first time in nearly a year.

'In that case, let's talk business, shall we?' he said, beaming.

Chapter Eighteen

'You've got a job in Rudy's café?' exclaimed Eve when her mother came round to see her that evening, full of it.

'Yeah, isn't it exciting?'

They were in Eve's kitchen, Dot sitting at the table drinking a cup of tea, Eve sorting through some washing she'd just got off the line. Josie was aleep in bed.

'If I'd known you were looking for a job, I'd have found you something to do at the boutique,' was Eve's impulsive response.

'I wasn't looking for a job . . . this one just happened to come up,' said Dot, surprised at her own assertiveness. 'And I don't need anyone to find me something to do. I'm quite capable of doing a job that needs doing, not something created just to keep me occupied.'

Eve was amazed at her mother's spiky reaction, and realised that she could have been more tactful. 'Sorry, Mum,' she said. 'I didn't mean to be patronising. It's just so unexpected. I mean, you haven't been out to work for years and, well . . .' She paused, choosing her words. 'Rudy's café is a bit rough.'

'So what if it is? It's clean, and the food's good.' She gave Eve a sharp look. 'It isn't like you to be snobbish.'

'And I hope I'm not being,' Eve was quick to point out. 'I wasn't casting asperions on Rudy's cuisine or hygiene standards. It's just that with most of the customers being working men, you might feel uncomfortable. They won't always watch their language, you know.'

'Mm, there is that,' said Dot in a warmer tone. 'So, I

shall either have to get used to it or tell them to watch it if I hear anything offensive. Because I really want this job. I need to do something useful, Eve. I'm fed up with filling in time at home, trying to find ways to occupy myself just to get to the end of the day.'

There was a quiet determination about her mother that Eve hadn't seen before. 'Oh, Mum,' she said with a surge of compunction, 'I should have done more to help. But I've been so busy with the shop and everything . . .'

'You couldn't have done more than you already have since your dad died, so you've nothing to reproach yourself for,' Dot cut in. 'But there's only so much other people can do when you lose your partner . . . as you very well know.'

'Yes, I do,' said Eve, remembering.

'For the first time in almost a year, I felt human again this afternoon,' said Dot, her eyes gleaming with a new light. 'And it was such a good feeling.'

'I can imagine,' said Eve.

'I feel as though I have something to get up for in the morning again.'

'As long as it isn't too much for you,' said Eve in concern.

'Come off it, Eve,' admonished Dot. 'I'm not in my dotage.'

'I know that.' Eve had become very protective towards her mother since her father's death. Dot seemed so lost, so vulnerable, it hurt Eve to see it. 'Take no notice of me. I'm just being the fussy daughter, afraid you'll overdo things.'

'I appreciate your concern for me, love,' said Dot. 'But I've been relying too heavily on you and George for company . . . it's time I got on with my own life now.'

'If this job is what you want, then good luck to you.'

'Thanks, Eve.' Dot paused thoughtfully. 'Funny how things work out, innit? I've been worried sick, knowing I should be doing something useful with my time but not having the nerve to actually look for anything. Then this job found me. And because of the way it happened, I didn't have time to think about it and get nervous. I just got stuck in.'

'Good for you,' said Eve. 'What are the hours?'

'Nine till three, but I've agreed to work longer if Rudy asks me to for any particular reason,' she told her. 'I'll be able to pick Josie up from school if you need me to.' She threw Eve a look. 'I've told Rudy that I'll probably want some time off during the school holidays, so I'll still be able to help out with Josie.'

'We'll work it out between us, don't worry,' said Eve.

'The extra cash will be useful,' commented Dot. 'I'll be able to spoil the kids now.'

'Spend some money on yourself,' her daughter suggested. 'Buy some clothes that fit you. You could go for something a bit more fashionable now that you're slimmer.' Eve's tone was light. Having tried, without success, to improve her mother's appearance for most of her adult life, she didn't seriously expect to succeed now.

'I thought you'd given up trying to modernise me?'

'Helping people to look nice is my business, it's in my blood,' Eve laughed.

'I'll be wearing an overall all day, anyway,' Dot reminded her.

'Okay, I won't nag you.' Eve walked round the table and gave her mother a hug. 'I'm really proud of you, though. Going out to work after all these years takes some bottle.'

'I haven't started yet.'

'As good as,' Eve pointed out. 'You've had a trial run.'

'True,' said Dot, in such a positive manner Eve hardly recognised her.

The wind of change that had begun to flutter through the Granger family when her father died was gaining strength, Eve observed with a touch of nostalgia. She'd never envisaged the day when Dot would go out to work. But she would give her mother every support. God knows, Dot had supported her often enough!

*   *   *

Lil seemed preoccupied when Eve went to collect some work one golden autumn morning in September. Shafts of sunlight beaming through the living room window made patterns on the wall, dappled by the net curtains, the shape of the cat sitting on the windowsill silhouetted at the bottom.

'Is anything the matter?' enquired Eve after they'd been through an order for some black evening tops.

Lil concentrated on the crocheting she was currently working on, seeming reluctant to answer the question.

'Lil, what is it?' Eve persisted.

The older woman gave Eve an odd look. 'I had a telephone call from Bart last night,' she said.

'Is something wrong with him?' Eve felt a stab of fear.

'No.' She chewed her lip. 'Oh dear, I hate having to tell you this, Eve,' she blurted out, her voice quivering slightly. 'But he's gone and got himself engaged. To Ann.'

Hearing the words was a physical pain to Eve. 'Well, we both knew he was seeing someone, so it isn't entirely unexpected,' said Eve, struggling to be adult about this.

'I suppose not,' said Lil. 'He's asked me again to go to Spain for a visit. Wants me to meet his fiancée.'

'That will be really nice,' said Eve.

'He knows perfectly well that I won't go, though.' Lil was adamant.

Bart had been trying to persuade his mother to go with Nora to Spain for a holiday ever since he'd been there. Lil had told Eve all about it. Eve secretly thought a fear of flying was the reason he hadn't succeeded, but Lil claimed it was due to the fact that travelling would be too difficult for someone in her circumstances.

'Won't you even consider it as it's for a special reason?' Eve gently enquired.

'How can I when I'm in this thing?' Lil said, looking towards her wheelchair.

'Arrangements can be made on the aircraft for that, as you very well know,' Eve pointed out. 'The crew would look after you. You'd be with Nora. And I'd take you to the airport and make sure you were in safe hands.'

'It's kind of you to offer, dear,' she said 'But I just can't face it.'

'Think how nice it would be to meet your future daughter-in-law,' said Eve with enormous generosity since her own heart was breaking at the thought of Bart having a wife.

'I'll wait until he brings her home to see me,' was Lil's reaction to that suggestion.

'It isn't like you to be beaten by anything,' remarked Eve. The other woman was usually so indomitable, and Eve had a sneaking suspicion that she wanted to go very much indeed but needed encouragement to help her find the courage.

'I'm not beaten by it,' she denied sharply. 'I'd do it if it was absolutely essential. But it isn't, and I really think it will be too much of a palaver.'

'You'll have a smashing time once you get there, and the weather should still be nice at this time of year,' persisted Eve. 'It'll be worth the journey to see Bart perform at a decent venue too.'

'I'm not going, so you can save your breath.' Lil's crochet hook was moving at such a speed, it might have been battery-powered.

'Most people would jump at the chance of what you're being offered,' said Eve. 'A holiday in Spain, all paid for by your son.'

'Yeah, yeah, I know I'm being an ungrateful old bag, but I'm not going and that's that,' was Lil's firm reply.

'It would be a terrific achievement for you,' Eve pointed out.

The crochet hook lost speed while its owner lapsed into thought. Eve's hopes were raised but dashed again when Lil said, 'I know you mean well, dear, but I'm not going and that's an end to it.'

'I'll make the travel arrangements for you and get you to the airport on time,' offered Eve.

Lil shook her head. 'It's very kind of you, but I'm not

going and that's that,' was her final word on the subject. 'Now, about these evening tops . . . how many do you want, and in what sizes?'

A few evenings later, Eve received a telephone call from Spain.

'Bart,' she said, her heart racing, 'how lovely to hear your voice.'

'Likewise.'

'I understand that congratulations are in order,' she said.

A pause. 'That's right,' he said eventually. It wasn't a good line, there was a lot of hissing and crackling. She pressed the receiver hard against her ear.

'All the best for the future, Bart,' she said, shouting above the interference. 'I hope you'll both be very happy.'

There was a crackly pause, then, 'Thanks, Eve . . . Actually, I'm just calling to thank you for persuading my mother to come to Spain for a visit.'

'You mean she's agreed?' Eve was astonished.

'Yeah, she telephoned me just now . . . said you'd talked her into it.'

'I thought I'd failed completely,' Eve told him. 'I had no idea she'd changed her mind.'

'Well, she has, and from what I can make out, it's all down to you.'

'That really is good news,' she said.

'Yeah.'

'Will it be easier for you if I make her travel arrangements this end?' she said.

'I can arrange a flight for her and Nora from here once I know exactly when she wants to come,' he said. 'But it would be a real help if you could take them to the airport. I'd feel easier in my mind if you did it, rather than have them going by taxi . . . she said you'd offered.'

'I'll be happy to do it,' she said.

'Thanks, Eve . . . she'll reimburse you for your expenses. I'll make sure there's enough money in her account.'

'There's no need for that,' she said. 'But don't worry, I'll sort everything out with Lil.'

'Thanks a lot, Eve.'

'It's a pleasure,' she said. 'And many congratulations again.'

'Thanks . . . 'bye for now.'

''Bye.'

She was trembling when she replaced the receiver, weak from the pleasure of hearing his voice, but sad that all hope had now gone. He was soon to be married and lost to her forever.

Bart was also feeling shaky when he put the phone down. He leaned back on the sofa in his Mediterranean-style lounge, white wall units and occasional tables contrasting with brightly coloured soft furnishings in contemporary patterns. He was alone. Ann was on late shift at the hotel. He was due in at work himself soon.

Eve still had the most disturbing effect on him, no matter how hard he tried to be indifferent. In theory you put the past behind you and stopped loving one woman when you got engaged to another. But it hadn't happened that way for him.

His engagement had come about because Ann had given him an ultimatum. Make a definite commitment to me or lose me, had been her uncompromising message. It had seemed easier to go along with her than not. After all, it was time he settled down. So he'd allowed himself to be swept along by events.

He was looking forward to seeing his mother and determined to give her a good holiday. The fact that he didn't have to go to work until the evening meant he'd be able to spend the days with her and Nora, showing them the sights and introducing them to the Spanish way of life.

Convincing his discerning mother that he was happy would be less simple than providing her with a good holiday. But convince her he must, because she'd worry if she knew the truth, that he'd made a terrible mistake in getting engaged to Ann. There would be no need for his mother ever to know about this, because he was determined to make a go of things.

Bea Myers wasn't impressed by Dot's job. 'It sounds ghastly to me,' she said. 'I can't imagine anything more revolting than serving food to bus drivers and sweaty navvies.'

'I enjoy it,' Dot told her, adding wickedly, 'and they're not all drivers and navvies, you know. We get the odd small-time criminal in too: burglars, shoplifters, pickpockets and the like.'

Eve wanted to laugh, and stared at her plate to hide her amusement. Her mother was getting to be quite forceful lately, she thought. Having a job had done wonders for her spirit.

It was late autumn, and Eve, her mother and Josie had been invited to George and Meg's for Sunday lunch. Meg had decided to make a double family occasion of it by inviting her parents too. Optimism gone mad, in Eve's opinion.

Having the sensitivity of a floor tile, Bea missed Dot's joke. 'How dreadful,' she said, interpreting this contact with criminal types as further proof of the Grangers' inferior status. 'You should report them to the police if you know they're breaking the law.'

'Dot was joking, Mother,' Meg informed her patiently.

'Oh . . .' Bea tutted, obviously feeling foolish, but still continuing with her belittlement of Dot's new occupation. 'Doesn't working with all that fried food make you feel sick?'

'No,' said Dot evenly. 'Anyway, it isn't all fried food. We do meat and two veg at lunchtimes.'

Bea – matronly as ever in a brown tweed winter dress – gave Dot a pitying look. 'It must be terrible for you, *having* to go out to work.'

'Yeah, I did consider the idea of begging outside Bentall's, but I thought it might be too cold for me in the winter,' she said with a deadpan expression. 'So I took the job at the café instead.'

The silence was agonising. George coughed to hide his mirth, Eve concentrated hard on her roast lamb, biting back a giggle. Meg turned scarlet and looked worriedly towards her mother. Frank was preoccupied with his thoughts and hadn't been following the conversation so didn't react at all, and Dot stared at Bea defiantly. Eve was proud of her mother. Not so long ago, she'd have sat back meekly and let Bea Myers get away with it.

'There's no call to be sarcastic,' said Bea, glaring at Dot.

'You did rather ask for it, Ma-in-law,' put in George.

'I've told you not to call me that . . .'

'Sorry.'

'Can we get on with our meal?' interrupted Meg, in an effort to smooth things over.

Seeing a look of desperation in Meg's eyes, Eve gave her a sympathetic look. 'Yeah, let's do that,' she said supportively. 'It's a lovely meal and deserves our full attention.'

Becky made a welcome intervention. 'Can I leave my meat, please, Mummy?' she asked.

'You should try to eat a bit more,' Meg told her firmly.

'But I don't like it,' said Becky with a look of such persuasion it sent shivers through Eve because it reminded her so vividly of Ken. Becky was very much like her mother to look at, but Eve could sometimes see her father in her mannerisms.

It occurred to Eve that had she not happened to meet Meg at the antenatal clinic that day and struck up a friendship with her, she'd never have known that Josie had a half-sister. She'd probably have spent the rest of her life deluding herself about her marriage to Ken, too, despite what she'd learned from her ex-workmates. The trouble with knowing the truth was that it blotted out memories of the happy times she'd had with Ken, which was a pity. But for all that, she was glad she knew.

'Put some mint sauce on it,' advised Josie, who was sitting beside Becky. 'It tastes lovely then. Better than school dinners.'

'School dinners, yuk,' said Becky. 'They taste like sick.'

'Really, Becky,' rebuked Meg.

'You mustn't say disgusting things like that,' added Bea authoritatively. 'It isn't nice.'

'But it's true, Grandma,' said Becky, pouring mint sauce on to her meat rather cautiously. 'Everyone at school says so.'

'Well, we'd rather you didn't, if you don't mind,' said Meg firmly.

'Sorry, Mummy,' said Becky, sighing.

The childish chatter removed the focus from the conflict between Dot and Bea and the adult conversation began to flow again, albeit that Bea retreated into a sulky silence.

'More potatoes, anyone?' said Eve, having helped herself from the tureen. She looked around the table, her glance resting on Meg's father, who didn't seem to be eating anything and was just playing with his food. 'Frank?'

No reply.

'Dad,' said Meg.

'Frank,' said his wife in a loud, disapproving voice, 'what *is* the matter with you today?'

'What?' He seemed startled, obviously deeply engrossed in his own thoughts. 'What is it, what's happened?'

'I was just asking if you wanted more potatoes,' explained Eve.

'Oh, no thank you, dear,' he said, giving her a watery smile, and she thought how pale he was looking, and thinner than he used to be.

'You've hardly eaten a thing, Dad,' said Meg with a mixture of concern and reproof.

'Sorry, dear,' he said. 'It's a lovely meal and you've done us proud. But I haven't much of an appetite today.'

'I don't know what's got into you lately,' said Bea critically. 'You never seem hungry. When your daughter goes to all this trouble to cook a meal for us, you could at least make an effort.'

'It's all right, Daddy,' said Meg, smiling and winking at him. 'Don't worry.'

At last the meal limped painfully to a close, much to everyone's relief, Eve suspected, and after coffee the guests departed.

'Not exactly the social gathering of the year, was it?' Meg remarked to George; they were in the kitchen doing the dishes together, she washing, George drying.

'Through no fault of yours, though, love,' he was quick to assure her. 'The meal was lovely, it was the atmosphere that spoilt it. My mother has become quite assertive.'

'So I've noticed,' said Meg. 'Going out to work has given her confidence.'

'I thought she and your mother were gonna come to blows at one point,' he said.

'Yes, it did get a bit heated,' Meg agreed.

'What was the matter with your father?' enquired George, frowning.

'I've no idea. He was in a very strange mood.'

'He didn't seem to be very well to me,' said George. 'He was as white as a ghost, and very quiet.'

'Things on his mind, I expect,' said Meg. 'Business matters if I know Daddy. He keeps things to himself, though. I managed to get a few minutes with him on his own and asked him what was the matter. He pretended he didn't know what I was talking about and said that everything's fine.'

'Whatever's troubling him, we won't get to know about it, then?'

'Shouldn't think so,' she said.

'Talking of business problems,' remarked George, drying

some cutlery and putting it away in the drawer, 'I've got one myself this coming week.'

'Really?'

'Yeah. There's a car auction I'd like to go to in Birmingham,' he explained. 'But it means my being away from the show-rooms all day.'

'The staff will look after things for you, won't they?' she asked.

'After a fashion,' he said.

'You don't sound very confident.'

'I'm not,' he told her. 'I don't like to be away for that long. Joan only knows so much, and the salesman's good at his job but he *is* only a salesman.'

'You need a manager,' she said.

'Yes, I think I probably do.'

'Someone you can trust to look after things while you're away from the site. A right-hand man.'

'That was what Dad was,' he reminded her, his mood darkening. 'No one could ever replace him.'

'Of course not, George, but you need someone to back you up,' she insisted.

'Mm.'

'Couldn't you promote the salesman to manager and get someone to replace him?' she suggested.

'Not really,' he said. 'He's a good salesman but I don't think he's up to taking responsibility for the business when I'm not there.'

'Pity.'

'It is. I shall have to put my mind to finding someone, though,' he said. 'It's hard for me to leave the place now that Dad's not around to look after things for me. Trouble is, I have to go out on business more than ever now that the firm's bigger.'

'They say that the art of good management is delegation, and you're gonna have to do more of it. And learn to switch off when you're away from the showrooms,' she advised him. 'I've had to do it. If I allowed myself to worry about all the disasters that might be happening at the boutique while I'm not there, I'd be a complete nervous wreck, and that wouldn't be good for Becky.'

'You're right,' he said. 'I must get it sorted.'

Becky appeared, asking if they could go to the park.

'What do you think, Meg?' George said, looking from one to the other. 'Do you fancy a walk in Walpole Park?'

'Yes, that would be nice . . . Go and get your coat and shoes, darling,' instructed Meg, 'and Daddy will help you get ready while I finish this.'

'Okay,' trilled the little girl, heading for the hall with her stepfather behind her.

Meg wiped the worktops and dried her hands, smiling at the sound of George and Becky talking and laughing together in another part of the house. Thank God she and George had come through that bad patch and were happy again. As traumatic as it had been at the time, it seemed somehow to have strengthened their relationship.

Bea Myers sat in stony silence all the way home in the car. As soon as they got inside the house, she launched an attack on Frank.

'I don't know what the matter is with you these days,' she declared, dragging her coat off and hanging it up in the downstairs cloakroom. 'There was a time when you would have taken my side against anyone. But nowadays I get no support whatever when people insult me.'

'Who insulted you?' he asked wearily as he removed his own coat.

'George's mother, of course,' she said, marching into the lounge and sitting down heavily on the sofa. 'You were there, you heard her.'

'I can't say that I noticed,' he confessed, sinking into an armchair near the fireplace. 'I must have been thinking of other things.'

'The woman's a monster,' Bea ranted. 'Like the rest of that damned family.'

'Don't start that again . . .'

'I don't know why Meg invites them when we are going to be there,' she went on, as though he hadn't spoken.

'Isn't it because Dot is on her own now?' Frank suggested reasonably. 'It can't be easy when you lose your other half. Meg is just doing her bit to help.'

'Well, I shall tell her not to invite that awful woman in future if we're going to be there,' she said. 'The Grangers are not in our class.'

'George *is* our son-in-law, dear,' he reminded her. 'You really ought to respect that.'

'I see no reason why I should. As far as I'm concerned, he isn't good enough for our daughter, and that's all there is to it.'

'They seem very happy together,' Frank pointed out. 'And he's a wonderful father to Becky. Surely that pleases you.'

'Why do you disagree with every single thing I say lately?' Bea asked, giving him a fearsome look.

'I don't.'

'Yes you do,' she argued. 'Sometimes I wish I'd never married you.'

Frank fell silent, his mouth twitching slightly. His face was ashen.

'So what do you have to say to that?' she asked when he didn't respond. She didn't enjoy being made a fool of by someone like Dot Granger, and as usual, her husband was taking the full brunt of her bad temper.

'Well?' she persisted, her beady eyes narrowed on him.

'The feeling is mutual, I can assure you,' he said at last.

Bea thought she must have misheard him, because he never, *ever* spoke back to her. 'What was that you said?' she wanted to know.

'Sometimes I wish I'd never married you,' he announced, standing up and glaring down at her, his body rigid with tension, eyes bright with temper. 'You're a selfish, mean-minded woman with no thought for anyone but yourself.'

Open-mouthed, she stared at him. 'How dare you speak to me like that?'

'I'll speak to you in the way you deserve,' he said, completely beside himself, the financial strain he'd been under for months finally telling on him. 'After the years of hell you've given me, I think it's time I spoke up for myself.'

'Years of hell . . . ?'

'That's right,' he said, his voice distorted with emotion. 'It's been nothing short of purgatory for me all these years, trying to meet your constant demands . . . putting up with your damnned snobbery.'

'Don't you dare say such things to me,' she uttered shakily.

'Oh, shut up for once in your life, woman,' he said, and stormed from the house, leaving his wife sitting on the sofa in a state of shock. In all of their life together, she had never known him behave like this before.

Frank walked through the well-kept grassland of Gunnersbury Park, trying to work off his temper, which eventually lost its fire, leaving him feeling miserable, with a dull ache in the pit of his stomach. The air was cold and still, a heatless sun glinting on the Round Pond overlooked by the eighteenth-century garden pavilion with its fine pilasters and columns supporting the beautifully ornamented stone pediment. He stared into the water, the surface rippling with the movement of a cruising family of ducks.

He walked on past the museum. A group of people were coming out, chattering enthusiastically about what they'd learned about local history. How he envied them. He couldn't remember the last time he'd enjoyed such an ordinary activity as that. In fact, he couldn't remember the last time he'd enjoyed anything.

On through the trees, almost bare now, past the deserted tennis courts and the fishpond. He was cold now, shivering. He'd left the house in such a hurry he'd not even stopped for his overcoat and was wearing just a sports jacket over his shirt and tie. The sun disappeared and the damp autumn chill of the advancing afternoon seeped into his bones.

Oh well, time to go home and face the music, he told himself. It was also time to do something he should have done a long time ago.

When he walked into the room, Bea was sitting straight-backed on the sofa, looking through a homes and gardens magazine. She didn't glance up or acknowledge his arrival in any way.

'I'm sorry I lost my temper and stormed out,' he said, standing with his back to the fire, looking at her.

'I should think so too.'

'But I'm not sorry about the things I said,' he continued.

She looked up sharply. 'Well, really . . .' she began.

'Before you start bitching again, I'm going to have my say,' he informed her.

'I thought you'd already done that,' she said with a sob in her voice. 'Years of hell, you said . . .'

'That was said in anger,' he pointed out.

'I hope you didn't mean it.'

He didn't reassure her on that point, but said instead, 'Now that I'm calmer, there are things that I must tell you . . . very important things.'

She looked at him, worried now for all her front. 'I've done enough listening to you for one day,' she proclaimed. 'All you do is insult me.'

'You must listen to me, Bea,' he urged. 'It's crucial that you do.'

'I'm looking for ideas for a new kitchen,' she said casually, ignoring his plea and turning her attention back to the magazine. 'Ours urgently needs updating.'

Patience tried to the limit, he marched across the room and snatched the magazine from her grasp. 'There'll be no new kitchen,' he said, throwing the magazine to the floor.

'There'll be no new anything for us. Not for the time being, anyway.'

'What are you talking about?' she demanded, too shaken by this news to rebuke him for taking the magazine.

'I've been trying to tell you for years that the business isn't what it used to be,' he said. 'But would you listen? Oh, no. Nothing I say ever warrants your attention. I've asked you to cut down on spending, told you we had to economise. But you wouldn't do it, would you?'

'I didn't think there was any call for it,' she said lamely.

'Well, I can spare you from the truth no longer,' he told her. 'You have to accept the fact that the business isn't doing well . . . in fact, things are very bad.'

'In other words, you're making a mess of things,' she said.

'It's the changing times we live in, can't you understand that?' he pleaded with her. 'Big corporations are taking over from individuals, who simply can't compete. More small shops are going out of business every year, every week even. The orders from those shops are my bread and butter and I'm losing more all the time.'

'There must be something you can do,' she said. 'You're an experienced businessman, surely you can work out a way to put things right.'

'I'm doing everything I possibly can,' he assured her. 'I've cut down on my staff . . . I'm trying to get new customers. I've even approached the supermarket chains with a view to supplying them. But they've got it all sewn up.'

'You will make it all right, though, won't you, Frank?' she said, frightened now for her comfortable lifestyle.

His instincts urged him to protect her from harsh reality, as he'd always done before. But that was no longer possible.

'As I've said, I'm doing everything I can to turn the business around,' he said. 'But I can't alter the way things are developing in the marketplace. I can't stop progress.'

'So . . . what are you actually saying?' she demanded.

'I'm saying that things could get worse,' he told her flatly.

'How much worse, exactly?'

He gulped hard and forced the words out. 'We could lose the house.'

She leapt up, terrified now, because her home and her status in the community were everything to her. 'You can't take my house away from me, Frank,' she said with genuine anguish. 'Tell me what you're saying isn't true, please.'

He stared at the floor, riddled with guilt for letting her down and being such a disappointment to her. He'd known she would take the news badly, but for a fleeting second he'd allowed himself the luxury of imagining that she might stand by him in this. You did hear of wives being supportive to their husbands in times of trouble.

In his heart, though, he'd known Bea would give him nothing but trouble. For himself he couldn't care less about the downturn in their fortunes. A big house with all the trappings wasn't essential to his happiness. But failing his wife so completely caused him pain like nothing else could. Despite her crushing contempt for him, which had become such a habit she wasn't even aware she was making it so obvious, he still felt very deeply for her. True, it sometimes felt more like hate than love, but it was all part of the same thing. 'I can't tell you that it isn't true, nor am I saying it will happen,' he told her gravely. 'I'm just warning you that it is a distinct possibility.'

Her eyes filled with tears. 'Well, I'll tell you this much, Frank Myers,' she said, half sobbing. 'If I lose my home because of your incompetence, I'll *never* forgive you.'

'No, I don't suppose you will, Bea,' he replied in a tone of weary resignation, and left the room because he couldn't bear to see the look of bitter resentment in her eyes.

Chapter Nineteen

In January of the following year, the death was announced of the woman who had revolutionised women's fashion in the 1920s, the legendary designer Coco Chanel. She died in her suite at the Paris Ritz at the age of eighty-seven.

Eve read about it in the newspaper the following evening, but was too preoccupied with another matter to pay it much attention: she was worried about her mother, who wasn't answering her telephone.

'I can't think what's happened to her, George,' she said to her brother on the phone. 'She never goes out of an evening unless she's with one of us.'

'Perhaps she's gone next door and stayed for a chat,' he suggested.

'She wouldn't stay there all evening,' Eve pointed out. 'I've been trying her number for hours.'

'It does seem odd for her not to be in at this time of night, I must admit,' he agreed.

'She could be in the house but lying on the floor, unconscious,' said Eve, panic rising.

'Now you're just letting your imagination run wild,' he warned.

'Such things do happen.'

'Not very often, though,' he reminded her. 'But I'll pop round to Marshall Gardens to make sure, if it'll put your mind at rest.'

'Thanks, George,' she said gratefully. 'I'd go myself but I can't leave Josie.'

'No problem,' he assured her.

'You've got a spare key to the house, haven't you?'

'Yeah . . . I'll keep you posted.'

Half an hour later, he rang Eve's doorbell. 'She's not there,' he said. 'The place was in darkness. Not a sign of her.'

'You looked in every room?'

'I went all round the house,' he informed her. 'I called on several of her neighbours, too. No one's seen her this evening.'

'Where on earth can she be?' Eve was beginning to get desperate. 'It's nearly eleven o'clock. She wouldn't be out on her own at this time of night.'

'It's bitterly cold out, too,' mentioned George, also becoming concerned now. 'I don't like the idea of her walking the streets on her own.'

'Perhaps she's had an accident . . . got run over or been taken ill on the way home from work,' said Eve, dry-mouthed with anxiety. 'We'd better start calling the hospitals.'

'We'd have heard if anything like that had happened,' George pointed out.

'Not if she didn't have any identification on her,' said Eve.

'She would have, though.'

'Yeah, I suppose you're right,' conceded Eve, combing her fringe back off her face with her fingers, her brow damp with nervous perspiration.

'We'll have to do something if she doesn't show up soon,' said George.

'I'll just give her number another try,' suggested Eve, though without much hope.

The relief was so great it weakened her when her mother answered the telephone, sounding remarkably cheerful.

'Mum . . . thank God!' Eve exclaimed.

'Whatever's the matter, love?' asked Dot. 'Are you ill? Has something happened to Josie?'

338

'We're fine,' she said. 'I thought something had happened to you.'

'Oh? Why's that?'

'I've been trying to get hold of you all evening,' Eve explained. 'I was worried when you didn't answer the phone. You never go out at night.'

'No, I don't usually,' Dot agreed in a matter-of-fact tone. 'I'm sorry you've been worried.'

'So, where have you been?'

'Out with Rudy,' said Dot, sounding very pleased with herself. 'The boss took me up the West End for a meal.'

'What!'

'Is there something wrong with that?' asked Dot, puzzled by Eve's tone.

'I've been tearing my hair out and you've been out enjoying yourself with Rudy,' said Eve, the strain of the evening venting itself in anger. 'You could have let me know you weren't going to be in.'

There was a long silence. 'It was a spur-of-the-moment thing,' Dot eventually explained. 'Rudy rang me about six to ask if I fancied a night out. He came to pick me up at half past, so it was all a bit of a rush, what with having to get ready and everything.'

'I see.'

'Did you want me for anything special?' Dot enquired.

'No.' Eve bristled. Since when did she have to have a particular reason to call her mother? 'Just wanted to make sure you were all right.'

'That was thoughtful of you, love,' Dot said, 'but you really shouldn't worry so much about me.'

'George and I were both concerned . . .'

'George?'

'He's here with me now,' Eve told her. 'He's just come back from your place, actually. We thought perhaps you were ill and that's why you weren't answering your phone.'

'Oh, Eve . . . I'm so sorry that you've both been worried.'

339

'If only you'd told us you were going to be out,' Eve said.

Silence echoed down the line again, then, 'I'm really sorry you've been worried and I'll try to remember to let you know in future if I'm going out anywhere.' A pregnant pause. 'But I don't want to feel as if I have to ask your permission.'

Eve was shocked at her mother's attitude. 'Well, of course not,' she quickly assured her. 'What a thing to say.'

'That's what you're making it seem like, Eve,' Dot informed her.

'I didn't mean to.'

'Look, love, I have to go,' she said. 'Rudy is about to leave.'

'Rudy's there?'

'That's right. He brought me home and saw me safely inside,' she explained. 'So I must go and see him out and thank him for the evening. I'll tell you all about it tomorrow.'

'Oh, Mum, before you go . . .'

'Yes, love?'

'Did you have a good time?'

'Wonderful,' she said happily. 'I haven't had so much fun in years.'

'I'm very pleased for you,' said Eve, wishing she meant it. But this astonishing change in her mother's behaviour made her feel oddly deserted.

'Rudy's a dear, and ever such entertaining company,' she said. 'But I'll give you all the details tomorrow. 'Bye, love.'

''Bye.'

Eve put the receiver down and turned to her brother, who was waiting to hear all about it.

'Well, George,' she said, sounding slightly bemused, 'while we've been at home worrying about her, our mother has been living it up in the West End.'

'I don't believe it.'

'It's true,' she said.

George burst out laughing. 'Are we going to punish her for staying out late?' he joked.

'You are a fool,' she said, smiling to hide her confused emotions.

Eve wasn't normally judgemental about other people's relationships, but she just couldn't warm to the one that seemed to be developing between her mother and Rudy, with Dot reporting outings with him to the cinema, the theatre and the pub.

She had nothing against Rudy. He was warm-hearted, kind and amusing, and was obviously making her mother happy. In fact, the novelty of a busy social life was making Dot jollier than she'd been when her husband was alive. Maybe that was the problem, Eve thought with a stab of compunction; perhaps she wanted her mother to stay as she was before, reliable, predictable and always at home. Was she really so lacking in generosity, or did the problem lie in the fact that she just couldn't bear the thought of anyone taking her father's place in her mother's affections?

Despite her efforts to conceal her feelings so as not to spoil her mother's new lease of life, Dot knew her too well.

'I know you don't approve of me and Rudy,' she blurted out one evening in February when Eve called to see her after taking Josie to Brownies.

'It isn't that I don't approve, exactly,' Eve tried to explain. 'It's just that I can't get used to the idea of your being with a man who isn't Dad.'

'Rudy will never, *ever* take your father's place,' Dot stated categorically.

'No?'

'Of course not.' She was emphatic. 'No one could ever do that. Rudy and I are seeing each other because we're both on our own and we get on well. He's a good friend. He makes me laugh, and that's something I never thought I'd do again.'

'I'm pleased that you're enjoying life again, of course . . .' began Eve.

'But you still don't like the idea of my going out with him,' Dot finished for her.

'I can't help it.'

'Look, love, I know how much your dad meant to you, and his memory will never die as long as I'm alive. Not a day goes by when I don't think about him,' she said. 'But he'll have been dead two years this summer, and life goes on. I'd been feeling lonely and . . . sort of isolated within myself, even when I was with people, until I got to know Rudy. He's taken that horrible feeling away.'

'I shall just have to try harder to get used to him being around then, won't I?' said Eve.

Dot gave her daughter a solemn look. 'It would mean a lot to me if you could accept it, love,' she told her. 'I don't want to hurt you, but I enjoy my friendship with Rudy and I really don't want to go back to how I was before, relying on you and George for company.' They were standing in Dot's kitchen, waiting for the kettle to boil. Dot took her daughter's hand and squeezed it. 'I'm still here for you and Josie, you know. You'll always come first.'

Eve was deeply ashamed. 'I never doubted that, Mum,' she said, blinking back the tears. 'You're entitled to go out with whoever you wish.'

'Ever since I've been widowed, I've had this awful fear of becoming a burden to you and George,' Dot confessed.

'You never could be,' Eve assured her.

'I might be if I don't have any friends of my own,' she said.

'Not you, Mum. But I can see your point, and I've had an idea,' said Eve, eager to make even more of an effort. 'Why don't you bring Rudy to lunch at my place on Sunday?'

'That would be lovely,' said Dot, beaming. 'I'll find out if he's free.'

'This is lovely, Eve,' said Rudy, referring to the roast beef and Yorkshire pudding they were having for lunch that Sunday. 'It's been a long time since I've had a Sunday roast. It never seems worth the bother just for one.'

'That's why Mum and I usually team up on Sundays,' Eve told him. 'I have to make the effort because of Josie, but I suspect that Mum might be tempted not to bother just for herself.'

'You're right about that,' agreed Dot. 'Mind you, I don't have to bother cooking for myself during the week now that I get a meal at work, all cooked for me and free.'

Eve looked from one to the other. 'Do you lose your appetite when you work with food?'

'Not likely,' said Dot. 'I've got my appetite back with a vengeance since I've been going out to work.' She gave a wry grin. 'So much for that slim figure I had after your dad died.'

'You're looking a lot better for it.' Whatever Eve's personal feelings about her mother's friendship with Rudy, there was no denying that it had been good for her health.

'Working does bring you out of yourself,' said Rudy. 'The café has always been a friend to me in times of trouble.'

'Talking about the café, how have you got on with decimal currency?' asked Eve. The new system had come into being only that week.

'Don't ask,' he laughed. 'I don't think I'll ever get used to it, and I'm damned sure my customers won't.'

'They will, though, and so will we. In time we won't even remember what a shilling or half a crown was worth,' remarked Eve. 'But it does take some understanding at the moment, I must admit.'

'Some people are worried that shopkeepers might use the confusion to mark up prices,' remarked Dot.

'I suppose some unscrupulous traders might try it on while people are still unsure as to how much the new coins are worth,' said Eve. 'But they won't get away with it for long.'

'I wouldn't dare try it on my customers,' grinned Rudy. 'I value the use of my limbs too much.'

Eve smiled. 'Mum tells me you've given up your theatrical agency,' she remarked.

'Yeah . . . I lost interest after Bart went away,' he said.

'Do you still keep in touch with him?' she enquired casually.

'We communicate through his mother,' said Rudy. 'I go to see her every so often to make sure she's all right. She gives me his news and passes mine on to him. I'm no letter-writer, and it's too expensive to get on the blower to Spain.' He ate a mouthful of food. 'Do you hear from him?'

She shook her head. 'Like you, I hear his news through Lil, though I did actually speak to him just after he got engaged,' she said. 'I managed to persuade Lil to go out to Spain for a visit and he called to thank me for that.'

'I heard all about that trip to Spain,' said Rudy. 'She seemed to enjoy herself.'

'Yeah, I got that impression too,' said Eve. 'The highlight of the holiday seemed to be seeing Bart perform. She said he was brilliant.'

'She was full of that when I saw her, too,' he remarked. 'But she didn't say much about Bart's fiancée.'

'I noticed that,' said Eve. 'I thought she was just being sensitive to my feelings . . . didn't want to say too much about Bart's love life, you know, with us having once been close.'

'It couldn't have been that, as she was cagey about it with me too,' Rudy said.

'Perhaps she didn't hit it off with his fiancée,' suggested Dot.

'Could be.'

'We'll probably never know,' said Eve. 'Not our business, anyway.'

'No. But you can't help wondering when you're fond of someone.' Rudy pondered for a moment. 'I probably shouldn't say this, but I was disappointed that you and Bart didn't make a go of it. I always had you two down as an item.'

'I thought they were right for each other too,' added Dot.

'I wish Uncle Bart would come to see us sometimes,' said Josie pensively, slowly forking a piece of roast potato. 'He's nice.'

'He lives too far away, love,' said Eve, rather than go into a lengthy explanation.

Rudy seemed to want to linger on the subject. 'He thought the world of you, Eve,' he told her, helping himself to more horseradish sauce.

'What makes you say that?' She couldn't help being curious.

'When a performer as hungry for success as Bart was gives up the best showbiz chance he's ever going to get for a woman, he must think a hell of a lot of her.'

Eve looked at him, puzzled. 'What chance was that?' she enquired. 'I know of no lost opportunities on my account.'

'Oh dear.' He frowned. 'Maybe I shouldn't have said anything.'

'You've said this much, you'll have to tell me the rest now,' she said.

He concentrated on his food, carefully spreading the sauce on to his meat, before looking up rather sheepishly. 'I remember him telling me to keep shtoom about it now, but I don't suppose it matters after all this time,' he said. 'It's all water under the bridge now.'

'Yes, yes, Rudy,' said Eve, impatient to know. 'But what big chance?'

'Ooh, it's a few years ago now . . . it was a New Year's Eve.' He paused meditatively. 'Must have been about 1967 . . .'

'Get on with the story, for goodness' sake,' urged Dot in a friendly manner.

'Sorry.' He gave a wry grin. 'Anyway, Bart had the chance to stand in for the cabaret star at Peaches Club in the West End.'

'Blimey,' gasped Eve. 'That's where all the celebrities go, isn't it?'

'Exactly,' Rudy confirmed. 'He would have been seen by people who matter in the business. But he wouldn't do it.' He looked at Eve. 'He said you needed him that night and he wasn't prepared to let you down. I tried everything I knew to persuade him, but he just wouldn't have it.'

The memory of that terrible New Year's Eve of 1967 came crashing into Eve's mind. She'd been traumatised by the discovery of the affair between Meg and Ken and had had to get through a family party at which Meg had been present. And Bart had been with her every step of the way.

'I was livid,' Rudy continued. 'The only time I ever get the bloke a really good booking, and he turns it down. I just couldn't get him to change his mind. He put the phone down on me in the end.'

'Did you call him at his mother's on the afternoon of New Year's Eve to tell him about it?' Eve wondered, memories of that awful day flooding back.

'Yeah, I believe I did,' said Rudy, looking into space as though thinking back. 'I couldn't get hold of him at home and I was getting into a panic about it. That's why I remember it so well.'

So did Eve. She could still feel Bart's strong arms around her as he'd comforted her, huddled together in his van on that bitterly cold afternoon. Knowing how much a career break had meant to him, she was now fully aware of the enormity of what he had given up for her. She was racked with guilt. The full force of what she'd lost when she'd rejected that second marriage proposal really hit home.

Okay, so she hadn't thought it fair to uproot Josie and drag her off to Spain on the strength of something as insecure as a performing job on the Costa del Sol. She'd also been in turmoil, having just ended her partnership with Meg, and had been keen to prove herself capable of succeeding on her own. But she and Bart could have worked something out between them . . . got married and seen each other when they could until either he came back to London or she joined him in Spain.

But she had slammed the door in his face, left him with no hope of a future for them. And now he was engaged to someone else.

'I remember it too,' said Eve in a small voice. 'He told me you had a booking for him for the following week. Nothing special, he said.'

'He knew that if he told you the truth you'd insist he take the job, and he reckoned his place was with you that night,' Rudy said. 'He didn't want you upset. He's that sort of a bloke.'

'Yes,' said Eve in a solemn tone. 'He is that sort of a bloke.'

Eve's annual accounts had just arrived from her accountants, and she was studying them in her office one morning that spring. They made good reading. Her turnover was up on last year and profits were healthy. Although she wasn't the type to wallow in self-congratulation, she did feel rather proud of herself. She'd been in business on her own for just over two years, her loan was paid back to the bank, which meant that her house was safe, and business was booming.

Although she'd been determinedly positive about setting up on her own, she had also been desperately frightened. But it had worked, and that was immensely gratifying. It was hard going at times, though. Just when things were running smoothly, something unexpected would happen, like staff sickness coinciding with the school holidays which meant she had no back-up at the boutique when she needed to be at home with Josie. On rare occasions, she'd even been forced to close the shop during trading hours.

Caroline, her assistant, a smart brunette in her mid-twenties, came into the office now with a query.

'Are we having any more satin trousers in?' she asked. 'I've got a customer in the shop desperate for a pair.'

'Has all our stock gone?'

'Yeah, we've sold out of all sizes.'

'As quick as that?'

'Satin trousers and hot pants are a craze at the moment,' Caroline reminded her.

'Yes, they are popular. I'll get on to the manufacturer and see if I can get hold of a few more,' said Eve. 'Tell the customer we'll have them in in the next few days.'

'Right you are,' Caroline said cheerfully and went back into the shop.

Eve's bruised faith in human nature following Theresa's treachery had been somewhat healed by Caroline, who had proved to be a reliable and loyal assistant. Things were definitely on the up at the moment, Eve thought, putting the accounts into the filing cabinet and going out into the shop, which was bright and modern, well stocked and – most importantly – filled with customers.

Despite all the problems, having your own business was worth it, she thought. She had a shop she was proud of and was planning for it to stay that way into the future.

A few miles away from Eve's boutique – in the office of a wholesale warehouse in North Acton – Frank Myers was feeling much less pleased with himself. In fact, he was practically suicidal as he stared gloomily at a letter from his bank.

His debts had built up over the years and had now reached the stage where the bank were not prepared to let the situation continue. There was no way out of this impasse. Even the sale of his house wouldn't save him from bankruptcy, not after the mortgage had been paid off. Everything he'd worked so hard for was about to slip from his grasp.

Six months ago he'd told his wife he would try to turn the business around. That hadn't been possible. He had stock in the warehouse that he could neither pay for nor sell. Bills were piling up and the bank were refusing to honour his cheques.

He now had to do what he should have done a long time ago – put his house on the market. If he didn't do it of his own accord, the bank would do it for him; he'd had to let them have a second charge on the house when he'd had his overdraft raised.

Far more frightened of his wife's reaction than he was of losing his business, he told his secretary he was going home and left the premises, sick with nerves.

Bea didn't scream at him. She sobbed her heart out, which made him feel even worse.

'But I can't lose my home,' she wailed, pushing him away when he tried to comfort her. 'It's too hard to bear, especially at our age.'

'I'm so sorry,' he said in a subdued tone. 'If there was anything I could do, I would do it.'

'There must be something.'

'There isn't,' he said miserably. 'I've reached the end of the line and we both have to accept what's happened and get on with what must be done.'

'We'll have to move to a small house in some terrible area, I suppose,' she surmised.

He stared at the floor, hardly able to force the words out. 'I doubt if a house will be possible, dear,' he blurted out.

'Not a house!' She looked bewildered. 'Oh no, you don't mean a flat. I can't live in a flat, Frank. It would kill me.'

'If I'm declared bankrupt, we'll only be allowed a certain amount to live on, so we'll be ruled by that,' he informed her. 'It might not even be enough for the rent on a flat. A bedsit, maybe.'

'Bankrupt? Renting a bedsit?' she gasped, the words filling her with loathing and shame. 'Surely it won't come to that?'

'It might well do,' he said. 'We have to prepare ourselves.'

'What's to become of us?' she asked him in a pathetic tone.

'We'll come through it somehow,' he tried to assure her, despite the fact that he was feeling desperate himself.

'Without your business, what will we live on?' she asked, eyes red and puffy from crying.

'I'll have to get a job,' he said with a confidence he didn't feel. He was fifty-four years old. Who would employ him? 'Try not to worry, I'll sort it out somehow.'

'Oh, the shame of it,' she cried, clutching her head. 'The unbearable shame!'

He tried to put his arms around her to comfort her, but she shrank away, as though she couldn't bear him to touch her. 'I have to go now,' he said, almost beyond pain. 'I've got to start things moving. Will you be all right here on your own?'

'I'll never be all right again,' she said bitterly. 'Thanks to you!'

When Meg received a telephone call from her mother at the shop, ordering her to come over right away, she dropped everything and did as she was told.

'We'll have to do whatever we can to help him,' she said gravely when Bea had got to the end of an hysterical account of what had happened.

'Help *him*?' queried Bea with a sob in her voice. 'I'm the one who needs help . . . losing my home because of him.'

Rage whipped through Meg, white-hot fury at the utter selfishness of this woman, who had constantly demanded of her husband and never given him one iota of support. 'Daddy's always done his best for us both,' she said, managing to control her temper. 'Now he's the one who needs help and we are going to make sure that he gets it.'

'I don't know what you expect *me* to do,' said Bea miserably.

'You can give him support and sympathy, for a start,' announced Meg.

'Sympathy . . . when this is all his fault?' her mother wailed.

'It isn't his fault.' Meg was fiercely protective towards her father. 'He's been driven out of business by forces beyond his control. You're his wife, for heaven's sake. It's up to you to be at his side at a time like this. You've had plenty of good times, now it's time to show what you're made of when they're not so good.'

'I can't believe my own daughter would be so horrid to me,' wailed Bea.

'I've seen this coming for years,' Meg continued emotionally. 'I've watched you drive my father into an early grave with your greed . . . sneering at him while he struggled to provide you with the sort of lifestyle he could never really afford.'

'This is all too awful,' objected Bea tearfully. 'My own daughter turning on me.'

'If you hadn't demanded so heavily of him over the years, this might never have happened,' Meg pointed out.

'Oh, so now it's my fault, is it?' Bea said, her voice distorted by tears.

'Nobody is to blame for the failure of Daddy's business,' Meg replied. 'That's down to the changing times. But if you hadn't been so demanding all these years, living beyond your means, he'd have had some money behind him – something to fall back on, instead of being threatened with bankruptcy.'

'Don't say that word in this house,' Bea said. 'I can't bear it.'

'Oh, for heaven's sake, lay off the self-pity and think about Daddy and what that poor man must be going through,' Meg reproved sternly. 'I've noticed how ill he's been looking lately; now I know why. He'll drive himself into a nervous breakdown if we're not careful. And he won't be able to look after you at all if he's in a mental hospital.'

'Don't say such things,' said Bea.

'Bankruptcy, nervous breakdowns, they're all things that *do* happen to people,' said Meg. 'You won't protect yourself by keeping quiet about them.'

'There's no need to make me feel worse,' said Bea mournfully.

'I'm just trying to get you to face up to things,' Meg told her.

'And there was I thinking I'd get a little sympathy from my daughter.'

'I'm sorry for you, of course I am,' said Meg, her tone softening. Whatever her mother's faults, Meg's filial feelings were still quite strong. Her mother was the product of indulgent parents. Meg thanked God she hadn't allowed herself to develop in the same way. 'But right now I'm more worried about my father. He's the one with all the problems to sort out, poor thing.' She stood up. 'I'm going to look for him at his office. I'll see you later.'

And she hurried from the house, leaving her mother feeling very sorry for herself indeed.

'You mustn't even consider it, Meg,' said Frank Myers, after hearing what his daughter intended to do to help him.

'I've been thinking about it in the car on the way over here,' she informed him, 'and I've made up my mind.'

'Oh, Meg, love,' he said, his eyes wet with tears. 'I'm really touched by the thought. But I can't let you sell your business to raise cash to help me.'

'I'm going to do it whatever you say,' she declared. 'So you may as well accept it.'

'But you've worked so hard to get your boutique established,' he said. 'You can't sell it just because I'm in trouble.'

'Who lent me the money to get started in the first place?' she reminded him.

'I did that because I wanted to,' he said with profound sincerity. 'It wasn't a favour that needed returning. You've paid the loan back, so that makes us quits.'

'I can't count the number of times you've helped me in the past,' she reminded him, 'and I want to help you now.'

'My business is beyond help,' he said.

'But an injection of cash would save you from actually being declared bankrupt, wouldn't it?' she suggested. 'Even if there wasn't much left over after you'd paid your creditors.'

'Well, yes,' he said. 'But I still can't let you do it.'

'If you tell the bank that help is on the way, they'll give you more time before pulling the rug from under you,' she said.

'But Meg . . .'

'No arguments,' she said. 'I'm going to get in touch with the estate agent as soon as I get back, put the boutique on the market.'

'And what will you do when you have no business to provide you with an income, and a child to bring up?' he enquired gravely.

'George will look after us. Anyway, I can get a job,' she said. 'I'm young . . . and very experienced in fashion retail. It shouldn't be a problem.'

'No, Meg.'

'Yes, Daddy.'

He turned away, his shoulders shaking, and she knew he was crying. Almost choking on the lump in her throat, she slipped her arms around him, her head resting against his back. 'You'll come through this, Daddy,' she whispered soothingly. 'And you're not on your own, just remember that.'

'I'm not crying because of the problems,' he mumbled, turning to her and burying his face in a handkerchief.

'What then?' Her tone was gentle.

'I'm crying because you've grown up to be so kind,' he said in a muffled voice. 'And I'm so very proud of you.'

'If I do have a kind heart, we both know who I've inherited it from, don't we?' she said.

And they hugged each other, tears rolling down their cheeks.

When Frank got home that evening, bracing himself for

another tongue-lashing from Bea, he found her in a surprisingly subdued mood.

'Shall we have a drink before we eat?' Her tone was noticeably friendly.

Unaware of the scolding Meg had given her, he was puzzled by her change of attitude but wise enough not to question it. 'That'll be nice,' he said.

'I don't suppose either us has much of an appetite.'

'No.' He poured a whisky for himself and a sherry for her.

'Might as well make the most of it while we can,' she said as they sat down in armchairs by the hearth. 'I don't imagine we'll be having luxuries like this for much longer.'

'You're right there,' he agreed. 'When this booze has gone there won't be any more, not until this mess is sorted out, anyway.'

'Did you contact the agent about getting the house on the market?' she asked.

'Yes, they're sending someone round to take details tomorrow.'

'Oh,' she said.

His heart lurched at the real pain in her eyes. He told her about Meg's offer of help and she brightened considerably.

'So we could be saved after all?' she suggested hopefully.

'Only from being declared bankrupt,' he said. 'We'll still have to sell the house. And the business is no longer viable.'

'Meg's money would help, though?'

'I've told her she mustn't do it, but she seems determined.'

'I think we should let her go ahead,' said his desperate wife.

'But she'll lose her business, Bea,' he pointed out worriedly.

'She's young enough to start again,' she said. 'We're not.'

He swallowed his drink quickly, looking away from her in disgust.

'You think I'm being selfish, don't you?' she asked him.

'I don't know how you can bear to have your daughter give up something that means so much to her to help us,' he said, meeting her eyes. 'I'd rather go under than have her lose so much. And if I were the only one involved, that's what I'd do.'

'It's a question of survival,' his wife explained wearily. 'I can't cope with what's happened. If Meg has the means to help us, I think we should thank her with open arms and let her do it. After all, if the situation was reversed, we'd help her.'

'I still don't like the idea.'

'Needs must when the devil drives,' she said. 'We're not young any more.'

'All the same . . .'

'I know I was quick to blame you, Frank,' she said in a softer tone. 'But I know what's happened isn't really down to you.' She stared at her hands, unused to admitting to being at fault and embarrassed by it. 'You've obviously done everything you can.'

'You really believe that?' This surprising admission made him feel better.

'Of course,' she confirmed. 'I'm not a fool. I know that things are changing, that progress means hard times for a lot of people. You only have to watch the television news to know that machines are taking jobs, supermarkets are wiping out small shops.'

'But you seemed not to realise . . .'

'It suited me not to,' she cut in. 'It's the way I am. I'm used to a certain standard of living and want it to continue, so I pretended it would. I'm not the stalwart type, the sort of woman who'll say, "Never mind, darling, we'll manage somehow." I want things to be as they've always been. But I have now reluctantly accepted the fact that they can't be.

I expect I shall do a whole lot more complaining before this thing is through, because I simply won't be able to help myself.'

'I bet you will too,' said Frank, but he did recognise the fact that his wife had made an effort to be supportive. A glimmer of hope lifted his heart. With back-up from Bea, however insubstantial, he could endure anything.

Chapter Twenty

Eve made it a general rule not to go into the shop on a Saturday because being at home with Josie at the weekend was her greatest joy. While her daughter was at dance class in the morning, she would whizz around the supermarket for the weekly shop, and later on would catch up with a few chores while Josie played with her friends. Then off to visit Grandma in the afternoon. Nothing special. Just a day of blissful ordinariness touched by that liberated feeling of holiday.

Dark-eyed and tall for her age, Josie was a lively seven-year-old with boundless energy and an affectionate nature. The bond between mother and daughter was a great source of pleasure to Eve but sometimes painful in its intensity, and stretched almost to breaking point at times because Josie could be as wilful as the next child when the mood took her. Eve took a firm line on discipline, especially as she had no partner to back her up. But through it all they adored each other and Eve cherished the times they had together. All week she looked forward to the weekend.

Things didn't always go to plan, however. Sometimes she was forced to go to work by some unforeseen circumstance, such as Caroline suddenly falling sick, as happened one Saturday afternoon in spring. Eve had to dash to the shop, leaving Josie with her grandmother. Whilst this was no problem for Josie or Dot, who got on like a house on fire, occasions like this were always times of self-reproach for Eve in that they caused her to question her wisdom in taking on the awesome responsibility of her own business when she was the mother of a young child. This kind of agonising was a pointless exercise, since she knew she was doing what was right for her particular circumstances, but still the doubts came.

When she finally closed the shop and got back to Marshall Gardens in the late afternoon, Josie was playing in the garden with some local children and George had called round on his way home from work to fit a new lock to Dot's back door.

'I thought Rudy would do your odd jobs now,' remarked Eve.

Dot roared with laughter. 'The place would fall apart if he did,' she said.

'Not a handyman, then?'

'Changing a lightbulb is about his limit, bless him,' she said lightly. 'He's a dab hand with a frying pan in the café kitchen on the cook's day off, but I wouldn't let him loose with a screwdriver, not in my house anyway.'

'Each to his own,' said George, who got on very well with Rudy.

'Any tea going, Mum?' asked Eve.

'I'll make a fresh pot,' said Dot, filling the kettle.

'I've been rushed off my feet at the shop this afternoon,' said Eve, flopping down on a chair at the kitchen table. 'God, I hate having to go in on a Saturday.'

'One of the drawbacks of having your own business is that you can't just walk away and forget it at the weekend,' said George.

'You're telling me,' said Eve 'Anyway, George, how are things with you?'

'Mustn't grumble, I'm managing to earn a crust,' he said, turning a screwdriver in a screw in the lock frame to attach it to the door.

'And the rest,' laughed Eve, her dark eyes sparkling with fun. 'You're doing more than just earning a crust, I bet.'

He finished the job and turned to her. 'I won't deny it,' he grinned.

'It's just as well you are doing well,' said Dot in a

more serious tone, 'now that this thing with Meg has come up.'

'What thing?' enquired Eve.

'Meg's selling her boutique,' George informed her.

'To buy a larger one?'

'No, she's finishing in business altogether,' he explained.

'I don't believe it.' Eve was very shocked.

'It's true.'

'Why on earth would she do a thing like that?' she wanted to know.

He told her the reason.

'Oh, George, that's terrible,' she said with emphasis.

'You don't have to tell me,' he agreed. 'I don't mind Meg selling up in the least – I'm more than happy to support us – but I know it's breaking her heart to have to do it.'

'It must be,' said Eve. 'I know how much that business means to her.'

'You and me both,' he sighed. 'I'm really worried about her.'

'Surely there must be some other way of getting her father out of trouble?' suggested Eve.

'Not that I know of,' he said.

'But she's worked so hard to make Trend into a success,' Eve went on. 'It was her way of proving to herself that she could do something in her own right after her pampered upbringing. She really loves that shop.'

'I know,' said George. 'If I had the dough I'd bail her father out myself. But I'm overstretched at the moment. The showrooms really set me back.'

Eve leaned on the table, chin on fists. 'Poor old Frank,' she said. 'He doesn't deserve something like this.'

'He certainly doesn't,' agreed George, who had been to see Frank at his office to convey his sympathy, sorry he couldn't offer anything more practical. 'He feels terrible about Meg giving up her business because of him. He'd rather go bankrupt than have her do it. But she won't listen to him . . . she's absolutely determined to go ahead. And, of course, Bea is all for it.'

'Typical,' said Eve.

'Meg thinks the world of her dad,' George continued. 'She says that she was given the best of everything when she was growing up because of his hard work, and now it's pay-back time.'

'How's Frank in himself?' wondered Eve.

'He's putting up a front, but the poor bugger looks ill,' said George. 'He's been worrying about something like this for years. I remember him talking ages ago about the way his line of business was being hit by the supermarkets.'

'I bet his wife isn't helping much either,' remarked Dot, pouring boiling water into the teapot 'She won't like having to lower her standard of living.'

'If I'm any judge, she'll be giving him hell,' said George. 'But he'd never say so. He's intensely loyal to her.'

'I can't help thinking there must be another way around the problem,' said Eve, pondering. 'Surely there's a solution that doesn't entail Meg having to lose her business?'

'If there is, I don't know of it,' he said.

'What a mess,' said Eve.

They moved on to other topics as they drank their tea at the kitchen table. Then Eve, Josie and George departed, leaving Dot to get ready for an evening out with Rudy at the cinema.

Eve was still thinking about Meg's troubles as she drove home through the sunny suburban streets, the shadows lengthening at this time of day. There must be some other way, she thought, there had to be!

Having spent the rest of the weekend mulling the problem over, Eve came to a decision on Monday morning. She closed the shop at lunchtime because Caroline was still off sick, and drove to Ealing Broadway through the back streets to avoid the traffic on the main road. It was a wet day, the soft spring rain dripping through the trees on Haven

Green, the grass luxuriantly verdant beneath the leaden skies that hung oppressively over the town.

'I came on the off-chance of your being here,' Eve explained to Meg. They were in the office at Trend, with the door shut.

'Have you come to tell me what a fool I am to sell my business?' Meg asked defensively.

'No, of course not,' Eve said at once. 'I'm here because I've thought of a way you can help your father without doing that.'

'There isn't an alternative,' said Meg gloomily. 'I've thought of everything and there's just no other way.'

Eve studied her fingernails for a moment, then looked up, meeting Meg's worried blue eyes. 'There is if I sell my boutique and buy back into partnership with you,' she told her.

'What!'

'That would give you cash to help your father,' Eve continued, enthusiasm growing, 'and you get to stay in business but with me as a partner.'

'I couldn't let you do that,' protested Meg emphatically. 'This is Myers family trouble, not your problem.'

'I realise that,' Eve assured her. 'But what I'm suggesting makes good business sense for both of us. Obviously you wouldn't get as much money from my buying in as you would from selling up altogether, but it would probably be enough to get your father out of trouble.'

Meg doodled on the blotter pad with a biro, her hand trembling slightly.

'At least you wouldn't lose the shop,' Eve persisted when Meg didn't reply. 'Provided, of course, you could stand having me as a partner again.'

'Why would you do this, Eve?' Meg enquired, looking up quickly and meeting her eyes. 'Why would you give up your business for me?'

'I wouldn't be giving up anything,' Eve pointed out. 'I'd merely be selling one business and buying into another.'

'And I'd have to be eternally grateful to you for coming to the rescue,' said Meg, her skin so pale it seemed almost transparent, her eyes smudged with shadows. 'When it was you who walked out on the partnership in the first place.'

'We both know that was the only thing I could have done at the time,' said Eve, lowering her eyes for a moment, then raising them to meet Meg's without shame. 'I know we're not the best of friends these days but I don't believe you really think I would expect gratitude from you.'

'No, I suppose not,' admitted Meg. 'But I would still feel beholden.'

'There would be no need,' said Eve, excitement rising. 'Because this arrangement would benefit me just as much as you.'

'How?'

'We both know that running a business on your own when you have a young child to bring up is a permanent dilemma,' said Eve. 'What with school holidays, child and staff sickness and the fact that school finishes long before either of us shuts up shop for the day.'

'Yes, it does get difficult at times,' agreed Meg.

'But it was a whole lot easier when we were working together and sharing the responsibility and the hours,' Eve pointed out.

Meg nodded soberly.

'So it would be a relief to me if we went back to our old arrangement,' said Eve.

'But your shop is doing so well,' Meg reminded her. 'You can't just give it up because of me.'

'I've told you, I would be doing it for both of us,' she said. 'This is a sound business idea, not just a sentimental gesture.'

'I'm not at all sure . . .'

'Think about it, Meg,' Eve urged her. 'My shop has done well. I should get a good price for it and make a decent profit, so I won't lose out. If I didn't have a child, I might prefer being in business entirely on my own. But there are so

many drawbacks when you're going it alone and trying to be
a good mother too, a partnership is much more sensible.'

'Are you trying to make out that this is all for your own
benefit?' Meg asked. 'That it isn't motivated by altruism?'

Eve looked at her across the desk, their eyes locked, the
atmosphere highly charged. She knew that if Meg was
going to allow her to save her business, she would have
to convince her of the advantages to them both, though it
was only in trying to save Meg that Eve had realised that
a renewed partnership might now be possible, and would
also be advantageous to herself. 'We were friends once,'
she reminded Meg. 'Just because we no longer are doesn't
mean I don't care what happens to you. But, at the same
time, this proposal of mine could be the solution for us both.
Until things went wrong, we were a great team.'

Meg clasped her hands on the desk and stared at them
meditatively. 'But things *did* go wrong, didn't they?' she
said, and Eve noticed a slight quiver in her voice. 'If we
weren't able to work together then, how will we manage
it now?'

'By making sure our partnership is strictly a business
arrangement,' proposed Eve. 'It failed before because we
let our personal feelings intrude into our working lives.
This time we leave all that behind when we come to the
shop. I've been thinking about this ever since George told
me about your family problems on Saturday, and I believe
it could work.'

'I'm not so sure . . .'

'Time has passed, Meg,' Eve pointed out. 'We've both
calmed down.'

'That doesn't mean that the problems of the past won't
erupt again,' said Meg cautiously.

'That won't happen if we don't let it,' said Eve. 'There'll
be too much to lose. We can't fail a second time.'

'I admit, the idea is tempting,' said Meg.

'I'll leave you to think about it,' said Eve. 'Talk to George.
See what he thinks. I definitely want to go ahead, so if you

decide you want to too, let me know and I'll get my shop on the market right away. I don't expect any trouble in selling it. Smart, inexpensive clothes are still the hottes thing on the high street, and my shop's in an excellen trading position.'

'I'll be in touch,' said Meg.

Getting up to leave, Eve said, 'I'll look forward to hearing from you then.'

'Sure.'

Eve walked to the door.

'Oh, and Eve . . .'

'Yeah,' she said, turning.

'Thanks for the offer,' Meg said, her cheeks brightly suffused. 'Even if I decide against it, I'm still very grateful to you for making it.'

'Gratitude isn't necessary,' Eve said with a half-smile. 'I would be a venture of mutual benefit, remember.'

Meg managed a smile too. 'I'll bear that in mind and le you know.'

''Bye, then.'

''Bye.'

Deciding to walk down to the Broadway for some shop ping before she went back to her car, Eve belted her whit 'wet-look' raincoat, put her umbrella up and made her wa through the hordes of rain-soaked people in Haven Gree Parade, getting caught in a crush when a crowd surged ou of the station. Intending to cut across the green, she darte through the traffic to cross the road, passing the taxi ran and the long queue of people at the bus stop opposite.

Striding out along the footpath through the trees, inhalin the sweet, earthy scent of wet grass, she realised that he teeth were clenched with tension, her nerves pulled tight Now that she had actually taken the plunge and made he proposal, she wanted Meg to accept it, *so much.*

'That's the best news I've heard in a long time,' said Lil week or so later when Eve told her that she and Meg wer going back into partnership. 'You two made a smashing team. I always did think it was a pity you split up.'

'Yeah, well, we're back together now,' said Eve, moving on quickly because she didn't want to drag up the past. 'With a bit of luck we'll be in business by the end of the month.'

'Have you found a buyer for your shop already then?' enquired Lil with interest.

Eve nodded. 'A man who already has a few boutiques in and around London is buying it. So, provided it doesn't fall through, I'll be back at Trend very soon.'

'And still wanting plenty of crochet work, I hope,' said Lil.

'You bet,' said Eve. 'Shall I pass your name on to the new owner of my shop? In case he wants to use you any time?'

'Yeah, you might as well,' she said. 'I've got used to supplying two shops.'

'Okay.'

'It's good to hear of something nice like a reconciliation,' said Lil, looking gloomy suddenly. 'I could do with something to cheer me up today.'

'In the doldrums?' said Eve, giving her a shrewd look. 'That isn't like you.'

Lil sighed. 'I've had rather a sad letter from Bart in the post this morning,' she said. 'He and Ann have split up.'

'Oh dear,' said Eve, unable to stop her heart leaping. 'For good?'

'Sounds like it,' said Lil. 'She's gone off with the drummer in the club's resident band.'

'That's terrible,' said Eve. 'He must be devastated.'

'He doesn't say much about how he feels,' Lil told her thoughtfully. 'Just says he's all right and it's probably all for the best. But he would say that, wouldn't he?'

'Bart'll be okay,' said Eve reassuringly. 'He's a survivor.'

'No mother likes to think of her child being miserable,

no matter how old they are,' she remarked. 'You'll find that out for yourself when Josie grows up.'

'I'm sure.'

'How is young Josie?' asked Lil, who was very fond of Eve's daughter.

'She hasn't been well these last few days, actually,' said Eve. 'But she's better now and back at school today.'

'What was the trouble?'

'Some sort of a virus, the doctor said,' Eve told her. 'Usual flu-ish symptoms, headache, high temperature, aching limbs. It pulled her right down.'

'Poor little love,' said Lil. 'Still, as long as she's better now, that's the main thing.'

'It certainly is,' said Eve, thinking tenderly of her daughter.

Bart was right off women and didn't want to get involved with one again. It just wasn't worth the pain and aggravation, he thought, as he waded into the sea for some hard swimming in the hope of shaking off the blues. Half an hour in the sun afterwards should relax him before he headed back to his apartment to get ready for work.

The water felt cool and soothing as he struck out through the breakers into deeper waters to ride the waves. Mulling his situation over truthfully, he could feel only relief that his relationship with Ann was over, despite its humiliating end; he'd gone to her room in the hotel unexpectedly one night to find her *in flagrante* with Al, the drummer.

It had never really worked for Ann and Bart. He hadn't been able to forget Eve, and Ann had sensed a holding back on his part, despite his very best efforts to commit himself to her. It was hardly surprising she'd found someone else. He just wished she'd had the decency to break it off with him first.

His pride had take more of a hammering than his heart. The pain of rejection was nothing compared to the agony he'd suffered when he'd finally accepted the fact that there was no future for him with Eve. He'd never forget how traumatised he'd been when he'd arrived in Spain. He doubted if Eve had realised the depth of his despair.

But all of that was behind him. He'd finished with relationships. He would be a damned sight happier on his own. He swam until he was pleasantly exhausted, then waded out on to the hot sands, which burned the soles of his feet. He dried himself, applied sun-tan cream and lay down on the lounger, luxuriating in the warm sunshine soaking into his skin.

He felt empty and alone, but it wasn't Ann who occupied his thoughts as he lay in the sun. It was someone with a much darker complexion altogether, and striking brown eyes.

'Can you fold those sweaters and and put them away on the shelves, please, Bea?' requested Eve one morning that autumn.

'I beg your pardon?' said Bea, in a manner suggesting that Eve had asked her to dance naked among the mini-skirts.

Eve repeated the request, adding, 'You can't leave them all over the counter like that.'

'I had to take them out to show to the customer,' explained Bea, with an edge to her voice.

'And now the customer has gone, so they need putting back.'

'I sold one,' said Bea, as though this eliminated her from any menial task.

'Yes, I know, and that's good,' said Eve patiently. 'But the ones that weren't sold have to go back on the shelves.'

'The junior can put them back,' declared Bea.

'The junior has gone to the bank to get change,' said Eve. 'And even if she was here, she wouldn't put those sweaters back.'

'She would if I told her to,' was Bea's categorical reply.

'That isn't the way things work at this shop,' explained Eve. 'We're a team. We each do our share and we don't expect other people to clear up after us. So, if you could just get on and do it before we get a rush of customers, I'd be much obliged.'

'Who do you think you're talking to?' Bea wanted to know.

Eve took a slow, deep breath. 'As far as I know, I'm speaking to a member of my staff,' she said through clenched teeth.

'I am the mother of the proprietor,' Bea corrected haughtily.

'You are the mother of *one* of the proprietors of this establishment,' countered Eve. 'I am a part-owner, and when I'm on duty, I'm in charge.'

'You're nothing but a common upstart,' was Bea's reaction to that.

'Common I may be,' said Eve, determined not to fly off the handle, 'but I do happen to be running this shop, and if you want to continue to work here, I'm afraid you'll have to do what I say.'

Ever since Bea had come to work at Trend a few weeks earlier, Eve had been biting her tongue. She'd wanted to give Bea a chance, but now the time had come to assert her authority, and she knew she had Meg's blessing in this. They had been of one mind about Bea's being treated like any other member of staff, with no special privileges. Eve had only agreed to give her a part-time job on condition that she pulled her weight. She wouldn't have employed a woman so lacking in charm and dress sense at all had she not been Meg's mother. But it was only for a few hours a week, so it couldn't do much harm. And the woman did need the money.

The lowering of Bea's status wasn't reflected in her attitude. If anything, she was even more arrogant, though Eve realised that this could be just a defence mechanism because her drastic change in circumstances must have been a terrible blow to her dignity. Frank's business no longer existed, and in the absence of a position suited to his management skills and experience, he was working as an odd-job man in a supermarket for very low pay. Bea had been forced to show willing and make some sort of contribution to their domestic budget, and working for her daughter was a softer option than trying her luck elsewhere in the harsh world of employment, especially as she had no particular skills or work experience.

Poor Frank was in a low state and deeply ashamed of failing his wife in such spectacular fashion. Both Meg and George were worried about him. At least his debts had been cleared with the balance from the sale of the house and the money Meg had given him.

But now Bea was making a vociferous protest. 'I shall telephone my daughter about this,' she threatened. 'I'll soon have you put in your place.'

'Go ahead,' invited Eve, waving a hand towards the telephone on the counter. 'She'll only repeat what I've said.'

'Oh, really?'

'Yes, really.' Eve studied the other woman, whose face was gaunt, her eyes showing all the signs of sleepless nights. She'd lost a lot of weight too. The strain of the past few months had obviously taken their toll despite her queenly manner. Bea wasn't an easy person to like and an even harder one to pity. But for all that she didn't deserve it, Eve felt a surge of compassion. It must be hard for her living in a tiny rented flat in a shabby part of Acton after that beautiful house near Gunnersbury Park. And having to go out to work for the first time at her age couldn't be easy either, especially after such an exalted lifestyle.

'We'll soon see about that,' she said, scowling at Eve.

'Don't let's fight, Bea,' said Eve in a conciliatory manner, because she felt she had so much more than this infuriating but pathetic woman who'd been plunged into the real world for the first time in her life. 'Since we're going to be working together, let's try to get on, shall we?'

Bea's answer was an indifferent shrug of the shoulders.

In the absence of a positive response, Eve went on, 'As I said just now, we're a team here at Trend. We treat each other with respect. I know it must be difficult for you to fit in with other people after so many years of pleasing yourself at home. But I'm sure you'll find the job easier if you abide by our rules rather than arguing the toss over what you will and won't do.'

'I naturally assumed that the junior would do the clearing up.'

'She's only junior to you in age,' Meg pointed out. 'In terms of the pecking order, she's higher in rank because she's experienced and a full-time member of staff. But even so, she wouldn't expect you to clear up after her.'

Bea seemed uncharacteristically lost for words. She lowered her eyes, but not before Eve had spotted real pain there. Realising that it would be easier for Bea to climb down off her high horse if she could do so unobserved, Eve left her to it and went to the office. Turning to shut the door behind her, she noticed that Bea was folding the sweaters and putting them away. For some reason this triumph gave Eve no pleasure at all. But it did bring a lump to her throat.

Later that morning all thoughts of Bea Myers were pushed to the back of Eve's mind by a telephone call from the secretary at the school to say that Josie wasn't well and needed to be taken home.

Eve telephoned Meg at home and explained the situation.

'I'm on my way,' said Meg without hesitation. 'Just leave everything and go and get Josie.'

'Sorry you've been lumbered when it isn't your day to come into the shop,' Eve apologised

'Don't worry about that,' Meg told her. 'Your daughter comes first.'

'Thanks.'

'No problem,' said Meg amicably. 'I expect I'll have to ask you to do the same thing for me before long, with winter bringing its usual crop of ailments. Situations like this were one of the reasons we went back into partnership, remember?'

'Yeah, I know,' said Eve.

'I'm sure Josie will be all right.'

'Let's hope so,' said Eve.

'What's the trouble, exactly?' Meg enquired with the natural interest of a mother.

'She's feverish again, apparently,' explained Eve. 'It'll be another bug that's doing the rounds, I suppose, or the same one come back. She always seems to be going down with something just lately.'

'That's how it goes with kids, though, isn't it?' Meg pointed out reassuringly. 'They get one thing after another for a while, then they seem to have a clear run for ages.'

'That's true,' agreed Eve. 'Anyway, I'd better get going now. I'll let you know when I'll be back at work.'

'Okay.'

'Thanks again.'

'A pleasure.'

Driving across Haven Green, the trees ablaze with glorious russet tones, Eve thought what a relief it was to be able to hand the shop over to Meg at a time like this. The unexpected had been so much more of a problem when she'd had her own boutique.

Her relationship with Meg wasn't so much fun as it had once been, because they kept it at a business level as planned. They were determinedly pleasant and polite to each other, but distant. Eve doubted if they would ever regain their former closeness because of what stood between them. It made her sad. But the events of this morning proved that going back into partnership had been the right thing to do.

Chapter Twenty-one

One cold and misty November evening – after the showrooms had closed for the day – George was sitting at his desk, feeling miserable and churned up inside, having just been through the traumatic experience of firing his manager. Dismissal had been George's only option, because the man had been grossly negligent in his duties, proving that he wasn't to be trusted.

The manager's blatant disregard for company policy had come to light because of a series of complaints from customers about faults on purchased vehicles, faults that should have been corrected before the cars got anywhere near the showrooms. It was the manager's responsibility to have every incoming car checked by a local mechanic with whom George had an arrangement, and repaired if necessary, prior to being put up for sale. There was more than just George's reputation at stake here; this was a matter of public safety.

Why couldn't people do what they were paid to do? he thought, irritated with himself for misjudging the man's character when he'd taken him on. He simply couldn't afford to employ anyone who cut corners when it came to safety. Sod it! Now he had all the bother of hiring a replacement. And it wouldn't be easy to find someone he could trust to take charge when he himself was out on business.

As well as the car auctions that George regularly attended, and meetings he had with the big garages for trade-in vehicles that were being sold off to dealers, he also went out among the trade, locating vehicles for customers who wanted something in particular. It was a special service he offered. The success of this business depended on him being able to get out and about, and he couldn't do that unless he knew the place would be properly looked after while he was gone. He didn't need a high-flyer, just someone honest, reliable and good with people.

An unexpected candidate popped into his mind and he leaned back in his chair, mulling it over. I wonder, he thought, tapping the end of his pen on the desk. After some more cogitation, he picked up the telephone and made a call.

'Nice to see you,' said Frank Myers, shaking George's hand when they met in a pub in Ealing Broadway an hour or so later.

'You too, mate,' said George. 'What are you having to drink?'

'A Scotch, please,' requested Frank. 'I'm in need of some anaesthetic after a day at that damned supermarket.'

'Demeaning for a gent like you, is it?' asked George after he'd ordered the drinks.

'It isn't that,' Frank explained. 'But unpacking deliveries, sweeping the storeroom floor and collecting trolleys all day isn't exactly challenging for someone who's been used to running their own company.' He leaned on the bar, heaving a sigh. 'God, the days seem endless at that place.'

'It's a shocking waste of experience,' commiserated George.

'Exactly,' agreed Frank. 'I've forgotten what it's like to use my initiative.' He paused, shrugging his shoulders. 'I'm still applying for managerial jobs, but I don't hold out much hope.'

'No?'

'No. There's no demand for people of my age in today's management market. Dynamic thirty-somethings are what's wanted.' He paused as the barman put a whisky on the counter. 'Anyway, that's enough of my troubles. What did you want to see me about? You didn't say on the phone.'

George grinned. 'As a matter of fact, I think you and I might be able to do each other a bit o' good,' he explained.

Up went Frank's eyebrows. 'Really?' he said with interest.

'You need a management job and I urgently need a manager at the showrooms,' George informed him. 'So how about giving it a try?'

Frank looked astonished. '*Me*, work for *you*?' he queried.

'No need to sound quite so enthusiastic,' said George with irony.

'*Enthusiastic!* I'm positively ecstatic,' muttered Frank, who was too overcome with relief to behave like a true professional and go easy on the eagerness.

'That's good.'

'I'm surprised you want to offer me a job after the mess I made of my own business, though,' said Frank.

'We all know that wasn't your fault,' George reassured him.

'Thanks for the vote of confidence.' Frank took a large gulp of whisky. 'You know I've no experience of the motor trade?'

'Management experience and integrity are far more important to me,' George told him. 'Obviously you'll have to learn how the trade works, but you can do that on the job. I must have someone I can trust to look after things without my being here the whole time, someone I can leave in charge with an easy mind when I'm out.'

'That won't be a problem for me,' said Frank. 'I'm used to taking responsibility.' He gave George a shrewd look. 'Thanks for giving me a chance, old boy. I won't let you down.'

'Hey, hang on,' said George, with a warning look. 'This isn't an act of charity. I'm offering you the job because I need someone and I think you'll fit the bill. I remember you once telling me that you've always fancied the car game.'

'I have,' said Frank, looking brighter than he had in years.

'Of course, the job will have to be on a trial basis to start with,' George explained. 'If we suit each other after a period of, say, three months, we'll make it a permanent position, yeah?'

'Suits me,' said Frank.

'Four thousand a year and I'll fix you up with a company car after the trial period, if all goes well and you stay on.'

'That's fine with me.'

'I need you to start sharpish, though,' said George. 'I'm tied hand and foot without someone to stand in for me.'

'I'll have to work a week's notice at the supermarket,' said Frank, 'so it'll be next week.'

'Fine.'

Frank lifted his glass, smiling, his cheeks flushed with excitement. 'Here's to us making a successful team,' he said.

George raised his glass, tilting his head at an angle. 'I'll drink to that.'

They talked some more about the job until George looked at his watch and said, 'Well, time I was on my way . . .'

'Or you'll have my daughter giving you a hard time,' Frank finished for him.

'No, it isn't that,' George corrected. 'I told Meg I was meeting you and I'd be late home, so I won't be in trouble there. But I want to call in on my sister on the way. Young Josie isn't well again and I think Eve's getting herself into a bit of a state about it, although she's at pains to hide it. She's wonderful the way she keeps cheerful.'

'What's the trouble?'

'The doctor doesn't seem to know,' said George, his dark eyes troubled. 'That's the worrying part. The kid keeps going down with one thing after the other. No sooner does Eve get her back to school than she's off sick again with another so-called virus, or the same one back again, nobody seems sure which. It's pulling her right down, and she's tired and listless even when she isn't actually ill. No energy at all, and she used to be such a live wire.'

'What a shame.'

'It certainly is,' agreed George, looking grave and shaking his head. 'And it's been going on for far too long.'

'It's probably nothing serious,' said Frank, hoping to

reassure him. 'When children get run-down they tend to pick up everything that's going around.'

'That's quite true, and I don't think it's anything much to worry about, myself,' said George, draining his glass. 'But Eve needs all the support the family can give her at the moment. It's hard enough bringing a kiddie up on your own when they're fit and well, let alone when they fall sick.'

'I'm sure it must be,' agreed Frank.

'Anyway,' said George, pulling on his leather gloves, 'I must get off. I'll see you bright and early Monday morning.'

'That's a promise,' said Frank.

Bea's reaction to the news of Frank's new job was much less enthusiastic than her husband's.

'I don't know what things are coming to,' she complained. 'As if it isn't bad enough that I'm forced to take orders from that awful Eve woman, now you're going to be working for that dreadful brother of hers.'

'He isn't dreadful,' defended Frank. 'He's a nice chap, and you'd see that for yourself if you'd only try to get to know him. As I've often reminded you, he *is* our son-in-law.'

'That makes it even worse,' she moaned. 'I mean, it's usually the father who gives the son-in-law a job, not the other way around.'

'It doesn't matter how unusual it it, it's a management position,' he pointed out. 'A job I can really get my teeth into, and I'm looking forward to it.'

'But hardware wholesaling is what you know,' she pointed out in a doom-laden voice.

'Business is what I know, whether it be cars or kitchenware,' he informed her. 'I'm very grateful to George for offering me the job.'

'Don't let him know you're grateful,' Bea warned him fearfully. 'We don't want to give him cause to feel any more superior than he does already.'

'George isn't like that . . .'

'Of course he is,' she contradicted. 'Those blasted Grangers are having a whale of a time gloating over our misfortune.'

'I'm sure George isn't the type to gloat,' insisted Frank.

'You're too naïve.'

'Maybe I am,' said Frank, 'but this job is a chance for me, and anyone who wants to gloat is welcome to. It won't put me off.'

'You should have more pride.'

'If it goes well and becomes permanent, you'll be able to give up your part-time job at the boutique,' he informed her.

'Oh.' This made her see the situation in a whole new light. 'Oh well . . . maybe it isn't such a bad thing then.'

'It's the best thing that's happened in ages,' he told her.

'Let's hope so,' she said, warming to the idea considerably. 'God, how I hate working at that boutique. I know it's only a few hours a week, but I'm like a fish out of water.'

'Not really your sort of thing, is it?'

'I'll say it isn't,' she affirmed. 'It's very hard for a woman like myself to have to take orders from people half my age.'

'I know, dear,' he said. 'Let's hope it won't be for much longer.'

Eve found it hard to raise any enthusiasm for Christmas when the run-up began to get underway at the beginning of December. Watching her daughter's health deteriorate was like having the life beaten out of her every minute of every day. The rosy-cheeked child so full of vitality was now pale emaciated and exhausted. Even during the times when she appeared to recover, Eve knew she wasn't right. Her eyes were heavy; her breath smelled of illness.

When it had first started, back in the summer, Eve was given the distinct impression that the doctor had put Josie's regular attendance at his surgery down to paranoia on Eve's part. He'd blamed the recurring symptoms on a stubborn virus but had sent Josie to the hospital to be tested for glandular fever just as a precaution. The result was negative and Josie was prescribed yet another course of antibiotics. And still the illness continued to come and go.

On this particular December evening, as Christmas trees glowed in front windows the length of Daisymead Avenue, Eve and her mother sat with Josie as she burned with fever. Eve had made up a bed for her on the sofa so that she didn't feel isolated upstairs in her bedroom.

Eve could hear the low murmur of Rudy on the telephone in the hall to the doctor. 'Sorry to call you out at this time, Doctor, but this child needs medical attention urgently . . . No, I'm afraid it can't wait until morning.'

Dear Rudy had been an absolute rock these past few months. Calm, kind and in control, he was a reassuring presence. It hardly seemed possible to Eve that she'd once found it hard to accept her mother's friendship with him, since he now seemed like one of the family.

'Will we be going to see the Christmas lights and the big Christmas tree in Trafalgar Square like we usually do, Mummy?' asked Josie weakly.

'When you're better, darling.'

'Will I be going to the Christmas party at school?' she said.

'I hope so, love.'

'I'll have to take some fancy cakes,' Josie reminded her mother. 'Everyone has to take something.'

'I know, sweetheart, and I'll make some nice ones for you,' said Eve, holding her hot little hand. Josie's eyes were feverishly bright, her cheeks unhealthily suffused. Eve gently mopped her damp brow with a cool cloth, noticing how dry and cracked her lips were.

'And I'll make some of my special iced biscuits for you to take, too,' added Dot.

'Will the doctor give me some medicine to make me better?'

'I'm sure he'll give you something,' said Eve reassuringly.

Rudy came into the room with the news that the doctor was on his way.

'Thank God for that,' said Eve.

'I'll make some tea,' offered Dot.

'You stay where you are,' he told her. 'I'll go and do it.'

'You're spoiling us,' said Eve.

'Making tea for people has kept me in business for many years and I'm an expert,' he grinned, bringing a welcome touch of normality to the atmosphere, albeit briefly.

Although Eve had known things couldn't go on as they had been, and was desperate for something positive to be done about her daughter's condition, when the doctor actually did take action, she felt buffeted by it.

'*Hospital?*' She was talking to him in the kitchen, out of earshot of Josie. 'She has to go into hospital?'

'Yes, she needs to go in for observation and tests, Mrs Peters,' said the doctor, a quietly spoken man with thinning hair and horn-rimmed glasses. 'We need to know what's causing this.'

Eve had turned pale with fright, and the doctor perceived her anxiety.

'You can go in with her, Mrs Peters,' he explained. 'You'll probably have to sleep in an armchair by her bed, but at least you can be with her. We encourage that these days.'

'That's a relief,' said Eve, though she felt only slightly better about the worrying situation. 'Will she go in tomorrow?'

'I'd like to get her in tonight if possible,' he said. 'Get her settled ready to see the consultant in the morning.'

'What . . .?' Her mouth was dry with terror. 'What exactly will they be looking for?'

'The doctor at the hospital will talk to you about that,' he said, evasively it seemed to her. 'I've done all I can as your GP, it's time now to involve the specialists.'

'You think she might have leukaemia, don't you?' Eve said, forcing herself to put her worst fears into words.

'I don't know what the problem is,' he said patiently. 'I'm keeping an open mind.'

'It is a possibility, though?'

He hesitated, looking at her, his expression impossible to read. 'Yes . . . yes, that is a possibility.'

It felt like a fist in her chest. 'I thought so,' she said.

'But it is *only* a possibility at this stage, Mrs Peters,' he was quick to point out. 'One of several. It could be any number of things.' He looked thoughtful, as though choosing his words. 'Obviously, though, you can't rule it out.'

'I understand,' she managed to utter through parched lips.

'Try not to worry too much,' he said kindly. 'She'll be in very good hands.'

'Shall I take her in the car?' Eve asked.

'No, I'll arrange for an ambulance. She isn't really well enough to travel by car.' The doctor took an address book out of his bag and flicked through the pages. 'May I use your telephone, please? I need to organise her admission into hospital, and arrange transport.'

'Certainly,' she said, and led him to the phone in the hall.

Between the doctor leaving and the ambulance arriving, the tension almost reached breaking point. Josie – who had shown remarkable stoicism for one so young during this lengthy illness – began to cry at the prospect of going into hospital.

'I'll be with you, love,' said Eve, gently wiping the tears from her eyes. 'I'll be by your side every step of the way.'

When she was calmer, Eve went to put a few things in a holdall for them both. Through the months of Josie's intermittent illness, she had forced herself to be strong and positive. No matter how worried and afraid she'd been, she'd tried not to show it and she'd never allowed herself to be discouraged. Now, as she took the bag into the hall, her mother and Rudy hovering behind her and the headlights of the ambulance shining through the glass panel at the side of the front door, her iron discipline wavered. 'I've never been so scared in my life,' she said in a low voice so that Josie couldn't hear.

'Keep a grip, love,' said Dot.

'It's for the best,' Rudy reminded her. 'They have to find out what's causing the trouble.'

'That's the part that's scaring me,' she told him.

'You're bound to be anxious,' said Rudy. 'We all are.'

'I wish Bart was here,' she said, almost without realising she'd uttered the words. 'God, I miss him.' She looked at them both. 'You've both been great and I love you to death, but Bart and I . . .' Her words tailed off as she bit back the tears. 'Oh well, mustn't get maudlin.'

'We'll come to the hospital tomorrow,' said Dot. 'But you'll keep us posted in the mean time?'

'Course I will,' promised Eve. 'You'll tell George and Meg what's happened?'

'We'll take care of everything here,' said Rudy. 'You go and be with your daughter, and we'll see you tomorrow.'

'Thanks.' She opened the door to the ambulancemen, forcing back a feeling of despair and managing to evince a confident air.

Over the next few days, Eve's world was reduced to the Dettol-scented confines of the children's ward at the King Edward Memorial Hospital. Josie was prodded, pressed, pierced with needles and given a thermometer to suck at regular intervals. Eve was told by the nurse that it would be several days before the results of the tests came back from the pathology laboratory.

There were a couple of terminally ill children in the ward, as well as the tonsillectomies and other routine cases. Eve was humbled by the bravery of the parents of these children, as well as that of the children themselves, and full of admiration for the nurses, whose dedication never faltered. There was such warmth here, such spirit, despite the ineffable sadness.

Eve was imbued with a plethora of emotions. Compassion, selfish gratitude because there was still hope for Josie, terror that the tests might prove otherwise and guilt for wanting fate to be kinder to Josie than it had been to some of her fellow patients. Eve would sometimes sit with one of the other children while its mother went outside for some fresh air or to have a cigarette. There was a strong sense of camaraderie among the parents, who found themselves thrown together in a kind of limbo. Eve herself had a brief daily respite from the antiseptic atmosphere when her mother stayed with Josie while she went home for a bath and a change of clothes.

Her state of mind fluctuated with her daughter's condition. When Josie seemed well enough to venture out of bed on her thin little legs to talk to the other children, hope soared in Eve's heart. But it was always short-lived, because the child was soon back in bed again, weak and exhausted, the pattern of the illness remaining consistent. Eve read to her until her throat ached, and helped her with jigsaws and colouring books, though Josie could make only a perfunctory effort. Eve wasn't particularly religious, but she prayed and prayed.

Late one night there was a lot of activity at the far end of the ward. Screens were put around a bed and there were people coming and going. The next day Eve was told that the little boy in that bed had died. He'd been suffering from leukaemia. Eve's sorrow for him and pity for his parents knew no bounds. And her fear for Josie became even more intense. She remembered how frightened she'd been when she'd thought she might lose her in pregnancy. This was much worse

That night, when Josie was asleep and Eve settled in the chair at her bedside, the ward quiet, lights dim, the night nurse at her desk at the end of the room, Eve's thoughts turned unexpectedly to Meg, who, together with George and Becky, had been to see Josie every day. Eve found herself recalling the joy of their friendship, its absence still a void in her life, especially at a time like this. How unimportant the reason for their rift now seemed. Compared to the possibility of losing Josie, it was nothing at all. Something like this really put things into perspective.

Closing her eyes, her thoughts drifted on to Bart, who was often on her mind, especially since Josie had been ill. She needed him, longed for his reassuring presence. Yesterday she'd been so desperate to speak to him, she'd almost made a long-distance call to Spain when she'd gone home for a bath. Just to hear his voice would help sustain her through this ordeal. She could be herself with him, the frightened woman instead of the brave mother she acted out for everyone else so they wouldn't get downhearted.

But it wouldn't be fair to worry him about Josie's illness. He wasn't a part of their life any more. Probably had quite enough problems of his own in the aftermath of his broken engagement. Anyway, she was a mature adult. She had to face up to the test results like the responsible mother she was. But she dozed off to sleep thinking of him, and of Meg. They were linked somehow by their importance in her life at a particular time.

Driving home from Dot's that same night, Rudy was wrestling with a dilemma that had been bothering him for several days. Should he interfere in something that was none of his business just because his instinct told him it was the right thing? Or should he do the sensible thing and keep out of it altogether? It was a well-known fact that affairs of the heart were best left to the people concerned. But he couldn't stop fretting about it.

He'd thought of discussing it with Dot but had finally decided against the idea because this had to be *his* decision. If he did act on his instincts and it proved to be a disaster, he didn't want anyone but himself to be blamed. That was why he'd not said anything about it to anyone.

At home in his small house in Acton, he poured himself a whisky and paced the floor. Interfering in other people's affairs was not something he would normally consider. But he was haunted by the thought of Eve at the hospital, so alone somehow, despite a caring family around her. Surely if you really were acting in someone's best interests, a small intervention was permissible? And anyway, all he would be doing was passing on some information. It was up to the recipient to do as he saw fit.

He finished his drink and went to bed still undecided. For most of the night he thrashed about in the sheets, mulling it over. It was still worrying him the next morning as he drove to the café. When the early-morning breakfast rush was over, he could stand it no longer. He went to the office and looked through his address book until he found the number he wanted, then he placed a call to Spain.

Bart was devastated by the news of Josie's illness and telephoned the local travel agent as soon as he came off the phone to Rudy. They rang him back to say they couldn't get him on a flight to the UK until late Sunday night – that was almost three days away. No, they told him briskly, it didn't matter how urgently he needed to get to England or how much money he could offer for a ticket – there was *not* a seat available on any aircraft to the UK until Sunday night. Did he want to book the ticket or not?

He briefly considered the possibility of going by car and boat, but that would take two or three days so he wouldn't get back any sooner. He reserved the ticket and arranged to go into the office and pay for it later.

A great deal of patience was going to be required to get through the time until Sunday without losing his sanity. Still, at least it would give him time to square things with his boss, who wasn't going to be pleased at having to find a replacement at such short notice. He would also call Eve to let her know he'd be there as soon as he possibly could, he thought, picking up the telephone. But after a brief pause he replaced it without even dialling the operator, because he knew with sudden certainty what would happen if he spoke to Eve. She would feel guilty for having him travel all that way and insist that he mustn't drop everything on her account. Better he just turn up and surprise her.

Going into the kitchen to make some coffee, he realised that it was only ten thirty, early for him to be up and about. Poor little Josie, poor Eve. His mother had mentioned something in one of her letters about Josie not being well lately, but he'd just assumed it was one of those kiddies' ailments that cleared up with no harm done.

Alarming thoughts poured into his mind, knotting him up

and making him feel sick. He poured himself a cup of coffee and went back to bed to drink it, trying to curb his fears and frustration at not being able to get to London sooner. Rudy had told him that Eve had mentioned him, said she wished he was there with her. But people said all sorts of things they didn't mean at times of acute anguish. He had no plans for the future. All that mattered was to be with her at this worrying time. Whether she needed him or not, he felt compelled to be there. Right or wrong, he was going home to the woman he loved.

When he'd finished his coffee, he put a call through to Rudy with the details of his travel arrangements, because the other man had offered to meet him at the airport.

'Should get into Heathrow about one o'clock on Monday morning,' Bart told him, 'but don't worry about coming to pick me up at that unearthly hour. I'll get a cab.'

'Oh no you won't,' insisted Rudy. 'I'll come and collect you. And you can use my spare room for as long as you need it.'

'I owe you one, mate.'

'See you about one on Monday morning, then,' he said.

'Yeah, cheers, Rudy.'

Monday morning just couldn't come quickly enough for Bart.

Eve had been told that she would be getting the test results any day now, and she was very worked up about it. Every time a doctor came in her direction her heart pounded and she broke out into a sweat. On Saturday things were made more definite when she was told by a nurse that the consultant would be seeing her on Monday morning and would have the results then.

By Sunday afternoon, although ostensibly calm, Eve was in a state of complete and utter panic: erratic heartbeats, nausea, the lot. Ironically, Josie seemed a little better, but Eve didn't read too much into that, expecting the recovery to be temporary, as usual. There was an influx of visitors that afternoon: Eve's mother and Rudy, George and Meg with Becky, some neighbours of Eve's. Even Meg's parents put in a brief appearance.

There was such a crowd around the bed, Eve went outside into the corridor to make space, because the ward sister didn't like too many visitors at one time.

'Everyone's turned up today,' remarked Meg, following her out and sitting down on a chair in a row opposite. 'I thought I'd leave them all to it for a while.'

'I'm glad you did, actually,' said Eve, 'because I've been meaning to have a word with you.'

'Oh? What about?'

'I just wanted to thank you for working my days at the boutique,' she explained.

'No need to thank me for that.' Meg was most emphatic. 'It's the least I can do.'

'I've had to have so much time off these past few months, I'd be out of business altogether by now if I'd still been on my own,' Eve pointed out. 'I just want you to know that I appreciate your doing my share without a word of complaint.'

'It's nice of you to say so. But the partnership is a safety net for us both,' Meg reminded her. 'I have the security of knowing that you're there for me if Becky gets sick or if I have to take time off for any other reason.'

'There is that,' agreed Eve. 'I think you ought to take a holiday to make up for all the extra days you've had to work, once . . .' She paused, swallowing hard. 'Once this is over.'

'We'll see,' said Meg. 'And in the mean time, forget the shop and concentrate on Josie.'

They lapsed into silence and the atmosphere became highly charged as Josie's condition dominated their thoughts again.

'It's tomorrow, isn't it, when you get the results of the tests?' asked Meg.

Eve nodded. 'I'm seeing the consultant sometime tomorrow morning,' she said. 'They're not sure exactly what time because he has such a busy schedule and sometimes runs late.' She made a face. 'I'm absolutely terrified.'

'I'm sure you are,' said Meg.

'I just don't know what I'll do if it's . . .' She cleared her throat, her voice shaky. 'I just can't imagine life without her.'

'Don't even think about it,' urged Meg.

'I feel I have to prepare myself,' said Eve. 'Just in case.'

'I can't say I know what you're going through, because no one can know that exactly,' said Meg, 'but having a daughter of my own, I can imagine.'

Eve studied her boots, which she was wearing with black flared trousers and a white polo-necked sweater. 'Josie's illness has really put things into perspective for me, you know,' she said, still looking at her feet.

'About life, you mean?'

'Life, death, people I care about,' she said, looking up.

'Something like this is bound to bring things sharply into focus,' said Meg.

'It's made me realise what's important, and the mistakes I've made.'

Meg gave a wry grin. 'We all make plenty of those,' she said.

'Yes, we do.' Eve fiddled with her fingernails. 'Things that seemed important before don't matter at all now.'

'I can imagine.'

'What I'm trying to say is . . .' Eve looked up, her eyes hot with tears. 'Oh, Meg, I've missed you.'

'I've missed you too,' said Meg softly.

And suddenly they were on their feet, hugging each other, copious tears falling, any lingering resentment finally melting away.

The Jamaican nurse who worked on the children's ward came out carrying some papers. 'The cafeteria is open,' she told them in her rich velvety voice. 'Josie isn't gonna miss you while you take a break, Mrs Peters, not with all the visitors she has to keep her company this afternoon.'

'Fancy a cuppa tea, Meg?' asked Eve.

Meg nodded, and they walked down the corridor together.

Discussing their broken friendship over a cup of tea in the cafeteria gave Eve a much-needed break from talk of Josie's illness.

'It's such a shock to find out that your best friend has been sleeping with the man you were married to,' she said. 'As well as the whole betrayal thing, I felt so exposed, as though my privacy had been invaded.'

'I felt like that too, when I realised who you were,' Meg told her. 'The whole situation was bizarre, us both expecting his baby, and within days of each other too.'

'And me having no idea.'

'That's right.'

'When the truth finally came out, I couldn't see why you hadn't told me before,' Eve explained. 'All I could think of was that you were my closest friend and you'd not been straight with me for all that time.'

'Can you accept now that I thought I was doing the right thing?' asked Meg.

Eve nodded. 'You were in an impossible position,' she said.

'Ken couldn't have known that we'd ever meet and become friends,' said Meg. 'It was an amazing coincidence.'

Eve managed a half-smile. 'Not so much of a coincidence when you think about it, though,' she said. 'Given what had been going on, it was more or less preordained that we'd both end up at the antenatal clinic.'

Meg giggled. 'The man had stamina,' she said. 'I'll say that much for him.'

'He was a liar and a cheat,' said Eve, 'but he left us both the most wonderful legacy.'

'Our girls,' smiled Meg.

'Our darling daughters,' said Eve.

'After I met George, I couldn't understand what I'd ever seen in Ken, yet I loved him so much at the time,' said Meg.

'Funny how someone so vital to your life at one point seems so completely unimportant later on. And I'm sure it would have been that way for me even if he'd lived.'

'I was in love with Ken for years, but compared with what I felt for Bart later on, it seems really quite lightweight.' Eve drank her tea slowly. 'And one of the reasons I lost Bart was because I let Ken's memory complicate my emotions.'

'I was never sure if you and Bart split up because you couldn't get Ken out of your system, or if it was because you didn't want to go to Spain,' said Meg.

'There was that too,' said Eve. 'I didn't want to uproot Josie. But Bart and I could have worked something out if I hadn't been such an emotional disaster at the time. When he asked me to go to Spain, you and I had just ended our partnership and I was still in shock about that. I felt as though I needed to get my life together. Looking back on it, I can see that I couldn't quite let Ken go. As a result, I lost Bart altogether.'

'A wonderful thing, hindsight,' said Meg.

Eve nodded, looking at her friend. 'Oh, it's so good to be talking to you like this again, Meg,' she said.

'Friends again?' smiled Meg.

'Definitely.'

'Good.'

'We'd better get back to the ward now, though,' said Eve, her brow furrowing as the diversion came to an end. 'Josie might be wanting me.'

Finishing her tea, Meg stood up. 'I hope all goes well tomorrow,' she said as they headed back to the ward. 'You'll let me know as soon as there's any news, won't you?'

'The minute I know anything, I'll give you a call, I promise,' said Eve.

'Bloody airline,' cursed Bart as he piled his luggage into the boot of Rudy's car outside the terminal at Heathrow on Monday morning. It was bitterly cold, a sharp wind blasting through his leather jacket. 'First a six-hour delay, then we had to wait nearly three hours after that. I was able to ring you from Malaga to let you know about the first one, but I never dreamt we'd be kept hanging about for so long after that. They kept saying we'd be boarding soon. Sorry you've had such a wait.'

'I rang Heathrow and they said there was another delay, so I came later,' explained Rudy. 'So I haven't been waiting too long.'

'That's all right then,' said Bart, closing the boot. 'I really appreciate your coming to pick me up.'

'No problem,' said Rudy, who was genuinely delighted that his old buddy was here. 'It's really good to see you.'

'Likewise, mate.'

They got into the car and headed towards central London. The skies were grey, pinpricks of rain dotting the windscreen.

Rudy fiddled with the heater. 'We could die of hypothermia while we're waiting for this thing to warm up,' he complained.

'Car heaters are all the same,' said Bart. 'But tell me, is there any news about Josie?'

'Only that Eve is seeing the consultant sometime this morning,' Rudy replied. 'He'll give her the test results then.'

Bart looked at his watch. 'It's half past ten already,' he said. 'Step on it, mate, I'd like to be there for her.'

'She might already know the worst by now,' Rudy suggested.

'Let's hope we get there in time,' said Bart. 'Just in case it isn't good news.'

'I'll get you there as soon as I can.' He peered ahead as the traffic slowed and came to a halt. 'Oh, bloody hell, I hope we're not gonna be stuck in this jam for too long.'

Bart held his head. Never had a journey felt so ill-fated.

Eve was sitting in the corridor outside the consultant's office, waiting to go in, when, to her astonishment and pleasure, Meg appeared.

'What are you doing here?' asked Eve.

'Thought you might want some company,' she explained.

'That's really kind of you,' said Eve, warmed by this act of friendship, despite the fact that she was sick with nerves.

'I managed to persuade the nurse to let me stay with you,' Meg told her.

'They're pretty good here,' said Eve. 'As long as people don't go on to the ward and get in the way outside visiting hours.'

'That's understandable,' said Meg.

'Who's looking after the shop?' Eve enquired, glad of a change of focus.

'I've left the staff to it,' she said. 'There's never much business about on a Monday morning. And I asked my mother to go in just to give some extra back-up.'

'How's she getting on?' asked Eve.

'Still doing the job under sufferance,' Meg told her. 'But if George takes my father on permanently, she'll be able to leave. She can't wait.' She gave a wry grin. 'And I don't think the rest of us will be sorry.'

Eve nodded in agreement. The conversation was a mere distraction from the matter that filled both their minds. Eve's heart fluttered and jumped, her hands damp with nervous perspiration. She felt quite faint when the door of the consultant's room opened and he appeared.

'Would you like to come in now, Mrs Peters?' he invited.

'Good luck,' said Meg, who was almost as nervous as Eve.

With legs like jelly, Eve followed the man into his office.

Chapter Twenty-two

'You'll give yourself a heart attack if you don't calm down,' warned Rudy as the two men sat in the barely moving traffic, Bart sighing and cursing and peering out of the window every few seconds. 'There's nothing we can do except wait until it starts moving. There must have been an accident or something that's snarled things up ahead.'

'I need to get to the hospital today, not next week,' muttered Bart, agitatedly combing his hair with his fingers.

'But as we don't have a helicopter to go in, you'll just have to be patient,' reproached Rudy. 'Anyway, as Eve doesn't even know you're on your way, she won't be fretting about your being late.

'That isn't the point,' said Bart. 'I want to be there for her.'

'I know, mate, I know,' said Rudy patiently. 'And you will be. She might have already had the news by the time we get there, but you'll still be there for her. So stop getting into such a panic.'

'Am I being a pain?' asked Bart, calmed by the other man's steadying influence.

'No more than usual,' joked Rudy. 'You always were an impatient sod when you wanted to do something in a hurry.'

Bart chuckled, realising just how much he'd missed Rudy's down-to-earth company. He looked out of the window at the leaden skies and the tailback of traffic stretching ahead for as far as the eye could see. Ugly factory buldings lined the road in places, with modern airport hotels etched against the skyline in the distance. This dreary grey scene was in stark contrast to the bright Andalusian landscape he'd become used to, with its pretty white dwellings and golden beaches. But Bart was suddenly so pleased to be home, hot tears rushed into his eyes. 'It's so good to be back,' he said impulsively.

'I've missed having you around,' said Rudy.

'Me too, mate,' said Bart. 'Me too.'

'The job's going okay though, is it?'

'Yeah, the job's fine,' he confirmed. 'Steady employment, regular money . . .'

'Do I sense a *but* in there somewhere?' Rudy enquired.

Bart nodded. 'But it isn't the same as making it here in the UK,' he said. 'That's still my dream.'

'You might stand more of a chance here now, having gained experience as a full-time professional,' Rudy pointed out. 'You could get on to the books of a really good agent.'

'You're not offering your services then?' smiled Bart.

'No fear. I'm out of the theatrical business altogether now,' Rudy told him. 'Not that I was ever in it properly. I'm best off sticking to what I'm good at.'

'Running the café?'

'That's right,' he confirmed. 'And it's a lot more fun now that Dot's working with me. We run the place together.'

'You do a bit more than that, from what I've heard,' mentioned Bart. 'According to my mum, the two of you are a bit of an item these days.'

'I suppose we are, sort of.'

'You sly old dog,' said Bart. 'But good luck to you.'

'It's the last thing I expected to happen,' Rudy told him, his manner becoming more serious. 'But as Dot and I are both on our own and we get on so well at the café, it seemed like a good idea to team up outside of work as well.'

'So, shall we be hearing wedding bells?' asked Bart lightly.

'It has crossed my mind, to tell you the truth,' admitted

Rudy, surprising Bart, whose question hadn't been a serious one. 'But I haven't said anything to Dot yet. I'm not sure how she'll react.'

'Well, well,' said Bart. 'And how does Eve feel about you and Dot, given that she was so devoted to her father?'

'She wasn't keen at first,' he said, 'but I think she's got used to the idea now. She knows I would never try to take her father's place and looks on me as a friend.'

'That's good.'

'Yeah, it does makes things easier,' he said. 'And I'm very fond of her and Josie.'

At last the traffic began to flow.

'Thank God for that,' said Bart jubilantly. 'Perhaps we will get to the hospital before the new year after all.'

The consultant was about forty, a slim man with a distant manner and a worried look about him which did terrible things to Eve's nervous system. She sat stiffly on the chair opposite him, Her gaze fixed on his pale face. His grey eyes peered at her through rimless spectacles.

He glanced at some papers on his desk, then looked across at Eve. 'We've got your daughter's test results back now,' he said.

Her chest felt tight and her heart was beating so erratically she thought she might have a cardiac arrest. 'Yes, I thought you would have,' she said in a small voice.

'Hmmm,' he muttered, studying the papers again.

Eve stared at his bent head, the scalp shining through the thinning hair. She was so tense, she wanted to be sick. Why was he taking so long to come to the point? It must be bad news or he would have told her quickly.

And then his words seemed to fill the room. 'They're normal,' he said.

'What . . . ?'

'The tests showed no abnormality,' he told her.

Because he still looked worried, she thought she must be

misunderstanding him in some way. 'You mean she doesn't have leukaemia?' she said.

'That's right.'

Hot, sweet relief surged through her with such intensity, she felt dizzy, tears burning beneath her lids. But she had to make sure. 'The recurring exhaustion . . . the feverishness?' she heard herself mutter.

'Very uncomfortable for her, but not serious,' he informed her.

Noticing that the doctor didn't seem particularly jubilant, she said, 'Have you found out what *is* actually the matter with her?'

'It seems that your doctor's original diagnosis was the right one,' he said. 'It's a virus, an especially stubborn one.'

'A virus,' she repeated numbly.

'That's right.'

'Oh, I can't believe it,' she said, closing her eyes for a moment and pushing her fingers through her fringe distractedly. She felt quite weak with reaction. 'I've been nearly out of my mind.'

'Yes, I'm sure it must have been a very stressful time for you,' he said, in a manner suggesting that Josie was only one of many patients he saw every week, some of whom wouldn't have such a happy prognosis. 'The problem is . . .'

She was back in the depths. 'Problem?' she echoed, her voice squeaky with fear.

'There isn't any special treatment,' he said. 'Antibiotics aren't the answer.'

Relief surged through her for the second time. Compared with the possibility that had tormented her for months, this seemed like nothing at all.

'So how will she get better then?' she enquired.

'Nature will have to take its course, I'm afraid,' he said. 'You'll just have to be patient, and so will she.'

'That'll be no problem to me now I know she'll get better eventually,' she said.

'The symptoms will probably continue to recur for a while, until it finally burns itself out,' he informed her.

'And then she'll get better?'

He nodded.

'Does this mean she can come home?' asked Eve, her whole being seeming to hum with joy.

'She'll probably be better off at home. There's nothing more we can do for her here now,' he said, managing a hint of a smile. 'You'll just have to carry on as you have been, giving her plenty of liquids and Disprin when she's feverish, nourishing food when she isn't. If you get worried about her again, contact your own doctor.'

'Thank you,' she said, rising to leave. 'Thank you very much.'

'You're welcome, Mrs Peters,' he said, closing Josie's file and putting it to one side on top of a pile of others.

Eve left the room struggling to control her emotions. As soon as she was outside in the corridor, she burst into tears.

Meg rushed over to her. 'I'm so sorry, Eve,' she said, misreading the situation.

'There's no need to be sorry . . . because she'll be all right,' said Eve through her sobs. 'Josie is gonna get better. It's just a virus that will go away in time.'

Now it was Meg's turn to collapse into tears. 'Thank God for that,' she said thickly, putting her arms around her friend and holding her close. They wept together.

Standing back to mop her tears with a handkerchief, Eve thought her imagination much be playing tricks on her as she stared at a figure striding towards them down the corridor. It couldn't be. It wasn't possible. But it was! She'd recognise that swaying gait anywhere. 'Bart,' she gasped in disbelief. 'It's Bart.'

Seeing both women in tears, Bart thought the worst. 'Oh, Eve . . . I'm *so* sorry,' he said.

Eve flung her arms around him, fresh tears falling. 'I don't know how it is that you're here, but I'm *so* pleased to see you,' she said.

'I'll go and give George a call to tell him the news,' said Meg, making a diplomatic exit.

'How bad is it?' asked Bart gravely, drawing back slightly.

'It isn't bad at all,' she said. 'Josie's going to be fine.'

'Oh.' His face was wreathed in smiles. 'But you were crying, I thought . . .'

'Tears of joy,' she said, feasting her eyes on his tanned countenance. 'Oh, Bart Baxter, you really are a sight for sore eyes.'

Having heard the good news about Josie from his wife on the telephone, George was feeling in a happy and generous mood. Making a decision about something he'd been mulling over these past few days, he rang through to Frank's office and asked him to come and see him as soon as he was free.

'That's the best news I've heard in ages,' said Frank after hearing about Josie. 'Your sister must be very relieved.'

'You bet she is,' he said. 'It's a load off my mind an' all.'

'Thanks for letting me know so promptly,' said Frank, turning as if to leave. 'I really appreciate that.'

'That wasn't why I wanted to see you,' said George. 'There's something else.'

Frank's brow furrowed. 'That sounds a bit ominous,' he said.

'Quite the opposite,' said George. 'I'm very impressed with the way you've been working this past month or so. You seem to have taken to the job like a duck to water.'

'I've still got plenty to learn about the car trade, but I feel as though I'm coping,' said Frank, who had a new vitality these days.

'I think you're doing a bit more than just coping,' George told him. 'You seem to me like a man in control.'

Frank smiled, something he did more of lately than he had in years. 'Thanks, George,' he said. 'That's nice to hear.'

George leaned back in his chair. 'I know that we originally agreed on a three-month trial . . .'

'That's right.' Frank looked uncertain, wondering if George was about to extend it.

'But as we're both happy with the way things have worked out, I'd like to make the job permanent as from now,' he announced. 'It'll make us both feel more secure.'

Frank was astounded. Things hadn't gone as well as this for years. 'You won't hear me complaining about that,' he said.

'I don't wanna risk losing you,' explained George. 'I want to be able to go out on business confident that things will be looked after by the right man here. So, if you agree, I'll get a permanent contract drawn up right away.'

'The sooner the better,' said Frank.

'Wine?' said Bea with a hint of disapproval when Frank arrived home that night clutching a bottle. 'I'm glad someone feels like celebrating.'

'You heard the good news about Eve's little girl, I suppose?' he said.

'Yes, Meg was full of it when she came back to the shop from the hospital.' She gave him a watery smile. 'Naturally I was as pleased as everyone else about it. I don't like the Granger family, but I don't wish illness on anyone.'

'You don't look as though you've had a good day, though,' he remarked.

'I haven't.'

'Why?'

She gave an eloquent sigh. 'Nothing in particular,' she said miserably. 'Just that working at that damned boutique is driving me mad. I don't mind helping out on the odd occasion, but having to work there on a regular basis is really beginning to get me down.' She paused. 'I feel so out of place there, and I know everyone else thinks I am.'

'I've got some . . .'

'The worst part is having to take orders,' she interrupted

in full flow. 'Do this, do that, do the other. It's really *too* awful.'

He could contain himself no longer. 'Aren't you going to ask what the wine's in aid of?' he burst out, his eyes sparkling.

She looked at him. 'I just assumed it was because of the news about the Granger child,' she said.

'It's wonderful news about her, of course,' he said. 'But I've got something else to tell you, something more personal to us.'

'Oh?' She smiled uncertainly. 'Well, don't keep me in suspense then.'

'You won't have to work at the boutique any more,' he announced triumphantly.

'But you haven't been in the job three months yet,' she said, hardly daring to hope.

'George is so pleased with how I'm getting on that he's cut the probationary period and made the job permanent as from now,' he told her proudly. 'So I can resume my position as sole bread-winner.'

Bea had never been much of a smiler; even in the good days she'd usually been straight-faced. But she smiled now, a broad grin that lit up her features. 'Oh, Frank,' she said, hugging him for the first time in years. 'That's such a relief.'

For the first time *ever*, he thought his wife might be just the tiniest bit proud of him. 'I'll open the wine then, shall I?' he asked, beaming.

'Oh, yes,' she said. 'This really is cause for a celebration.'

Later that same evening, Eve and Bart were also celebrating with a bottle of wine, and eating Chinese takeaway on trays by the fire. It was the first chance they'd had to talk properly. Josie was asleep in bed, the improvement Eve had noticed these past few days continuing.

'Now that I know there's no cause for alarm if she's poorly again, I can cope,' she said.

'It must have been dreadful for you, not knowing what was wrong,' he said.

'I can't tell you how awful it's been, the constant worry when the thing wouldn't go away. But worse for her, of course,' she reminded him. 'She's the one feeling ill, poor little thing.'

'I wish I'd been here to give you both some support,' he said, forking a piece of sweet and sour pork.

'I wished you were with us too, many times,' she told him. 'And I really appreciate your coming all this way now.'

'I didn't hesitate for a second when I heard what was going on.' He had already explained Rudy's part in his return.

'I'm sorry things didn't work out for you with Ann,' she said.

He put his head at an angle and sighed. 'Just one of those things. Ann and I were never right for each other.' He went on to give her more details.

'That must have been terrible, finding them together like that,' she said.

'My pride took a battering, that's for sure,' he admitted. 'But I soon got over it. I'm a tough old bugger.'

She ate some beanshoots, savouring the flavour and realising that this was the first morsel of food she'd tasted since the onset of Josie's illness. Her appetite wasn't the only thing that had improved with the removal of the worry either. Her mind was functioning properly again too, and there were things she needed to say to Bart. 'I know that your life is in Spain now, and mine is here in England, but I want you to know that I regretted not being able to marry you. Still do.'

He put his fork down and looked at her. 'You do?' he said.

She nodded 'I wanted you to know that, even though there still can't be a future for us together,' she said. 'It would be even more impossible now. I mean, I couldn't uproot Josie by taking her to Spain to live, not after all she's been through lately. She's already had enough disruption, time off school, time away from her friends. I couldn't bear to cause her more upheaval by moving away from here.' She looked at him seriously. 'Of course, I'm being really presumptuous here, since you haven't even asked me to go back to Spain with you.'

'Eve . . . Eve,' he said, putting his food down on the coffee table and standing up. 'You must know how I feel about you.'

'Well . . . the fact that you dropped everything and came all the way from Spain to be with me does tell me something, I must admit,' she confessed.

'Exactly,' he said. 'I came because I still love you. And I want to be with you. I never loved Ann because I couldn't stop loving you.'

She put her tray down too and went into his arms. 'I love you too, Bart, and I've missed you more than you could ever know.'

'Likewise.'

'But how can we have a future together when we live so far apart?'

'We'll find a way,' he said, kissing her. 'We'll find a way.'

One evening two years later, Eve and Josie were settled in their seats near the front of the stalls at the London Palladium. On Eve's other side, at the end of the row, were Lil and Nora, the end seats having been removed to make room for Lil's wheelchair. Sitting next to Josie was Becky, then there was Dot and her husband Rudy, and Meg and George with Meg's parents, who were here this evening, Eve suspected, because Frank wanted to be. Nowadays the Myers often attended social events at which the Grangers were present, unheard of in the days when Bea had reigned supreme.

From what Eve had gathered from Meg and George, Frank had much more of a say in what he and his wife did these days. His job as George's manager had enabled them to move back into a house, albeit only a very small one. Frank was determined they wouldn't live above their means again, and he made the rules now, apparently.

'When will Uncle Bart be coming on the stage, Mummy?' asked Josie.

'Not long now, darling.'

'Goody,' she said excitedly. 'I can't wait to see him.'

Eve looked at the programme. Bart was the third act on in the first half, and he had another spot towards the end of the second half. Just seeing his name on the programme gave her a thrill. Her husband on stage at this world-famous theatre, where some of the biggest names in showbusiness had appeared. Wow! He wasn't top of the bill, but just to be appearing here was proof of the direction his career was taking. He'd come a long way from the working-men's clubs and rough back-street pubs that were once his platform.

She looked behind her. Not an empty seat anywhere. An expectant buzz filled the auditorium as people chatted among themselves, waiting for the entertainment to begin. As the curtain went up and the show opened with a group of dancers, Eve found herself reflecting on the events of the past two years . . .

After their reunion, Eve and Bart had decided they couldn't bear to be parted again, and came to a mutual agreement that it would be better for Bart to come back to the UK. They had got married soon after his return.

The lack of a regular income was Bart's biggest worry, because he still had responsibilities to his mother. Eve offered to support him while he concentrated on his showbusiness career, taking bookings all over the country if necessary. Even if he was away from time to time, at least they would see more of each other than they would if he went back to Spain.

At first he wouldn't hear of living on Eve's earnings and said he would go back to window-cleaning as a day job. She'd pointed out quite adamantly that that would be a backward step he mustn't even consider at that stage. He should give himself at least a year in which to try to earn his living as a showbusiness performer. Only if that failed should he think about window-cleaning as an option.

With a great deal of difficulty she'd persuaded him to agree. At first the plan had seemed doomed to failure. With no agent to find him work, he was back treading the boards in rough clubs and seedy pubs. But working as a professional in Spain had improved his technique, made his act more polished, and this finally persuaded a well-known agency to put him on their books. The venues got better, money began to trickle in. He was booked for a summer season in Bournemouth. Eve and Josie had gone down at weekends to be with him, and for longer spells during Josie's school holidays. Work had led to more work, and he'd played in some of the northern theatres. And now the London Palladium!

The dancers were followed by a trio of jugglers in sequinned costumes who did a lightning-fast routine and left the stage to a roar of applause. Josie was nudging Eve and holding up a bag of toffees that had been passed along to them from Dot.

Eve took one and looked along the row to her mother, mouthing a thank-you. Her mother smiled. She did a lot of that since she'd married Rudy about a year ago. Eve gave the bag of sweets to Josie to pass back along the row, catching a glimpse of Meg and George, who were happily chatting while the applause died down. Their marriage still seemed to be rock-solid, she thought. Reflecting on her own friendship with Meg, she came to the conclusion that it was all the stronger for having been lost to them so agonisingly for a while. Neither of them would let that happen again, it was far too precious.

As they settled for the next part of the show, Eve glanced at her daughter and was imbued with love and gratitude for her return to good health. The virus had taken a while to clear up but had finally done so, and she'd been well ever since. Having had her eyes opened to the disease that Josie had mercifully been spared, Eve was now a keen supporter and campaigner for a charity to raise funds for research into the illness.

Returning to the present, she heard the compère introduce Bart as 'a performer we're going to be hearing a lot more of in the future.' As he walked on to the stage, looking stunning in a black dinner jacket and dazzling white shirt, his thick brown hair combed into place, her heart swelled with pride. She was terrified for him, though.

Her hands were clasped tightly together on her lap, her breathing shallow with nerves as he began his act with some humorous observations about life based on his own experience. When nobody laughed she wanted to die. But he didn't panic or dry up, he simply carried on. Somebody laughed, then another. It turned to a ripple. Then suddenly a warm, encompassing roar of laughter filled the theatre. Bart had done it; he'd won them over!

When he launched into the song he'd sung the very first time she had seen him perform, at the motor traders' dinner dance, Eve was mesmerised, her eyes shining with tears. Her husband was going places, and wherever his talent took him she would be with him – as it said in the words of the old Sinatra hit he was putting over so beautifully now – all the way.

Miss You Forever

Josephine Cox

One winter's night, Rosie finds a woman who has been severely beaten by thugs. At a glance, Kathleen looks like an unkempt, aged vagabond, carrying all her worldly possessions in a grubby tapestry bag. Her only friend is the mangy old dog who accompanies her; the sum of her life is in the diaries she so jealously guards. Yet close up, Rosie can see that Kathleen has a gracious beauty – the 'look' of a respectable lady of means.

Moved by Rosie's care and compassion, Kathleen entrusts the precious diaries to her. In the soft glow of a night-lamp, Rosie opens the first page. Captivated through the small hours, she uncovers a heartrending tale of stolen dreams, undying love, heartache and loss. Once, a lifetime ago, Kathleen had a promising future, a family and a reason to hope. But is this really the end of her dreams?

'Vivid characters' *Express*

'Guaranteed to tug at the heartstrings' *Sunday Post*

'A heartwarming tale' *Sunderland Echo*

'Another sure-fire winner' *Woman's Weekly*

0 7472 4958 X

HEADLINE

As Time Goes By

Harry Bowling

Carter Lane is an ordinary backstreet in Bermondsey and, for Dolly and Mick Flynn, it is home. When Dolly's boys volunteer for the armed forces and her daughter Sadie seems determined to throw her life away on a married man, Dolly's neighbour, Liz Kenny, is there to offer words of advice and a shoulder to cry on.

But when a bomb uncovers a skeleton in the yard of Gleeson's leather factory, their own lives are thrown into turmoil. As the Blitz takes its toll and the inhabitants of Carter Lane endure the sorrows and the partings which they had dreaded above all else, they find comfort in one another and solace in the knowledge that their wounds will heal – as time goes by.

'The king of Cockney sagas packs close-knit community good-heartedness into East End epics'
Daily Mail

0 7472 5882 1

HEADLINE

Katie's Kitchen

Dee Williams

When her friend and business partner Edwin Brown dies it seems like Katherine Carter's own world has ended. Not only has her closest companion been taken from her, she's also lost the successful restaurant they built up together, as well as the comfortable home they shared with her young son. Now all this has been snatched away, for Edwin has left no will and his lecherous brother Gerald presumes he's inherited Katherine along with the house.

With little money but full of determination Katherine escapes Gerald's violent advances and takes lodgings in Rotherhithe, with her cook's sister Milly. Despite its poverty, Docklands London is full of hope and friendship and, in helping her new neighbours through their difficulties, Katherine finally begins to tackle her troubled past. But even as she rebuilds her life around the pie-and-mash shop where she works, a terrible shadow is hanging over the country. And little does anyone know the horrors 1914 will unleash . . .

'A cosy chair and a Dee Williams book is a little bit of heaven' Lesley Pearse

0 7472 5537 7

HEADLINE

If you enjoyed this book here is a selection of other bestselling titles from Headline

When Tomorrow Dawns

Lyn Andrews

1945. The people of Liverpool, after six years of terror and grief and getting by, are making the best of the hard-won peace, none more so than the ebullient O'Sheas. They welcome widowed Mary O'Malley from Dublin, her young son Kevin, and Breda, her bold strap of a sister, with open arms and hearts.

Mary is determined to make a fresh start for her family, despite Breda, who is soon up to her old tricks. At first all goes well, and Mary begins to build up an understanding with their new neighbour Chris Kennedy – until events take a dramatic turn that puts Chris beyond her reach. Forced to leave the shelter of the O'Sheas' home, humiliated and bereft, Mary faces a future that is suddenly uncertain once more. But she knows that life has to go on . . .

'Lyn Andrews presents her readers with more than just another saga of romance and family strife. She has a realism that is almost tangible' *Liverpool Echo*

0 7472 5806 6

HEADLINE

How to Beat
Panic Disorder

One Step at a Time